CONSTANT
HEART

SIRI MITCHELL

A CONSTANT HEART

BETHANY HOUSE PUBLISHERS
Minneapolis, Minnesota

Cover design by Jennifer Parker
Cover photography by Mike Habermann

Published by Bethany House Publishers
11400 Hampshire Avenue South
Bloomington, Minnesota 55438

Bethany House Publishers is a division of
Baker Publishing Group, Grand Rapids, Michigan.

Printed in the United States of America

Library of Congress Cataloging-in-Publication Data

Mitchell, Siri L., 1969–
    A constant heart / Siri Mitchell.
      p. cm.
    ISBN 978-0-7642-0431-9 (pbk.)
    1. Elizabeth I, Queen of England, 1533–1603—Fiction. 2. Nobility—Great
Britain—Fiction. 3. Great Britain—History—Elizabeth, 1558–1603—Fiction.
I. Title.

    PS3613.I866C66   2008
    813'.6—dc22
                                         2008028163

SIRI MITCHELL has written five novels, two of which (*Chateau of Echoes* and *The Cubicle Next Door*) were named Christy Award finalists. A graduate from the University of Washington with a business degree, she has worked in many levels of government and lived on three continents. Siri and her family currently reside in the Washington D.C. metro area.

ENGLAND

during the last decade of the sixteenth century

under the reign of Queen Elizabeth

1

*B*ut how could he *not* like you?"

"He is an earl, Joan!"

"And you, Marget, are to be his countess."

The Midsummer Day sun was hot and absent any breeze. We were sitting on a log at the marsh's edge, our skirts drawn up to our knees, caps resting on the ground beside us. The marsh birds would warn us of any intruder, but there were unlikely to be any wanderers this festive day. We had slipped away from the city's merriment to ponder my rapidly approaching marriage.

In several short months I was to exchange my life as a knight's daughter for life as a countess. That thought still had the power to drain the blood from my face as if January's salt-laden winds were whipping in from the Wash, stealing my breath as they continued on their way.

"Think you. For how many years now have you trained for this?"

"Twelve." It had begun at the age of five. If I whispered the number it was only because, of a sudden, I did not wish for the training to end.

"And now you can . . . what *are* all those things you can do? 'Tis been some time since I heard your father recite them all at my father's tavern."

"He has been busy."

"Aye. The pride of our fair city. The noble merchant-turned-landowner. He has been turning himself in circles, sending hither and thither across the kingdom to catch you a husband. You should be rejoicing at his success."

"But what if—"

"What if what? What if you cannot please him?" Joan's voice was rising, as if my worries were trifles too small to warrant her attentions. "Do you not know a dozen ways to dance? Can you not sing like a songbird? In how many languages can you read? And how many stitches can you work upon a canvas? How can you fail to please him, Marget?"

"If only I could meet him . . ."

Joan shrugged. "And what good would that do anyone?"

"What if he is . . . aged?"

"Then you will spend less time in bed and more time in delighting yourself with . . . all the means of a countess at your disposal."

I could not keep a blush from spreading through my cheeks. "But his first wife—"

"The marriage was annulled. Is that not what you told me?"

"Aye. 'Tis true."

"Then she was no wife to him at all."

"But what if—"

"What if horses could fly? Would that not be marvelous? What if the Queen herself were to trade places with me? Would that not be grand?"

I grabbed her arm and made her stop. Made her turn toward me. "Truly. What if I cannot please him?"

"Are you meaning to ask me if you are to play the role of your mother?"

My fingers tightened around her arm.

"He will *not* be your father, Marget. You *will* please him. He *will* stay in your bed. Is that what vexes you?"

I could not bring myself to nod, but Joan knew me almost better than I knew myself.

"Hear me: there is nothing in you that could make him cast you off."

"But—"

"Hush you. Last time I noticed, earls were still men." She said it as if that settled everything. As if there were no reason for the worries that churned in my belly.

"But—"

"And last time I looked, Marget, you still had the face of an angel." Her gaze softened before she continued on. "'Tis nothing like my own."

Her words asked for no comment and none was needed. We both knew the truth, had known it since we became friends. God had doled out looks to me with a generous hand, while he had been overly judicious with Joan. Her eyes seemed perpetually tired; her mouth drooped constantly in apparent fatigue. She hunched at the shoulders as if expecting a blow at any moment. Her strengths were abundant— loyalty, honesty, good humor—but they registered not upon her person. My poor, sweet Joan was less than plain. But it seemed not to matter to her one whit. She had always been my protector. I had assumed she always would be. But fate had decreed that in a few short weeks I would be embarking upon a new life without her. And at that moment, that seemed the worst part of the impending change.

"Come." Joan bent to pick up our caps and then took my hand, pulled me from the log, and began to run toward the city's walls, toward the bonfires and the singing and the dancing.

I could do naught but follow.

It was enough to drive a man mad!

Any nobleman worth his title could write poetry. That was what my tutor had taught me long ago. That was what I had always believed. But then came Philip Sidney and Edmund Spenser, and now rumors of some person named Shakespeare. They had ruined it for us all. It was no longer acceptable to just dash out a sonnet. One must employ mythology *and* politics, and work for days to cultivate allusions aplenty.

But now, all I needed was a rhyme for *carriage*.

Her Majesty's comportment, her carriage, could be compared to . . . Bah! It had been at the edge of my mind the entire forenoon. Carriage . . . carnage.

Nay.

Carriage . . . cleavage.

There was no hope for it. It would come. I could feel it, but I might as well do something else, something more productive, until it did. Why did poetry have to require so much work? I was replacing the quill in the inkwell when a knock sounded upon the door, and then it opened forthwith.

It was Nicholas. He was carrying something in his hand. "For you, my lord." He straightened from a bow and extended a document toward me. "From the east, my lord."

The east. Perhaps . . . I made quick work in breaking the seal, but then found my eyes could not deal so deftly with the words contained inside. If only my hands would stop shaking.

I spread it on the desk before me but still could not focus on the words long enough to read them. Pushing away from the desk, I gestured Nicholas toward the paper. "Read it."

"My lord." He stood beside the desk and took the letter into his hands. " 'Tis dated King's Lynn this twenty-second day of June. 'To Simon St. Aubin, most gracious lord, Earl of Lytham, I humbly take my pen in hand to—' "

"Aye, aye. Does he accept the terms or not?"

A C O N S T A N T H E A R T ❦

"It seems, my lord that . . ."

"An aye or nay will suffice."

"If you could find the patience to allow me the opportunity to simply—"

"You vex me."

Nicholas's lips twitched into the briefest of smiles. "If *you* would rather have the reading of it, my lord?"

"Nay! And may the devil take you."

"Then . . . it would seem as if . . ."

"Aye?"

Nicholas held up a finger to stay my words. If he had not been my most trusted friend, I would not have forborne the insolence, but he was my Gentleman of the Horse. And I had marked him as mine in my younger days. Had it not been for my youth's ill temper and the sharp end of a stick, he would now be absent a star of a scar that marred his left cheek.

"What say you?" I asked again.

Using that same finger, he reached down and slid it beneath a line of text. And then, finally, he lifted his eyes to mine. "Aye. After all of that, in the very last phrase, he agrees. You shall have the hand of his daughter in marriage."

"Thank heaven!"

"Congratulations, my lord. It is my fondest hope that the young lady will bring you nothing but happiness."

I looked at him. Though his mien revealed nothing but innocence, I knew him too well. "You mean to say, as opposed to the first young lady?"

Nicholas merely stood there.

I frowned as I regained my desk and removed my quill from the inkpot. "The young lady is of no importance."

"I beg to argue, my lord."

"You have never begged for anything in your life, Nicholas." I looked up just in time to see him hide a smile by tucking his chin into his chest.

"Be that as it may, that young lady shall soon become your countess."

"Aye. 'Tis the manner in which these things generally occur."

"A countess who will represent you. A countess who may bear you an heir."

I put the quill back into the inkpot and turned to look at him. "Pray, be plain."

"As a knight's daughter, her only wish will be to please you. You must not punish her for another's mistakes, my lord."

"Do you think me some cruel tyrant?"

"Nay, my lord. But it was you who said she was of no importance."

"*Relatively* speaking, Nicholas. 'Tis her dowry that I am after. Her knight-father's riches will allow me to regain Holleystone. If there is anything to rejoice over, 'tis that fact. You and I shall both be going home. 'Tis for *that* God is to be praised."

After being sold to pay for another's destitution—my brother's, the former earl—Holleystone was once again to be held by its rightful owners. And never again would it leave the family's possession.

Coaxing the lease of my other estate, Brustleigh Hall, from the Queen had been a victory, but the return of Holleystone would be a triumph. It was a shame I would have to marry for that pleasure, but the return of Holleystone was worth any tribulation. Surely the girl could not be so bad as my first wife, Elinor. I gathered those thoughts before they could gallop away from me. Though I had taken Elinor to wife, Parliament had recently annulled that marriage and so, in fact, I had no wife. Had never had. But the Act of Parliament that had expunged a marriage had failed to obliterate the memories . . . that the face of an angel could hide a heart so duplicitous . . . that beauty could be so deceitful.

It still cost me to think of the ways, all the very *many* ways, in which she had betrayed me. Though I had tried everything I knew to mend the wound, each thought of Elinor pulled at the edges, threatening to start it bleeding once more. And now I was to bind myself to another woman.

At least this one was just a knight's daughter. Surely I would not be expected to keep her long at court. Just as soon as I was able I would hide the horse-faced young girl away at Holleystone. Would that I could send her to Brustleigh and keep Holleystone for myself, but it seemed it could not be helped.

If Holleystone was personal, a family wrong to be righted, then Brustleigh was for the Queen. The renovations were nearly complete, and with what would be left of the girl's dowry, the remaining work could be finished sooner rather than later. And when it was, I would persuade Her Majesty to visit. With that sign of preference, along with some small sign of the Queen's preferment, then I could finally be first among her courtiers.

Nicholas cleared his throat, a sure sign that I had been ignoring him. "The young lady, my lord."

"What of her?"

"You will not neglect her, my lord?"

"Certainly not! Luck's chosen vessel must be looked after . . ."

My thoughts turned toward all the ways in which I might, very soon, become lucky. I might be selected to receive a venerable Garter Knighthood. I might be asked to take a seat on Her Majesty's Privy Council. I might be given another estate or even a chance to purchase a monopoly.

Nicholas coughed.

"What is it?"

"The gifts, my lord."

"The gifts?"

"If you are to be married in several months, then I have only several months to attend to the preparations, my lord. First among them, the gifts."

"What gifts?"

"For the betrothal, my lord. And the morning after."

"Morning after what?"

"Your *wedding*, you great dunce!"

I waved him away. "Choose something you deem adequate. And since you concern yourself with the girl's welfare, take the gift there yourself."

I am certain he thought I did not see him shake his head over my words; I did. But I could not care. Fortune had finally smiled upon me. My ship had turned its sails toward home. That I would soon be married and have some girl by my side as I sailed could hardly matter.

Marriage.

That was it! Carriage, marriage. Her Majesty's *carriage* could be compared to a *marriage* of . . . grace and virtue? Of grace and . . . beauty? Grace and something. Why did poetry have to come in fits and starts? My only hope was that the more I practiced, the more I wrote, the easier it would become.

As Nicholas left the room, I reviewed the portions of the sonnet I had already written. I had been writing on the subject of Her Majesty, but as I contemplated my future, I decided to write instead about Fair Fortune.

I put the one sonnet to the side and began anew.

2

The Earl of Lytham sent a letter agreeing to the terms of the marriage. Along with the notice of his concurrence was sent a betrothal gift. It arrived in a small chest, carried by a messenger clad in the earl's colors of azure and red.

"Perhaps a gift of coin!" My father had never been able to shed the gowns of his trade, and a merchant's interests were both singular and constant.

"It could hold a prize other than gold. It might be jewels." With those words, my mother had come as close to scolding Father as ever she had. "Go on, Marget. Open it!"

I did not want to. I did not wish to know what it contained. A gift always reveals its giver, and I was afraid that it would tell me something I did not wish to know about the man, the earl, who was soon to be my husband.

Were it coins, I would know he was assuming me to be some ill-bred spendthrift, concerned only for the state of my purse. Were it some piece of frippery, I would know he was assuming me to be a wanton, bent only on frivolity.

I walked toward the messenger who held it; he dropped to one knee at my approach. As soon as I had closed the distance between us, he lifted the lid of the chest and then offered the whole of it up to me. But not without first meeting my eyes. I found his gaze filled with understanding. It was oddly reassuring.

I did not relieve him of his burden but took only from the chest what the opening of the lid had revealed: a letter and two packages, one large and one small.

As I began to open the letter, my mother grasped my arm. "The gifts first!" She took the letter from me and replaced it with the smaller of the packages.

My fingers fumbled with the ribbons that bound it, so I handed it to her.

She made quick work in revealing the contents. "I was right— 'tis a ring!" She tried to give it to me, but I did not want it. "Rubies. And . . . sapphires? They are strangely blue."

"Azure." I looked toward the messenger and he nodded. " 'Tis a ring of the earl's colors." There had been enough messengers going back and forth between the earl and King's Lynn that if I knew nothing else of him, I knew the St. Aubin family colors.

"Well, 'tis . . . 'tis fine, then. Put it on, child."

If I had not held out my palm for it, she would have dropped it to the floor, so great was her eagerness to have me wear it. But I did not yet wish to be marked like some prized mare.

"And the other? The larger?" My father was leaning across the table in his impatience to discover the contents of the remaining package.

I took it to hand and was surprised by its weight. This one was easier to open, contained inside a velvet pouch. Upon being released from its tether, the gift, a golden disc, slipped out into my hand. I turned it over. Its flat surface was marked by a winding of golden scrollwork and its edges measured off in regular increments. It was divided in two by a golden bar.

"What is it?" My father had no use for things which had no purpose.

"Let me see!" My mother was standing upon her toes, trying to see over my shoulder.

The messenger cleared his throat. "'Tis an astrolabe, my lady."

"An astrolabe?"

"An instrument, my lady, for navigation."

"Navigation?" I could not treat this man any longer as a mere servant. In this matter, clearly, he had more knowledge than I.

Above a star-shaped scar, his eyes seemed, for a moment, to twinkle. "Perhaps if the lady read the letter . . ."

I put the gifts on the table and returned to the task I had first undertaken. I broke the seal and spread the letter before me. But in this, at least, the messenger was mistaken. It was not a letter. It was a poem. A sonnet.

"What does it say?" My father was squinting in his attempts to read it.

I began to read. "It says,

> Every man who claims a destiny
> Is giv'n a ship of fate on which to sail
> Some guide their course by basest treachery
> While faint hearts anchor far from life's travail
> But take to hand the Astrolabe of Love
> And soon you find that your course does run true
> Through day and night, gales thundering above
> All the sailing leads to naught but you
> To you alone I give Love's astrolabe
> That in your sailing you might find the same
> Gale winds that blew my soul to you to save
> Might in return give you to me to claim
> Coupled, may we kneel before love's altar
> Clasping hands that bear faith's ancient color."

At the end of its reading, I discovered myself to be smiling. A quick glance at the messenger told me he had discovered the same. Trying to turn my lips into a frown, I returned my attentions to the poem. If the earl were true to his words, he was a man who seemed to want to love me. Or, at the very least, to respect me.

I could wear a ring given me by such a man.

While my father tugged the sonnet from my hand, I turned to question the messenger. "Ancient color?"

"Azure, my lady."

"And faith?"

"'Tis the Earl of Lytham's motto, my lady: *fortiter fideliter*."

"Bravely, faithfully?"

"Well said, my lady."

"I am not your lady."

My words were inexcusably sharp, but the messenger met my gaze with one of mild amusement. "Nay, madam. You may not be *my* lady, not yet, but you are one just the same."

I refolded the poem and put it back into the chest with the astrolabe. Then I took the ring from the table and pushed it onto my thumb. It was heavy but it fit.

Our banns, the Earl of Lytham's and mine, were read at church three weeks in succession. With each reading, the knot within my belly that had eased upon the delivery of the earl's sonnet began to tighten once more. I felt a giddy excitement about leaving the marshes of Norfolk for the storied opulence of the Queen's court. But lying beneath it was a pressing anxiety. In spite of Joan's attempts to buoy my spirits, I felt as if I were an impostor. Who was I to launch myself upon the royal court as a countess? And, more importantly, how was I to survive upon my own?

With each twisting of my innards, I read the earl's poem anew. Surely life would not be so bad if it were lived beside the man who had written such a poem. After two months' time, the parchment had grown soiled from my fingers and worn from being folded and refolded. But it had also become fixed in my mind.

And my heart.

I was given leave by my father to take a servant with me from his household, but in my new life I desired more than a servant. I wanted a companion. My old nurse had died. I had my own maid, but she was a simple girl and cowed by the least change in daily routines. I might have settled on one of the maids-of-all-work, but to what advantage? I had almost resigned myself to leaving alone when Joan saw me passing her father's tavern and begged a word. In private.

"My father searches a husband for me."

I clasped her hands, excited by the prospect. "But surely this is good news!"

Her face became even more drawn than normal. "How can it be good? Who would want me?"

I restrained my sigh but could think of no reply. Who indeed would want her? Her father, a publican, was not so rich that a dowry would long distract a man from Joan's face. "Does he . . . has he mentioned any names?"

"Only John Stump."

"Of Fisherfleet?"

"The very one."

"With seven children?"

"Aye. And three wives buried."

Three wives buried could not be held against a prospective suitor . . . unless those wives had been helped toward death by the back of a man's hand.

We looked at each other in a long silence.

"Could you come with me to London?"

"Could I go with you to London?"

I could not say whose petition was presented first.

It took, however, no little amount of persuasion to convince Joan's father to let her come into my service. My father's first request to him was denied.

I questioned him about it at supper. "He said, 'Nay'? But why?"

He shrugged, then tugged at his ear. "I cannot account for it. You do not offer her a position as a scullery servant. She is to be your personal companion!"

"And you told him that?"

"I did, the obstinate dogfish! And I talked to him in monies too. In keeping Joan from marriage, he could save what he might have paid out for a dowry."

"And?"

My father threw his hands into the air. They came down around a tankard of ale. He took a long draught, then wiped his mouth on his sleeve before he continued. "He has not the sense of an ass. And he has never operated his trade according to how much money he can make but according to how many enemies he can create. So one cannot hope that talking sense to him would change his mind."

"But how can this not benefit Joan? And she so clearly does not want to marry John Stump . . ."

"Who would?"

"Her father cannot have her interests in mind."

"For certes he does not! Any man worth the name marries off a daughter for his *own* interests. And any man who does not should consult a physician. But the thing of it is, I cannot see how Joan's service to you could fail to benefit him."

I despaired of ever gaining her when, two weeks before my marriage, well past supper, she pounded upon the door and was shown up into my room. I was already abed but folded back the coverlet so she could join me.

She slipped in, thin as an eel, and curled herself into a ball.

"Are you cold?" I questioned.

"Nay."

"Are you well?"

Joan's voice was barely a whisper. "I will be in two weeks' time. Once we have journeyed far from here."

"Is here so very bad?"

She slipped a thin hand around my forearm and tugged at me until I turned to look at her. "I will never make you sorry you took me with you. Only promise you will never hit me and I will stay with you until death. Mine or yours."

"Hit you? Why would I do such a thing?"

"Promise."

"What has—"

"Promise!"

I had no choice but to agree if I hoped to quiet her. But still, I wished I knew the source of her desperation. "I promise."

3

And so Joan came into my service. On the day I was to put on my marriage gown, she put on a livery of the Earl of Lytham's colors: a red gown with azure sleeves. I fingered the material as I helped her pull it down over her head.

She shook out the gown to arrange it over the farthingale hoops. "I have never seen anything finer."

Neither had I. And to think that it had been provided for a simple servant!

"Come! 'Tis my turn to help you." With Joan's assistance, I came to be dressed in a shift of fine linen. While Joan occupied herself with finding my corset, I pulled silk stockings up over my knees and tied them just beneath with a length of gilt ribbon. We wrestled with the corset, finally cinching it tight to flatten my breasts. And then my farthingale hoops and petticoat. And finally the gown.

Made from crimson satin, it was embroidered with gold and pierced with pearls. Joan worked around me to fix the folds of the ruff with pins. And then, when I could no longer see my feet for the ruff, she helped me push them into my shoes. When she at last combed out my hair and pronounced me perfect, we went downstairs, where my mother placed a garland of rosemary and red roses into my hands.

I felt, that day, as though my stomach encaged some mad beast that was using his claws to find a way out. I recited the sonnet to myself *ad infinitum*, hoping that like some charm of magic it would soothe my nerves. It was only when I saw the Earl of Lytham that my belly began to fashion itself back together. Joan had spied him from a window of the great hall as he stood talking to my father.

"There, now! He does not look so very old, does he?" Joan must have read my mood, for her voice was colored by false cheer.

I joined her at the window, pushing back a curtain so I could see more clearly. He did not look old, though he did seem closer to my father's age than my own. His hair was dark and curly. His brows were still black. His beard had been tamed, clipped close to his chin, leaving his jaw clear. And his mustache followed the wide curve of his mouth.

We kept watch as he spoke to my father.

"His eyes are kind." Joan said it as if she begrudged him that quality.

"Are they?"

"Aye."

I stayed for a while and watched and indeed, it seemed to me that there *was* kindness in the way he held his lips and in the lines around his eyes. And I decided then that I would rather meet him in my own courtyard than in front of the church.

When I stepped out of the door, the earl left off conversation with my father and looked upon me.

I smiled.

And at that, he seemed to recoil. His eyes darkened in alarm, as if, instead of comeliness, I offered him some sort of misshapen horror.

———

I blinked. And blinked again. The girl's father continued to speak, but I no longer heard his words, for standing before me was a vision of . . . Elinor . . . as she had been ten years before. Still possessed of grace, still infused with innocence. Change the black hairs for red and . . . this girl was even more lovely than my wife who had never been.

And she expected me to marry her. This day!

I clamped a hand around Nicholas's arm, wheeled us around, and took us toward the stables, sword slapping angrily against my thigh. "I cannot marry that girl. And why is she wearing my mother's ring?"

"A betrothal gift, my lord. You said to find something I deemed adequate."

"That you would give such a girl the ring of my beloved mother . . . !"

"She is to be your countess."

"Nay. I will not marry her."

"You must, my lord."

"I will *not* marry that girl."

Nicholas opened his mouth, then closed it. He leaned to my left, looking, no doubt, at the girls standing behind me. "Is there something . . . wrong with her, my lord?"

"Aye. Everything! She is too young . . . she is too . . . beautiful."

Relief colored Nicholas's smile. "As I told you when I had returned from delivering the betrothal gift."

"But I thought that surely . . . surely you had exaggerated. That a knight's daughter could possess such . . . perfection . . ."

"You would have the other, then? The one who stands beside her?"

I turned and looked to where the girls waited. Standing beside the one I was pledged to marry stood precisely the sort of woman I had hoped for. A horse-faced, tired old-woman-of-a-girl. "Aye. That is exactly whom I wish to marry!"

"But you have pledged yourself to—"

"To a devil in women's weeds! I will not do it. Not again! Beauty is deception. Beauty is . . . 'tis nothing but a lie!"

Nicholas stepped near and laid a hand upon my arm.

I shook it off. "You forget yourself!"

"She is not Elinor, my lord."

"I am being punished. May God help me . . ."

"She is *not Elinor*. I have observed her, my lord. I have spoken with her. She will not disappoint you."

"How could she do anything other? You should have told me."

"I did, my lord."

"You should have made me listen."

"I thought you were. My lord."

I sighed, closed my eyes, and turned my face toward heaven and prayed for God to give me strength. I do not know why I bothered; He clearly was not listening to me. There was no help for it: I had to talk to her. Had to meet her. Courtesy demanded it of me. Oh, to have worked so long and so hard to shed myself of one siren only to arrive once more at the beginning of the nightmare. It was not to be borne. Yet what could I do?

Like Odysseus, I would take every measure to keep myself from her. I would stop my ears to her voice. I would turn my eyes from her face; I would do what I must. I would not have my life's blood drained from me again.

I would not do it.

My father had ceased talking, and together, Joan, my father, and I had watched as the earl stalked away with his messenger. If truth be seen, with someone who was clearly *more* than a simple messenger.

Something was wrong. I knew it. My hand found Joan's as we stood there watching. Waiting.

The men had argued. The earl had quieted. And now he was walking back toward us. Back toward me.

My right foot stepped backward. My left foot joined it. Were it not for Joan's hand grasping mine, I would have fled from the anger, the rage I saw in his eyes.

But he did not come on the attack. Once before me, he removed his hat and swept it toward the ground, its crimson feathers trailing in the dust. He followed that gesture with an elegant bow. Then he took my hand in his.

"Mistress Barnardsen, you have done me a great honor by pledging to become my wife."

I would not have thought it by his tone, nor by the way his fingers barely grazed mine. What had I done to disgust him? And where was the man who had written the sonnet?

After the signing of the wedding contract, we proceeded from my father's house to the church. The only two people who did not speak or sing or tell jokes were the earl and me. Around us rang out laughter and good wishes to the accompaniment of instruments. And then we reached the church.

Standing before the altar I pledged, in front of the rector, my friends, and my God, that I would take the earl to be my wedded husband, to have and to hold, from that day forward, for better, for worse, for richer, for poorer, in sickness and in health, to love, to cherish, and to obey, till death us depart, according to God's holy ordinance.

———

It was over. I was bound to the girl for time and all eternity. Until death us depart. I could not think a gloomier thought.

Aye.

I could.

I could think on the night's festivities and what lay ahead.

God, please help me. Help us both.

Sliding a look toward her beneath my cap, I saw a face too young to hold such . . . misery. She was thinking thoughts no happier than my own. Perhaps then all would come right. I was no beast. Perhaps if I smiled.

There. I tried.

And was rebuffed. Hibernia never saw a chillier maid. It would take a tankard of ale for me to do . . . what must be done.

Holleystone.

I must think on Holleystone. Holleystone was worth any trial. Holleystone was worth any harpy. With Holleystone regained, I could set my thoughts on other things. Things such as Brustleigh and the Queen's favor and all that would follow from that triumph. Holleystone was worth even this . . . Aphrodite.

It had to be. Until death us do part.

————

The earl never spoke one word to me. Though he did leer at me. Once.

The ceremony finished, Joan took the garland of flowers from my hands and fixed it on my head. As we stepped out of the church, the bells tolled noon. The return to my father's house was even more raucous than our departure. Once there, we dined on peacock, replete with its feathers; on capons and veal in pomegranate sauce; on pig and sturgeon; on wafers and jellies; on grapes and quinces. The barrels of wine my father had imported were drained by evening, but that stopped no one from imbibing in ale.

Later that night, after still more feasting and dancing, we were placed into bed together, the earl and I. He did what I was told he must do and then he left my chambers.

At least he had not stayed long enough to see my tears.

I sought the corner of the bed farthest from the door and pulled my knees up toward my chest to staunch my trembling. At some time during that long night, Joan climbed into bed beside me and circled me within the fortress of her arms.

When I could find my voice, I spoke to her in a halting whisper. "Is this then what a marriage is . . . one person conquering and the other being conquered?"

"Hush you, now. 'Tis the way of a man with a maid."

I could not stop my tears. They were unquenchable, ushering forth from a fount sprung up inside me.

"Hush, now. You must not begrudge him a thing he had to do."

"He . . . hurt me."

"Aye. But tell me true: 'tis your soul that hurts more than your body, is it not?"

"How do . . . how did you know?"

She took a long time to answer, and during the interval, curiosity overcame my tears. I turned to face her.

She turned away, and it was then she spoke. "You do not know me, Marget."

———

I knocked on Nicholas's door. Waited. Put an ear to the wood and heard a sonorous snore. Knocked again. The snore stopped . . . and then started once more.

I had already been to the stables to chase up a game of cards, but my men were nowhere to be found. And the stable grooms were sleeping off their ale.

Knocking a third time, I threw the weight of my shoulder into the motion. At this rate I would soon awaken everyone in the house!

I turned from the door and considered returning to the girl's room. Nay. I could not do it. And just as well. For as I began contemplating taking myself to the stables once more, the door swung open and Nicholas appeared.

He stepped out into the hall and glanced both up and down its length with bleary eyes. "My lord?"

"I have need of a place to sleep."

Wisely, he made no comment as he stood aside for me to enter . . . though he did look a bit forlornly toward the bed he had just vacated as he kicked the rushes covering the floor into a pile. He lay down on them, threw his cloak about himself, and soon resumed his sleep. Along with his snoring.

It did not matter, for I could not sleep. I loathed myself.

Perhaps God would grant me just one request. If there could be a child come from this horrible night, then I would never have to touch the girl again.

That I should be one to make a girl weep.

She had tried to hide her tears, but I had seen them. I had only done what I had to. And it had taken tankards of ale in order to do it. But I had been as gentle about it as I could. And in the end, Nicholas had been right. The girl was not like Elinor. Elinor had always been more than willing . . . and that was the problem. Who had not sampled of sweet Elinor's delights?

I stopped myself before I could think on it further. Holleystone: there was a happy, happy thought. I had Holleystone. Holleystone was mine. And this night's . . . events . . . meant that the girl would not be able to dissolve the marriage. She would not be able to do what I had done to Elinor. At least not unless I lost my senses, and I was not planning to.

Nay, Holleystone would be forever mine.

But as my eyelids closed and I drifted toward sleep, the thought occurred to me that I might have sold my soul to obtain it.

The next morning there came a knock at the door while I was being dressed. I was startled to discover myself cowering, clutching my shift to my chest while Joan went to answer. She talked for a moment with a person in the passage, then closed the door and walked back to me. "A gift."

"For what?"

"From the earl. 'Tis the wedding gift." She opened her hand and held out her palm. Nestled within were a pair of bracelets. Matches to the ring I had received upon our betrothal. "Shall I help you with them?"

"I do not want them. I will not wear them." Their glinting, glittering jewels were fixed to nothing more than a pair of shackles. And I did not wish to wear a constant reminder that I had bound myself to the earl until death us depart.

"You must." Joan eased them over my wrists, and when I began to cry, she clasped me to her chest.

I was expected to sit a horse, something I did not often do, and ride all the way to Downham Market, some ten miles away. Accompanied by Joan, the earl, and fifty of his men, I gritted my teeth and did as I was bid. But, oh, the humiliation that was driven deep into my soul. All who looked upon me could not fail to know what had been done to me.

At least the earl's messenger, who had turned out to be his Gentleman of the Horse, a man called Nicholas, was solicitous of my well-being. A tall and balding man with the look of a scholar about him, he rode beside me most of the forenoon and I learned that he had been attendant upon his master since boyhood.

"Boyhood?"

"Infanthood, my lady. His, at any rate. I came to the earl's house as a squire."

"You are of noble birth, then?"

"The second son of a baron, my lady. I could tell you many stories." Though he waited for my reply, his tone made it clear that he hoped I would prompt him to do so.

"Certain though I am that you could, they are not of any interest."

"I do hope there might come a time, my lady, when they will

be. I remain at your service." He doffed his hat before he trotted away to join the earl.

It was the greatest courtesy I had been shown that day.

———————

"As one who has known you from birth, my lord, I cannot keep myself from speaking."

"You will whether I wish you to or not. Be brief."

"The countess, my lord."

"What of her?"

"If you would only speak a word to her, my lord."

"Why?"

"To cheer her, my lord."

"I? Cheer her! You misread the situation, Nicholas. She hates me."

"My lord, she cannot hate you. She does not know you."

"She hates me. Watch you this." I pulled my horse from the front of the column, gesturing for it to continue and then joined the girl. "Good day to you."

She shrunk from me, her horse jogging the legs of the maid riding beside her.

I waited until the girl had checked her horse before I spoke again. "I hope you travel well this day."

She neither looked at me nor deigned to speak.

"Well . . . only several miles further." I doffed my hat before leaving to rejoin Nicholas.

"She does hate you!" Nicholas's hand hovered above his scabbard. "What did you do to her?"

"If you are going to draw your sword on me, I will do more than scar your cheek."

"What did you do?"

"Only my duty."

"Only . . . but . . . did you speak no word of kindness? Was there no tenderness?"

"I never wanted her."

"And now she knows what she might only heretofore have suspected. Well done. And they call *you* the nobleman." He wheeled his horse around without taking leave of my presence and went to join the back of the column.

But his words reverberated in my head. He should have stuck me through with his sword. It would have been more kind.

4

*I*t took us five more days to reach London, and the earl gave us not an easy ride on any of them. The country we rode through had been left dull by autumn's frost. It was stripped of trees and thus of shade. There were bushes aplenty, but the woodlands had been deforested to supply the navy with ships during the previous year's fight with Spain.

The skirt I had drawn over my gown as a safeguard had been irretrievably dust-streaked by the third day, but I did not have another. As we approached the city, I sought the earl to gain some indication of his expectations.

"My lord?"

"What is it?" His reply could not have been more ungracious.

"I wanted only to know . . . when we reach the city, what are we to do?"

"We are to join the court."

"Immediately, my lord?"

"Why would we wait?"

"I had hoped . . . I had thought that perhaps . . ."

"Perhaps?"

"Perhaps I might be allowed to change into something less soiled, my lord."

"It is already late and I had meant to have gone to Whitehall yesterday. Excuse me." At that, he spurred his horse and made quick work of leaving my company.

I returned to Joan's side and shook my head at her inquiry. "I am not to be allowed to change."

———

"The girl wants to change."

"Your countess, my lord?" At least Nicholas was speaking to me once more.

"I am overdue to the palace."

"And towing her into court looking like a lamb dragged through the countryside will earn you no favors with the Queen, my lord."

"I suppose we could stop at Lytham House."

"You do not have to profess your undying love to her, but it would not hurt relations between you to be gracious, my lord. And as Lytham House sits in the middle of your path to Whitehall, you might be accused of being unfeeling if you did not."

Curse the man, he was right. I had been known to show more kindness to mere servants. But if I looked on her, if I talked to her, then how could I escape the enchantment of her beauty? "If we stop, it will be you who oversees the unloading."

"Of course, my lord."

"And it will need to be done with all haste."

He nodded.

"And it is you who will show her to her chambers." I had not been in them since Elinor had gone. And I saw no use in visiting them now.

"The rooms have been redone, my lord." He paused. "As you had asked."

Nicholas gazed at me in expectation. "If you have a question, then ask it!"

"The countess might feel more warmly welcomed to Lytham House if it were you who did the welcoming, my lord."

"There is no time. Perhaps on the morrow . . ." Perhaps on the morrow she will have grown ugly. Perhaps on the morrow I will have grown blind.

————

I saw the city long before we entered it. It had smudged the horizon with its walls and soiled the sky with the smoke of coal. We entered the city through Bishopsgate after a short delay due to a waiting line of carters. The farther into the city we went, the greater was the assault upon my senses. Voices in all tone and timbres shouted their wares. Around me dodged all manner of people, some porting goods on their backs, others driving livestock before them. And from all sides of the street rose a stench so great it threatened to smother me. Trapped in a maze of buildings, absent any breeze, the reek of rotting food and human waste thrown out into the streets invaded the air. And the hooves of our horses and the feet of the sellers only served to mix it into the mud lying atop the pavement and drive it further into the foundations of the city.

Joan lost short time in retching.

By clamping my teeth together and endeavoring to ignore the filth around me, I was able to preserve my own dinner. We came to an intersecting of five streets, where the buildings had been pushed back to save room at their center for a market. A place of flesh and fish, it was vibrant with odors and blood, flies thick upon the sellers' offerings. We rode round the stalls and still we kept going. But quite soon the earl turned off onto a quieter street lined with enormous houses. At one of them he turned into the gate and trotted up into the courtyard. And there, at last, we could escape the worst of the stench.

Grooms came out to collect our horses, and as I sat there, staring about me in amazement, the earl walked up the stairs to a massive door and disappeared inside.

Nicholas reined his horse beside my own, dismounted, and then offered me his hand. "Welcome to Lytham House, my lady."

I placed my hand in his and he helped me gain the ground. After having ridden so hard for so many days, I should have wanted only to collapse upon a bed, but the sight of the magnificent building in front of me swept all thoughts from my mind.

It was a new house and handsome, built of brick with a cobbled courtyard. The roof was heavy with huge, fantastical bricked chimneys and a cupola in the middle that flew the earl's coat of arms. The arched windows were outlined in dressed stone and echoed the shape of both the arched gate and door.

"It was built to honor the Queen."

I looked for some sign of that honor but could find none.

Nicholas cleared his throat, and I turned back to find his eyes sparkling. "It was built in the shape of an E." He gestured me in front of him. "And so, my lady, would you like to step in upon her backbone?"

I smiled and then, on legs made wobbly from riding, I took him up on his invitation, walking through the door into a sort of short hall. To my left was the great hall, projecting two stories in height with large expanses of mullioned windows playing a game of shadow and light on the floor. Nicholas bid me walk farther into a long corridor that stretched away from me on both my sides. To my left was a grand staircase, and it was there that Nicholas led me.

Up those stairs and off a long gallery, the twin of the corridor beneath it, were my rooms. Two of them. An inner and an outer chamber. I reveled in the luxury of painted wainscoting and intricate tapestries, the fabulous curtains at the windows and the woven matting beneath my feet. There was a great bed with its four posts carved in flowers and vines and topped with indigo feathers. The mattress was covered with azure damask fringed with gold, and crimson velvet bed curtains hung from its rails. As soon as Nicholas left us, Joan and I went and sat on it, falling backward into its softness.

"I could spend the rest of my life in this very bed."

"And I could spend the rest of mine right here beside you." Joan spoiled the sentiment by poking me in the ribs with her elbow.

"Stop."

"Move."

"I command you to stop."

"And I command you to move."

"You are a worthless servant."

"Perhaps, but you have trained for this for years. And if you do not move, the earl will have to wait on you."

Nothing could have made me move faster.

Joan helped me out of my traveling clothes and into my best dress, my marriage gown, as quickly as she was able, but still the earl was waiting for us, pacing the corridor as we descended.

We rode in the same manner as we had come: accompanied by Nicholas and the earl's men. We entered the palace grounds through a crenellated gate and rode wide around some painters working a golden drapery upon the walls. The area was bustling with people and animals, and even the horses were dressed in finer livery than most of the people I had beheld in London.

We left our horses in Nicholas's care and entered the palace.

The earl offered me his hand, though he did not look at me, and we walked, hands held before us, down the long gallery that ran the length of the building. His silk-clad arm, embroidered with silver love knots, matched my own in color. We traveled between groups of men whispering and scowling, shuffling sheets of paper in their hands. They were clothed in all the colors of a summer's flower garden. And around them, like bees careening from blossom to blossom, ran pages. Sun had doused the passage with light, glinting off jewels and causing stiff lace ruffs to glow. It made the men look like the very flowers they resembled. There stood a plump, frilly carnation-colored gillyflower. And there, a French marigold dressed in cloth of gold, turning toward the sun so he would sparkle.

A smile played with my lips, but I swallowed it when we entered the Presence Chamber. The finery in the gallery was gaudy in comparison.

The whole of my life had been focused on getting me to court. All of the lessons. All of the money. All of the advantages I had been given. But none could have prepared me for the scale of this grandeur. The throne was worked in brown velvet, embroidered with gold, and set with diamonds. All about were instruments of music made of glass, of silver, or of gold. The walls themselves were laid with gilt. Light blazed from myriad gold chandeliers, hung from golden cords. Everything glittered, from the jewels on the ladies' dresses, to the mantel of the fireplace, to the gown of Her Majesty, the Queen.

The earl led me forward toward the dais, then paused to whisper to one of the women clothed in white attending Her Majesty.

The woman nodded and approached the Queen, curtsied, and, when acknowledged, stood and spoke to her.

Her Majesty leaned back slightly and eyed us, behind the woman's back. Then she sat forward once more and gestured to the woman.

That lady returned and bid us approach the throne. I felt my belly tighten.

The earl bowed.

The Queen extended her hand toward him.

He took it and kissed it. Then he extended his other hand to me and introduced me to our sovereign as his wife.

As the Queen turned her attentions toward me, the smile she had bestowed upon the earl slid from her face. She raked my form with her eyes and then fastened them upon my face.

———

"What have you brought us, Lytham? A Moor with darkened skin? A gypsy child?"

My smile died as I comprehended Her Majesty's words. She did not like the girl! What had gone wrong? I threw a glance toward the girl at my side, but everything seemed as it should. She was already bent in a curtsey; she had not uttered one word.

But I needed words. And quickly! "Your Majesty . . . compared to your alabaster beauty . . . the very moon would be suspect as a gypsy."

There was no response from the throne.

I chanced a glance at the girl. God, help me, she was going to cry! She could not cry. She would make me a laughingstock.

Thank heaven, in the next moment my prayers were heard, for there came the suggestion of laughter from the Queen. All was well. And then, she spoke. "I shall take note: I must banish the moon from the kingdom. And, Lytham?"

"Your Majesty?"

"Have a care. Warn your wife. It is not wise to gaze too long at the moon."

To gaze too long at the moon was to risk the loss of one's sanity. Warn my wife? It was a warning meant for me. Parliament had granted me one annulment. It would not grant me another. And should another wife of mine take leave of her senses, then my career as a courtier would be over.

———

The court gasped.

In my surprise, I did not think to gasp. I did not even think to breathe. Had she just warned me from . . . from madness?

The earl's hand, suddenly moist, squeezed mine, forcing it toward the ground.

I bent still further, feeling the stiff busk in my corset press into my belly. I trapped my breath inside my chest.

"You may go."

Beside me, Lytham dipped even further, pulling me with him, urging me to do the same. But I could do no more.

Taunted by laughter, we backed away from the Queen and left the Presence Chamber. In laughing, she had made a royal joke of us.

I will not cry. I will not cry.

What good would my marriage do my father or husband if I sniveled in front of the Queen like a child? But still the tears would not stop gathering. I was soon in danger of spotting my gown with them. I felt them gather behind my eyes, felt a drip form just inside the tip of my nose.

Her Majesty's dark, glittering eyes had sent a message, if I could only decipher it. Had I glimpsed mistrust? Suspicion? Hate?

How could she hate me? She did not know me.

But her smile had ceased the moment the earl had made my introduction. The moment her eyes had come to rest upon me.

The ride back to Lytham House was made in great haste and complete silence.

Once inside the courtyard, the earl dismounted quickly. I tried to follow him, but my feet became tangled in my skirts. Nicholas helped me loose myself and held my hand as I dismounted. I nearly forgot to thank him in my rush toward the house. But my hurry was justified; the earl was waiting for me inside the front hall.

"Does Her Majesty have any reason to despise your family?" His tone was not accusatory. But neither was it kind.

"None, my lord."

"Does Her Majesty have any reason to despise you?"

Do not cry. Behind the skirts of my gown, I fisted my hands into balls, driving my fingernails straight into my palms. "None, my lord."

He frowned, then turned and strode toward a door. He shut it firmly behind him after he had walked through, leaving me standing in the middle of the hall, alone, still wearing my marriage gown.

5

I had fifty men to ride with me and fifty men to serve me, but never had I felt so vulnerable, so . . . alone. Was the whole world against me? God, the Queen, the entire court?

Without Her Majesty's favor, I had nothing. As a courtier, everything hung in the balance of her affections. And it seemed to rest on the fulcrum of the girl.

But why?

And was there any way to undo what seemed to have been done?

Perhaps. If I could but figure out what it was.

"Nicholas!" I called out to the house in general, knowing that if Nicholas were not in a position to hear me, then word would make its way to him that he was wanted.

Once I gained my room, I unfastened my scabbard and handed it to a chamberer, threw my doublet in the direction of another, and gave my hat to still a third. Then I dismissed them all.

Taking up an English horn, I began to play a melancholy tune as I let my thoughts work.

The Queen was not pleased.

Were she not pleased, she would never visit Brustleigh.

Were she never to visit Brustleigh, I would have no sign of preference.

Had I no sign of preference, I would never receive any signs of preferment. No Garter Knighthood, no seat on the Privy Council; no estates, no opportunity to purchase a monopoly.

Should I never receive any signs of preferment, my resources might never be replenished and I would end up where I had started: facing the possibility of selling Holleystone. And if I could not retain Holleystone, then I would never be able to restore my family's honor.

That the fate of the Earls of Lytham should rest upon the shoulders of one young girl! But then, had not my own brother traded away our good name and our fortunes for one of that same sex? I would not, could not, do the same. I had a chance to restore all that had been lost. It would not do to let everything slip away just when the means to regain it had been placed at my disposal.

I worked back and forth through the logic of the facts, trying to find some reason to change my conclusions, but the fact remained that Her Majesty was not pleased. And so there could be no other outcome.

The horn was mellow, but it lacked a certain note of misery, which I very much wanted. I put it away and took up a treble viol instead.

———

I walked up the grand stairs in search of my rooms. And Joan.

After a while I happened upon my chambers, but from a direction opposite of the way I had been shown to them before. And when I finally reached the refuge of those walls, I did not find Joan within them.

My return had not been anticipated, for the curtains had been drawn and the windows shuttered. There was a single candle set upon a table beside the bed. It threw the rest of the room into darkness. I thrust aside the bed's heavy curtains and sat down on the brocade coverlet. I smoothed my skirts as I sat, habit not allowing me to let them wrinkle.

If only I knew what I had done. I tried to place my thoughts in order to decipher the puzzle of what had happened at court.

We were a good match. *I* was a good match. Everyone had thought so. Ours had been the union of Northern English money to the time-honored respectability of an English peer. There was nothing of which to disapprove.

Had he truly said the Queen despised me?

My eyes cast about the room, looking in vain for something upon which to fasten. I ended by staring into the candle's flame, letting my thoughts find their own channels. As I watched, a gray moth came to rest upon the candleholder. It climbed the candlestick, undaunted by the flame, until it encountered the dripping wax. And then it was too late to retreat. Once its foot was caught, it could not be unfixed. The moth fluttered its wings faster and faster with urgent imperative. Then the draft in the room shifted and the flame swept horizontal, setting first one wing, then the other ablaze. A crackle when fire met substance, a slender spiral of rising smoke, and the moth was gone.

I watched as the drippings made steady progress down the face of the candle. They slid over the charred insect one by one, until all traces of its fate were obliterated.

A prickling sensation swept my spine and I was overcome by a need to be rid of the wedding clothes. To rid myself of the reminder of a marriage that had been thrust upon me. If I could remove the stiff ruff around my neck and rid myself of my corset, then I could pretend that I was a maiden once more and that none of indignities that had assaulted my person had taken place.

I pulled at the ruff, grasping at one of the hundred pins that held it in place, but it stuck into my flesh. I pulled my finger away and watched a droplet of blood rise from my skin. I sucked at the blood, unwilling to let it mark my clothes.

Pulling at the ruff with the other hand only resulted in pricking those fingers as well. Turning, I meant to release the laces that fastened my gown at the back, but I could not place my hand to them. I could not free myself from anything.

I stood then, turning and pulling, tugging at my gown, desperate to rid myself of its constraints. I heard lace tear and jewels fall but could not rid myself of the desire to be free. Finally, reason prevailed and I stopped, panting, wrapped in the shreds of a marriage gown that had cost a veritable fortune. A gown that was part of my dowry.

What had I done?

And more importantly, what was I to do?

Had I not curtsied soon enough? Had I not curtsied well enough?

There in my chambers, I closed my eyes and bent in reminiscence of the homage I had paid the Queen.

I had done . . . just . . . so.

I opened my eyes and my gaze fell on the same stretch of hem that it had in the Presence Chamber. I closed my eyes again, reliving the audience with the Queen. The earl had urged me to curtsey further. And that I had done.

I closed my eyes and bent again in imitation. Opened my eyes to survey my form as well as I could with the ruff still fixed about my neck.

It was perfect.

I rose and curtsied again. And again. And again. It mattered not that the front of my gown flopped open, giving plain view of the corset beneath. It mattered not that my forepart dangled drunkenly from my kirtle's skirt. I was searching for some flaw, sought some sign of betrayal in my limbs, searched for anything, any reason to explain the Queen's ire.

But I found nothing.

I closed my eyes and curtsied once more. And then I remembered that at the last, the earl had forced my hand to the ground, urging me to bend further. But I had not done it. Had thought it impossible to bend further. But perhaps . . .

Bending forward, I felt my busk strain. And then it snapped. The sudden absence of restraint pitched me forward and I fell to the floor.

It was evident that I could not have done more. And lying there alone, with my face to the ground, I cried.

By and by, Joan returned. I heard the door scrape, heard her steps cross the floor. And then, a pause. "Marget?" She soon knelt at my elbow, gripped my forearm to help me up. "What has happened?"

"It was . . . horrible. The Queen did not like me. Everyone . . . laughed . . . at me." My voice caught on the last word and my eyes overflowed once more.

"They cannot have laughed! Why would they have laughed?"

"She called me a gypsy."

"The Queen?"

I could only nod.

Joan helped me to a stool. She removed the French hood that adorned my head at a tilt, then pretended to smooth my hair, succeeding only in wiping away my tears. When she left my side to pour me a glass of wine, her work was ruined, for new tears issued to take the place of the old.

I tried to save what remained of my ruff when it became apparent that the tears were flowing from some font that would not be stopped. I scrubbed at them furiously, but it made no difference. I succeeded only in chafing my cheeks and my neck, making me look even more like the gypsy Her Majesty had called me.

"Stop pawing at that ruff. Let me get a chambermaid to help you."

"Nay! Please. I have no wish for anyone to see me."

So she removed the pincushion from my jewel casket and proceeded to unpin the ruff even as I tried to hide my face from her. She approached me to fasten a second ruff in place, but I waved her off.

"I cannot wear this gown."

"Which other do you want?"

I did not know. Neither did I know what I should do. I had examined my every action and found nothing wanting. The Queen despised me, my husband detested me.

What I wanted was to go home to King's Lynn.

My father could disown me, my mother cuff me, but anything would have been better than being here. My chin began to tremble on its own accord. The harder I tried to still it, the worse it became. My lips began to convulse as sobs wracked my body.

Joan came near.

I shook my head, willing her to go away, but she ignored me, gathering me to her chest like a child.

I threw my arms around her waist and clung to her.

After some time I quieted and Joan brought me more wine. After several sips, my thoughts became sharper and I turned them toward the task at hand, toward something I could do. I concentrated my efforts upon choosing a gown and answering Her Majesty's only complaint.

"The indigo. I will wear the indigo." Crimson would have only enhanced the red in my cheeks. I needed pallor. I wanted the alabaster skin for which the earl had praised the Queen.

Never before had I been accused of being common. My skin was transparent, translucent, marred by neither pox nor freckle. My black hair only made me seem more pallid; my blue eyes, it had been said, shone like the palest of winter skies. I had been born with the complexion every woman in the kingdom used artifice to obtain.

And yet, she had called me a Moor.

———

Fortunately, Nicholas found me before I had wallowed too long in melancholy. As it was, he walked into the room as I was playing an especially dismal rendition of "Flow My Tears."

"My lord?"

"There is to be a banquet at Whitehall this night. Make ready my horse for leaving, Nicholas."

"And the countess's, my lord?"

"What of it?"

"Shall I order her horse readied?"

"Nay."

"She does not go? Is she ill, my lord?"

She was not ill and Nicholas knew it. He just wanted to hear me say the words. To have me give voice to my own injustice. Only this time, my actions could not be seen by him to be objectionable. "I took her to court. I introduced her to the Queen. The Queen laughed at her. Everyone else laughed at her. I think I have done my duty by the girl."

"Why did they laugh, my lord?"

"Because the Queen called her a gypsy."

"A gypsy? But she is as pale as a corpse . . ."

"I know it. But the Queen said it. What would you have me do?"

"I would have you go to the banquet with your countess on your arm, my lord, and force everyone to respect her."

"That would require a great assumption on your part."

"And what would that be, my lord?"

"The assumption that I care to *have* her on my arm."

"So you mean to abandon her? To have her first dreadful experience at court be her last? My lord, that does not become you!"

"I mean to do nothing more with her at all."

"You must not do it, my lord. What has she done to deserve such ill-mannered behavior?"

"She has . . ." *come to me with the face of an angel and the innocence of a lamb.*

"Aye?" Nicholas prodded.

"She has . . ." *been used terribly by the Queen and all of the court.* "She has . . ."

"In truth, my lord, she has been born beautiful to a wealthy father whose fortune you happened to need *and* she's had the misfortune to follow behind Elinor."

That was not what I had been thinking! "You make me out to be a blackguard."

"Then, please, my lord, prove my suspicions to be unfounded."

———

Later, the earl sent word to me, through the steward, that we were needed at the palace for a banquet.

"I will not go."

Joan glanced at the door behind which the steward had disappeared. It was closed. "You have to go."

"There must be something good about being a countess. Why cannot my wish be also my command?"

"Because you would be making a grave mistake in not attending."

"In not giving them more reasons to laugh at me?"

"If you do not go, whatever they imagined they could laugh at will only become proven in their eyes. If you do not go, they will laugh at you forever. Was there no one there who was kind to you?"

"Not one."

"Then you must make them be kind to you. You are a countess. If they will not like you, they must at least respect you."

They did not have to be kind to me, neither were they required to respect me. But Joan had not been present at my introduction, and she had no way of knowing what it had been like to be chewed up and spit out by those glittering nobles. Before I left I bid Joan find the betrothal ring and the bracelets the earl had given me. Though he was the least of my friends, it was he who provided my title, the reason for my being there. And tonight, it seemed, I had need to belong to someone.

When I appeared as requested and joined the earl in the hall, he made no comment on my change in garment. Indeed, he made no comment at all.

As we rode back to Whitehall, I gathered my courage for the evening ahead. Joan was right. To have absented myself from court would have been to admit defeat, to have sacrificed everything my father had worked to gain. To have forgone my duty would have made an admission that the earl had made a grave mistake in taking me to wife. It would have announced to all present that he would have done better with no wife at all.

Though the earl sat beside me at the table, I was isolated from those around me by a barricade of silence. To him, at least, our tablemates were polite. After sliding surreptitious glances toward the Queen, they leaned toward him in conversations of quickly whispered words. It only succeeded in confirming my suspicions: the trouble with our coupling was me.

But the indifference of others leant me invisibility. With no partner to talk to, my thoughts floated back to my introduction to the Queen. Before she had looked into my eyes, she had looked at my gown. Was it for that she had despised me?

It had been styled in the latest fashion so that I would not cause the earl shame. Indeed, it had proclaimed his wealth and his royal favor with its decorations of the finest pearls. Its colors and materials were well within my right, as a countess, to wear. I had not tried to climb above my station, to be batted at like a common fly.

My French hood? The veil that covered the back of my head?

Glancing down the table, I saw other women wearing the same. Both those seated above me and those seated below me.

My glance passed the table once more, and I found one thing of note: of all the august woman at the table, only *my* face lacked white ceruse paint. Only *my* hairs were not orange. Surely they could not all be related to the Queen? Surely they did not all come by the Tudor hairs naturally. Was mine the only skin unmarred by disease? Mine the only hairs not hidden beneath a wig?

I turned my attentions to my plate and ate of stewed oysters. I lifted my eyes again, reluctant to confine my gaze to food when around me nobles wore a veritable treasure chest of gems and jewels. I had never before seen such a vast exhibit of wealth.

As I glanced down the table, the earl's eyes trapped my gaze. His dark eyes were devoid of warmth, his thoughts unreadable.

Breaking from his look, I lifted a nutmeat to my lips. But as I ate, realization dawned that to a person, every noblewoman was eating only custard or jelly. So I left the remainder on my plate.

In the following days, I vowed I would be more careful to match my actions to those among whom I moved. I had no need to paint myself, nor did I wish to wear a wig, but my best hope was for Her Majesty to forget that she had known me. To blot the memory of me from her mind. Until I could return the earl to her good graces, I would try not to remember myself to her at all.

6

dressed with great care the next morning as I thought about claiming my place among Her Majesty's nobility. That place was mine to claim, by right of marriage, unless the earl indicated otherwise. But if the previous day's experiences were any guide, I could only assume that place would not be given unless I asserted my right to have it. It was imperative that I show my presence. To remain at Lytham House would be to relinquish my position, to forfeit any hope I had of being useful to the earl. For how else could I determine which ladies were most influential and whom I must befriend? Whom I must invite to supper and whom I must avoid? It was at court that my talents for singing and for dancing could be best displayed.

Since I longed to be part of what I had been trained for, I wanted neither to be the first in fashion nor to be among those wearing the previous year's styles. I wanted to look like all the other courtiers' wives.

A chambermaid helped me put on my shift, corset, and silk stockings. Then Joan motioned me to stand on a stool, and together she and the maid raised the farthingale hoops above me so I could push my head through them.

I took some bread as the maid fastened the farthingale to the bodice. That done, there was the question of the kirtle. Since I would wear a French gown with the front of the skirt cut away, the front of the kirtle would be revealed. "I want the gold gown, I think, and so the cloth of gold kirtle." But after it had been taken to the sempstress, I changed my mind. It would seem dull to wear too much gold. "Could I . . . I think the cloth of gold forepart should be replaced with the carnation."

As I sipped at wine, Joan found the sempstress and told her to detach the remainder of the cloth of gold forepart from the front of the kirtle and join the carnation forepart to it instead. The forepart replaced, she brought it back to my chambers. The chambermaid aided me into the gown and arranged it over my farthingale.

But I stopped her. "Leave me think a moment." Instinctively, I had chosen to wear my gold gown, the only gown I could see in the dim light. But it would be the first gown any would notice in the bright-lit Presence Chamber, and that would not do.

I could wear the indigo once more. Or the one my mother had ordered made in gray. The gray gown was wretched, the color of ashes. But it symbolized repentance. At my mother's insistence, a gray gown of satin had been part of my dowry. She had advised that a proper wife should always have a gray gown in which to mourn a death or beg forgiveness from a husband.

Perhaps gray; I could play the penitent. Surely that would please the Queen.

"I shall need this gown replaced by the gray."

Joan cast a long look at me before she gestured the maid to pull the gown from me.

"And with it, not the carnation forepart, but the cloth of silver in its stead." If I was to make myself humble, at least I could do it in a gown worthy of my new station.

The maid removed the gown and then the kirtle I had just put on, handing it to Joan.

Joan disappeared, no doubt to take it to the sempstress once more. I felt bad that the woman would have to unpick the stitches that had just been sewn.

I took more bread while I waited for Joan's appearance.

When she returned with the forepart replaced, I lifted my arms to be dressed once more.

"Sleeves, my lady?" The chambermaid curtsied as she asked.

"The gray." Much as I would have liked the silver which matched the forepart, I chose for the Queen's pleasure, not my own.

The maid laced the sleeves to my gown. I stood straight as she laced the gown up the back.

"A hat, my lady?"

I preferred my tall hat for its gaiety but had chosen a more traditional French hood for my introduction the day before. I settled, finally, on a caul. It needed but a simple arrangement of hairs, and the netted cord that would gather my tresses in back was dotted with pearls.

A second chambermaid parted my hairs in the middle as I sat on a stool. She twisted them away from my brow and then captured them in the net. After she finished, she curtsied. But before she left my presence, I stopped her.

"This morning, I will want vermillion."

"My lady."

Joan found the casket and lifted the lid for the maid as she painted my lips and dabbed at my cheeks. After she had finished, Joan held a mirror for my viewing.

I surveyed the results and was pleased. I looked sober. The vermillion paint had made my skin seem paler. No one would accuse me of being a gypsy.

I was ready for whatever the day might hold.

Upon leaving my chambers and asking for the earl, I was told he had already left for the palace and had taken Nicholas with him. Unsure of what I was to do, I stood there at length until Joan made the decision for me.

"My lady will want a horse to take her to the palace and twenty of the earl's men to ride with her."

I would? I turned toward her, brows raised. Had she gone mad?

She smiled. When I said nothing in response, she inclined her head ever so slightly toward the front hall. And then, when still I had not moved, she curtsied before me, straightened, tucked her hand around my arm, and dragged me forth.

"What have you done?" I was furious with her. What did I know of commanding twenty men? And what was I to do with them once I reached the palace?

"I have done nothing but asked for an honor due someone of your rank."

"And what am I to do with them?"

"Whatever you please."

Whatever I pleased. I contemplated that thought as we waited for my horse to appear. I could probably have saddled her faster myself. I began to wish of a sudden that I had not been so set on upholding my position at court. For surely no one cared whether I made an appearance. No one but the earl, of course. And perhaps then not even him. I sighed. "What is the earl to say?"

"Whatever it is, certain I am that he will not be so hasty in leaving you behind next time."

I frowned at her.

She crossed her eyes at me.

An unseemly giggle threatened to bubble from my throat, but at that instant we heard the sound of a great thundering of hooves. The earl's men rode into the courtyard in formation, a vision of azure and red, wrapped in dust. The man in the lead was holding the reins of my horse.

None of the men looked overly happy at having been summoned from whatever it was they had been doing.

"I wish . . . Could you not accompany me?"

"'Tis not my place. 'Tis yours. And you had best be about the taking of it." Joan raised her chin and looked toward the men. "They await your order." She nudged me forward with an elbow.

I descended the steps and walked to my horse. The man holding on to her reins dismounted, and I allowed him to help me mount.

"My lady." He bowed deep in gracious homage.

I looked one last time at Joan, wishing for all the world that I might stay by her side.

She frowned.

I cleared my throat to find my voice. "I would go to the palace."

The man made no move.

Was there some secret word? Some special phrase that would make them do my bidding?

"You would go to . . . Whitehall, my lady? Or to Greenwich?"

I looked at him sharply to discern if he was making sport of me. But he was not. He only wished to fulfill my command.

"To Whitehall."

"My lady goes to Whitehall!"

The men rode their horses round the courtyard and waited in formation in front of the gate. But what were they waiting for?

The man who had helped me mount gestured that I should go first. "My Lady Lytham."

I felt a blush spread across my cheeks. They were waiting for me. But I did not remember how I was to get there. "I should be quite . . . grateful . . . if I did not have to think too hard upon where it is that I am going."

"Perhaps you would allow us the honor of seeing to your

protection. You could, my lady, ride perfectly at ease if you rode in the middle."

And so I rode forth, in their center, in relative ease, for the pace was not too fast. Neither was it too slow. But upon our approach to the palace, I began once more to worry. What was I to order them to do? It would not have been correct for me to return to Lytham House on my own. But neither did I think it prudent to have the men wait for me, since I could not know how long I would be at court.

I hoped it would become evident once we had reached the palace. Perhaps I would see companies of other men in livery.

But I did not.

And although the man who had helped me mount also helped me dismount, he provided no cues, no sign of what he expected me to say or to do. And so, coward that I was, I walked into the palace without so much as a backward glance, willing them all to disappear.

7

As I twisted and turned through the labyrinth of halls and passageways, I forgot about the men altogether as I neared the Presence Chamber. My thoughts turned instead toward what must lie ahead. I paused in the gallery, in the gloom of a shadow, and then slipped into the room behind a group of other women.

To the right side of the room, I could see the earl, engaged in conversation with a knot of peacock-hued men. One of them, looking toward the door, saw me and then quit the group, slinking away to join another. At his movement, the rest of the men melted away, leaving the earl standing, suddenly, alone.

He turned and saw me. He neither honored me with a bow nor shunned me with a turned back; therefore neither claiming nor disowning me.

To my left, ladies clustered in loose groups, standing as close as their farthingaled skirts would let them, speaking softly and observing much. Their faces, painted white, brought to mind the memory of a childhood Madonna, a relic from Queen Mary's reign. Carved of marble, her beauty had been frozen as if it were glazed with ice. Her chief attribute had been disregard. It had not mattered how long I stood and gazed at her, she had never turned to look at me.

Wanting for guidance, I tried to signal the earl.

He would not acknowledge me, and I would not cross the room to him. Receiving no direction, I made my own decision and walked toward the nearest group of women.

I stood, silent, listening to their conversation and waiting for a sign of recognition. Some indication of welcome. I knew not a single one, although I was certain most had been present for my introduction to the Queen. But without some person to introduce me, I was casting myself upon their sympathy. Though I could not enter their circle, they could invite me in. And so I prayed for an opening in that formidable hedge of skirts. Prayed that God would establish my feet firmly on this new path I was to take.

I tried to catch an eye, but they were as difficult to trap as butter-flies; never still, those gazes constantly fluttered away from me. I tried to smile, but it left me feeling like a simpleton, beaming only for the empty air in front of me. I could, however, hear snatches of their low-voiced conversations.

". . . introduced her to everyone. Even those who had known her from . . ."

". . . I assure you. A love match from the very first . . ."

". . . an annulment. I was there. I saw all, I swear to you . . ."

". . . quite mad. But they say that it goes well with her in . . ."

From the women's gowns, a dozen swaying pomanders diffused the scents of amber, nutmeg, and roses long dead. The wafting of breeze from a multitude of ostrich feather fans whorled the odors together and swirled them around me. In the cloying air, I suddenly felt ill. I deployed my own fan and tried to sweep the smells away.

When I could breathe again with ease, I pretended still to be part of the group. In desperation, I smiled, no longer caring if it made me look the fool. I laughed when the other women laughed;

hysteria thrust it forth from me. To an observer, I must have appeared quite gay.

". . . within a fortnight, you can be sure. He only waits until . . ."

". . . and look you. Next time the Queen . . ."

". . . retire to the country. Heed my words . . ."

No one paid me any attention and yet I felt as if every eye in the chamber was turned in my direction, as if every word they spoke was made in reference to me. And then I heard an odd noise. It sounded like the nickering of a horse. But surely, there could be none inside the room. As I twisted to the right to try to identify its source, a soft neighing came from my left. And another from a group in front of me.

Feathers fanned the air again, at once both hiding faces and revealing eyes. And that time, they were all turned toward me. And then I understood: this knight's daughter would not be extended any welcome in this place.

Alternate waves of heat and chill struck my face.

The women quite deliberately turned their shoulders to me and migrated toward another area in the room. I stood alone for some moments, reeling from the snub. Then I did the only thing that I could do.

I fled.

I wound through the halls at Whitehall Palace until I burst through a door into the frigid air and found myself inside a pleasure garden. Deserted in the chill weather, rosebushes pruned to flower late offered up blooms unseen by any other human eye. I found solace in their beauty and relaxed in the luxury of seclusion. My breath began to slow.

A single medlar tree hunched beside the garden wall, its fruit providing billaments for the branches. I walked closer, inspecting the tree, looking for the medlar most like a rotting apple. I removed my gloves and plucked a promising fruit. Piercing the skin with my teeth, I sucked out the flesh as the juice dribbled down my chin. Soft as a cooked apple with the spiciness of cinnamon, it wanted only a glass of port to attain perfection.

"If I might suggest . . ."

I started at the voice and turned to discover a man extending a handkerchief toward me. He was extraordinarily tall and dressed in the vivid array of a courtier. His flat cap flopped forward over his right eye, a pearl dangled from his ear. But even so, his beard was scraggly and his clothing marked more by disregard than by fastidiousness.

"This kind must be plucked hard, else it will shrivel as it keeps."

Although I did not like the glint in his eyes, I let the medlar skin and seeds fall to the ground and took the handkerchief from him. I wiped my chin, then gave it back. "I do not know you."

"Nay, you do not." He was amiable in his agreement. "Your husband has not been kind enough to make an introduction." He peered more closely at my chin, then stepped forward to grip it between his thumb and forefinger. "You have a spot just . . ." He brought his head still closer, looking all the while at my lips.

I tried to withdraw, but the force of his grasp rooted me to the earth. My limbs began to tremble.

———

I had been watching the girl all morning. To her credit, Marget managed to look paler than she had the day before. Also to her credit, she entered the Presence Chamber with the look of a warrior about her. I watched mostly to see what she would do. And what would be done to her. She turned toward me once or twice for guidance, but I could give her none. As in fencing, the society of the court was marked by conversations. Each action must inspire a reaction. To fail to react was simply . . . to fail. But as in fencing, no one could fight for you. Battles among courtiers had to be fought *corps à corps* or not be attempted at all. What was illegal in fencing was expected in these circles. I might have demanded a place for her, but it would have disappeared the moment I turned my back.

Still, even I was shocked by the cruelty with which the noble ladies suddenly separated themselves from her. Could they not have been kind for nobility's sake? Would she always have to flee a laughing court?

It took quick stepping and the direction of several servants before I found her. She had somehow stumbled upon Her Majesty's private pleasure garden. I hastened to remove her from it, then slowed my steps. She had already been discovered.

By the Earl of Essex.

Not only did she look like Elinor. She *was* Elinor. She was Elinor come back to haunt me.

As I watched, Essex pulled her close. And I could not separate what I had seen of Elinor, in my very own bed, from what was happening in the garden before me. Was my fate to be forever plagued with feckless women?

Revulsion rose as bile in my throat. I was about to turn away when I thought the better of it. Did he think my wives were his for the plucking?

————

"I would suggest, Lady, that—".

"May I suggest, Essex, that your best strategy be retreat?"

Heat washed my face as I recognized the earl's voice.

Apparently the courtier also recognized it. He released my chin and then he bowed, turned on a brightly clad heel, and left.

"Are you so generous with your affections that you would encourage the attentions of the Earl of Essex?"

The heat drained from my face as I recognized the insult to my virtue. "You, of all persons, should know that I am not." Although

I would have liked to have forgotten our marriage bed, I am quite sure that he had not.

"It does not take much to tempt one such as him." His eyes probed mine.

"I have done nothing! I did not know him. I know no one. I may not introduce myself; moreover, if I could, I would not know to whom I should. You have given me no guidance. You have deserted me!" To my eternal shame, tears leaked from my eyes, disguising my anger as weakness.

I turned my back to him and, stumbling, reached out an arm toward the medlar tree, seeking the strength of a trunk rooted deep within the ground.

He came near but offered me nothing more than had the Earl of Essex, only pulling a handkerchief from his doublet and flicking it toward me. "Dry your tears." His eyes spoke of impatience rather than concern.

By the time I had done with drying them, he had disappeared. I turned and surveyed the garden for his whereabouts, but he was gone.

I did not want to be offered a handkerchief; I wanted to be invited into his world. I wanted to be his wife, to assume the role for which I had been trained. To be of some service, to serve for some use.

Tears threatened to spring anew, but I had grown tired of them. I turned, threw the handkerchief to the ground, and stalked toward the palace door.

As I reached to pull it open, I thought the better of my actions and turned back to fetch the material. If I could not help the earl advance his position, then at the very least I could help him manage the things he still possessed.

I returned to the palace with reluctance, having no desire to offer myself up as entertainment for the other women. Perhaps . . . perhaps I had done what I could that day. Perhaps a greater impact might be made on the morrow, when I returned myself to their presence. Perhaps that would make the greater statement of my tenacity. Having decided upon that tack, I spent some time in discovering a way to leave the palace and finally broke out into the vast courtyard from which I had earlier entered.

The earl's men, all the twenty of them, were waiting as I had left them . . . only they had been joined by two others. The earl himself was talking with great animation to the man who had seen to both my mounting and dismounting. And Nicholas stood to one side, watching them both.

I wanted to turn aside and creep back into the palace, but those men not watching the amusement the earl was providing had fixed their eyes fast upon me.

The leader of the twenty saw me and made a swift bow. "My lady."

The earl turned toward me. His lips were crimped into a frown. "You commanded twenty of my men to accompany you here? And then gave them no leave? They have been sitting here for more than three hours! Precisely the amount of time I have been laughed at—again—by everyone at court!"

I curtsied as deep as I was able. "I had hoped you might accompany me, my lord, but since your presence was required by Her Majesty, I only thought to bring myself to your side as quickly as possible. I did not know the roads in the place. I did not know what kind of villains might await me. I only knew you would have no wish for your own wife to be overtaken by some rude person. If I have erred, please count it as ignorance and seek to remedy the fault through education. I would only do what brings you the most honor."

"What would do me the most honor is to have you return yourself to Lytham House forthwith." He held out his hand, ostensibly to help me mount.

I placed mine into his and took advantage of our nearness to say one thing more. Though it destroyed me to do it, I heard myself pleading with him. "You must help me. I will be any kind of wife you want. You must only tell me what it is that you expect. I have no wish to see you laughed at. My sole desire is to see your honor grow. You must believe me!"

He only hoisted me up into the saddle rather rudely, made a stiff bow, and then turned on his heel and left.

Nicholas handed me my reins. "My lady, he is not the man you think he is."

"Please do not tell me that he is less, for I do not know how I could bear it."

The last thing I saw in leaving was Nicholas's face. His eyes. Their gaze was softened by great pity.

———

Nicholas began to flay me with words as soon as we reached Lytham House. At least he waited until I had gained my chambers.

"You kick at her at every turn as if she were an unruly pup. Even the most obstinate of beasts can be trained. And she is not a beast, my lord, she is a lovely girl. To please you is her only wish."

"Then she wishes for the impossible."

"Truly, my lord? Are you truly such a misanthropist as that? Did Elinor leave you nothing in her going?"

"Do not speak to me of her."

"I do not understand, my lord. It is not as if you had loved her."

Love. "Nay. I committed a worse crime than that: I trusted her. I trusted her and she turned me into a cuckold. Had she not lost all reason, then I could never have gotten an annulment. Parliament would only have laughed at me and instructed me to tie her up like some animal in heat to keep the mongrels from coming round."

"So 'tis for want of trust you keep her at some distance, my lord?"

"Aye." Trust was a valuable commodity at court. Traded by

everyone, but possessed by no one. Its rarity was surpassed only by love. For love implied commitment, and how could any of us commit ourselves to any but the Queen? Love implied singularity, and how could any of us benefit another if our affections were bound to one in exclusivity? Love was never looked for and rarely found. When it was, it always ended badly. Far better not to confuse love with pleasure. That way, one could love the Queen with abandon and pursue carnal bliss, as exemplified by Essex, at leisure. I had learned my lessons. In both love and trust.

"Forgive me for asking, my lord, but how can you learn to trust her if you do not first learn to know her?"

"And that, you see, is why I will not know her. Find some other dead horse to beat."

Still, the girl's words haunted me during the dark of the night.

"My sole desire is to see your honor grow. . . . You must only tell me what it is that you expect."

How was it that at every turn she seemed to disappoint me? By being beautiful? By being moldable? By desiring to be a wife I actually wanted? One that I needed? What was it that I expected?

I expected Elinor. That is what I expected. And if she met that expectation, then she could never fail to disappoint me.

8

At night, those first weeks at Lytham House, I dreamt of my home. Of King's Lynn. When I woke from those dreams, I could still smell the sea in the air and hear the gulls cry. I could lick the corners of my lips and taste salt upon them. But I knew it was just the memory of my tears.

In London there was the River Thames and there were ships aplenty, but it was not the same. Where the sea winds sweetened the smells of King's Lynn, there was no breeze stiff enough to cleanse the streets of London. And winds skimming up off the Thames brought the river's own stink with them. Scavengers employed by the city's wards wandered the streets, making certain that people were disposing of their refuse responsibly. There were public cisterns for emptying the contents of closestools and chamber pots. But still the streets were filled with ashes and kitchen stuffs. And though there were common privies aplenty, every alley was used as a latrine. Building crowded against building and together they all leant forward to meet at angles above the centers of the streets. There were corners in London the sun would never reach.

But there was one thing which enchanted me about the city: I loved the swans that floated on the river with their long elegant necks, ever curving, ever swaying, swimming about in games, like so many nobles upon the water. They were so populous that at times the wherries transporting people from one side of the river to the other seemed to part and swirl them into snowdrifts.

One day, as Joan and I were rowed to Southwark to stroll in Paris Garden, the lure of their down proved irresistible.

"May I . . . would they let me . . . pet them?" The oarsman had probably never heard a request more daft.

"Pet them? They'd let you feed them. Daresay they'd let you take them home, except see those nicks in its beak? There's five. Means that's Her Majesty's bird. She catches you, you'll spend a year in Newgate." He barked a laugh, then bent to rummage in a sack. "Here, lady." He tossed a crust of bread onto my lap.

I reached out a hand to the swan and she reached out her neck toward me. She nuzzled my hand, looking for the crust, and allowed me to pet her for the briefest moment before taking possession of her prize and heading back to her game.

I wished all my hours could have been spent so pleasantly.

Most days I accompanied the earl to court. At least after that second disastrous appearance, he waited for me. And if he could not, then he made some provision for my transport.

In time I became accustomed to my role. It was not a difficult one to execute. I had only to stand, for the better part of the day, at court. Often there was dancing or other entertainment in the evenings. Occasionally there was a state dinner, presided over by the Queen, at which I would take my place at the table next to the earl.

I observed the swift changes in fashion that swept the court with the regularity of the tides. Had some lady worn a particularly pleasing shade of yellow with indigo? Then in the next days, the fashion was echoed by all the courtiers and their wives. Had some lord added extra buttons to his doublet? Then so did another, only he had them done up with emeralds. And another in rubies. And then a third had both emeralds and rubies worked into the hem of his cloak and a new fashion for cloaks had been created. I did not know how the Earth could contain enough jewels to supply Her Majesty's court.

I also soon discovered that there was one lamentable gap in my training, one area in which I had been left ignorant: I had been told nothing of the life of a courtier. But then perhaps it was because there was nothing of substance to be told.

As I watched the court, day after day, I came to the conclusion that if it was the duty of the women of the court to display the wealth of their husbands, then it was the courtier's job to seize every opportunity and turn it either to his advantage or to another courtier's disadvantage. Did the others, like the earl, practice the courtly arts of dancing and playing music, jousting and leaping? I was certain that they did, for how else could they have given such brilliant displays of their talents? The monies lavished on clothing and accoutrements was astounding to my provincial eyes. Even more astounding was the fact that the expense was undertaken only so that the Queen might give the courtier an opportunity to spend even more money on leasing a crown estate or purchasing a monopoly. There seemed no end to the amount of time and monies exhausted for appearances' sake alone. It was a way of life that seemed to produce nothing of worth and yet consume everything of value.

The first few weeks, when I returned to Lytham House to fall upon my bed in exhaustion from sheer boredom, Joan would rub my feet to draw out the aches.

We spoke to each other in whispers, never sure of who else might be listening. It seemed in this place that one could never be sure when they were being observed. The room could appear empty, then in the blinking of an eye it could be filled with servants. They appeared, silent as apparitions, and left the same way.

All but one. All but the slopswoman. She always seemed to be cackling to herself, muttering a tuneless song as she went about her unsavory task. Joan could perform a perfect imitation. She would run her fingers through her hairs to bedraggle them, and then she would draw her cheeks into her mouth, fold her lips into each other, and hobble around the room. The only thing she could not duplicate was the servant's red, bulbous nose.

"You should not do such things, Joan!" I could hardly speak for laughing.

"Why? Do you fear my face will be stuck this way?"

"Aye. Nay! Stop—'tis unseemly!"

At that moment, the servant in question entered the room. Joan straightened, but the woman was ignorant of the game we had been playing. She went about her work in her normal way.

"What is it that she sings?" Joan had seated herself on the bed beside me, so I did not have to speak very loud.

"Do you want me to find out?"

Before I could reply to the contrary, Joan had pushed herself away from the bed and was stalking the servant on cat's feet, an ear turned in an obvious manner toward the woman.

I stopped my breath, hoping the servant would make no sudden movement, but she did not. Joan dogged her until she left.

"And?"

She shook her head. "Mutter, mutter, mutter, WHITE. Mutter, mutter, mutter, GRAY. Mutter, mutter, mutter, TIGHT. Mutter, mutter, mutter, DECAY . . ."

For some reason the recitation made me shudder. But then Joan drew up her skirts and began to dance a jig. "And a hey nonny, nonny."

"That was not part of it!"

She dropped her hold on her skirts and came back to sit beside me. "Maybe it was and maybe it weren't. But you will never know!" She took my foot back into her lap. "Did they laugh at you today?"

"Nay."

"See then?"

"Neither did they talk to me, any of them."

"They are afraid of you."

I scoffed. "Aye, beast that I am."

"They are."

"Afraid of what?"

"They are like all those fishwives in King's Lynn that mock the fairest maids, afraid that they will never regain what it is they once had."

"I only wish I could stop going."

Joan stopped rubbing my foot. "Never say that!"

"Why not? 'Tis true."

"When you stop going, the earl will have no use for you."

She was right. She was always right. "Is there no way I could have what I want and do what he wants?"

Joan raised her eyes to mine. "There is one. You could have his babe."

His babe. That would require the sharing of a bed. But after our wedding and my introduction to the Queen, the earl had never touched me again. I cannot say that I much minded. "I could. But it requires two for such . . . things."

"Why should he take you into his bed if you claw and spit at him every time he comes near?"

"If I do, 'tis only because he claws and spits at me."

"Sheathe your claws."

"If I sheathe them," I protested, "then I go about unarmed."

"If you do not, then he . . . simply . . . goes about."

It was the first time I had considered such a thought. I had worked so hard at protecting myself from him. Might I only have succeeded in driving him into the arms of another? If he were steadfastly ignoring me, then on whom was he bestowing his attentions? I knew him to return home quite late. "Joan, is he . . . has he been . . . ?"

"I do not know. But why should he not?"

I could not let myself think too long on what he might have been doing with his time and attentions. But I could start to consider the cost of reversing my own course.

I *must* reverse my course.

My father had populated the countryside of Norfolk with his bastards. The one thing I hoped from my marriage was that my own husband would not do the same.

9

The celebration of Her Majesty's Accession Day, the day she had ascended to her throne, arrived. I attended the tilts at the palace and watched as the earl took his place among the other nobles. Some of them had their lady's glove fixed to their helmet or their sleeve, but the earl had asked for nothing from me. And had he asked for something, I confess I do not know what I would have given him.

What kind of man was he that he could ignore his own wife? That he was more solicitous of his servants' interests, of Joan's even, than my own? I could not call him unkind, just as I could not call him unhandsome. His dark curls were pleasing. And his beard was quite precisely trimmed. His mustaches were long enough to make themselves known, but not so grown as to be overlarge. In short, he looked the perfect courtier. In fact, he courted all but one.

All but me.

And I could not understand why.

Not that I wanted to *be* courted.

———

I had sent my armor to the armorer's to be polished and had commissioned a new spear. I commanded that a new gown be made for the girl as well. All seemed perfect. Except that everywhere I looked, the ladies of the court were bestowing tokens upon their husbands or lovers. Sometimes both. I may not have a lover, but I was a husband, and my wife had given me nothing. Not a look nor a word nor a token of any kind.

Not that it mattered.

Oh, but it did!

I intended to wait no longer. "Nicholas!"

"My lord?"

"I would that you request a handkerchief from the . . . my . . . countess."

"My lord?" He offered his own handkerchief to me. "Please, do me the honor."

"Thank you just the same, but I will not fix *your* handkerchief to *my* helmet."

Knowledge lit his eyes. "Of course not, my lord."

I kept watch on Nicholas as he made his way toward the girl. I could not hear their conversation, but I was able to read their gestures.

At Nicholas's approach, she smiled. The red of her gown made her skin glow like a moonstone. Nay. In truth, it could not be the red, for there was something that ever glowed from within. There was such . . . goodness about her. It flowed forth like a moonbeam.

There now! Was that not magnanimous of me?

Could the nobles around me hear my thoughts, they would think me daft indeed.

As Nicholas spoke, her smile grew broader still. She pulled a handkerchief from her sleeve and offered it to him with a laugh.

And then, he betrayed my interest. He pointed in my direction.

Her smile withered.

Our eyes met.

I bowed.

She held my glance for a long moment, then turned back toward Nicholas and spoke to him.

He bowed in leaving and made his way back to me.

"She would not have offered it had she not thought it was for you."

"She sends it with her regard, my lord."

"Regards?"

"Regard."

Then she sent it with nothing. For I already knew that she had looked at me. What I wanted to know was what she thought of me. But I took it from Nicholas and ordered my squire to tie it to my sleeve.

It was such a dainty, delicate thing.

Not entirely unlike its owner.

———

I watched as the earl had my handkerchief tied to his armor. I must admit that my first inclination when Nicholas had told me of the earl's request had been to snatch the handkerchief from him. But Joan's words, having become a constant chorus in my head, had made me reconsider.

I had decided to sheathe my claws.

Not that I wanted . . . In truth, I did not know what I wanted. But I could at least pretend to be a respectable wife. I could watch as the earl trotted into the tilting yard. I could take an active interest in his sport.

He won the first match. And the second. And the third. And it was only then I realized my hands were fisted tight. I opened them to find the imprint of my nails driven deep into my palms. I frowned at the marks. And as I sat there trying to detach my emotions from the earl, he lost.

Still the crowds cheered him. But he sought only one's glance. When he raised the visor of his helmet, he was looking directly at me.

As soon as was allowed, the earl joined me. He looked quite . . . dashing . . . in the pieces of armor he still wore. His cuirass covered the great expanse of his chest, and a snowy ruff blossomed from the gorget that encircled his throat. The sun found the gold-filled engravings and touched every one of them. He dazzled.

What did one say to an earl who had just lost at the tilts? Did one congratulate him on having succeeded in matches one, two, and three? Did one express hope for better luck in the next year's tournament? Did one say anything at all?

"I thank you for your kindness in allowing me this token of your person."

God solved my dilemma. The earl had spoken first!

I turned on my cushion to face him. My handkerchief lay in his palm. "It gave me great pleasure to have been asked for it."

"Then perhaps I might be allowed to keep it?" His hand closed around it.

I could not keep a blush from coloring my cheeks. "As you wish. Forgive me, my lord, for not having thought of it first, before you . . . had to . . . request it of me."

———

I had not made a bad showing at the tilts. Everyone knew it was for the Earl of Cumberland to win, but I had made it through my third match without trying very hard. I should have made it to the fourth, but I had happened to glance up at the stands as I was spurring my horse to a gallop, and I saw the girl frowning. At me. It put me off my rhythm. And my being put off my rhythm threw my horse off his stride.

The result might have been foreseen. My opponent broke a

spear on me. I suffered still from its blow and might have rubbed at the spot if I had not still been armored.

The day was not unpleasant, the girl beside me not uncomely. In fact, she was tripping over her words like a foal newly born. Her blush was rather becoming.

"Perhaps then, you would cede to another request?"

Her gaze quivered as it met mine. "And what might that be, my lord?"

"Perhaps you would grant me the pleasure of your company as we return to Lytham House?" I had not tried to ride beside her since our journey from her home to London after our marriage.

"It would be my . . . pleasure." The fire in her cheeks flared once more. "An honor. Thank you, my lord."

"The honor is mine, Lady Lytham." I reached for her hand and kissed it, watching her face grow more ruddy all the while. Aye. Those cheeks were ablaze. It was too easy a game to be called sport, but it was amusing nonetheless. It had been years since I had seen a woman blush. The paints used by the court women hid the blooming of their cheeks, making them seem quite brazen. I had forgotten how enchanting a blush could be. "You cheered for me, then?"

Surely her cheeks must ignite into flame! That cerulean gaze sought refuge once more in her skirts. "I did, my lord."

"Must that sound like a confession?"

"I confess, my lord, that I was so intent upon the sport that I forgot to cheer."

"I value your interest above your plaudits. Raise your head. Look around."

She lifted her head at my command.

I gestured to the throngs around us, evaded the perimeter of her ruff, and brought my lips closer to her ear. "What do you see?"

Her eyes swept the crowds, lingering here and there. She glanced toward the tiltyard, then back at the crowds.

"See you not how those who shout the most sometimes watch

the least? Look you there." I turned her head to the side with a nudge from my own. "Watch the woman in green." I observed the girl while she watched the woman and saw the instant knowledge light her face.

She clapped a hand over her mouth to stay her laugh.

The woman, a baroness, did everything but watch the tilts. She fed herself with sweetmeats. She talked with the women seated beside her, and when she thought no one was looking, she picked at her teeth. In terms of sport, she took her cues from those around her. She cheered only after she heard them start, and kept at it long after they had finished.

"Do you think she knows she cheers her husband's enemy?"

The girl's head turned in my direction, her eyes sought my own. They were shaded with concern. "She does?"

"Do not worry yourself. His mistress does the same."

Her eyes lit with alarm as she looked around. "And where is she?"

"Who?"

"His mistress?"

"Right beside her. They sit together."

The girl's skin went pale, as if I had drenched her with a bucket of water. It took an eternity to coax the bloom back into her cheeks, and by then I had nearly tired of the game.

10

The pageantry of the tilts, the crush of the crowds, and the earl's attentions had overwhelmed me. I wanted only to ride home in peace. To let my thoughts wander to the jostling of the horse, but I had forgotten that I had made a promise. The earl had asked to ride beside me. And I had told him it would be an honor.

It was.

But I had no resources left to engage him. To converse with a courtier was to play at conversation, and I had not the wits left to be charming or gay. And if I could not be charming, he might come to think I was a dullard. I was not one. I had thoughts aplenty. I had spent them all that forenoon in wondering what it would be like to have a close friend be the recognized paramour of your husband. I had used all my strength in examining the gazes of the women who had looked in our direction, wondering which of them might be my rivals for the earl's attentions.

I did not delude myself.

There was a choice to be made in my marriage . . . if it had not yet already been made. It was within my power, perhaps, to influence the outcome. Was the cost so very great that I could not pay it?

Many women did. Why could I not be one of them? Was pride any reason to allow a bed to grow too cold? So cold that it could no longer be considered a refuge?

"You think too much."

"My lord?"

"Your thoughts mar your face. If you keep them within you, it might ever thus be so." He pulled his face into a frown that, I am certain, was calculated for my amusement.

I permitted myself to smile.

"And now the lady bewitches me!"

I knew I was to have responded with some pretty phrase or other, but my thoughts had taken up too much room inside my head. And I could say nothing other than what I was thinking. I had never been especially adept at prevarication. "You do know, my lord, that I consider it an obligation of marriage to fulfill my duties. And I cannot consider my obligations met if I do not fulfill them all."

His eyebrows rose at my words.

I felt my cheeks flame but ignored them. Those words had cost me, but the absence of them might have cost even more.

He looked at me with something akin to interest in his eyes. "Of which obligations do you speak?"

My regard faltered. I could not keep it from doing so. "Please, my lord . . . you must . . . help me."

He had said nothing further during that ride back to Lytham House. Indeed, I almost wept from shame long before we reached the courtyard. But once inside the gates, he took the reins of my horse and helped me from the saddle with his own hand.

But instead of releasing mine, he kept it within his grasp. When I expected him, once inside, to drop my hand and turn aside to linger in the Great Hall, he escorted me instead up the grand stairs.

To my own chambers.

My stomach performed a curious trick. A kind of simultaneous dance of celebration and a careening tumble of regret. I did not dare to look at him.

But before he released my hand, he bent to whisper in my ear. "I will return."

He would return!

As soon as the door shut behind him, I began pulling the pins from my ruff with shaking hands.

Joan appeared and put her hands to mine. "Let me get help for you. I can call for a chambermaid. Or would you that I do it myself?"

"Nay. I do not want—he is to come back, Joan! I have followed your advice and he has said he would return."

"Then we need all the help that can be summoned." She stepped out of the room and returned several minutes later, followed by an army of maids, which she proceeded to command.

"You there, warm the bed."

"You: find herbs to freshen the rushes."

"And you: stir the fire!"

"Wine for my lady. And cinnamon for her breath."

As Joan ordered her maids about, I was turned this way and that by my own maids relieving me of my ruff and gown and changing out my chemise.

Finally, all stood ready. All met Joan's approval. She dismissed the maids and then, finally, she went, herself, to leave.

I clutched at her arm as she left. "I do not know what to do."

She detached my hand and then squeezed it. "Have no worries. I am certain that he does."

Aye. He did. He knew. And I knew too. That was the problem. How could I forget what I already knew? The pain. The shame. The humiliation.

And . . . how was I to wait for him? Was I to . . . to sit? I placed myself into a chair. Sat upon my hands. Banged my ankles together. Bolted to my feet when I thought I heard a sound.

Nay, I would not sit. Perhaps . . . was I to be found abed? It would be warmer.

I crept toward the bed and plucked at the curtains. I decided there would be time aplenty to spend there. No need for haste.

Instead, I started across the room toward the fire. But then what would I do once I got there? Indecision rooted me to the center of the room. I closed my eyes, calmed myself, and repeated words I knew by heart.

> To you alone I give Love's astrolabe
> That in your sailing you might find the same
> Gale winds that blew my soul to you to save
> Might in return give you to me to claim

I had nothing to fear from the man who had written those words. I had nothing to fear. But then, I heard the door scrape open and the time for deciding was done.

———

She stood in the center of the room, shimmering as the firelight played off the folds of her chemise. She was standing there, shoulders squared, doing nothing at all but waiting. For me.

All the arguments I had wrestled with. All the warnings I had given myself. All the lessons I had learned about women . . . everything but longing fell away. I could almost believe that this girl was nothing like Elinor. Are not all things possible to those who believe?

O God, please, help my unbelief! Help this marriage to be different.

———

He smiled at me.
I smiled at him.
He took my hand in his.

I placed my other on top of it.

But as our actions unraveled to an unmistakable ending, I did not know if I could read the part I had set before myself.

"You are willing?" He put a warm hand to my shoulder.

"I . . ." Even as I laid my head on his hand, I knew I could not do it.

———

She fluttered away from me before I knew to stop her. And before I could intercept her, she had gone and hid herself among the shadows.

Curse the girl!

She had sat that morning among the crowds watching me, apprehension turning her turkey stone eyes into sapphires. Concern had colored her cheeks at my losing. Her hands had quivered like little birds. She had half risen from her seat before she realized that she should not move. Not in advance of Her Majesty.

Well-spoken in conversation, her voice had been pleasingly low. She had even blushed charmingly at my profession of interest. And continued to blush for the whole of the forenoon.

And then, she had propositioned me. Plainly. Clearly. Shamelessly.

How else should I have interpreted her words?

And now, she had made a fool of me!

I should . . . nay. I would not take the girl unwilling. I would not. Could not. Some men might, but not me.

Without sparing her another glance, I stalked from the room, throwing the door shut behind me.

———

"Do not tell me you refused him!"

"Go away. Leave me be." I tried to tunnel beneath the coverlet, but Joan would not let me. She pursued me.

"You refused him?"

"I did not."

"Then why did he return to his chambers?"

"I did not refuse him."

Joan pulled the coverlet from me, exposing me to the fire's glow. She sat on her knees beside me, peering at me through the flickering light. "If you did not refuse him . . . did he refuse you?"

"He did not." I pulled the corner of the coverlet from her, wanting nothing so much as to be hidden when the truth was revealed.

"If you did not refuse him and he did not refuse you, then . . ." I knew the moment she had discerned the answer. I heard it in her voice. "You simply ran away?!"

I had simply run away.

"You cannot invite a man into your bed and then refuse him once he has come! You have made a fool of him . . . and he will not soon forget it. God help you, Marget; 'tis plain enough you will not help yourself!"

I could not weep. My tears had frozen from fear. I had made the choice for my marriage. In spite of all my best intentions, in spite of all my desires, all my dreams, I did not do what I should have done. And now, all was lost.

All had been lost because I had been afraid.

11

*L*ytham."

I turned and just barely kept myself from frowning. Bowing instead, I brought the woman's hand to my lips. "Lady de Winter." I had not seen the countess for several months, but she still had the same look of a predator about her. Her cheeks were still sunken, her teeth still rotting, and her hooded, unblinking eyes still made my skin crawl in revulsion. I might have ignored her, but she wore the unmistakable scent of influence. She knew everyone and she knew everything. Secrets were her currency of trade. Thankfully, she did not know mine.

She was staring at something beyond my shoulder.

I turned and looked in that direction. It was easy to guess the object of her fascination. She was staring at the girl.

"She has the look of Elinor about her. But . . . she is not Elinor, is she?" Lady de Winter paused. "There is something I have always wondered. Why did you marry Elinor when you could have married me instead?"

I could not keep my lips from curling. Why indeed. There cannot be much difference between two serpents.

"Everyone knew she was a faithless whore. The only surprise was that you allowed yourself to fall in love with her."

I had *not* fallen in love with Elinor. If Lady de Winter had been a man, I would have called her out.

She must have known it. "Or was that the *only* surprise?"

How had she learned of my secret? "What do you want?"

"She is young enough to be my daughter."

"Pray, say what you will and be gone."

"I could teach her. I could make her . . . useful. Show her how to meet the Queen's expectations."

"Why?"

"I made a promise to Elinor before you had her put away. Did you not know it?"

"Nay."

"I promised the poor girl I would commit myself to your success."

"I thank you for your troubles, but Destiny is a ship better sailed alone."

"As you wish. Some might tell you differently, but I did make a promise and I do intend to fulfill it. There are, however, two ways in which I might do it. I could commit myself to her success in your success or . . . I could just simply commit myself to . . . you."

It took all my skills as a courtier to keep my distaste from showing. Propositioned by two women in two days. Oh, the irony. "I would be pleased by anything you might be able to do with the girl."

"So it *is* to be the girl? Well. You cannot blame a woman for trying. I will see what can be done."

————

I escaped from court one day after dinner to sit on a bench in a corner of the pleasure garden, though not, of course, the one meant for Her Majesty. My Book of Hours dangled from my waist; I placed it unopened on my lap, letting my eyes take a tour of the grounds.

This late in the season, the medlars had lost their leaves. Their branches, bent at weird angles, reached toward the sky. They had such a lovely, desolate beauty. In the center of the garden, the monthly roses had recovered from their pruning and had pushed new arms up toward the bleak sun. At the tip of one of them, a rose of deepest crimson had blossomed.

A flurry of wind dove beneath my skirts, reminding me that reading out of doors in December was a short-lived pleasure. I opened my book and turned the well-read pages, looking for comfort in those eternal words.

"I am Lady de Winter and *you* are quite fetching."

I looked up to find a woman rolling the stem of the crimson rose between her hands, staring intently at me over the tops of its petals. Although she had the same ceruse-painted face, vermillioned lips, and orange hair as all the women at court, I was certain I had never seen her. And just as certain, from the dazzle of jewels ringing her skirts, that she was also a noblewoman. "I beg your pardon?"

"But you are. The whole court is talking about Marget the knight's daughter, the raven-haired witch from Norfolk."

Marget. I had not thought that anyone knew my name. At least no one save Joan. "How is it that they talk about me but never to me?"

"Ah, but you are new at court, are you not? When no one is talking to you it signifies that everyone is talking about you. And everyone is talking about the Earl of Lytham's new bride."

"Pray, what are they saying?"

"They wonder when you will realize Her Majesty is jealous of you."

At that, I snorted and cast my eyes significantly at my book. Unladylike, perhaps, but I could not help myself. Soon though, curiosity got the better of me and I lifted my eyes toward the woman's. "The Queen, jealous of me?"

"The Queen would be jealous of any woman who attracts her courtiers' interest."

"Surely you jest."

"Surely I do not. I know about the Earl of Essex."

I felt flames flicker at my cheeks. During my time at court, I had occasion to watch the Earl of Essex and I had come to know, as my husband had said, that he was free with his affections. "The Earl of Essex would try to lift any woman's skirts."

"Nay, you err. He may disregard station, but he never disregards beauty." She snapped the bloom off the rose, leaving a short stem beneath it. She bent and fixed it behind my ear, beneath my tall hat and just in front of my caul. Then she put a hand to my jaw and turned my head, admiring her handiwork from every angle. "Nay, you are every courtier's dream, even if it is not prudent for him to admit it."

"Every courtier? I have never said one word to . . . any of them."

Her painted lips parted to expose discolored teeth and a raucous laugh. I wondered if she were quite sane, for there was a strange light in her golden eyes and a peculiar pitch to her laughter. "They are to have eyes only for the Queen. And, perhaps, a chambermaid or two. Here . . ." She gestured to me to leave her room on the bench and then proceeded to sit beside me. "I shall give you a lesson. The Queen is every man's mistress—nobleman and courtier alike. You and I are just here for propriety. So long as everyone agrees the Queen is the most beautiful woman in the realm, she remains perfectly benign. For how many other naturally dark-eyed, red-haired women are there at court?"

My mind cast through the ranks of noblewomen I knew by sight. "None?"

"Correct."

I was unsure where her speech was leading, and she must have glimpsed the confusion upon my face.

"Most of us were not born with those Tudor flame-colored tresses, were we?"

"Nay."

"Nay. And yet, why do you think most of us leach the color

from our hairs, pluck our foreheads, and then frizzle the rest?" She looked at me with anticipation.

"I do not know."

"Could it be, perhaps, that we are trying to imitate someone?" She cocked her head and let her eyes bore into mine.

"Her Majesty?"

"Very good. Bravo. And why do you think that is?"

"I am sure I do not—"

"Because any woman would want to imitate the beauty of the most beautiful woman in the kingdom. There can only be one. Do you understand?"

I started to nod, but then decided I could not. "Nay."

"We all compete as in a pageant, but we compete at the Queen's pleasure. You may be beautiful, girl, when it comes to black-haired, pale-eyed beauty, but there is only one kind of beauty in Queen Elizabeth's court. She brooks no rivals. She is always first among the red-haired, dark-eyed beauties because everyone else is but a poor imitation."

"What are you trying to tell me? Pray, speak plain."

"When you came to court, you came without entering the competition. You are quite beautiful. You are quite young. You have no pox marks to ravage your skin. You do not paint yourself."

"But I have no need of ceruse."

She slammed shut the book upon my fingers and my vision shimmered with unshed tears. "One must never admit that one has something the Queen does not. Listen well: You are not allowed to be beautiful. Not as a black-haired nymph. You must enter the pageant. You must help bolster the vanity of Her Majesty, our Queen. It is our first and only duty as the wives of our husbands. To advance them, we must retreat."

12

efore I could revel in the friendship of Lady de Winter, I learned that with Her Majesty's removal to Richmond Palace, the earl was removing us to a place called Brustleigh Hall. We were given the news, Joan and I, by Nicholas as we sat embroidering in my outer chamber.

"And where is it, Nicholas?"

"In Berkshire, my lady."

"Berkshire? To the west, then?"

He nodded.

"And how long are we to be there?"

"I do not know, my lady. But it is thought that you will stay for some time when my lord returns to attend court."

"I am to stay . . . in Berkshire . . . without him?"

His eyes failed to meet my own.

Joan rose from her chair, letting her embroidery tumble from her lap. "He has dismissed her, then?"

"Joan." There was nothing to be done about it if the earl had made up his mind.

"He is retiring her to the country?"

"Joan!"

"Is that what he is doing?"

"I could not really say."

If Joan would not be quiet, then I would do the talking. "*If* that is what is being done, then I am certain he has some good reason. And I presume Brustleigh Hall will prove an adequate accommodation."

At that, Nicholas smiled and seemed to check a laugh. "I do not think you will find it lacking, my lady."

There was much to be done in preparation for leaving. London, while not friendly, had been my home for the months since my marriage. And if I had no friends, save the prospect of one in Lady de Winter, I had become accustomed to my life in the city.

Indeed, there was much that I liked about being a countess. I ate my food from a silver plate, scooped into my mouth with a silver spoon. The first time I discovered the largesse at Lytham House, Joan and I had laughed in delight. I had my every need satisfied by an army of servants. I sat whenever I wanted, and when I did it was on a chair, not a stool. And Joan had a chair for herself too. There were chairs in abundance! And, luxury of luxuries, I slept upon a feather mattress, with my head upon a feather pillow, the sheets heated each night with a warming pan.

And I slept by myself. At least nearly.

I had asked for a bed to be made up for Joan within the thickness of the wall of my chamber. But with the curtains drawn around my bed, I could imagine myself to be quite alone. It made up for the rest of my hours, when someone always waited in attendance upon me.

And so it was with no little regret that I bid good-bye to Lytham House, a sense of failure about me as I rode beneath the city's gate. For in truth, it would seem that I was being banished. Retired to the countryside. And who could say what my life would be like there?

We rode for one day. And then we were given word that the

next forenoon would see us at Brustleigh Hall. I presumed it to be some ancient manor house that had long been in the earl's family. And I put it out of my thoughts, knowing I would have time enough to contend with it when we arrived.

———

I was tiring of Nicholas's arguments. He had been at them since we had left London the day before, and now that we had almost arrived at Brustleigh, the number and intensity of his words had only increased.

"You drag her from the only home she has known, have me tell her that she is expected to stay there when you return to court, and then you do not have the courtesy to speak to her? My lord!—"

"Nicholas, you have no knowledge of what you speak."

"I might, my lord, if you would but tell me."

"That girl is nothing but a . . ."

"What, my lord? A scared young girl far from home?"

"Nay! She is a—" Propriety kept me from saying the words I wished to speak. But I could think them: seductress, temptress.

"My lord, could you not at least speak one word to her? Perhaps in welcome to Brustleigh Hall? You would do the same for Essex should he ever chance to visit."

I couldn't keep from smiling. That I would, if only to aid him in understanding how superior Brustleigh Hall was to his own estate.

I trotted back to where the girl was riding and turned my horse to walk beside hers. "You would wish to see your new home?"

The girl blushed at my voice, but that sight no longer had any power to charm me.

"At the rise ahead, you shall be able to see it."

She nodded and set her horse to follow my own as we turned off the road and mounted an incline. Below us lay Brustleigh.

"*This* is Brustleigh Hall?"

"Aye." All two hundred acres of it. All one hundred rooms of it.

"It is quite . . . large."

"It was once a monastery."

I watched as her eyes roamed the sight before her. Then she turned them toward me. "If it was a monastery, then it cannot be your home."

"Nay. This is not my home. It belongs to the crown. I pay rents."

"So you do not have a home of birth?"

"I do. Once more. An entire estate to the west and the north."

"But you prefer to live here?"

"I would prefer that Her Majesty visit here. Brustleigh is a place fit to entertain a Queen. And soon it shall. Soon I shall."

As I sat there and watched the workers scurry around the hall, it gave me great pleasure to imagine Her Majesty looking upon the same sight. Could there be any finer estate in all of England . . . save Her Majesty's own?

"Forgive me for asking, but it is here that I am to stay, my lord?"

I turned at the girl's words and surveyed her face. Her eyes were troubled. Indeed, of a sudden they appeared too large for her face. "It does not please you?"

Her eyes dipped from the estate down to her saddle. "It is the grandest house I have ever seen."

I am sure her words were true. What other grand estates would she have seen having been hidden away in King's Lynn? Yet, though it may have been the grandest house she had ever seen, her words did not convey any pleasure at that thought.

He wheeled away from me and galloped back down the escarpment. I hoped he had not taken offense at anything that I had said.

It was just that Brustleigh was so . . . large. So massive. So unmoving and cold. How could I ever make a home of that place?

It was the first time he had spoken to me since . . . that night. I blushed to contemplate what he must think of me. Of how I must have appeared to him. To have proposed something so . . . forward . . . and then to have failed to . . . oblige.

It shamed me to think of it. I turned my thoughts instead toward the estate. I had felt a queer relief in knowing that the earl too had not been accustomed to life within the walls of a building so immense.

It was so large that a part of it could lay in disrepair without adversely affecting the rest. An entire wing of the structure looked in imminent danger of falling in upon itself while men swarmed about the walls elsewhere, wrenching great stones away in some places and raising up new ones in their place. Workers' tents dotted the landscape. Fire pits marred the earth. I would not have been surprised to have counted a hundred men at work before me.

It was of this that I was to become mistress. I did not want it. Not any of it. But my future had already been determined. My feet had been placed on a path that was not of my own choosing.

13

With the echoes of work swirling about us, Joan and I settled ourselves into my chambers. Brustleigh had been created from layers of luxury. From marble in a rainbow of colors. From window after window, expanse after expanse of glass. I did not understand how the walls could stay up when they had been sliced so often to make windows. Some walls had even been pierced for no reason but perfect symmetry, for it was not to a room that they offered light, but to the back of a chimney or a small closet within the walls. No detail had been overlooked. No expense had been spared.

" 'Tis like a palace, Marget." Joan whispered her words. In fact, we had both been whispering since the moment we had arrived.

" 'Tis meant to be." Though I had started the sentence normally, *still* my voice had transformed into a whisper. I could not help it. I could not cast off the feeling that I did not belong here. That soon someone would come to order me out. "The earl means to invite Her Majesty to visit."

"The Queen herself!"

"Aye."

"That I should live to see the Queen."

Once that thought had made my own heart quicken.

"We could practice for her."

"Practice?"

"We could hold our own court, you and me. With the chamber-maids as the nobles and the slopswoman as a page. You could be the Queen, and I could be . . . a princess!"

"Shh! Someone will hear you."

She placed her fists on her hips and thrust her nose toward the ceiling. "You do not think me fit?"

"I think you . . . foolish!"

But it did not take long to discover the truth in Joan's game. Brustleigh *was* a court. And I *was* to be its Queen. For in coming to that estate, I found that I had acquired much more than a title. I had acquired a whole circle of maids from all corners of the realm who were to be attendant at my every amusement. There was one baron's daughter as well as several from viscounts' families who were anxious to receive training and possibly find a husband while living in a countess's household.

In that new world of mine, I was their lady and they were sworn to uphold my interests and be my constant companions. But when looking into their eyes upon introduction, I found a cool reception. Who was I but a knight's daughter, who had taken from their ranks a position to which they might have aspired?

From the first, I tired of their presence. If I found it difficult to amuse myself in such great quarters, then how was I to find amusement for them? If it was daunting to find my place among such splendor, it became doubly difficult to do so under the eyes of those who either assumed I knew my way or hoped that I would fail. Each new morn was an exercise in discipline as

I forced myself from bed with a smile and a greeting for those who waited upon me.

I had become a reluctant Queen at my own court.

After I had dressed and broken my fast one morning several weeks into my time at Brustleigh, I stepped into my outer chamber to find my own small court gathered before me, waiting upon me for some indication of what we might do. Flustered, I cast glances about the room, looking for that which might occupy. I seized upon the idea of embroidery and started for my canvas.

Before I could take two steps, Joan stayed my arm.

"Your handiwork, my lady? I shall retrieve it for you." If I could not respect my position, she was determined to.

My maids quickly busied themselves with their own work and we sat together, all of us on chairs, one luxury which, if truth be told, I enjoyed. A stool made hard work, after some hours, at remaining upright. But by the time dinner was announced, I had tired of handiwork and had caught my head nodding over my hands.

After dinner, there loomed nearly an entire afternoon. Aside from seeing to the household accounts, I had no idea with what to occupy myself. And my maids. In truth, I knew what I would have liked to have done. I had a new book, *Rosalynde*, unread in my chamber, though I could not neglect my duties for solitary pleasure. However, Joan, bless her soul, had a diversion.

" 'Tis a fine afternoon for a walk, my lady."

"Is it?" I had not thought upon it. I walked to a window, and indeed, the sun had gilded the hill before me. Though it was still winter, the day was mild.

And so I marched my maids around the gardens, such as they were, once, twice, before Joan reached out to touch my arm. Turning, I saw her gesture as if to stay a pony.

Slow your pace.

In turning my head, I could see that, indeed, apples had risen on my maids' cheeks. I moderated my pace while chastising myself. I was no longer some country knight's daughter who had to hurry about her business. I was a woman of nobility with naught but time. And if I sped through that leisure, I would only force myself to think up another. Haste was no virtue here.

I went to my sleep satisfied that night, for I had happened upon a pattern for my days: handiwork in the morn, followed by the accounts, and then a walk in the afternoon. And if I should let my assigned companions retire early to their beds, what of it?

But the rains of the next day, and the next, and the one thereafter scuttled all of my plans. By the third day, after having spent hours devoted to embroidery, my thumb and my fingers were pricking as if stuck with pins. And glances at the work of the others told me I would soon have to find other amusement, for their work was almost completed. As was my own.

In desperation, I asked Joan to retrieve the new book from my room. I commended it into the hands of one of the maids with the instruction that she commence reading.

She stared at it as she might have looked upon a serpent.

"Pray, begin."

She looked up from it and then offered it back to Joan. "I am most sorry, Lady Lytham, but I cannot."

I could not help but sigh. "Does your taste not run to romance? Would you prefer *The Book of Martyrs*, then? I have no favorites."

"I would prefer no book at all."

No book at all? Such presumption! I forced my lips into a curve. "I wished only to offer some diversion from the needle, but no matter. Perhaps one of the others will be kind enough to read for us." Since she, so plainly, was not.

The next maid blushed and refused the book even as Joan pressed it upon her.

"Sweet heaven! If you do not wish to acknowledge me as your

mistress, then please go and be a blight upon some other house! I have never witnessed such condescension from a maid so young. I give you leave and make you free!"

"It is not that, your ladyship. It is only that I cannot."

"Cannot what? Cannot be kind? Cannot be agreeable? Cannot be gracious?"

"Cannot read." The words were spoke so faint I scarcely heard them.

"Nor I." The second maid added her confession so quickly it might have been one and the same.

"Cannot?—but surely . . ."

The one shook her head as did the other.

"Cannot read? But how do you hope to manage accounts? How do you hope to correspond with your own family?"

"We—" The first maid glanced at the others. "I read enough to do that, of course, but not sufficiently to . . ."

"Read aloud?"

"Nay, your lady."

"And the rest of you?"

They shook their heads with wide eyes and none of the shame they ought to have felt.

Well. If I could not be predominant by birth, I found myself to be preeminent by education. I commanded Nicholas to find my maids a tutor. And I made it known that until they could read in my presence, I would not have them. For what good were attendants if they could not fulfill my wishes?

I ordered the door of my chamber shut withal and then I fell upon my bed, fully clothed. Sweet relief! It felt as if a millstone had been loosed from my shoulders.

But the maids were the least of my problems. The windows of Brustleigh had continued to haunt me. To their number had been added still more. In order to suffer such luxury, those of us living on the inside were obliged to cover them from wandering eyes and pretend they did not exist. I was happy to do so until winter's chills began to seep in earnest around their panes. And then, I scarce could stand them.

The cold was constant and so chill that I could stand three paces from a fire and still see my breath. I wore all the clothes I could, adding a waistcoat under my bodice, wool stockings, thicker shifts, and several old coarse wool petticoats. And still I felt the cold. I would have given my feather bed in exchange for a closet of a room with a fireplace and no windows, exactly the sort of room Joan had, but it would not have been seemly. And I could hardly have fit all my maids within it.

By February it was too chill to do my needlework, and I was too numbed by the cold to care. Quite simply, I lived through each day only for the pleasure of retiring to the warmth of my bed. Supper proved to be the worst part of my day. It might have been borne had we kept a large table, but with only me, the maids, and on occasion the earl, there were not bodies enough to heat the vastness of the room. And the table, in the middle of that great hall, was too far from the warmth of any of the fires. The food, as always, was cold by the time it reached our plate, but that winter I was grieved by that common offense. To counter the trembling of my limbs, I drank ale in abundance.

I had just wiped my nose with my sodden handkerchief one forenoon when the earl and his steward entered the chamber.

"You have the rheum?"

"Nay. Why?"

"Your nose drips."

"My nose drips constant. If I rubbed it every time there was a drop, I would soon have no nose left." I was too cold to give any care to my words. The chill had embittered me.

"You are ill then?"

"I am *cold*."

The earl glanced toward the fire. The flames blazed as high as the mantel.

"Shall I find a physician to attend you?"

"Nay. I only ask that every window of this place be dashed to pieces and brick put up in their place. I might as well move in with a crofter, for they already live little better than out of doors."

"You cannot mean it. This is the grandest estate in all of England!"

"And the coldest! I would sacrifice finery for warmth in an instant."

"Get up, walk the gallery. Walks are what it is meant for."

"I am so frigid that the thought of moving makes me colder still. Leave me in peace. I shall thaw in the spring with the fields."

"Why have you not asked for a warming box?"

I lifted my skirts enough to allow him to view the box upon which my feet rested.

"And still you complain?"

"Have you a box for my nose?"

The earl rolled his eyes and then knelt beside me. He took one of my hands between his own. " 'Tis ice!"

"As I have said."

He reached out a finger and touched my nose with it. "How can it not fall off your head? It is not a nose, 'tis an icicle. Get you to bed!"

"I shall stay there until March."

"Do what you must."

————

I bring the girl to the finest estate in all of England and what does she do? Complain! She complains of the cold, she complains of the maids, she complains of the windows. Was she not, of late, but a knight's daughter? Should she not be . . . grateful? Thankful? Pleased? Should she not at the very least be content?

I was down the hall and on the way to the covered gallery before I thought to throw a cloak around myself.

The cloak be hanged!

I took several turns of the gallery before I could force my thoughts from the girl's pallid face and blue-tinged lips. She looked like some wretched urchin!

I stopped my pacing and leaned out over the rail to get a better view of the work being conducted below. The work yard had long ago been churned into a field of mud. But as I watched carts move back and forth across its length, I realized the mud had frozen; yesterday's cart tracks and footprints had been pushed up from the morass by frost.

I cupped my hands to my mouth and blew on them to persuade feeling back into my fingertips.

By summer the construction would be finished. And then the decorating could commence. This year, the next, and then finally Brustleigh would be ready. Two years. *If* I were lucky. Two years of great effort, and even greater expense, but then years of great reward would follow.

I took one last look at the work and then hastened back inside to my chambers. Nicholas met me with my cloak.

As I hesitated in taking it from him, he moved forward to place it around my shoulders. I noticed, with surprise, that he wore one as well.

"You feel the cold, then?"

"As do we all, my lord."

"One expects such weather in February."

"Aye, my lord, though to feel such weather, and feel it so acutely inside, is not as commonly expected."

I frowned and shrugged the cloak from my shoulders as I took to the chair at my desk. Some minutes later, however, I asked Nicholas to retrieve it for me. "And Nicholas?"

"Aye, my lord?"

"Make certain the girl's hearth is well supplied with wood."

———

Joan and I, and my maids when they rejoined us, kept our feet fixed to the warming boxes and our tongues loosed in conversation those long, chill weeks while around us rang the sounds of a building under renovation.

Sitting in the countryside in Berkshire, I observed the rhythm of the year to have been altered. And with it my assurance of what I knew the world to be. For though I was no longer a knight's daughter, I did not yet feel like an earl's wife. I was living and moving in a world with unknown boundaries. A world operating according to rules of which I seemingly had no knowledge, despite my lengthy training.

At Brustleigh we went to church, but it was not the same. I did not know the people. I did not know the rector. There was no one to talk to save those of my own household, so there was no reason to stay and linger. And so, we never did. Church became a function to attend rather than an event to take part in. I was a countess. And since I was in the country, outside of court, I had no real peers.

But I had no sooner settled into the rhythms of life at Brustleigh when the earl announced we were to move back to Lytham House. That set my maids to chattering. And so loud were their voices that I was obliged to leave my chair and place myself closer to the earl so that I could understand him.

"Am I to go as well?"

"You would rather stay, then?"

"Nay! I had been given to understand, however, that when you returned to court, my lord, I would be staying here."

"You may stay if you like. It makes no difference to me."

Looking into his eyes, I knew him to be speaking the truth. But it made a very great difference to me. I would go where he went and in time, if heaven granted my wish, he might learn to seek my presence too.

14

$\mathcal{I}$ returned to London, if not with high hopes, then at least with anticipation. My four maids were atwitter the whole way with thoughts of the glittering society they would soon enter. Though they would not be presented at court, they would, in time, certainly be presented to those who called on us at Lytham House.

If any chose to call on us at Lytham House.

When I made my return to court, it was if I had never been away. No one looked at me. No one spoke to me. No one paid me any mind. I was granted a sort of invisibility even as I listened to the conversations around me. My days continued, one the same as the next, until one day I had a visitor. Lady de Winter announced her presence in my chambers at Lytham House with a stomping of her foot.

"Girl, I have not seen you!"

I rose from my chair and curtsied, caught unawares. "And I have not seen you." I dismissed my maids, gesturing to them with my hand behind the skirts of my gown.

"You look . . . the same. Did you not understand what I told you?"

"I did, but then, before I could see you again, the earl took me away to Brustleigh Hall."

"Brustleigh Hall. But you have returned. And have you nothing to say to me?"

"Above all else, I desire your help. I would . . . retreat."

Her eyes fastened upon mine and she smiled. "Splendid. Then you must first become more pale."

Paler still? "And how might I accomplish this?"

"You will want a paste of flour or the whites of eggs."

"I would be the most pale of ghosts."

"We could bleed you. That always achieves a paleness in skin, although it has the unfortunate effect of inducing a faint."

I could not keep myself from shuddering. "I want nothing to do with blood."

"Then you will want ceruse."

She directed her attentions to Joan. "Do you know how to paint, girl?"

Joan lowered her eyes and shook her head.

Hoping to rescue Joan from the lady's attentions, I answered before she could reply. "I have never had need to paint. Not ceruse. For vermillion, one of the chamber—"

"You have the need now. And a chambermaid will not do. Send to the apothecary for ceruse and vermillion. Tomorrow I will bring my woman and have her show your girl how to paint."

The next morn, before dinner, Lady de Winter and her woman were shown to my chambers.

Joan and I rose when they entered.

Lady de Winter walked toward me and did not stop until the hems of our skirts met. Then she held out a crooked finger and lifted my chin toward the light, turning it as her eyes inspected my face. Her head trembled slightly and so did her finger as it pushed against my chin.

"The eyebrows will need to be plucked."

"I have never—"

"I had thought you in need of help, but if you will not listen, I will not aid you."

"Do not think me ungrateful."

"Then do as I instruct you."

As I sat in a chair, Lady de Winter's woman proceeded to rid me of my brows. Every last hair of them. It did not take many pluckings before my eyes had begun to spill tears.

"Had you done this in your youth, it would not prick so badly."

I would have nodded, but her woman was brandishing the instrument before my eyes. I clenched them tight so I could not see her.

After my brows had been erased, Joan held a looking glass out to me.

In the reflection, Lady de Winter appeared by my side. "Much better."

I ran a finger across the skin made smooth by the absence of hairs. The lightest of touches drew pain.

"It will not hurt long."

"And the reddening of the skin?"

"We will render it pale with the ceruse."

Joan returned the mirror to its coffer and stood behind me while Lady de Winter and her woman stood before me. The woman dipped a brush into the white paint, then applied it to my face. Again and again, she drew the brush across my skin. As the paint began to dry, it tightened the skin beneath it.

"Should it itch?"

"If it does not itch, there has not been enough applied."

The woman paused and looked at Lady de Winter.

"Close your eyes, girl." Once I had done as she had said, she turned her attentions to Joan. "You, girl. When you paint the eyelids, take care not to brush the paint into the eyes. It would not go well for your mistress. Nor for you, I would warrant."

After having painted my eyelids, Joan held the looking glass once more before me.

"The paint must be thick and it must be even to cast the illusion of youth."

"I am not so very old."

"I do not wish to be reminded. And neither does Her Majesty."

"My lips?"

"We paint them with vermillion."

"But should they not be white to start?"

Lady de Winter looked at them for a moment, then tilted her head. "If that is what you wish." She stepped back so her woman could continue to paint. When it was done, Joan held up the glass again.

I was as pale as a corpse. Paler still.

"You will want red for your lips. Do you want it for your cheeks as well?"

I looked at my reflection, captivated by the stranger who stared back at me. "Nay. Nay, I think not."

"Then I have supplied what was lacking. Do you not forget it, Marget the knight's daughter. That country maid is heretofore banished. I never wish to meet her again."

———

The time at Brustleigh had been a good diversion, but being back at court in London was stimulating. There was news to be had and power to be gained. Sir Walter Raleigh's influence as one of Her Majesty's favorites was on the wane. The Earl of Essex's was on the rise. There was so much to be heard and to do that I had nearly forgotten Lady de Winter's curious offer to help the girl. But then, the girl began to paint.

She appeared for supper one day, looking the very picture of a courtier. Except for her hair, of course, which was still as dark as midnight. Gone was the knight's daughter. Banished was any trace of provincial innocence.

"You were saying, my lord?"

It took Nicholas several attempts to turn my eyes from the girl to his own. And even then, I could not remember what it was that I had been saying.

"She is trying, my lord."

"I can see that for myself." Would wonders never cease? She *was* trying. And perhaps she might prove herself to be useful after all. I left Nicholas for the girl. Bowed and then took her hand, escorting her into the hall for supper.

———

The application of the paints was tedious and trying and Joan did not want to do it.

"But I cannot do it myself," I pleaded.

"Then do not do it at all."

"I need you."

"To turn you into a corpse?"

I tried a different tactic. "I command you to."

"Then I shall go home."

"Please, Joan!"

"Marget, you are asking me to take your beauty, take something God has given you, and turn it into some sick, diseased, dying mockery of loveliness."

"This is what I have to do."

"You do not have to. And I do not trust that woman."

"I do. She knows of what she speaks. You have not stood in court for weeks . . . months . . . with everyone pretending they do not see you. You have not been laughed at. Made fun of . . ."

"Aye, but I have. Who in King's Lynn has not made fun of my

father, Humfrey Hybby? Who has not laughed at the Green Griffin Tavern? And who has not mocked me? Poor Joan Hybby of Ratten Row."

"You do not—"

"I *do* understand! I understand what they do not, and that is that you can only do with what you have. With what God has given you. If you try to be anyone else, then that is the worst that can happen, because you cannot ever be them—and then you give up being you. And then, Marget, you are nobody at all. If you cannot be who you are, then who can? I may be whey-faced Joan Hybby from King's Lynn, but at least I am somebody. And at least I am who I have a right to be."

"Joan, please."

"I fear for you. I truly do. This is not right. 'Tis not right to paint a dead person's face onto the living. And if I do it, then who knows but that it will come true."

A shiver crept down my spine at her words, but I shook it off. I took up the brush. "If you will not do it, then I will have to."

She watched my poor attempts at painting for several long minutes, then sighed and took up the brush. "I will do it."

After scrubbing the paint from my face the night before, Joan needed several attempts to fix it adequately to my face anew. The previous day's application had left my skin rough and dried. But eventually we declared her work satisfactory and I went, as was my habit, to court.

It was a day unlike any other, for it seemed that in assuming the mask of the paint, I had assumed some other identity. I had become a person upon whom it was permitted to look. The circles that had never opened to my presence on previous days contained women who wished, this day, to acknowledge me. The Lady de Winter first among them.

She grabbed my arm and pulled me as close as my skirts would allow, right into a conversation she was having with another lady.

I saw that woman give my gown a swift glance. And I also saw her eyes linger on my jewels, especially on my brooch of bees.

"You cannot have heard the news about Essex."

I blinked. "Essex? The Earl of Essex?"

"Which other? He has married."

"Whom?" For certain though it was that he was the Queen's favorite, he was also notorious for his debaucheries.

"Guess." A smile played with Lady de Winter's lips.

The other lady named several among the Queen's maids.

"Nay. Frances Walsingham-Sidney."

The other lady gasped. "He has not! How could he and still retain Her Majesty's attentions? She is the spymaster's daughter—his liaisons will be reported direct to her father's ear!"

Even I, in King's Lynn, had heard the name of Walsingham. And it had been spoken, always, in a whisper. In fear. For Walsingham had eyes everywhere. And he knew every man's business. I tried to convey the same shock as the other woman, but the paint allowed my face no emotion. My absent brows had no strength to raise themselves against the ceruse. My lips found difficult work turning, in any direction, beneath that white mask.

Lady de Winter's eyes gleamed bright. "Might that not be the point? But perhaps I misspoke. To all of us, he is indeed married, but to Her Majesty alone, he remains unencumbered."

"Her Majesty does not know? He lies to the Queen? It must be by omission . . . ?"

"At the moment. But should she ask him, he would swear he had not done it."

"What can he hope to gain? For certes she will find out the truth."

"Hope to gain? Nothing. To prevent? The axe of Her Majesty's wrath. And he may yet for some weeks. Watch and learn how one can lie to one's sovereign and still come away with head attached to shoulders. I predict after a show of rage and an explosion of rhetoric, Essex will be back in her good graces."

"You cannot think so."

Her lips folded themselves together. "I know so."

It happened just as Lady de Winter had predicted. Many months later, when Her Majesty discovered the news, she exploded. When her rage finally cooled, she welcomed Essex back toward the throne with open arms. His wife, however, was another matter. Essex's reconciliation with the Queen had everything to do with his wife's permanent retirement to the country. Out of court, out of mind.

Gradually, as Lady de Winter began to show her favor toward me, I became a member of her group. A part of court. And for a while it seemed there was a fashion for bees. Every lady had a piece of jewelry fashioned in that image from amber.

And I had started it.

The women circled around Lady de Winter, and from her place at their center she would direct her comments to me. The others would listen when I answered, but still few cared to converse. I had followed Lady de Winter's advice. I had heeded her suggestion. My face was the palest in the Presence Chamber. But still there was needed something more. And apparently she knew it too, for soon we received an invitation to sup at My Lord and Lady de Winter's. Perhaps it would be this, then, that would finally cause the court to accept me.

ℐ 15 ℰ

ℐ took great care in choosing what to wear. I wanted a gown that would glow and sparkle by candlelight. Nothing too dark. Nothing too dull. I decided upon silver tissue, knowing that the threads would give back the light. For my sleeves, silver tissue embroidered with gold. For jewels, I forsook diamonds, rubies, and emeralds, knowing they would not cast the smallest gleam. I wanted the glow of pearls. The sempstress spent hours attaching them to sleeves and gown and fixing a length of silver tinsel around the hem of my skirt.

Lord de Winter had a French cook and so we feasted first on a stewed broth. Then, a boiled pig, a capon and bacon, a roast of beef and all of its sauces. And next, a roasted lamb and baked venison with a tart. Several pasties, another tart, and a gingerbread packed in gold leaf completed the meal.

When supper was over, instead of separating, male and female, we all retired to a smaller room. We seated ourselves in chairs that formed a circle in the middle of the chamber, first a man and then a woman, every person seated next to his own spouse.

Lady de Winter announced the evening's entertainments to be a round of clever questions. Each person was to propose one, and she would choose the most amusing. But before she could say anything further, Lord de Winter stood, red of face, in all his corpulence, and bowed toward her. "Might I propose that by virtue of their sex, the ladies be first among us to offer their diversions?"

"Certainly, you may. Well said!"

Lord de Winter regained his seat as his lady wife's eyes settled on the woman to her right. "My dear?"

The woman rose before she spoke. "Seeing that the flower is chief among plants and that each one casts its own charming spell, I would know which flower and which attributes of that flower each one would assign to their beloved."

A viscount seated across the circle from her stood and bowed. "A good question, but shall we not all be punished if we do not assign some variety of rose, the queen of flowers, each one of us to his beloved? I fear your neat question might become a neater trap."

Lady de Winter frowned. "I did not guess you to be wearing women's weeds this eve, Lord Pinnock. 'Tis the ladies who will do the proposing."

Admonished, but not appearing unduly upset, the viscount took to his seat.

"And you, Lady Pinnock? Since your lord speaks so plainly?"

"A question of vanities, My Lady de Winter. And upon which object or trait the vanity of each one is fixed. Confession being good for the soul, the question is therefore one of self-improvement."

"Here, here." Beside me, a gentleman rose and bowed. "I pronounce myself to be most vain of my lady wife."

The woman beside him simpered and then stood and curtsied. "And me, of my lord's praise."

"How delightful," Lady de Winter said, looking not very pleased. "I can see we will find no great self-improvement here. Lady Blodwell?"

"I would know which virtue is best loved in each one's beloved. And then, in each case, which vice is most tolerable."

"A very clever question indeed. Lady Lytham?"

It seemed to me that the talk tended toward flattery when what was wanted was a discussion of real merit. "I would learn my lord-ships' thoughts on Her Majesty's peace for the Polonians and the Moldavians and how it has impacted trade."

The air among us immediately dulled and seemed to lose its sparkle as if I had suggested some new plan to drain the fens. Beside me, my lord the earl shifted and crossed his legs in a direction away from me.

Lady de Winter's lips pressed into a scowl for the briefest instant before she appeared to rally herself and smiled. "For this evening I most like Lady Blodwell's question on virtues and vices. And do be warned: vain flattery will only lead us to Lady Pinnock's question on vanity."

Lord de Winter cleared his throat and came to his feet once more. "Might I suggest that since the ladies have taxed themselves in creating this evening's amusements, that the men give their replies first?"

"This seems good to me but with one alteration: the man will reply first and then his lady." Lady de Winter extended a hand toward her husband. "My lord?"

"Of all virtues, I find myself most taken with cleverness. For it makes up for any lack in other attributes and serves us more the older we become. Of all vices, I find faintness of heart to be most tolerable, for it is the attribute most marked in women."

———

The supper's wine had created a pleasant warmth in my belly and a numbing buzz within my head. A game of questions. How delightful. The evening's diversions brought back memories from previous years. Memories of other evenings spent here in this very room. Evenings in which Elinor had flirted shamelessly with some of this night's same guests.

I tried to shake those buzzing thoughts from my head, tried to fix my ears on the words of those around me.

It was Lord Pinnock's turn to answer the question. "In my opin-ion, unaffected beauty is a virtue all love when discovered. And prevarication the most tolerable of vices. We only prevaricate when we do not wish to hurt those we love."

He should know. I am certain he lied to his wife quite regularly as he sought solace from her unsightly visage in the arms of his mistress, Lady Blodwell.

I chanced a glance in that lady's direction. Her paint could not divulge a blush, even if candlelight would reveal it, but her eyes were fastened on the form of Lady Pinnock. That lady, however, was as unaware as a mouse in a falcon's sights.

I stifled a belch.

Lady Pinnock dissimulated so well that she failed to answer the question entirely.

On to Lord Blodwell.

He fixed his eyes upon me as he spoke. "The virtue I find most pleasing in she I love is a generous spirit."

He could not be talking about his wife, for she was known to be not only parsimonious, but also a scandalmonger. I had not known him to have formed an alliance elsewhere, but he must have. I would have to find out with whom. I shifted in the chair. Hid a yawn behind a hand.

"As far as vice, I would have to say once more . . . a generous spirit."

As the rest of the room laughed, Lady Blodwell frowned. And once the words had made sense of themselves, the message became very clear. At least to me.

Elinor's generosity had been widely praised, in circles other than mine. And if her vice had wounded me, quite clearly it had benefited him.

The varlet!

———

The question had proceeded around the circle at a dignified rate, each one giving an answer and explaining, in increasing length, how they had arrived at it. And then, the question came to my lord.

He rose. "As for virtue, I must state my preference for a constant heart. And as for vice, beauty." He bowed and began to regain his seat.

But several men took to their feet at his reply. "Beauty? But surely, Lytham, all men would consider beauty a virtue!"

The earl stood and bowed in their direction. "Show me a beautiful woman with a constant heart and I will consider altering my opinion. As I see it, a beautiful woman at least gives one's eyes a pleasant face on which to fix as she plunges a dagger into your back."

My cheeks flamed as if they had been slapped. And in the guttering candlelight, I saw glances shifting toward me and then, quickly, away from me. I had been ignored by the earl, overlooked, and dismissed, but never before had I actually been insulted.

It was my turn to speak and I knew not what to say.

But the affront prodded my thoughts and the slight gave voice to my grievances. If he was trying to send me some sort of message, then I would send him one too. I could not keep myself from looking at the earl as I spoke. "I might have also chosen constancy as my virtue, but I discover my thoughts to have shifted. As a virtue, I much prefer flattery, for even when it speaks dishonestly, for the most part it speaks gallantly. And as a vice, I shall say honesty. Though it may pronounce worthy judgment, it has a blade which cuts deep. Though in time the wound may heal, I believe a scar will always remain."

———

Though I took to my seat immediately after I had spoken, it took some time for me to realize the girl was speaking. And then it took longer still to comprehend her words. And it was then I knew complete humiliation. For in seeking to keep Elinor's transgressions from haunting me, in seeking to answer Blodwell's taunt, I had succeeded only in wounding the one who sat beside me. Without prevarication. Without cause. Truly, I was the worst of clotpoles.

———

Lady de Winter clapped her hands and gestured to a servant. He answered by bringing round a box and urging us each to take from it a sheet.

"It is a new part-song that I would have sung. Here! Come away from your chairs and stand together as Lord de Winter plays the lute."

In the ensuing disorder that arose in arranging ourselves for a song, I found myself standing at the edge of the group, far from my lord, who was on the other side. I hoped to have left the episode behind me, but I did not. In between the words of the song, I heard words spoken in gossip.

"Do you think he meant *her*?"

"Who else could he have meant?"

"Well . . . then he is less a gentleman than I had thought. To have aired such views . . . and to do it in her hearing . . . !"

I lifted my head and voice in song even as I told myself that the only person the earl had dishonored that evening was himself.

As we took our leave that evening, Lady de Winter pulled me off to one side. "You are hopeless, girl! No one wants to talk of treaties. Things less taxing are what is needed in polite company . . . though I have to say you answered Lytham's insult admirably. And that will do you more good than you know. Now . . ." She crooked a finger toward a servant, who bowed and then offered her a book. She took it and placed it in my hands. "Read this before you speak to me again. It will teach you everything you must begin to know."

It was only after we left that I dared to look at it. The book was by Castiglione and the title was *The Book of the Courtier*.

We rode home in silence, surrounded by a dozen of the earl's men. I wondered how long it would take for the entire court to hear of the Earl of Lytham's insult to his lady wife. And I wondered to whom their laughter would be directed. Toward the earl or toward me?

16

oan must have read my mood that night, for she did not press me with questions. But with the morning's light, her words knew no end.

"What happened?"

"Supper."

"And?"

"Entertainments."

"Did Lady de Winter abuse you?"

My reply was forestalled by the drawing of a shift over my head. "Nay."

"Did the earl?"

My glance dove away from her own.

She placed herself in its path by relieving a chambermaid of my silk stockings and kneeling to tend to the task herself. "Did he?"

"He has no love for me."

"He cannot mislike you."

I winced as she tied the garter too tight below my knee, then bent and tugged at the ribbon with my finger. "He does."

"For what reason?" She chased away my finger and retied it.

"For my beauty."

"He mislikes you for your *beauty?*"

"Aye."

"You must be mistaken. You must have misunderstood."

"If I did, then so did the rest of the guests at Lady de Winter's last night."

"That makes no sense. What did he say? *Exactly.*" She said the words as if she doubted my own.

"There was a question put to every person to answer. What virtue does one most love and which vice is most tolerable."

"A vice? Tolerable?"

" 'Twas the game put before us. And each answered in turn. The earl said, 'As for virtue, I must state my preference for a constant heart. And as for vice, beauty.' "

"He said *beauty* was a vice?"

" 'Tis what he said."

"Why?"

The breath with which I might have answered was forced from my chest by the fastening of my corset. I took another, shorter and shallower. "He said that a beautiful woman could not possess a constant heart. And that at least when a beautiful woman betrays one, solace can be found in her face."

"Well . . ." Her face twisted as she thought upon the words, and then suddenly her features relaxed. "He cannot have meant you."

"Who else could he have meant?"

"I do not know." She shrugged as if it made no difference. "But it was not you."

"Everyone else thought it was. Even Lady de Winter was kind to me."

"She was not!"

"She was. She nearly embraced me."

"She did not."

I relented. "She did not. But she seemed to want to." And I wished she would have.

Joan pressed a cup of wine into my hands after the farthingale hoops had gone over my head and then she left my chambers. She returned in time to apply my paints. And when she did, she bent close to tickle my ear with her words.

"It is said the earl could not sleep last night."

"Good."

"It is said that his words weigh heavy on his heart."

"As heavy as millstones?"

"It is said he wishes he could unsay them."

"Aye. For then people might not have laughed at him . . . but they would still remain etched upon my heart."

"Marget? Hear me! You must be kind to him."

"When he has been so unkind to me?"

Joan swept the paint across my brow with a less than gentle hand. "Do you not wish to keep him from straying?"

"I would give him to any woman who wants him. And gladly!" Perhaps I said those last words a bit loudly, for several of the chambermaids turned in my direction. And even the slopswoman looked up from her odious chore.

I did not want to remember Joan's words, but I could not keep them from my head when I met the earl to ride to court. He took my hand himself to help me onto my horse. He rode beside me through the streets and did not leave my side even when we rode through the city's gate. His attempts at conversation were frequent though feeble. When I looked at him, he held my gaze only a moment before looking away. He made me feel quite as miserable as he looked. I might have offered words of forgiveness, but he never asked them of me. And I could not betray my knowledge of what Joan had told me of his remorse, though his actions corroborated every word.

It was with great relief that I walked into the Presence Chamber and left his side. I had never taken more delight in the women of the court. I was safe, in fact, until evening when we left for Lytham House together.

He said not one word all the long way home, though that in itself was not unusual. It was the feeling in the air between us that was uncommon.

———

I was mortified by my behavior of the previous evening. Still. The feeling had grown worse throughout the day. As I watched the girl I realized again, with each gesture she made, with each word she spoke, that she had nothing at all to do with Elinor. And no one but Blodwell and I knew of whom I had spoken. I had harmed the girl's reputation—and my own—for no reason at all.

My misery knew no words. But as we reached Lytham House, as I aided the girl to dismount and watched her walk away, I knew I had to say something.

"Wait!" A rude beginning, perhaps, but a start nonetheless.

She turned back to me. Stood utterly still just . . . waiting.

But what could I say? She knew only that I had been rude. Why did she have to be told of the horror that became my marriage to Elinor? Why should she have to learn of Elinor at all? And why should I have to make amends in front of God *and* the stable grooms? "Would you do me the honor of accompanying me to my chambers?"

Wariness crept into her eyes.

"I only wish to speak with you."

With seeming reluctance, she held out her hand to me.

I took it up with my own and we walked, together, into Lytham House. I slowed my steps up the grand stairs to match her own. Opening the door to my rooms, I stood aside for her to enter.

She did so with an air of trepidation, stopping just inside the room, her head turning first one way and then another.

Following her gaze, I realized little was visible in the gloom of night.

She drifted toward the window, beside which I had placed my desk. Her small hand reached out to touch a jeweled coffer whose gems gleamed in the fire's flickering light.

I followed behind her, but as my boots scuffed the floor and gave warning of my course, she withdrew her hand.

"Please." I picked it up and placed it in her hands. "'Twas given me by Raleigh."

"*Sir* Raleigh? Sir Walter Raleigh? You know him!"

She looked at me with such eagerness, such admiration. "Certainly."

"You have . . . spoken to him?"

"Spoken to him? I have beaten the man soundly at cards. Many a time."

"And he gave you this?" Her hand caressed it. "We used to play battles, at being Sir Walter Raleigh . . . down by the Wash. When I was a child."

"'Tis a bauble. A mere trifle from his spoils."

She looked at it as if it were Her Majesty's crown. "Spoils? Of war?"

"Aye." Were there any other kind?

"And he gave it to you?"

"Aye."

"Sir Walter Raleigh . . ."

I took the coffer from her with gentle fingers; it was heavy for one so small. I replaced it on the desk. Then I caught her hand and drew her toward the fire. "As you are interested in spoils, you might like to see this. I took it myself from a Spaniard at the point of my sword." I removed a gilt cup from the mantel. The cup had been engraved as a globe, and the pediment was supported by a sea nymph.

"During a battle?"

"Aye."

"When you were fighting with Sir Raleigh?" She had clutched the cup immediately to her breast but had failed to give it even one moment's notice. And truly, it was as fine a goldsmith's work as I had ever seen.

"Raleigh was there, though otherwise occupied."

"So you did not fight together, then?" Her eyes contained such hope.

How could I not fulfill that expectation? "Aye. Together at Smerwick. In Ireland."

"Smerwick." She said the word as some say the name of our Lord. With all veneration and reverence. "And what did Raleigh do?"

Enough of Raleigh! To hear her speak of him, he was some god come to earth as a man. "We laid siege to the garrison. And then we massacred the Spaniards and the Italians, the interlopers."

"And then he put them to the sword. All of them." She said it as if she were reciting some book.

"The better part of them, though he did have *some* aid in doing so." The aid of the Lord Deputy of Ireland and the commander of four thousand troops, Grey de Wilton. We had beheaded the men and some of the local Irish women as well . . . six hundred of them. It had taken two full days. If I closed my eyes I could still see soldiers at their work, tossing the headless bodies into the sea. Could still see the gruesome piles of heads, stacked in the fields, birds plucking at their eyes, their flesh.

"And you beside him!"

"Or perhaps he beside me."

To her credit, her cheeks blushed. "You fought as well."

"Aye. I did."

Her face went grave as her eyes met my own. "Forgive me."

" 'Tis I who have been truly ungallant. I wish to beg your forgiveness for yesterday's words."

"You have it."

"Truly, you astonish me with your kindness."

Her eyes refused to meet my gaze. "I should . . . go."

I did not want her to. But what was I to do? Say, "Wait"? Tell her, "Nay"?

She tried to hand the cup back to me.

I did not take it. Instead, I took one step closer. Perhaps what had gone wrong between us could be redeemed. Perhaps the pleasure that had been lacking at our first union could be established. I put a hand to her chin.

She closed her eyes but allowed me to raise her head toward mine. Such trust. Such innocence.

She opened her eyes and looked at mine.

Such resignation? Such . . . *fear*? Did she really think me such a brute? I could do nothing with such a vision of myself reflected in her eyes. Could do nothing when she assumed me to be so base. Her reactions had rendered me impotent from both shame and fury. Perhaps she was not so different from Elinor after all.

I took the cup from her and replaced it on the mantel, and then I bid her go.

———

As soon as the door was shut behind me, I fled toward the refuge of my rooms.

Joan stepped toward me through the shadows, causing me to jump at the sound of her voice. "Returned so soon? I was told the earl had summoned you." She spoke as if she wanted me to tell her it was an untruth. But it was not.

"He did."

"And?"

"He did not want me."

"How could he not want you?"

I rounded on her, fury giving heat to my words. "He did not want me! I am not wanted! How many times must I say it before you believe it?" Before I believed it? The truth was, my charms, my beauty, my person had been weighed by the earl and had been found wanting. And I could not know why. I had been willing. Afraid, perhaps, but willing. Could he not see my fear? Could he not have helped me? Said even one word?

17

If I had needed a sign to comprehend just how much the earl loathed me, I did not have to wait long to receive it. He came to my chambers one forenoon accompanied by a stranger and all of the household musicians.

"I have engaged a dance master to teach you the volt."

"The . . . volt?" But the volt was a scandalous dance in which men and women . . . clasped each other.

"It is often danced at court, and you must know how to do it."

"But—"

"It is one of Her Majesty's favorite dances." He signaled for the musicians to set themselves into place.

Once they were ready, the dance master came to my side and commanded the musicians to begin.

The earl entertained himself by settling into a chair and watching us.

"It begins, my lady, much like a galliard." The galliard, I already knew. We stepped together first right and then left and then joined hands. But he soon dropped them and used one of his own to grasp my busk near the waist and the other to embrace me.

I knew then I could not do it and wriggled from his grasp. "I am sorry, but I cannot do this."

"Come, girl, it is not as if you will be condemned to the stews for dancing a volt!"

"It is not . . . seemly, my lord."

The dance master bowed toward the earl. "Perhaps, my lord, the lady would feel more at ease if you would agree to demonstrate."

The earl sighed and then pushed to his feet.

———

We addressed each other as for a galliard and the music began. I lifted her by grasping her busk below the waist and propelling her upward with my thigh. She was so light of weight that I nearly threw her over my shoulder.

Her cheeks turned crimson with heat, but I had tired of that game as well. "You cannot pretend to be a blushing maid."

"My lord, I do not pretend. I know little of court circles and their debaucheries."

I clasped her to my chest with less than gentle arms. "When Her Majesty commands a volt, you *will* be able to dance it." When I turned her loose to take the next step, she stumbled.

I made her practice the dance with me once. Twice. A dozen times even, until she could dance it with ease. Though her rhythm had ever been impeccable, her movements became more proficient, more fluid. But still her eyes reproached me. Their misery spoke volubly of betrayal.

And that just made my mood more foul.

If I had not suspected she might prefer it, I would have yielded the lesson to the dance master. As it was, we danced the volt three more times.

When we were done she left as an enemy defeated, spiritless and pathetic, as if in fact I had succeeded in imposing my tyranny. I had wanted to teach her the volt? It seemed as if I had done naught but teach her just how right she had been to fear me.

———

As the weeks progressed, I realized that I had little control over whether the earl was peopling the city with his bastards. I was forced to admit to myself that my marriage might never become what I had hoped, that it had been doomed from the start to become the marriage that was my parents'.

I did, however, continue to have some small successes at court. Since having been introduced to paints by Lady de Winter, I had kept that regime faithfully, but Joan began to notice what I had noticed as well. Something was happening to my face.

"You'll want some cool cloths for your cheeks."

"Nay. Do not bother yourself. It hurts to touch them. They feel hot, but a cool cloth brings no relief." My skin was dry. And quite red.

"An unguent, perhaps? I can send a page to the apothecary."

I sat upon a stool, staring into a glass. My skin looked and felt like an expanse of mud, dried and cracked by the sun. I did not know what to do, except more of what I had been doing. The layers of ceruse hid the truth of what lay beneath.

The next morning Joan painted my face in the same manner in which she always had done. But when I went to court, I went to find Lady de Winter.

She kept me waiting at her elbow for some time before acknowledging my presence.

I curtsied, then came as close to her as my gown would allow. When I spoke it was scarcely louder than a whisper. "My face is flush. I feel it under the paint."

She peered at my face, her brow furrowed, and then at once it cleared. "It is dry? And red?"

I nodded.

"What is needed is a wash of mercury to leave the skin sleek and smooth. You will want a paste of gimminy and lemons to blend with it. Mix them with flowers of Brimstone and it will cure the red with pale. Apply it first, before the ceruse."

I sent to the apothecary for the required ingredients and had Joan do the mixing of them the next morning. The heat did not burn in my cheeks as before, but I still felt flush. I made care to remember to have Joan add more mercury to the paste the next morn.

Though the mercury had soon cured my ailment, my skin was not my only complaint. It seemed the attention paid to me at court rested chiefly upon the presence of Lady de Winter. When she was absent, which was more often than not, I could not get any lady to talk to me. My favor in the eyes of others clearly rested upon her good name rather than my own.

I was given more than sufficient time to ponder the situation one day in her absence. More than sufficient time to think on how I might be accepted for my own merits. The earl appeared to have returned to Her Majesty's good graces. His friends never had any lack of news to share with him.

I dared a glance toward the Queen when her back was turned. What did she want of me? What did any of them want of me? My gown sparkled with jewels, but those of others sparkled still more. I was neither the least nor the most fashionable in that court. I was as pale as a snow fairy. My ruff was as stiff as my busk. My hair was . . . still as black as a moonless night.

Perhaps . . . Was it as simple a thing to fix as my hair?

When Lady de Winter next showed herself at court, I made quick work of gaining her ear.

"My hairs. What can I do for my hairs?"

She smiled, revealing all the teeth she had remaining. "There are many things we can do to your hairs. First we color them, then we frizzle them, and when they finally fall out, then we have you made a periwig."

"And how do I have it colored?"

She recited a list of ingredients and, upon my return to Lytham House, I sent to the apothecary for them.

The next morning she came to Lytham House to help me. She directed Joan to undress me.

"But why? I have only just now been clothed."

"And I only want to color your hairs, not your ruff. Nor your robe." She gestured permission to Joan to begin and then walked over to my jewel box and opened the lid. "What wonders to behold!"

Joan had begun to pull pins from my ruff, so I could only watch as Lady de Winter plucked a jewel from the interior and held it up, close to her face.

"The light here is dim. Garnet or ruby?"

The light did not seem any less in her area of the room, but it seemed rude to remark upon it. "A garnet. From my father."

She placed it back into the coffer and came up pushing a ring onto her finger. "This ring?"

It was of sapphires and rubies. "From the earl. To seal our betrothal."

She turned toward me and smiled. "He always knew how to choose a jewel." She drew it from her finger and placed it back in the box. I heard her sift through the contents for a moment before she pulled forth my rope of pearls. "A lovely necklace." She drew the length of pearls across her hand, caressing the largest between a finger and her thumb.

She picked out other sundry pieces, holding them close to her nose to examine them.

Last, she pulled from the box the smallest jewel I owned. A brooch worked in gold which took the form of a beehive, and from it dangled several bees fashioned from amber. They looked to swarm whenever I moved.

"You must always wear this one."

I had worn it, several times with some success, but not of late. "It is the smallest of the lot."

"Aye. But this can be your fashion. You signal you are a bee, busy with the work of your Queen. Loyal. True. One of those who work while the drones merely dance." She punctuated the statement by shaking the brooch in my direction. She laughed at the animation and ran a finger through the bees to make them spin and turn. Then, of a sudden, she clasped it in her fist and dropped it back in the box. "You know the drones profit from your hard work. And so will the Queen. But what of you, honeybee?"

"My lady?"

"The honeybee forages for any kindness she can find. And then she dies."

"But, thank heaven, we are not drones."

"And what of them?"

"It is said that once they mate with the Queen, then their death is not far off."

She appeared to think on it a moment and then she burst into laughter. Laughter so merry it forced water from her eyes. When it had quieted, she was able to speak. "When they mate with the Queen, they will die? Just so. Certainly so for many of her favorites. Aye, better a honeybee than a drone."

18

*S*ome while later, once I had been stripped to my shift, Lady de Winter instructed Joan to mix the dye.

Joan began by adding some water to a mortar.

"Nay, girl! The quicklime first. Otherwise we risk explosion."

Joan did as she was bid. The mix began to bubble and boil.

"Is it . . . safe?"

"Safe? We all use this. At least we do until our hairs fall out."

Lady de Winter ordered up several ewers of water and a tub. The tub she had placed at my feet, directing me to kneel before it. And then she turned her attentions to Joan.

"Girl, you will douse your lady's head with this potion. You will let it rest for a time and then you will wash it clean with the water from the ewer."

Joan curtsied and as she did it she looked at me. Pointedly.

I gave her the smallest of shrugs. I knew that she did not want to do this. Knew that she nurtured a growing distaste for Lady de Winter. But what was I to do? If dyeing my hairs would gain me entrance to court on my own merits, then I could not be about it soon enough.

I knelt beside the tub. A chambermaid covered the rim with a towel and I placed my neck upon it.

I heard Joan take a position beside me and then I felt the potion drip onto my hairs. It was warm. It had a not unpleasant smell. But the longer it stayed on my head, the less I smelled of it and the lighter my head began to feel. There was an . . . odor . . . "What is it? What is in the mixture?"

"What is needed. Lead, sulphur, and quicklime, with a bit of water mixed in."

"Rinse it off!"

"It needs time to do its work."

"My head feels . . . far away. And I can no longer smell."

"Then consider yourself fortunate, girl."

I knelt there until my back had cramped and my knees had dug holes into the floor. Finally, I felt the cool relief of water cascading down my tresses.

"Keep your eyes closed or they will suffer."

I was afraid that if I closed my eyes, I might drift into a faint, but I clenched them shut and waved an arm for a towel. I heard Lady de Winter command one from a chambermaid. The water stopped flowing and a towel soon appeared.

"Does your head become clear?"

"Nay."

Again, my head was doused with water. And a third time. And a fourth until I began to feel I had possession of myself once more.

Joan helped me up and then dressed me in a loose robe.

Lady de Winter drew me toward a chair placed by the fire. "Sit you here and let your hairs dry."

She sat with me while Joan retreated and a chambermaid combed out my hairs.

"My head itches."

"And so it will for a time, but at least it itches under red hairs now."

When it had dried, we observed the color to be so pale it was hardly a color at all. Joan held up a looking glass to me and I saw my skin had been made sallow by the discolored strands. Nature had never intended me to have red hairs. But it had achieved my greatest hope. Would that my eyes were glowing orbs of gray like Her Majesty's, for the blue eyes blinking at me looked startling, like turquoise, when placed into a setting so wan. But there was nothing I could do about that color.

The maid curtsied before Lady de Winter.

"Now, we shall frizzle them."

The chambermaid bobbed once more and went to find the tongs.

"Frizzle?" I was hoping I had misheard her.

"Have you no tongs?"

"Aye, but—it cannot be waved? Or curled?" Either would have taken less time to accomplish than would contorting my hairs into those short, sharp frizzles.

"By all means, if you would rather not play for position at court. If this is your desire, then I will gather myself to go and not disturb you any further." Lady de Winter rose from her chair and took a step toward the door.

"Nay. Stay. Please."

"Very well. As you wish." She lowered herself once more into the chair.

The maid returned with the tongs, lit a candle, and began to heat them by holding them to the flame.

"Proceed, girl."

The maid glanced from Lady de Winter to me.

I nodded.

Standing behind me, she took up a length of hairs close to my scalp and grasped it between the tongs, twisting them with a force that misshaped my eyes. It did not take long for the marked stench of burning hairs to reach my recovered nose.

"Shall you read to me?" Lady de Winter's question sounded like a command.

I attempted a nod, willing to do anything that would pull my thoughts from those torturous tongs.

"Joan? *The Faerie Queene*?" I heard her steps swish atop the rushes as she searched for the book.

The maid released me from her grip and I saw Lady de Winter frown.

I looked round to find the maid holding a lock of hairs between the tongs. It had broken from my head.

"You must not use so much heat. And do not grip the hairs so long. With the coloring, they do not take the heat so well."

The maid stood as if frozen, staring at the hairs.

"Throw them to the fire, girl." Lady de Winter, done with the maid, turned and glanced over her shoulder, looking for Joan. "And find your lady her book!"

The maid removed the hairs from the tongs and cast them into the fire. Then she heated them by candle flame to begin her punishment anew.

I read through the first seven cantos, pausing only when the pain became too great, and then only to swallow a gasp.

After the whole of my head had been subjected to the tongs, Lady de Winter watched as Joan dressed me and then she stayed to direct the arrangement of my hairs beneath my hat.

Before she left, I asked Lady de Winter a question that had, until then, remained undecipherable. "Why do you help me?"

"Because a lovesick woman left Lytham in my care. I promised her to help him any way I could. I see what you want, girl, and we have the same goal. We both want him to succeed. So if I can aid in your success, then you can aid in his. It is nothing less or more."

I had grown so used to the girl's presence that I rarely noted it. She walked softly. She spoke softly. She . . . lived softly. If, as Nicholas had claimed, she had ever hoped to please me, she had, at last, stumbled upon a way to do it. She had nearly made me forget her very existence.

But that all changed one evening when I came down the great stairs for supper and found that a perfect vision of a courtier was waiting for me in her place.

After I had bowed, I took her hand to kiss it and looked into her eyes . . . which looked straight back at me. And it was only then that I realized it *was* the girl. For in truth, there was little of a girl left in her. And not a suggestion of a blush atop those painted cheeks. The change in the color of her hairs completed the illusion that the paint had begun to cast. And somehow it had emboldened her manner.

As I looked upon her throughout the meal, I began to see how she might be used to some advantage.

The next morning I commanded my tailor to come for a consultation. I commanded the draper, the furrier, the cobbler, and the glover as well.

———

The next forenoon, my presence was requested by the earl. Joan helped to repaint my face and a chambermaid restyled my hairs and fixed my hat to them anew before I went to see him.

I kept the image of the person I had become before me as I struggled to summon each new breath and keep my fear at bay. What did the earl want of me? And how would a courtier, how would Lady de Winter, choose to respond?

As I walked through the door to the earl's rooms, my trepidation soon turned to relief. It was not to a private audience that I had been summoned. The earl's rooms had been overtaken by people and fabrics, furs and fripperies, gloves and shoes. It was filled to overflowing with people. All of them, it soon became apparent, were waiting for me.

"My lord, might I suggest a damask silk in crimson?" The draper bowed before the earl, then approached me while holding out a length of fabric. His assistant took my hand, towing me further into the room. As he did that, another person proceeded to remove my hat from my head and a fourth to unlace the sleeves from my gown. A fifth went to work unpinning my ruff.

A sixth man, a tailor, grasped the end of the damask and arranged it across my chest, tucking it into my bodice and then tugging on the whole to bring it still lower. "Perhaps a style such as this, my lord?"

The earl rose from his desk and stood before me, turning his head first this way and that, examining me with narrowed eyes. "'Tis a vivid color . . ."

"Aye, my lord, and made with the very best of dyes."

"But I fear it too overpowering."

The draper dove for a length of azure-colored damask. "Perhaps in a different color."

The tailor whipped the crimson from my chest and used it instead to wrap around my skirts. "Perhaps in a different location."

"With a jeweled silk shoe?"

"Or a trim of sable?"

"A kid glove?"

"Perhaps . . ."

By the end of the forenoon, the earl had ordered from the tailor a dozen gowns in a rainbow's worth of colors; from the cobbler, a dozen pairs of shoes; and from the glover, a dozen pairs of gloves. But never, not once in all of the draping and wrapping, tucking on and pulling off, had any of them thought to speak to me.

Within a month's time, all that the earl had ordered had been delivered to Lytham House. And it was with great rejoicing that I learned, the next day Lady de Winter was absent from court, that all that toil had been worth the trouble. I had people aplenty to speak to and none turned from my voice.

19

The more I became part of the circles of the court, the more the earl began to turn his attentions toward me. Advised by Joan, I tried to do nothing that would turn them away once more. But it was not long before I knew his attentions to be perfunctory rather than personal. He played at being a noble husband and, having watched and learned from Lady de Winter and her friends, I played at being a noble wife.

But still, I was not a wife who could satisfy her husband. The earl found other delights to amuse him than my bed. And though he now spoke to me and laughed with me, he did the same with every lady in the court.

I learned to smile when I would rather grimace. I learned to laugh when I would rather cry. I learned to pretend interest in what bored me and to pretend indifference to those things which might have caused the lift of an eyebrow—had I had any left.

One forenoon, since the tides were against us, we rode across London Bridge to Southbank to stroll in Paris Garden. Upon our return, in approaching the bridge, I looked up too early and saw a rotting head leering from the first gateway. A swarm of kites were picking at the flesh. The top of the skull had been pecked clean to a knob of ivory.

Lytham glanced over, saw me looking up, and followed my gaze.

"A priest. Quartered. For treason."

My stomach roiled and I frowned against the surge of bile that erupted into my throat. Unable to help myself, I heaved and then leaned across the saddle and emptied my dinner into the street.

When we dismounted at Lytham House, the earl commanded wine from one of his men. When it was delivered, he handed it to me.

"Forgive me, my lord. I am sorry . . ."

"Never be sorry for possessing a woman's heart."

"It does not move you?"

"When a man commits to his path, as did that priest, his destiny is writ by his steps, and the best he can accomplish is to delay the hand of fate."

"And you, my lord? What of your path?"

He looked on me and smiled, but the warmth of the smile did not reach into his eyes. "My steps have led me to fair places indeed."

Such pretty words, but now I knew how easily they rolled off a courtier's tongue. They were as false as my own red hairs. But I returned the smile and drank some more. The earl was a courtier and would always be one. But then, perhaps I had become one too.

———

The girl had asked me of my path. Did I truly believe that my destiny was writ by my steps? That I could do nothing more than delay the hand of fate? I puzzled on my own words as I walked up the grand stairs and pondered them still more as I paced within my chamber.

They were pretty words, couched in pretty phrases. Pretty words were my currency, though I rarely gave any thought to their actual meaning. But these words . . . I could not help but wonder if I truly meant them.

By fate, did I not perhaps mean God? Were they one and the same, or did fate perhaps place herself into the hands of God?

Perhaps.

Surely when a man committed himself to a path, he must choose one destiny over another. My brother, for instance. Had he not committed himself to his lustful passions, then Holleystone might never have been sold. He might never have caught the great pox and died. Might, in fact, have lived on to marry some suitable woman who could have borne him an heir.

But then, where might that have left me?

What might have been a more judicious choice for his own destiny would have been disastrous for mine. Or perhaps not. Who is to say that I might not have made my own fortune had I continued in the wars? Or that I would not have become the sort of courtier that I was now?

I ceased my walking and placed myself at my desk. Took up a quill and dipped it into the inkwell.

No matter what my destiny might have been, it was fixed now. I had planted my feet firmly upon the path of the courtier. My family's honor, my own destiny, would rise or fall according to how well I trod that sometimes— oftentimes—disreputable path. There now was an irony: that my family's good name should rest upon my own duplicity! In my life Her Majesty seemed to play the role of the Most Almighty God. If I were to receive any benevolence, any sign of goodwill, I must look to her to receive it.

Blasphemy, all of it, but uncertain though I was of my own theology, I knew one thing quite well: I served Her Majesty, the Queen. And when that Queen dictated who God was and how He was to be worshiped, one might have a very hard time drawing any other conclusion than this: 'twas Her Majesty the Queen of England who determined the very nature of God.

How had religion come to be so mixed up in politics? And if I had been so bold as to observe such heresies, did that mean my soul was damned?

Perhaps.

But who would do the damning? Her Majesty or God? Perhaps one could place himself in the service of both at the same time. That was certainly what Her Majesty implied. But what could there truly be of faith when a Queen had dared to set herself above God? If indeed God was truly sovereign, if indeed I was leading a life unworthy of my family's honor, then it was He who would have to convince my own sovereign to loose me from the courtier's path. I could see no other way to live my life.

I sighed and then put the quill to the paper before me.

There was no point in thinking such melancholy thoughts. They could only lead to confinement in the Tower. If there was a destiny to be had, a fate to be influenced, then I might as well be about the doing of it. There was a letter that must be written to the steward at Holleystone, and later, entertainments to be had in Her Majesty's Presence Chamber.

———

A dance was commanded by Her Majesty one day for the evening's entertainment. As I stood in the Presence Chamber, praying I would not have to dance the volt, I heard some person address me.

"My Lady Lytham?"

I turned to find a courtier bowing before me. The knot in my belly tightened. Of all the courtiers present, it was he I misliked the most. His dress and demeanor were that of a courtier, but his eyes were those of a beast. And when they looked upon me, I felt hunted.

I sought the earl's help and found him to be watching me with unblinking eye, but he did not act in my defense. So there was to be no direction, no guidance, no interest.

Taking the courtier's arm, I let him lead me to the dance. We began with a regal pavane and then sprang into a lively galliard. But soon my worst fears were realized and I was drawn close in the steps of a volt.

His embrace was too close, his eyes too bright, his hands too busy. And so, after he had lifted me the first time, once my feet touched the ground again, I feigned illness and withdrew.

By the time I reached the door, my nostrils seemed too small for the breaths I needed and my head too small to contain my anger. I broke out of the palace and into the courtyard. But just when I would have called for my horse, the earl came leading her with his own hand.

It was the first true kindness he had ever shown me. But I could not open my mouth to thank him for fear all my sentiments would tumble forth. For fear that I would accuse him for leaving me susceptible to such indecent fumblings instead of thanking him for his thoughtful gesture.

And so I said nothing at all.

The next day, when I appeared at the stables to ride to court, the earl was having his own horse saddled. I could not think that he had waited for me, but I had no other way to explain our convergence in that place at the same time.

I nodded and he returned the greeting.

I could not stand long in the earl's presence without conversing, for it would be impolite. I opened my mouth to speak as he did the same.

He bowed swift and gave me to speak.

I did not know what I would say but opened my mouth once more. "Your ruff is very handsome, my lord."

He straightened with a stiff back. And in doing so, withdrew from me.

"A man could grow rich in starch."

He looked at me with keen eye. "Why would you say that?"

"As ruffs grow larger, so does the need for their stiffening. A man could grow rich if he supplied the stuff." Good heaven, could I sound any more like a merchant's daughter? I only wished I could stop speaking.

"*If* he supplied the stuff?"

"Aye. If one cannot supply it, of course, then one must buy it." There was nothing I could add to my words that could possibly make me sound more daft.

His smile, when it came, was dazzling. And it left me, for a moment, as befuddled as my words. "You are brilliant."

As brilliant as a dimwitted oaf.

The groomsmen appeared then with my horse and saved me from speaking any further inanities. But after that conversation, the earl's scrutiny grew more pointed. He watched me. Constantly. If I had once wished for his attentions, I wished for them no longer.

———

I had asked, in all of the ways that I could, for an appointment with Her Majesty. At last I was alerted by her secretary that my request had been granted. I dressed with particular care, in the white and black which Her Majesty favored. I had my hat replumed and selected my best cloak.

I was told to go to her privy chamber, where she would speak with me. I found her playing at the virginal. She played for some time before she turned her head and noticed that I was there. And still she began another song and finished it before she deigned to speak to me. But when she did, she rose and held out her hand for me to kiss.

"Lord Lytham."

"Your Majesty."

"Does your gypsy wife play so well as that?"

"She does not play at all, Your Grace."

"You ought to have asked my permission for your marriage, Lytham."

"I did, Your Majesty."

"I ought to have met her. In advance."

"It seems, Your Majesty, that you had met her father on your progress through East Anglia when you knighted him. I had assumed that you would not have bestowed such an honor on—"

"Do you not dare to assume what I might think!"

I bowed. Blinked hard when I faced the floor to try to clear my thoughts. How had the conversation gone so wrong? It was not of the girl that I had wished to speak. I straightened. "I beg your pardon, Your Grace, for having offended you with thoughtless words."

"Well. You are not the first to have been lured by such . . . base-born looks. Though most noblemen seem to have no need to legitimize such liaisons."

I could think of no words with which to reply. Perhaps . . . an apology? "I fear, Your Majesty, that I have made a very great mistake."

"I fear so as well, but perhaps we might yet find a way to rescue you. You have given me good advice on occasion." She leveled a look at me. "You have *almost* always told me the truth. I do not know why you do not sit on my Privy Council."

Her Privy Council! I bowed once more. "Your Grace."

"You have been begging to speak to me."

Begging was not quite the word I would have chosen. "On the matter of starch, Your Majesty."

"What of it?"

"It has come into my head, Your Majesty, that a large sum of money might be made for the . . . treasury . . . if a monopoly were sold."

"I have sold more than one monopoly. Monopolies are odd. They promise very much, but in my experience they deliver very little."

"But a monopoly for starch, Your Grace, might well be different.

The size of ruffs only continues to grow. And bigger ruffs require more in the way of starch . . ."

She paced the floor in front of me. And then stopped. Sat once more at the instrument and plucked a few chords. "How much do you think a person might pay for such a monopoly?"

"Two thousand pounds? Three thousand?"

Her hands fell to the keyboard. "As much as that?"

"*I* would, Your Majesty. Should you ever choose to sell it."

"Some more good advice, Lytham? And more truth? I shall keep that thought at hand."

————

Lady de Winter herself had noticed some difference in Lytham's demeanor. "You know he watches you?"

"Of whom do you speak?"

"Your earl."

"I did not know him to be present."

She made the smallest of gestures with her head.

I followed the movement with my eyes. And certes, past her shoulder, against the wall, stood the earl, watching. Waiting. Driving me mad. "First he will not claim me, and now he will not let me tarry long from his sight! He studies me as if I were some exotic creature."

"He exhibits pride of ownership. Methinks he wishes to tame you."

"That, I doubt. He wishes only to be sure I do not wander far."

"Perhaps. But you could change that."

I turned my eyes from him back to her.

She smiled. "I think it time, my dear, to change your feathers."

"But . . . he does not seem to want me . . . for anything more than my dowry. And he has already used it."

"Aye. But he is in need of an heir as well."

144

"A babe can hardly be made when he stays a room's width apart from me." Not that I was complaining.

"A room's width? You jest."

"I do not."

She probed me with her eyes.

"A table's width."

"At no time has he been closer?"

"There was the one time . . . in the stables . . ."

She smiled.

". . . when we *talked*."

"Talked?"

"Aye."

"Of what?"

I paused before answering. "Of ruffs."

"Ruffs?"

"And starch."

"What of it?" Lady de Winter looked perplexed.

I shook my head, willing the memory to go away.

She shook hers as well. "If he cannot see your beauty, then we must get him to feel his age. For then he will know an urgency for progeny!" She glanced around the room and then moved still closer. And when she spoke again, it was with lowered voice. "I know an apothecary who is very discreet. For the right sum, one can purchase a powder. If it is placed in the earl's cups, he will begin to feel all the pains of age."

"I do not wish to poison him!"

Her eyes threw darts at me. "Quiet your words! Those services are not widely known, and I wish to keep them that way. Besides, 'tis nothing which cannot be reversed."

"Nay."

"For just one week. And upon recovery, he will be so exhilarated he shall fairly leap into your bed."

"Absolutely not."

"A philter then, to induce love?"

"And have a raving beast loosed in my chambers?"

Her eyes narrowed as she looked at me. "You sound as if you despise him."

"I do not despise *him*. I despise his kind."

She took a step back and surveyed me. "How noble. And what is his kind? Are you speaking of the courtier? He is a perfect specimen. But how can you despise him for that?"

"I despise him for his flirtations. For lust unbridled that makes sons without fathers to claim them."

"You despise the lust? Then get you far from here. Lust is what makes this kingdom go round! 'Tis very useful."

"Useful! I come from a village where every third boy had the unmistakable look of my father about him. It was not useful; it was shameful."

"And so you refuse Lytham his just desires so you can drive him out into the city to satisfy himself there? I am far from a soldier, but that seems to me to be a poorly wrought strategy."

20

Perhaps my strategy was a poor one, but I could think of nothing to replace it. And I could think of nothing that the earl could be doing during the hours of night but frequenting the Southwark stews. I could think of nothing to stop him. Until one day I had been watched too well for far too long. Then my strategy turned to offense. I left the group with whom I had been speaking and went to confront the earl.

"What do you want of me?"

"I assure you, Lady—"

"Do you think me blind?"

"Nay."

"Do you think me deaf?"

"Nay."

"Do you think I do not know what you are about? At least have the decency to save my dignity. And do not expect that you will creep into my bed as easily as you do one of your maid's. I may be a knight's daughter, but you pledged a vow to me. And as far as I know, there is only one night that you have kept it."

His eyes flashed steel. "My bed, I assure you, has been cold as a grave."

"Then for that I beg your pardon."

"It is offered as freely as your indictment."

We were at the crossroads of accusation and incrimination, and neither of us would yield. But I was driven to make amends. I was haunted by the marriage that was my parents', and the fate that was my mother's. "What have I done to make you so mislike me?"

"I have been taught not to place my trust in beauty."

"You mislike me for my beauty?"

"I do not trust you for your beauty."

I lifted my chin. "You do not know me."

"I have already learned to what depths the feminine heart may descend."

"But you cannot have learned it from me. You punish me for a sin I have not committed."

"I seek to protect myself from a sin you have not *yet* committed."

"And so I must do penance for someone else?"

There was a longing, a loneliness at work upon his face. He gazed upon me with the yearning of a small child who is told that he may look but is forbidden to touch.

"What did she do to you?"

"Who?"

"Whoever it was that abused your trust. Was it your first wife? You must teach me how to keep from repeating her infractions."

He smiled then. A slow, sad, infinitely lonely smile. "You cannot help the person you are. And you cannot change your sex."

————

I watched as the girl left, wanting nothing so much as to see her stay. But to look upon her loveliness, to stand in her presence, to hear just one word spoken by those lips was such exquisite torture that I could no longer bear it.

She offered me everything I wanted, but nothing that I needed.

———

I had expected that confronting the earl would put my rage to rest. And it did. But it had also left me without hope. Would that my marriage could be buried, like a common cowslip, to grow once more and re-flower as a primrose. But the earl had set his heart against me; I had nothing with which to counter his sentiments. All I wanted to do was return to Lytham House, but I could not let the earl see how deeply his words had hurt me. I meant to slip from the Presence Chamber and walk the palace halls in solitude, but Lady de Winter found me first. She reached out and attached herself to me with a grip that bit like iron into my arm.

She drew me into a corner and sequestered us behind the feathers of her fan. "Lytham is speaking to anyone who will listen about starch. Why?"

I could not help my cheeks from coloring. "It was of starch that we spoke in the stables."

"The stables?" Her lips turned up in merriment. "The stables where you *talked*? Of ruffs?"

"Aye. And starch." Must that conversation haunt me forever?

"And what was it you said?"

"Only that a man could grow rich if he could sell the stuff."

"And so Lytham speaks of starch because . . . a man could grow rich . . ." She left off speaking for a moment, then she chortled. "Clever man! He seeks a monopoly for starch!"

"We did not speak of monopolies."

She gripped my arm even harder. "But if all who sell it must first pay him . . . here is the opportunity for you to help him!"

"He will not trust me."

"He cannot trust you."

"But we are wed."

The fan ceased its undulations as her eyes fixed upon mine. "His heart belongs to the Queen. As does the heart of every man at court. And any one of them would plunge a dagger into another's ribs if he thought he could do it without being jailed."

"But my greatest wish is to see him succeed. I am his wife!" Why could he not understand that?

"But before you are his wife, you are first a woman."

"And this must always be held against me?"

The fan took up its rhythms once more. "Listen well: Women are used of men. If we cannot court the Queen, then we can court the men who court the Queen."

"But how can I work for him if he will not use me?"

"You must evade his mistrust."

"By declaring myself worthy of his confidence? I have already tried!"

She pulled me closer. "Leave him his mistrust. He will not notice it when you present him with desire."

"Desire. Would that I could."

"You can. We must think on it. For 'tis no use presenting him your most obvious assets. As you say, he looks on them and is warned. You must coerce, not with your body, but with your mind."

"How?"

"You must give him what he most desires."

"I try! But how can I help him make new friends when he does not even include me among his circle?"

"You must gain entrance."

"Again I ask you: how?" It was easy for her to pronounce judgment and propose vague solutions, but I had not yet heard her offer any practical advice.

"With knowledge. With a piece of information more valuable than gold. It may not have anything to do with starch, or in advancing his case for a monopoly, but at least it will let him know you are to be trusted."

"And where do I look for it?"

"You must let it look for you. What have you to induce information in your direction?"

"Explain your meaning."

"Information will not come of its own volition. It must be lured. Have you any jewels? Some pretty thing which any courtier's wife would want? Or better, gold?"

"I have . . . something." I had my father's garnet ring.

"Very good. Then we shall obtain your information in due time."

I gave the ring to Lady de Winter, and before the week had ended, she had been given what was needed.

"Quick now, the French king has asked Her Majesty to send him four thousand more troops. The forces are to be levied and a person is needed to lead them. She favors Essex, but his youth could be made into a disadvantage. Go you now, tell Lytham!"

"But what is he to do with this information?"

"Whatever he will. Make haste!"

And so I soon found myself posting through the streets of London, bearing information said to be of great import, which I knew not how to interpret. I only hoped it would be used to turn the earl's sentiments toward me.

I found him at last in his chambers, and there I told him all I knew. After, when I anticipated certain triumph, he merely offered his thanks and went back to his work.

Unsure whether my words were of value, I hesitated in leaving.

The earl lifted his head from his page and told me he had no intention of keeping me from my duties. I had hoped that my words would spark some action, if not gratitude. In that, it seemed I was sorely mistaken.

———

The girl had come to me with information about Essex. Information that I had already obtained, but not so long ago that it would be known by all the court. Somehow she had worked to receive something of value, something which, had I not known it, would have been useful indeed.

It seemed that Lady de Winter had succeeded: the girl had become a courtier. And if she understood how to obtain information, what it cost and how it could be commanded, then maybe she understood about . . . everything else.

Now, though I could not still trust her, at least I knew how to predict her course of action. And she had tried to help me. She had tried to give me what she thought I needed. Perhaps then I might give in to what I so badly wanted. Perhaps I might be able to forgive myself my weakness.

21

*S*everal hours later, Lady de Winter called to visit.

She was shown into the hall. I offered her drink and cakes, but she refused them.

"So what did he say?"

"He thanked me."

"And?"

"And went back to his work."

"He went back to his work?" She took to the floor, pacing. "He went back to his work. We must ask ourselves, Why? Why would he not act immediately? Why would he not do . . . something? Take some action?"

While Lady de Winter continued to question herself, I picked up my needlework once more. I threaded indigo yarn through the needle and then pushed it through the canvas, wishing that it was the earl's eye instead.

"He wishes to confirm your information before he acts upon it! You were right to think he mistrusts you."

Of course I had been right. I had known it from the first week of our marriage.

"I must know if he sent a messenger out after you gave him the information."

I did not even raise my eyes from the canvas to reply, because the affair no longer interested me. "Ask what you will. Do what you want." It no longer mattered to me. I had played my best hand only to find that my opponent no longer remained at the table.

The next day there was to be a State dinner at which some ambassador was to be honored. My presence was required. I donned a gown of carnation-colored silk embroidered with a cobweb of golden thread and took my place beside the earl.

We were seated, as always, between two other earls and their wives. The one who sat next to me was too hard of hearing to carry on a conversation. The countess of the second, sitting at Lytham's elbow, was an unashamed flirt.

We collected what we could from the mess of dishes set before us. Further up the table, they had been served stag and veal. And further down, capons and mutton.

I stirred through my salad with my spoon. It was a collection of borage, bugloss, cabbage lettuce, bitter lettuce, olives, rosemary flowers, radishes, and winter savory. Some person's idea of a love salad. I lifted a leaf of bitter lettuce to my mouth. Chewed as I thought upon its meaning.

I do not love you.

I grasped the slippery ovoid of an olive and mulled its meaning as I isolated the flesh from the pit.

Your love annoys me.

I pulled the pit from my mouth and set it on the plate. Which sentiment was the more damning? To not have your love returned? Or to have it be considered a mere annoyance? I hardly knew. The earl was indifferent. Perhaps that was the worst sentiment of all.

I glanced in his direction and our eyes caught. His gaze slid toward his plate as he plucked a radish from it, and then fastened again on mine as he set it in his mouth.

A radish. *I am sorry.*

Would that he were.

I wanted only to please. I wanted only to be a wife of utility. I wanted the earl to be glad that he had married me. And I wanted him to be true to our vows.

Perhaps it was as Lady de Winter had said. Perhaps I hoped for too much.

I looked again at Lytham. Again, he lifted a radish to his mouth. I began to look away when a quick movement on his part drew my gaze once more. His hand reached toward the countess's plate and deposited one of his own olives upon it, then took from her plate a radish.

Your love annoys me . . . I looked from her plate into his eyes. Saw his brow lift.

I hid a smile in casting my eyes toward my own plate. But of their own decision, they soon lifted to him again. And as soon as they did, he placed the radish in his mouth and chewed upon it furiously.

I am sorry.

Perhaps, after all, he was. But what of it? To be penitent was one thing, but to be repentant was another. I looked at him boldly and lifted my brow.

He frowned. Then he turned his attention to his plate, examining the herbs. He pulled a leaf of borage from the salad and looked at me, triumphant.

I am made glad by you.

Well. That was something. At least he was no longer indifferent. I drew a leaf of bugloss from my own salad and ate it without looking at him.

You please me. For he did. He was not unseemly to look at. He was not unkind. At least not as a habit.

He countered with a leaf of cabbage lettuce.

Your love feeds me.

My love fed him? He did not have my love. Had not even asked for it. So he was only flirting with me? Well, I could flirt too. I took my spoon and rolled an olive to the top of the greens. Then I put my spoon down and stretched my fingers toward the olive, looking not toward my plate but toward him.

His eyes glinted and then he snaked out a hand toward the countess's plate once more. She was conversing with her husband and did not notice that the earl had stolen not one but two radishes from her plate.

I am sorry. I am sorry.

He grimaced as he swallowed them.

I hoped they were bitter.

He placed a hand over his heart and bowed his head, almost imperceptibly. Then he pulled a leaf of winter savory from his plate. Pausing before he placed it in his mouth, he looked straight into my eyes.

I offer my love.

His love? Was he flirting still or did he mean it in truth? As I tried to sort intention from flirtation, he again pulled a leaf of winter savory from his plate and ate it.

I offer my love.

And what was I to do? What was I to say? I glanced down at my plate to ascertain my choices, but fate had left me only one way in which to respond.

I fingered a rosemary flower, lifted it to my nose, and then put it in my mouth.

I accept your love.

Only after I had swallowed did I dare to meet his eyes.

Again, he lifted a hand to his heart and bowed his head. Then, with his head still bowed, he lifted his eyes toward mine. A smile played at the edges of his lips.

I felt my cheeks warm and was thankful the ceruse would keep anyone from noticing.

Later, after all the courses, strawberries were brought to the table.

I lifted one to my lips, as did Lytham.

I am yours.

And that time, the blush spread further than my cheeks.

After dinner, there was to be a pageant. As I rose from the table, the earl rose as well. He offered me his hand and escorted me from the hall. "I abhor radishes." The words were meant only for my ears.

I could not keep my lips from curving and did not look on him for fear of laughing. "Then, my lord, you must give care that you never have cause to eat them. It is a bitter fruit meant for bitter words."

"*However*, I would have eaten one thousand to rest once more upon your good graces."

In the watching of the pageant, the earl stood behind me, but he stood too close. The pressure of his stance was communicated through the strain on my farthingale's hoops.

I turned my head, as far as I was able, against the ruff, but I could not see him. I tried again, in the other direction, but failed at that as well. Advancing back, toward him, I hoped to signal him to my side.

He did not move and I felt the front hem of my skirt rise, as if, like a bell, it had been pushed from behind. I made a hasty retreat forward.

At last, the pageantry finished and the whole began to break into groups for purposes of entertainment. Here, a party to play cards; there, a party to sing with a virginal. The earl grasped my elbow and hastened me toward the door. I could not get him to slow until after we left the hall.

"Do you be good, my lord."

"Pray why, when being bad yields so much more gain?"

I reached out and rapped him on the nose with my fan, which did little good, being made of feathers.

"Come, you will have to do better than that to banish me from your sweet self."

"Count you not upon my sweetness. Have you not heard of the wolf that hid herself in a sheep's skin?"

"Aye. But the one howls while the other bleats." Of a sudden, he steered me into a darkened hall, leaned forward over my farthingale, and kissed me. I had no chance of responding, save a quick, indrawn breath.

"As I thought. You are a very lamb, my sweet."

I leaned forward and slapped him for making light of me.

He winced, then smiled. "I find I must amend my opinion. You are a lamb . . . with the heart of a tiger." He bowed.

I could not control the warming of my heart. "I shall eat a radish for that."

"There is no need. I have eaten enough for the both of us. Come." He offered his hand and I took it.

Later, back at Lytham House, he helped me to dismount. "Nicholas once told me you were not the woman I thought you were."

I smiled. "He told me the same about you."

"If it were the season for lily of the valley, I would give you them. In heaps."

Lily of the valley: *kiss me.* "Between two hearts, there is no room for flowers."

22

Once inside, he escorted me past my chambers and into his own.

"My . . . I do not . . . my clothes . . ."

He cast a glance at his chamberer, then approached me and began to pull the pins from my ruff. "A pincushion and my lady's box for ruffs."

His gentleman left the room and quickly returned with the same. Lytham deposited a fistful of pins into the man's hand. "A pox on the pinmaker! Lady, how many pins does it take to keep a ruff in place?"

"As many as your own. And one or two more. Perhaps my own chambermaid could assist . . . ?"

" 'Tis a sorry excuse for a man who cannot pull a pin from a—Ow!" He put a finger to his mouth and sucked on it. "They have treacherous points to them. Stand still. Stop your laughter."

I tried. And finally, he was done. As he unwound it from my neck, he kissed the skin as it was revealed.

My eyelids fluttered and then I remembered where I was. "Your chamberer?"

"You there! You may go." He did not even lift his head from his task.

I saw his chamberer bow and then leave the room. He closed the door firmly behind him.

Before that evening, all of the earl's gallantries had been perfunctory. But the earl in pursuit of a goal was a valiant warrior. When I put up a wall, he scaled it. When I set up some obstruction, he demolished it. He made quick work of all of my defenses.

I discovered that night where desire lives. And I felt her sigh. Ever so gently he prevailed upon me to yield. And when I did, it was not so much sacrifice as surrender.

———

She looked so peaceful. So . . . beautiful . . . sleeping as she was, one hand tucked under her cheek, the other curled up underneath her chin. I wanted to . . . in truth, I knew not what.

I wanted to lie beside her and watch her sleep until she woke. I wanted to stroke her silken cheek as if she were some prized pup. I wanted to . . . bask in the glow of her goodness as if she were the sun. But most of all, I wanted to be the first person she looked upon. I wanted to be the sight those fair eyes awakened to.

But I could not do it.

I had to go to court. The Queen would wait for no woman. And especially not this one.

Thinking upon our conversation the previous night caused me to nearly laugh aloud in delight. The number of radishes I had consumed! Perhaps . . . perhaps there *was* a memory that I could leave her with. A token that would cause her thoughts to be possessed of me throughout the day.

I slipped from the bed and stopped the chamberer with a hand when he would have come to my side. I crossed the room to him instead.

He aided me into my hose and shirt, but when he would have buttoned me into my doublet, I asked for a gown in its stead.

"My lord." He bowed, but I knew I had caught him unawares, for he had to put down the box of ruffs and leave the doublet he had laid out in exchange for a fur-edged gown which he helped me to put on over my shirt.

At this point Nicholas entered my chamber.

"My lord."

"Nicholas."

He eyed my clothing. "You do not go to court this morn?"

"I am off to the garden first. To find some forget-me-not."

"I can do it for you, my lord. It would be a pleasure."

"Nay!"

Nicholas's eyebrows shot up toward his hairs.

"But many thanks . . . I would do it myself."

"As you wish, my lord."

I descended the stairs and wound my way into the courtyard, where a small garden had been nurtured between the walls. By the time I had identified the flower that I sought, I had a contingent of servants trailing behind me. The gardener stood ready with his shears, one maid with a basket, and another with a cloth, presumably for my hands. Behind them all, with a bemused twinkle in his eye, stood Nicholas.

Could a man have no privacy?

I withheld a sigh and reached for a stem of the flower.

Before I could pull at it, a snip of clippers had severed it clean from the stalk. The gardener held it out toward me. For appreciation? For inspection?

I nodded.

He laid the stem in the maid's basket.

"Another, my lord?"

One stem would seem a miserly offering when I had promised her an armload of lily-of-the-valley just scant hours ago. I wanted the whole bush of blooms, but what would the gardener think of me? The lord of the house, standing outside at the sun's rising in his night's shirt picking flowers.

"My lord?" He held his clippers at the ready.

I nodded. The man clipped three more before I was satisfied.

"A different kind of flower, my lord?"

"Nay. That will be all."

The man bowed.

The girls curtsied.

But just before they left, I relieved the maid of her basket.

I extended it toward Nicholas. This foolishness had taken long enough. I needed to be on my way to court. "Would you see that the countess gets these?" I would leave it to his own discretion to figure out where she was and why.

Later, as I trotted toward the palace, I thought of her once more. Nay. Thought of her *still*, if the truth be known. Could one see my thoughts, I would surely be thought a chuckle-headed boy gone daft on love.

Love!

That word gave me pause. I could not, would not be in love.

Love was the one luxury I could ill afford. The one extravagance I did not hope to possess. The only reward for falling in love at this Queen's court was a cell in the Tower. Love meant a certain fall from grace. Love was the only sure way to destroy any chance of success that I had. I was not in love. At least not with the girl.

The only person one could possibly fall in love with was Her Majesty the Queen.

Aye. If I were in love, then it was with the Queen. She of gilded hair and . . . rotted teeth. She of alabaster skin and . . . sunken cheek. Of such noble carriage and such . . . cantankerous speech. Aye. *That* was my beloved. I would much rather pledge my heart to my Queen than my head to the executioner's axe.

Of course, that did not mean that I could not maintain a discreet liaison. If I had spent extra time abed, if I had gone about the garden in my gown, it was only because it was something any man would have done. Any courtier. To court a woman with whom one was . . . upon whom one bestowed . . .

Well.

I was a courtier. I courted. It was what I did. And I excelled at it. It mattered not that I courted one woman. It mattered even less that she was my wife.

————

When the gentleman of the bedchamber opened the bed curtains the next morning, the sun revealed me to be in Lytham's bedchamber still. And on the pillow a note: *Her Majesty summons*. But beside me lay a bouquet of forget-me-not bound up in crimson ribbon. I smiled. A doubled message. *Forget-me-not. True love.*

Or, perhaps, a third message.

Forget me not, my true love.

23

The days that followed proceeded as if they were a sequence in the best of dreams. I felt my cheeks flush at the very sight of the earl. Felt my limbs grow weak in the presence of him. I became a master at pretext. I learned ten thousand reasons to excuse myself from company so we could closet ourselves together. There was never enough time to be alone. In the presence of others, we tried to ignore what was growing between us. As Lytham kept reciting to me, a courtier was only to make love to his Queen. So in public, the Earl of Lytham remained a loyal and fervent devotee of His Majesty. But in private? Those loyalties were quickly, if shamelessly, discarded.

Though I seemed to walk in enchanted lands, not all in the Presence Chamber were as ignorant of our affairs as Her Majesty's Grace.

"He is enamored of you, and who could blame him?"

My eyes shifted from the earl to Lady de Winter. "Pardon me?"

"What have you done to Lytham, girl?"

A thousand things of which she must never know. I tried to smile although my cheeks burned. "I have only done as you suggested."

"As I suggested? And *I* suggested that you bewitch him to the detriment of his duties?"

"Nay. You suggested that I change my tactics."

"Aye. But you may have gained more than I had wanted. You need only produce an heir, not make him grovel at your feet like some lowly serf. 'Tis not long until Her Majesty will notice, and then we shall see where Lytham's affections take him. To the Tower for certain. To the executioner? 'Tis not rare."

My cheeks had been doused in iced water. "The executioner?" I could barely force the words from my mouth.

" 'Tis a game we all play, but there are rules. And the first is this: never make a fool of Her Majesty's Grace. She believes her courtiers love her? Then do nothing, *not one thing*, to destroy that illusion!"

My eyes had been straying toward Lytham, but the slap of Lady de Winter's hand against my cheek gained her my full attention.

"Do you love him?"

"I do not—"

"The only acceptable answer is nay. You may be fascinated, enthralled, and captivated by him. You may sleep in his own bed for all I care, but you must not fall in love with him. I will only help you as long as you help him, and you cease to help him the moment you fall in love with him. Do not do it!"

"I . . ." My cheek stung so much that I could hardly gather my words to speak.

"Understand this: to love him is to kill him. Men have been hung for far less."

I tried to avoid Lytham in the coming days. If I could not cease to love him, then I tried to protect him from my love. But he knew me. He knew all of my hiding places. And surrounding myself with my maids did no good. He only sent them away.

"Why do you hide yourself from me?"

"I do not hide."

"Neither do you lie."

My cheeks flamed. I bent my head to my handiwork.

"At least not with very great success." He pushed away from the door where he had been watching me and came to stand beside me. "'Tis a beautiful bird you work at."

I blinked. Looked at the canvas between my hands. Tried to hide a smile. "'Tis not a bird. 'Tis a fish."

"Oh. Aye. Fins, not wings . . ."

He walked to my table, opened my jewel coffer. Shut it. Walked to the window. Looked out. Turned his back to it. Started toward me. Stopped. "Do I . . . displease you?"

My work slid from my fingers before I could stop it. "Nay!" I bent to grope for it among my skirts.

"Do you not wish for my attentions any longer?"

I closed my hand around the canvas and the needle stuck into my finger. "Nay!" Wait. I had meant . . . What was the question? "Aye! I mean—"

He closed the distance between us with a few long strides. "Please, let nothing I have done come between us. Only tell me what it is and I will right it."

I shook my head. If I told him I was trying not to love him, it would only reveal how miserably I had failed at that task.

"Marget, my sweet. I cannot bear for there to be discord be-tween us."

Tears trailed down my cheeks. I moved to wipe them away, but he kneeled before me and wiped them away himself.

"You are unhappy. Is it Lytham House?"

I shook my head.

"Do you wish to go to Brustleigh?"

I smiled through my tears. If he only knew: never again, there.

"I will send you there, though my heart would suffer. You have only to ask."

I shook my head.

166

"Then what is it?"

"I have been told I must not love you."

"By whom?"

"It does not matter. I have seen the consequences of love all around me."

"But you can. We must only remain silent. We must only keep it a secret and never mention it again."

"I must keep my love secret?"

"As I do my own."

"You love me then?"

"Aye. God help me. I know I should not love you, but I do. I cannot help myself. And now that you smile at me like an angel, how can I not kiss you?"

He leaned over my knees and did what he could not keep himself from doing. And then he placed his head on my lap.

I put a hand to his hairs and stroked them.

"Never keep yourself away from me again. I could not bear it."

———

As I knelt there with my head in her lap, I could almost convince myself that there was no danger in loving her. That what we were doing, what we felt for each other, could not be wrong. That it would harm no one, that Her Majesty could not begrudge us this one small happiness. But the voice of experience would not be quieted. It howled at me to protect my person, safeguard my neck, and shield my assets. It cried at me to use wisdom, to play the courtier's game by the rules I knew so well. But how could I when my heart had already been exposed? When my love had been laid bare?

The wisest action might have been to send Marget away from me, far from court, to Holleystone. But who knew how long it would be until I could join her? And how did one go about living absent one's heart?

I sighed.

Marget's hand stilled.

Of a sudden I longed for home, for Holleystone. For a place removed from intrigues, from cares, from . . . the Queen. I tried to stop such foolish thoughts, for what was a courtier without a court? If I dreamed of such things, then I might as well fix my thoughts on Paradise; the one place was just as remote as the other.

But that did not mean I could not partake of temporal pleasures. I could visit Holleystone. And if I did it, if I went and returned within two weeks' time, then I would not have to ask Her Majesty's permission to absent myself from her.

I lifted my head, captured Marget's hand, and pressed a kiss into her palm. "How would you like to go home?"

―――――

That fall Lytham took me to Holleystone, the home of his birth. He was a native of Berkshire, and it took us some days to journey there. But it was a merry trip, filled with singing and laughter. We would start out of a morning, the ground and the trees grayed by frost, and then with the sun's appearance discover that everything frost's fingers touched had turned to gold, to crimson and ginger. We rode through a gilded fairy world.

And as we rode, Joan regaled the earl and Nicholas with stories of our own county.

"Have you never heard of Old Shuck, my lord?"

I could not believe her boldness! "Nay, Joan! Do not speak of him." I did not like the tale she wanted to tell. And it was nearing dark. We had yet to reach some place to stop for the night.

"I never have." Lytham glanced at me. "Although I cannot say that I would not appreciate another story of yours to tickle my ears."

" 'Tis no story, my lord. This one 'tis truth."

Lytham winked at me. "And the Weyborne Witches and Stiffkey Trolls were not?"

"You may mock me if you like, my lord, but Old Shuck is as real as you and me."

"Perhaps tomorrow, Joan. In the morning." I wanted illumination for this dark tale.

Lytham examined my face. "The tale scares you then, my sweet?"

"We had a friend die that saw him."

"T'were Little Mary Bailie. Within a twelve-month of the sight of him. She and her mother both!"

"Pray, tell."

"Old Shuck, he's a demon hound, huge as a foal with eyes that burn like fire."

"We could use him this night. Perhaps he could lead us on our way!"

Nicholas snickered at Lytham's word.

"You may laugh if you like, my lord, but just you remember Little Mary Bailie. All she did was pay a visit to her mother's father, who lived at Sheringham. She laughed as well when he told her the tale, but weren't none of them laughing when she died."

"Forgive me, Joan. Please continue."

"Did I tell you Old Shuck is dark?"

"Nay."

"Well, he is! Black as a moonless sky, my lord. Which serves him well as he sneaks up on you at night."

"Light of foot is he?"

"Not especially. Just sly. You could not know he stalked you except you can hear his feet. They thump. On the ground. After you. And then afore you know it, they sound from just behind you."

"And let me guess: if you turn around to look at him, you die."

"Nay, my lord. He does not kill so easy as that. You cannot see him at first, for he is darker than dark."

"Remind me, Nicholas, not to go sparring with shadows."

Nicholas tried to hide his smile, but I could see the flash of his teeth through the gloom. "Aye, my lord."

"The trick of Old Shuck is that first you see nothing at all. But if you keep looking long enough, you see those flaming eyes. And 'tis then you know that you will die."

An owl hooted in the twilight. The mournful sound sent a shiver creeping up my spine.

"And how does he kill you?"

"He does not, my lord."

"He does not kill you?"

"Nay, my lord. 'Tis the knowledge of him, my lord, that kills."

"Knowledge?"

"Aye, my lord. He *can* chase you toward danger. But worse, 'tis thinking upon the beast and knowing that he is real that always kills the one who sees him. Before a year is gone, he makes you kill yourself."

"Mary Bailie?"

"She could not sleep for seeing the hound in her dreams. And soon she could not eat."

"And her mother?"

"Well . . ." Joan looked toward me.

I shook my head.

She shrugged. "She was mourning her dead girl when she wandered into the Wash, my lord."

"Aye?"

" 'Twas *the Wash*, my lord."

"Aye?"

"Where King John lost all his gold?"

"And so?"

"The Wash takes what it wants and will not return it. The sands swallowed her, my lord. Though they say if you wander about at night, you can hear her cries for help. Terrible cries, my lord. You would not want to hear them."

We rode uneasy for the rest of the way. Nicholas turned several times to look at the road behind us. I nudged my horse closer to Lytham's. Joan tucked her mount behind mine. At least we rode with Lytham's men. Old Shuck or not, they would ensure we arrived safe at Holleystone.

But still, I could not keep thoughts of little Mary Bailie from my mind. I did not believe in ghosts or ghouls, but Mary's tale was different. She had been my friend, and whatever she had seen had haunted her. Perhaps, as some said, it was a wolf; or perhaps a bear escaped from traveling gypsies. But when she returned to King's Lynn, she brought a terror with her. The encounter had left her among the living. It was the illusion that had killed her. And perhaps it was that which unnerved us all. The truth might have been reasonable, plausible even. It was the lie that killed.

24

Several days later, long after the specter of Little Mary Bailie had faded, we reached Holleystone. When I saw the estate, I was charmed and overcome by sweet relief. There was nothing of Queen Elizabeth there, no structures built in the shape of an E. No royal crests, no royal colors. And, best of all, five of Holleystone's twins would have fit within the walls of Brustleigh Hall. If Brustleigh was palatial, Holleystone was familial; Holleystone was home.

The house was ancient. It still had a crenellated roof with five old-fashioned chimneys spaced along its pitch and a defensive tower at one end. I could have walked the length of it in thirty strides, it was that small. The windows, what few of them there were, had been set in panes, but not yet latticed.

"It is not of a size with Brustleigh." Lytham said the words as if an apology were necessary.

"I think it just right." I amended my opinion when I realized the house was built in the shape of a U. Behind the front stretched two wings in parallel that more than doubled in length the width of the front. But I could not long be disappointed. It was a house to love. And to trust.

I had been right to bring Marget to Holleystone. As she looked at the place, a smile lit her face and stayed there for the length of the day.

"'Tis perfect, Lytham. I can see why you love it here."

And then I could understand more why I loved her. She fit at Holleystone. Having been there just under a day, she had become part of it in a way that Elinor never had. We had visited, she and I, when my brother still had possession of the estate. She had disparaged it as unfashionable. Had spoken to my brother of a greater number of windows, a more elaborate construction of chimneys.

"Is something wrong?"

I had frowned without being aware of it. I inverted my lips to a smile. "Do you not think there should be more windows cut into the walls?"

"Why? It would ruin the place."

"What of the chimneys?"

"I adore them."

"You do not think such a place in such a county un-fashionable?"

"'Tis charming. And I would not change one thing."

Not one thing, when Elinor would have changed everything.

"Your face . . . 'tis grown so dark," Marget said.

"Bad memories, my sweet."

"Of here? I do not think they could long survive in such a place."

She was right. And so I banished them for the length of our stay.

We stayed less than a week at Holleystone and then we had to pack up and return to Lytham House, for we knew the Queen would install herself at Whitehall in time for Accession Day.

Unlike my time spent at Brustleigh, I wished the time at Holleystone would never end. And it was with no little regret that I installed myself once more at Lytham House. But I could not long be downcast. Lady de Winter called upon me the day after our arrival.

"The country did you some good, girl. You look positively ruddy."

Ruddy? I lifted a hand to my face and realized with horror that I had forgotten to paint. Had it taken so little time to fall out of the habit? "I was just—Joan!"

"Aye?" She came into the chamber at a run and only stopped to drop a curtsey when she saw Lady de Winter. "My lady."

" 'Tis time for the paints, Joan."

She frowned.

"Now."

As Joan painted, Lady de Winter continued to talk. "I hope you have thought on my words."

Words? Which ones? There was only one answer I could think to say. "Aye."

"Good. It takes time, certainly, to turn the heart from its course. No one can fault you for that. But while you are waiting for your head's command to be obeyed, you must pretend that it already has been."

"I must confess that—"

She sighed. "I see I must regain the ground your time in the country has lost me. I speak to you of love, girl!"

"Love? But . . ." I remembered the words Lytham and I had exchanged. Remembered our secret. "I cannot love him." I was cheered that my voice had not faltered at those words.

Joan's hand fumbled the brush, causing it to fall to my lap and streak my gown with paint.

"Mind your task, girl!" Lady de Winter turned her attention back to me. "Good, good! If you say it enough times, then perhaps your face will stop convincing me that you lie."

"I do not . . . lie."

"Come now, I know the truth. But be of good cheer. Though you may not be able to hide the truth from me, there *is* a way that you can hide it from the court."

"There is?"

"Declaim everything that is good about him. No one could believe that you love a person you do not respect."

"Declaim? *Every*thing good? But . . . that is . . . lying." And I preferred to keep a secret by saying nothing rather than denouncing the truth.

"'Tis not lying. Not truly. You must just tell yourself that it is not for everyone to know the truth. Besides, if you say such things enough times, your lie will soon *become* true."

"But—"

"You can be sure the earl does the same regarding you."

"He does?"

"You can be sure of it."

"Truly?"

"Why? Has he told you that he loves you?"

"I . . . he . . ."

She began to laugh. It was a terrible, horrifying laugh. A laugh so cruel that I wanted to slap her across the face to stop up the sound. "Oh, my dear, you are so very young! Let me guess. Did he say words such as, 'I know I should not love you, but I do. I cannot help myself!' "

He had. But when Lady de Winter said them, they sounded so . . . crass. And they made me feel so . . . cheap.

"I am certain that when he said them, it sounded as if he loved only you in all of the world."

It had.

"But remember, girl, he is a courtier. He must love only his Queen. He has words aplenty and they mean nothing."

Nothing?

"He will say whatever he needs to in order to accomplish his purpose. You might call it lying. We simply call it expedient."

Expedient.

"So hear me well, girl. If you wish to hide your heart while it is healing, you must say nothing that will give you away."

She took herself away soon after, but in her going she had left a bruise upon my heart and I could scarcely breathe for the pain.

Joan brought me a cup of wine, but I could not drink it. "Do not listen to her, Marget."

"But . . . 'tis what he said. They were his words precisely."

"And who is to say he did not mean them?"

"But how could she know them unless she had heard them herself? On some other occasion?"

"She is a mean-spirited shrew who only seeks to destroy what she cannot have herself."

"What do you mean?"

"She is jealous!"

"Of whom?"

"You, Marget!"

"She cannot be jealous of me. What is there to be jealous of?"

"Your youth. Your beauty. The earl."

"The earl . . . ?"

"He loves you."

"He is a courtier."

"Aye. In his words perhaps, but not in his actions. You have only to watch the man to know that he has placed his own heart at your feet. And the lady knows it. She tries to make you stomp upon it. Do not do it. He would not soon forgive you."

"But he must not love me, Joan. And that is the truth. He cannot. The Queen will begrudge him his affections."

"Then let him manage the politics of it. He has given his heart to you, so you must guard it for him. Do not let that lady tell you otherwise."

I went to court that day and spent my time in misery, knowing not whom to believe. But whenever I looked for Lytham across the Presence Chamber, I found him always looking at me. Soon I could do nothing for all the thoughts swirling in my head. I took myself outside to the pleasure garden to find peace.

But Lytham found me there instead.

He plucked a medlar for me, and after I had eaten of it, he used his handkerchief to wipe my chin. I could tell by the warmth in his eyes that he wished to kiss me, but it was not safe. And so the words he spoke next did not surprise me. "We should not be seen out here together, but I could not leave you alone while you were looking so morose. Come, we will go back inside."

I placed my hand in his and he helped me to my feet. But when he would turn to walk the path, I pulled his hand toward me.

He turned to look at me with concern.

"Are you quite certain that you wish to love me?"

He smiled, but it contained no cheer. "Nay. I am not certain at all. But I have naught to do with it. You have captured my heart and you have not yet told me how to ransom it."

"But what if—"

"What if God struck me dead on the morrow? How could I not thank Him for sending you to me?"

And then I remembered what I should never have forgotten. It was *this* man who had written my sonnet:

To you alone I give Love's astrolabe
That in your sailing you might find the same
Gale winds that blew my soul to you to save
Might in return give you to me to claim

And there was light now where there had been darkness. He could not be lying. He had ever proclaimed his intentions. But still, one problem remained. "What if someone at court knew, guessed at . . ."

"My love for you?"

"Aye."

"Then it could be very dangerous indeed. Depending upon the person. Whether they would use that knowledge to help us or to destroy us."

I felt my burden lighten further. Lady de Winter was already pledged to our success. If she did anything with her knowledge, it would only be to help us. I could trust her, just as I could trust Lytham.

25

After setting things straight with Marget, it seemed I could hardly go about court without a smile upon my face. Could I not do something soon to get rid of it, I would begin to be thought quite simple.

"My Lord Lytham!"

I glanced over my shoulder to see Katherine Mintingdon, newly become Viscountess of Extley. She was one of my childhood friend's youngest daughters. "Brickbat Kat!" She had ever been one to tell a person exactly what she thought. Of them and everything else.

"Do you not call me that!" She had colored delightfully. "They will think me unfit for court."

"Never that, darling girl. Court is unfit for you."

She tried to swipe at me with her ostrich feather fan, but the tendrils got stuck in a brooch she had fixed to her bosom. Her eyes widened as she looked at me. And then, she dissolved into giggles. "You must help me or I shall go about court for the rest of the day thusly. And what shall they think of me then?"

I tried to look at her sternly. "Only that you try to hide yourself from prying eyes. And rightly so!"

"Help me. Before the viscount sees me. He will think me utterly hopeless."

I sighed and proceeded to help.

————

I was bored with the ladies' conversations around me. They spoke of that which they always spoke: of which courtier had made himself look good by making which other courtier look bad. I passed my fan in front of my face to hide a yawn. I looked around the Presence Chamber for something of interest, only to see Lytham at the other end of the room, helping to free a lady's fan from a brooch. It had been fastened to the bosom of her gown at a point where very much lower would have been . . . too low indeed.

As I watched, by pushing his fingers down her bodice, he freed it for her.

She laughed. And then struck him on the nose with her feathers.

He only smiled and reached for her hand to kiss it. And then kept looking at her, adoration in his eyes, as she walked away.

And right then, all of my dreams died. I could look on him no longer. Turning, I left the ladies and made to exit the room. But in my haste, I reeled into a group of young dissolutes and began to stumble. One of them righted me with a hand to the elbow, only he did not take it away once my footing was secured.

"I do not believe I have had the pleasure of meeting you, Lady Lytham. I am Mr. Chilton, and these gentlemen are Mr. Greville and Mr. Stoughton."

I smiled, then tried to detach myself from his grip.

"Countess." The tallest of them bowed, then straightened. "I may not have had this pleasure before, but I have often wished for it."

"You are too kind." Truly, I wished they would stop speaking and leave me to go.

"It is you who are kind to take a moment to speak with us, although . . . perhaps we can provide more lively company than the earl's."

I remembered Lady de Winter's words. *"Declaim everything that is good about him. No one could believe that you love a person you do not respect."* I forced lips into a smile. "Aye. Perhaps you can."

The other man joined the conversation. "He cannot be as dull as they say."

"Oh, nay!" I remembered myself. "Nay. He is . . . much duller."

"They say he cannot write poetry worth his quill."

Oh, but he could. "He has not written any for me."

"I would write you sonnets by the dozens!"

I stood there alone, speaking with them for over an hour. By then my smile was flagging and I was filled with remorse for all of the dispersions I had cast upon Lytham's character. Just as that thought passed through my mind, I glanced off behind the men and noticed the earl.

He was watching me with a stricken gaze.

I saw myself then as he must see me. A lone woman, speaking intimately with a group of young libertines. What must he think of me?

But then, why should I care? Had he not just this morning spoken to me of love? And had he not then immediately turned his attentions to another?

———

She was Elinor all over again.

Is this what it felt like to see hope die? A dull, grinding despair in the gut?

Would that she had not hid her true character from me for so long a time. Would that I had not just professed my love.

———

Lytham did not accompany me home that night. In fact, he did not return home at all. And I did not know what that should mean. Was I destined to live my life in fear of what my husband might be doing behind my back?

I slept not at all, and in the morning's light all of my anxieties could be found upon my face. I stared into a glass, looking at a stranger; a stranger gray of face and aged of skin. I looked haggard. Harassed. Devoid of hope.

"Are you not well?" Joan squinted at my face as she began to mix up my paints.

"You can tell? By what? My pallor, my skin? All the many lines?" I threw the glass onto the table, not caring at all if it broke.

Joan leaned toward me and took a good long look at my face. "Your skin looks as it ever has. Since you began painting, that is." She paused as if trying to gauge the effect of her words. "Nay. 'Tis your eyes. They look bruised."

They felt bruised. The same as my heart. "He does not love me."

"I cannot believe it."

"At least not with constancy."

"You are certain?"

"As certain as you would be if you had seen him plunge his hand down the front of some girl's bodice."

"Perhaps . . ." She tried to come up with some explanation. I could see the traces of her thoughts upon her face. But she too failed, the same as I had the previous night.

She had nearly finished painting me when the steward knocked and then entered the chamber with a message. "Mr. Chilton, Mr. Greville, and Mr. Stoughton are asking for you, my lady. I will await your answer in the passage." He disappeared, shutting the door behind him.

I was blushing, though by that time, thanks to Joan's work, it was not able to be seen.

Joan paused in her application of vermillion and then bent close to my ear. "Tell me quick before the maids come to style your hair: what have you done?"

"Nothing!"

"There can be no good reason for three men requesting to see you."

"I have done nothing . . ."

"What are you playing at, Marget?"

"If I flirt, innocently, with the men of the court, 'tis my business. And certainly none of Lytham's."

"Sweet heaven! *You* may flirt innocently, but I am certain *they* do not. Men are all the same. They hope for something. What did you give them to hope for?"

"Nothing—I am not that kind of woman!"

Her cheeks colored.

For some reason, I felt . . . shamed. "They introduced themselves to me."

"And did you talk to them before or after you saw whatever it was you thought you saw between Lytham and the girl?"

"After." I felt like a child who had been reprimanded.

She set the paint on the table and stepped out into the passageway.

I followed after her.

"Now, listen well."

The steward nodded just as I would have done, confronted thus with Joan's formidability.

"You are to tell the men that she regrets she does not know them. Do you understand?"

"Regrets she does not know them. Aye."

"But—"

Joan silenced me with a look. And turned her attentions to the steward. "Go!"

The steward turned and walked down the hall, presumably to deliver the response.

"But I *do* know them, Joan."

"And after this morning, you will not. You can thank me later. Once you realize that I have saved your virtue. You do not want to know such as those."

"I might."

"Do not flirt with evils you know nothing of. There is nothing good that could come from knowing men who would press themselves on a lady at this hour." She pushed me back into the room, took up the brush, and finished her work upon my cheeks.

"So . . . what am I to do . . . about Lytham? Just let him wander? Without doing anything at all?"

"Why could you not just ask him about her?"

"And make my humiliation complete?"

Joan squeezed my hand. "It cannot be any worse than how you already feel."

I went through the day at court with Joan's words echoing in my head. And finally, I admitted that she was right. I could not feel any worse than I already did with anger, humiliation, and sorrow at work in my soul. So upon my returning to Lytham House, I waited, pacing in the Great Hall for the earl to return. I waited long past supper, yet he never appeared.

Shaken and despairing, I at last abandoned my post and went up the stairs.

Joan helped me from my gown and eased a chemise over my head.

"I waited for him. He has not returned."

Joan's gaze was marked by compassion. "Go to bed, Marget."

"Aye. To bed."

I burrowed under the sheets, but I could not stop my thoughts from burrowing into my heart. Was all truly lost? Had what we once shared truly disappeared? A longing for Lytham welled up inside me. A yearning for his laughter, his warmth, his presence. It was so fierce, so tangible, that I slipped from my bed and wandered through the passage to his chambers. I did not expect to find him there and I was not mistaken.

But behind me, I could hear his chamberers slip out into the corridor.

Let them think what they must. I *was* shameless. I *was* begging. I no longer had any pride. I would have crawled into his bed had I been sure of my reception. But I crept into a chair instead, pulled my knees to my chest, and began to weep.

I did not care if there was no place in the court for love. I had possessed it once. I wanted it again.

I do not know how long I sat there, but at some point in the night, long after my eyes and thoughts had been dulled by tears, he returned.

And he was not pleased. With anything.

"Where are my . . . ? Is there no one here to help me? By—Ow!" He fumbled with the pins of his ruff.

I might have offered to help him, but in his presence I had grown afraid.

And then he reached down to his thigh and drew a knife from some hidden scabbard. Holding the point to his neck, he drew it away through the ruff and pulled off the material, flinging it to the floor.

I gasped.

———

Sweet heaven! I had been tormented by thoughts of the girl all day. Did I have to be tormented by visions of her at night as well?

The vision shimmered. And then sniffled.

It was not a vision at all. It was the girl herself. What had I done to provoke such persecution? Was it not enough that she had thrown my love away? Embarrassed me by cavorting with the court dissolutes? Why did she insist on hounding me?

She lifted her eyes to mine as if it required some great feat of courage. Tears had worn a path down her cheeks. Her eyes seemed glazed by sorrow. She looked exactly as I felt.

"So. You think me blind? And dull as well?"

"Nay." Her eyes flickered fear.

I glanced down and saw I still held the knife in my hand. I sheathed it, stood before her. "It is said that you told Chilton, Greville and Stoughton that very thing."

"But to proclaim what I truly think, that you are a man above all men, would that not be precisely what I should *not* say? I am not supposed to love you. Tell me how not to love you. Because I cannot do it."

"You have a strange way of showing your love."

"As do you! How can *you* profess to love me and then dive into the front of some girl's gown?"

"The front of—"

"Did you think to hide it behind her fan?"

"Her fan?"

She pushed herself from the chair. "If you must be unfaithful, then at least have the decency to form your liaisons where I cannot see them. Could you not at least do that for me? I have tried to please you, I have painted myself like a . . . vixen for you. I have tried every way that I can to promote you in court. I have *loved* you! Is it not enough? Why do you have to seek the arms of another? Why am I not enough?"

I could not understand what she was saying. Was she saying I was . . . that I could . . . was she not accusing *me* of being Elinor? I walked as an aged man to the chair she had just left and placed myself into it. "What is it that you think I have done?"

Her eyes went bleak. And when she spoke, it was in a whisper. "Must I say it?"

"But how could you . . . ?" How could she think that? And more, why was she accusing me of something I was accusing her of? Was it not she who was starting off down Elinor's old trails? "How could you think me so despicable? And if I were so, why would you even care?"

A sob broke from her throat.

"It certainly seemed as if you found your own solace elsewhere, in the company of other men."

"If I did, it was only because I had seen *you*!"

"Seen me what?!"

"With that *girl*! With your hand down the front of her gown! Do not think to tell me you cannot remember."

But I could not.

"Do not think to tell me it meant nothing!"

But it must have if I did not remember it. A cold sweat broke out upon my brow.

Marget spit her words at me in fury. "She must be . . . enchanting. Does she worship you as you worship her? I could almost hear her giggle at you from across the Presence Chamber."

Gown. Fan. Giggle. I felt my body sag in relief. "Brickbat Kat."

"Is that her name? And you would tell me of it! Even my own father never stooped so low!"

Suddenly, I understood everything. "I would tell you of my friend's youngest daughter. Of a babe I once bounced upon my knee. A lass newly married who has every expectation that she will not succeed in this court. A lass not, may I add, entirely unlike *you*. She had got her fan stuck to her brooch and she asked me to help her unfix it. She asked an old family friend because she did not wish to be an embarrassment to her new husband."

By the time I had finished my recitation, I was smiling from sheer relief. From giddiness. Marget had misinterpreted my actions for cheating! But what havoc her thoughts had wrought. What havoc my own thoughts had wrought. I wondered how the love between us, which had seemed so strong, could also be so fragile. I reached a hand out to her. "Come here."

She stepped near. But she did not reach her hand out to mine.

"How could I ever look at another woman when you stand before me as you do this moment?'Without ornament, without paint, without anything at all?" My heart seemed to have such a ridiculous way of soaring. "You are more than enough."

Her head rose, her eyes shining. "And I could never think of looking at another man the way I look at you."

Her hand met mine and I pulled her into my lap. I had more in mind than just sitting, but why should it not first begin with a kiss?

26

With all well once more between Lytham and I, we greeted the cold with the indifference that comes only from the knowledge of a warm and congenial bed. Winter poured forth from heaven's gates in a freezing rain, which glazed all of London's houses and made the streets treacherous. But once the ice had melted and Her Majesty took herself to Richmond Palace, Lytham asked permission to return to Holleystone.

I awoke the first morning at the estate with cramps in my wrists. When Joan came to draw me from sleep, she observed me trying to shake them out.

"What is it?"

" 'Tis nothing. My wrists have simply decided to sleep longer than I am prepared to permit." The sensation was not unlike that of a person left too long abed, when the insides begin to ache for want of motion. By the time I had been dressed, the impression had vanished.

But the next week it returned. And by the end of February, it had become my constant morning companion. We tried bundling my hands in heated cloths. It did nothing for my wrists, but it reddened my palms.

I had become rather glum about the state of my hands when one morning Lytham tried to cheer me.

"Come! You are too melancholy. Sport is wanted. Change into your riding clothes and I shall meet you out front with your horse."

"Where are we going?"

"To the mews."

The mews? Then he meant to hawk.

Once Joan had helped me change, Lytham and I mounted and rode out to the birds.

A man dressed in a rough jerkin and hose emerged from the structure to meet us. He had the air of a man stepping out of his castle, his demeanor not unlike Lytham's when he stepped out of Holleystone. His nose was rather like Lytham's as well. But his face was bronzed and roughened by wrinkles, as if he had spent his life in the sun.

"Falconer, we wish to hawk."

"My lord."

"Is it not time to be finding you an apprentice?"

"Time enough once I am dead. My lord." He turned his back to us and disappeared inside the building.

"Falconer's the best in the county. Perhaps in the realm. I could not otherwise allow my person to be treated so disrespectfully." Lytham's words were apologetic, but his smile was not.

Upon entering the mews, the birds turned their heads and looked at us with unblinking eye. One of them shifted in its cage, setting the bells on its legs to jangling.

"I had always wondered how falcons were kept."

"You have never hawked?"

"You find me so masculine as that?"

Lytham bowed before me, then took my hand and kissed it. "Nay. I find you so clever as that!"

"My father loves the hunt, but he has never kept birds."

"Never?"

I relented. "He kept pigeons."

"Pigeons!" Lytham and the falconer exchanged distressed glances.

Lytham addressed the falconer. "Do you not still keep a merlin?"

"The Lady Elinor's?"

Lytham frowned.

The falconer recognized that he had made a mistake and tried to reduce it. "That merlin has gone."

"Then find another. The countess shall be trained a merlin."

"Aye."

I waited for Falconer to say "my lord," but he never did. I was surprised the earl would tolerate such impertinence. But perhaps, as he had said, the man was worth it.

The falconer handed Lytham a sturdy leather glove before pulling on a long, thick glove himself and removing one of the birds from its cage.

Lytham mounted his horse, then bent and reached an arm down toward the falconer. The bird, now transferred to Lytham's arm, was hooded.

We rode out into the hunting park, where Lytham set the bird to flying while the parks-keeper sent men out into the woods to scare up the game.

"They call this the sport of kings, for the falcon is king of all he sees. He can spy even the smallest of creatures." The bird, as if to oblige Lytham, paused in mid-flight, tucked his wings to his body, and plummeted toward the earth. Hardly stopping to sink his claws into his prey, he flew back to us and landed at Lytham's feet, his claws grasping a wriggling squirrel.

The bird released the prey and Lytham kicked it aside, then

sent him out to fly again. We spent several hours at hawking, and it proved a good diversion from thoughts of my hands.

As I progressed on my needlework that spring, back at Lytham House, I noticed increasing prickles and itching in my thumb and long finger. They felt dull and swollen, as if my skin were too small, though in looking I could perceive no change in their shape nor in their size.

Joan caught me trying to rub the tingles from my palm one forenoon.

"If I might . . . ?" She took my hand between her own and began to rub the palm with her thumbs. It helped for a time, but my ailment reappeared the next morning.

As if in answer to my prayers, it soon became apparent from what ill I suffered. If we were correct, Joan and I, the cure would show itself in six short months. I was to birth a babe! And there was much to be prepared.

I wrote to my mother for linens and she sent them back in abundance. I sent Joan back to Holleystone to find a wet nurse and a rocker for the babe's cradle. I began work upon a small cap, though it went slowly for lack of strength in my fingers. I collected a coral for the babe to cut its teeth on and bought a tiny ruff.

Lytham took great care that I not over-tax myself. No longer was I allowed to accompany him to Southwark to the theaters, though he would always search me out to tell me of the plays that he had seen. As my belly grew bigger, Lytham's concerns increased. Though every other woman in England continued her habits up until her lying-in, I could not. Though I would not allow myself to be barred from court, he forbade me to attend state dinners. He had seen me, once, pause in my handiwork and pull at my fingers, so that pleasure was denied me as well. Soon all I could do was sit at the house while he went about the city at his leisure.

27

With my activities so severely curtailed, I gave Joan little about which to worry. And so she set her thoughts on chilblains. Since I was spending so much time in the stillroom, laying up salves and remedies for the season and for the babe, I was exposed, more than was usual, to winter's chills. She insisted that I not tarry upon leaving but come first up to my chambers. And waiting there, she would heat stones upon which I could warm my hands and feet.

One afternoon the cloth in which she had wrapped one of the stones slipped. We did not discover it until she uncovered my hands and I lifted them from the rock. We both cried out when we saw the blisters.

She dropped to her knees, her eyes drowning in tears. "I beg your pardon! We can plunge it into water. I can cover it in unguent!"

"Aye, quickly. Go!"

Her distress was much worse than my own. For although it was my hand that had been burned, I could not feel the pain. I ran the edge of a fingernail across the blisters and felt still nothing. Not even when I pressed down against the bubble of my own flesh.

I lifted the palm to my cheek and it felt hot against my face.

Curious indeed.

I tried to hide the blisters from Lytham, but he discovered them at the first opportunity.

————

"Are you well, my sweet?" I bent to kiss Marget as she sat by the fire in her chambers. She had stayed at Lytham House that night while I had attended entertainments at court.

"I am well." Her eyes belied her statement.

I caught up one of her hands and meant to kiss it, but she recoiled at my touch. Opening my hand, I gasped at the sight before my eyes. "What have you done?"

"It is nothing. Just a blister."

" 'Tis more than one. 'Tis several!" I turned her hand toward the fire's light so I could see them more clearly. "How did you come by them?"

"I was heating my hands."

"Why?"

"I had been in the stillroom."

"Why?"

"To lay up unguents." There was exasperation at work in her voice.

"But you were there long enough for your hands to swell so?"

"You sound just like Joan!" She pulled her hand from me and tried to fold it into her other.

"And Joan is a woman with some sense in her head. You cannot do such things."

"Then what *can* I do? I cannot sing, I cannot dance, I cannot embroider, I cannot . . . do anything!"

"I only want you well. You *and* the babe."

"I *am* well."

"Perhaps . . . shall I ask the musicians to perform? Tomorrow night?"

She shook her head.

"I could . . . invite a group of players to come."

She shook her head once more.

"We could . . . play a game of chess!"

"I wish to *do* something, not just sit in a chair and watch something done."

"I can think of many things that do not require you to sit. One thing, for instance, that might require lying down. Upon a bed."

Her chin came up. "Nay. You will not have me so easy as that! Not when you cage me up."

"What if I promise to uncage you?"

"To do anything I like?"

"To do some things that you like . . . just so long as you promise me one thing: do not over-tax yourself."

"I promise. But I regret to inform you that your suggestion of entertainments for this evening is quite taxing indeed."

————

I might have kept my promise to Lytham, but Sir Walter Raleigh got himself placed under house arrest in May. And Lady de Winter told me Lytham would want to know. I found him in his chambers with Nicholas, surprising the both of them with my presence.

"What has happened?"

I took several moments to reply, lacking the breath to say anything at all.

Lytham led me to a chair and bid me sit.

" 'Tis Raleigh."

"What of him?"

"His marriage has been discovered . . . and his babe."

"His marriage?"

"To Bess Throckmorton. Her Majesty's maid-in-waiting."

Lytham's brows rose near to his hairline and I knew then the feeling of sweet triumph. I had told him something that he had not known.

"He has been married?"

"Aye."

"Are you certain? Surely the babe was just . . . an . . . accident. A singular occasion."

"It has been said that it resulted from a series of several . . . accidents." Such bold behavior by one of the Queen's maids would not be tolerated. Not if the love affair had been carried on beneath that very long, very aquiline, very jealous, vain, malevolent nose. Indeed, Raleigh was questioned for two days. And then Bess was taken and placed under house arrest with her babe, elsewhere in town. It could not go well for her.

And in some respects, it was not going well for me. My hands were swift becoming useless. And I knew it most upon dressing. One morning I asked Joan for my rope of pearls and a brooch.

She brought them to me and I inclined my head so that she could drape the pearls over it in several loops. She worked some moments to arrange them in cascading lengths. "And the brooch?"

"Fasten it to the sleeve."

She moved to pin it to the left sleeve.

I shook my head. "The right."

Once she had finished, she took up my paints, but my fingers had begun to prick. And in rubbing them, I realized they were unadorned.

"I still need a ring."

She returned to the box and lifted a hand to retrieve what I desired. "Which one?"

"Can I see them?"

She held the box before me, beyond the bounds of my ruff, so that I could look. I decided upon the emerald and reached in to the box to acquire it. It slipped from my fingers at the first. And then it fell away from them on my second attempt. I put my other hand to the box to steady it and tried again. In my scrabbling through the box after the jewel, Joan's hand came to possess it and she offered it to me in her open palm.

Maddened, I reached for it, taking it up between my thumb and finger. But it tumbled from my grasp before I could thread it upon my hand. "Blast the ring! I do not want it now."

But, in truth, I did. And later, after I had dismissed the chambermaid and Joan, I tried for the ring once more.

I opened the coffer and saw it lying upon a tray, hidden by nothing. But try as I might, I could not coax my fingers to possess it. I realized I had no choice but to go to court with my fingers bared. But in leaving the room, my attention was arrested by a pair of gloves I had carelessly cast onto the table. I thought to take them with me to hide my fingers from view. But again, I could not grasp them. Finally, I swept them into one hand with the other and went out into the day.

But the episode had kindled a cold flame of fear within me. If I could not pick up a ring or put on a glove, then how could I sit a horse? How could I eat at a table? And how would I be able to hold my own sweet babe once it was born? I might have sent for a physician, but to what end? He would only have wanted to bleed or purge me, and I did not want to absent myself from court. I took a deep breath and ordered the flickering of anxiety within my belly to cease. The pricking would pass. The clumsiness would end. Why should it not?

And so I left, clinging to my hope that the ailment would be cured with the birth.

28

With summer's long, languorous days approaching, the earl's thoughts turned to the pageant of Her Majesty's Progress about the countryside to visit her people. And to the preparations to be made for the journey. He tried to convince me to stay at Lytham House, but I would not be coerced. For six weeks we were to have the pleasure of becoming an itinerant court. But that did not mean activities would not continue as was their habit. And I meant to be a part of them.

In fact, we had hardly time to arrange ourselves at Nonsuch when gossip began to circulate. One morning there was a hum emanating from the Presence Chamber as if from a beehive. As I stepped inside, I snared not one person's attention. Courtiers were clustered in tight groups that did not invite guests.

Had Spain foresworn some new attack against Her Majesty? Worse, had France joined with them?

I knew there was one who would know what there was to be told: Lady de Winter. Seeing my approach, she waved me to her side with her fan.

"Is it Spain? France?"

Her eyes glowed with unholy glee. "Worse, even! 'Tis Bess Throckmorton."

"What has she done?"

"Besides have Raleigh's baby? She has been taken to the Tower."

"Why?"

Lady de Winter's lips thinned and her eyes narrowed. "What else is to be done to a maid who entices Her Majesty's pug onto her own lap?" She was shaking her head, pretending outrage when satisfaction was lurking all the while in her eyes. "Heed my words! There can be no love affairs at court. None but those pursued by Her Majesty. What can the girl have been thinking?"

I could guess. I knew. She had been bewitched. It had not mattered what she knew or what anyone else had thought. She had fallen in love.

Several days later the court was left reeling with the news that Raleigh too had found himself clapped into a cell in the Tower.

We spoke of it, Lytham and I, at dinner one noon as we ate at court of capons with spiced oranges, fish stuffed with currants, roast pig, parsnips and marigolds, and a spinach tart baked with rose water. In fact, it was the topic of everyone's conversation. "But now will she not have to take his estate from him?"

"The Queen? Why should she now if she has not before? She will forgive anything but being made a fool of. And Raleigh, God bless the man, is just the one to wriggle out of his responsibilities." He paused to work some meat away from a bone. "If Her Majesty asked him this day who was Bess Throckmorton, he would look her in the eyes and plead ignorance. And she would believe him! When has the Queen ever listened to reason where her heart is concerned? She is cuckolded by the very men she can never marry."

"But why?"

"Why can she not marry? Who would have her? She is past the

age of child-bearing. But more, who would she have? Any man she married would want the throne."

The countess sitting on the other side of Lytham leaned past him to speak to me. "And 'tis the throne, her true love. Besides, she never wanted to marry."

I leaned past Lytham to speak to the countess more directly. "Why not?"

"Look what marriage did to her poor mother." She drew a line across her neck with a finger. "And it did not seem to agree with her father." She shook her head. "Seven times he was married! He could not make up his mind."

Beyond the woman, her husband rose slightly from his chair to speak over his wife's head "She is more like her father than she knows! Why get married when—" He was stopped from speaking when his wife stuck an elbow in his gut.

Lytham merely shook his head and resumed eating.

Frustration was at work that summer upon every person at court. And not on Raleigh's account, but for cause of the weather. Wells had dried up across the kingdom and springs had stopped issuing water. Many beasts died that summer for thirst.

The birds could not be bothered to sing, though the earth gasped in relief at night to the rhythm of crickets' screeching. Even the bees seemed indolent, unwilling to go about their business in the oppressive heat. We began to leave off layers in our dressing. And when waving our fans caused more perspiration than it abated, we left off doing that as well.

The court grew insolent. It lacked patience, it lacked humor, it lacked, quite frankly, of rain. And clouds. Of those dark events that serve to underscore the brightness of the light. Light, unrelieved, unabated, had become light unappreciated.

We left one house early that Progress, ere the sun had woke, and rode early to dinner at the next. We came to despise the banqueting houses constructed for our pleasure. They may have blocked the sun, but they also stored up heat. To step into them for the partaking of a dessert course was to step into a smelter's furnace. At more than one estate, Her Majesty ate all of her dinner inside . . . and left the rest of us to blister in the smoldering temperatures.

A malaise began to spread through our ranks. A most mysterious and inconvenient disease that altered neither the appearance nor the constitution, but required the victim to retreat to a country estate to recover.

How I longed for water. How I wished to float upon the River Thames, making furrows in the water with my fingers, Lytham strumming upon the lute. If I closed my eyes, I could conjure visions of the swans and hear the watermen jostle for fares. But then we were told the river had dried up.

It was unimaginable. How could the city function without the river to supply transit? To cleanse it? How was one to visit a theater? The Courts or the Bear Garden? London without the Thames was unthinkable.

But October brought the worst news of the year. As the Progress came to a close, word came that the plague had overtaken London. There would be no hope of the court's return to the city. And indeed, a city without a river, a city that had closed up its theaters and quarantined itself against the plague, was a city to which there was no reason to return.

We found ourselves moored instead to the city of cupolas, turrets, and chimneys that was Hampton Court. At least we were not dancing on each other's toes as we had at Nonsuch. Lady de Winter once told me Hampton Court had eight hundred rooms. I knew her to tell tales, but that statement might well have been the truth.

We had just arrived when Lytham decided to send me back to Holleystone for my lying-in.

"But I am not ill! I am just breeding!"

"And I want you to do it at my home."

"There was one countess danced a galliard a week before she was brought to bed. At this very place."

"I will not have my heir bounced out upon his head for want of his mother's care."

"I care very much about the health of this babe! And it is one month still until he makes his appearance."

"A month I would know you safely at home." Lytham drew me into his arms and aimed a kiss at my neck, but his approach was blocked by the babe growing in my belly. "The boy stands between us even now."

He retreated to stand behind me and then resumed his sweet pursuits.

"How do you know him to be a boy?"

His lips paused. "Your belly wobbles a bit to the right, my sweet. Your right eye is more brilliant. Your right cheek more flush."

I felt my left cheek warm to match it. "And if you are mistaken?"

"Then *she* shall be the most beautiful girl in England and we will see her married to a future king."

It took all of Lytham's skills at persuasion to move me from Hampton Court to Holleystone. And in the end, he left court to accompany me there himself.

29

As I accompanied Marget with my men, the consequence of the drought was plain to see. England's tidy farms lay in waste around us. The furrows that usually organized the fields into regiments had degenerated into chaos. The wheat that had been first stunted and then scorched by summer's sun had been left to rot so that fields looked filled with corpses. Doors to huts hung open, creaking in the wind. Their roofs, which generally puffed with smoke, had fallen in. The landscape, bereft of trees, had no wood to kindle even the smallest of fires. We may have destroyed the Spanish Armada, but fitting out the navy had destroyed all of England's trees.

Around us, the poor wandered like a group of finches in search of food. And not always on the road between villages but through the brush. Yet not one person pursued them to demand why they did not keep to the roads. And we saw no one being whipped back to a home parish for vagrancy. Indeed, it was as if the people had no home parish at all. It was alarming. Always, they were walking. And no one seemed to know or care where. The only poor I saw motionless were those who had fallen into ditches, dead.

What was to become of England if people would not keep to

their places? If they felt free to wander wherever they desired and whenever they wanted? And if they did not keep to their homes and do the work of their fathers, then who would do it? The closer we got to Holleystone, the less often the vagrants moved off the way when we passed.

Finally, I halted in front of one such a group.

They made no reverence. And they made no move to leave our path.

"Please, my lord, a bit of bread?"

"Please, my lord, a swallow of ale?"

"Have you a license for beggary?" I questioned.

"Not in this parish, my lord."

"Then you are strangers. Why do you wander so far?"

"We have no home. We once had, but there is nothing to eat. And none left in the village, my lord."

"None?"

"None save us. We started with two children . . . but they . . . now they're dead." They were a ragtag bunch of six.

"You cannot just wander, man!"

"Then what shall we do, my lord? Sit down and die?" In his agitation, the man's hood had slipped down his head. His lank hair hung in shocks, an ear protruding between them . . . or what was left of his ear. At some point it had been burned, leaving the remnants to curl in toward his skull. It was the mark of a vagrant, caught not once but twice. And the penalty for a third offense was death by hanging.

"This is not the first time you have wandered afar."

The man straightened in a brazen manner. "And I will wander still farther if I must."

I looked them over once more, then nodded and set my horse into motion.

Marget urged her own horse forward to ride beside me. "But did you not see his ear? He is a vagrant. A sturdy one. And caught twice for his crimes."

"What should I have done? In this country, with no food in his possession, it cannot take long for him to die."

———

When we reached Holleystone, we were home barely a forenoon when the steward announced trouble at the gate.

"'Tis the poor, my lord. Those that were and those that are now. The countryside has turned to beggary. And now that you are here . . ."

Lytham replaced his quill into his inkwell and walked to the window. He stood there so long a time and looked so troubled that I soon put aside my book to join him.

To hands stretched through the gates, the gatekeeper gave bread. And for every hand that was satisfied, another soon appeared.

He turned toward the steward. "When is the soonest they can expect a return from spring's plantings?"

"If they have the strength to sow, then they could eat the roots of their crops, my lord, once they have sprouted."

"But then they will have no harvest next fall."

They shared a look that set a dog to gnawing at my belly.

Lytham's aspect brightened. "There are fish in the river."

"The river went dry in July, my lord. It will return this winter, if there is snow, once it melts, but there will be no fish."

"Then I have little to offer them. Do they think me God that I can turn three fishes into a feast? I have none! I have naught to give them. London is destitute. There is no trade, there is no commerce. And I can conjure nothing from plain air! It is too heavy a burden. This is what the Church is for! At least when we allowed monks, they cared after the people. This wandering about the countryside is shameful."

But the steward only sighed. "You could open the hunting park, my lord."

"And have the game run out? And the underbrush destroyed? Nay." He began to pace. Then he stopped. "But I could order it hunted. If it were hunted wisely, there may be enough to last until spring."

He looked toward the steward, who nodded.

"Then with God's help we will manage this. No one may have enough, but if I may say it, no one may be found to have too little."

Lytham returned to Hampton Court once my mother and aunt arrived. They were joined by Lady de Winter. And it was not many days later before the babe decided to come.

No time was wasted in sending for the midwife. So quick was she drug from her labors that she arrived in my chambers still bloodied from butchering her dinner. I wished for Joan's calming presence, but being still a maid, she had been pushed from my rooms at the first opportunity.

The midwife ordered the windows shut up and the candles extinguished. At first she made me stay abed. And then, as the pains increased, she plied me with drink. There were some moments of great peace, and then came the sensation of all of my insides pushing to get out.

At my mention of this, the midwife and my mother pulled me from bed and pushed me into the birthing chair.

I gripped my mother's hand as I strained.

"Why must it be so difficult?"

"Great joy is received from so hard a labor."

"How did you survive this?"

"The pain is quick forgotten."

In the cramps which then seized me, my mouth loosed words I might have sworn I never knew. Most of them blighted Lytham's good character. Suffering as I was in my travails, words ushered forth uncensored from my mouth. ". . . sends me away from his sight while he stays at Hampton Court cavorting with the Queen! Would that she suffer so much as I—" My words were drowned by my screams. When I once again found breath, I continued my tirade. "I shall never allow him to touch me again. I care not how many radishes he may eat!"

"So *that* is how he did it!"

My mother clucked at Lady de Winter and wrapped my head in a dampened cloth. "Do you not make promises you cannot keep."

"A pox on men and all their devices!"

"You cannot mean it."

"I do mean it! I curse them all. Every wandering, pox-bitten dog of them. Every one of them who leaves the countryside peopled with his likeness while his daughter and his wife pretend not to notice!"

The room had fallen silent. And every servant, every person attendant, looked at all things other than my mother and myself.

I clenched her hand and brought her close to me. "Why do they do it?"

"They cannot help it."

"Then why did you allow it? What did you do to make him not love you?"

Before my mother could reply, Lady de Winter provided an answer. "If he did not love her, then let the fault be with him!"

I gasped, and not only from the pain.

Lady de Winter pushed from her chair and poured a cordial, then came to my side and handed it to me. "A wife and lovers: the one is for empire building and the others for pleasure. You cannot hope to be both, girl. Love is a luxury most of us cannot afford."

But I did hope. And I wanted to be both.

And then pain seized me and I wanted nothing more than for the babe to be born.

He was so small. So very tiny.

I did not, at first, understand the gasps of those attending me. But I was not long in gaining their knowledge. He had come into the world too soon. And one hour after he was born, he expired.

ℳ 30 ℬ

*L*ytham could not get permission to leave court, but my friend, my mother, and my aunt stayed with me for the month. I cannot say that I was good company. Or a good hostess. I could not, in fact, say very much at all. Not without bursting into tears. Not when everyone was trying to console me.

"Have no fears, there will be another."

But I wanted no other. I wanted the one that had been lost.

"It happens. I lost four myself. Died ere they were born."

I knew it happened. Of course it happened. But why did it have to happen to me?

"There, girl. This time, next year, see if you are not lying-in again. Lytham will see to it."

Next year? Pain squeezed my heart tighter with every breath. How would I survive until the coming year?

When a month had passed, when it was time for my churching, I dressed with care and I dried my eyes. I asked the chambermaid to take pains with my hair that day and then I tried to add to my costume a smile.

Once at church, I knelt as the vicar thanked God for preserving my life during childbirth. It was true enough that He had, but why could He not have also preserved the life of my child? Why should I be celebrating my own good fortune while my babe slept in the cold tomb of the earth?

I did not give way to my melancholy. At least not outwardly. It was a day for drinking and feasting. For celebrating motherhood. And I had been a mother, if only for one short hour. It was also a day to send my guests back to their own homes. And I did not want them to leave if they would only worry about me the length of their journey home.

———

When Marget returned to Hampton Court, it was with pale face and subdued spirits. I longed to take her into my arms, to hold her, to comfort her, but I could not. Had we been at Lytham House, I would not have hesitated for an instant. But at court, who knew who could be watching? And since the news of Raleigh and Bess Throckmorton's marriage, everyone anticipating the next scandal, the next courtier who might betray the throne.

Had I been able to do as I wished, I confess that still I would not have known what to say to Marget. My own spirits were distinctly lacking in joviality. I had no wish but to mourn the tiny life who had been, for an instant, mine. And who better to mourn with than my wife? But then . . . had not our union been the cause of all of the sadness? I feared she might wish for nothing more than to be left alone.

———

Upon my return to Hampton Court, I resumed my role. Lytham never spoke of the babe and neither did I. In fact, he spoke to me very little at all. I longed to hide myself within the stronghold of his arms, but they were not opened to me. Lacking a safe port at which to anchor, at which to gain strength, I moored myself at court instead, though I had no great wish to be there. I had no great wish to be anywhere at all.

But there was much news to catch up on. And Lady de Winter was the first to fill my ears with it.

"The Viscount of Montacute has died. Much to Her Majesty's sadness."

"I cannot account for her emotion. Was he not Catholic?"

"A Catholic of the heart, not of the politic."

"And what is that to mean?"

"Simply that his body belonged to Her Majesty and his soul to his God."

"I do not see how a man could live divided when Spain provokes war against us, inciting all kinds of villains to assassinate our Queen. To be Catholic is not to be heretic, it is to be traitor." I was in no mood to dissemble. I no longer had any patience for the duplicity of the courtier. Could no one understand? My heart had been broken. I had a son. He had died. Babes died frequently, but that babe had been mine.

The only thing I wanted to talk about was the one thing no one would mention. Had none of the women in that Presence Chamber noticed my distended belly? Had none of the women noticed that I had, of late, returned to court from a long absence? Grief lapped at my heart like the waves of the sea. And there were times, like the coming of high tide, when I could do naught but feel its coming. I needed some place to retreat. Some place to hide, but there was nowhere to go in that great palace.

And Lady de Winter would give me no peace. She plied me with news and harassed me with questions.

"And what, your New Year's gift to the Queen?"

"I do not know. Lytham presents the gift."

"Then you must find out. And when you do, you must tell me."

I only did it so she would cease her harassments. And then I reported back for lack of any other diversion.

"He gives her an astrolabe." Just as he had once given me.

"Every person gives her an astrolabe; they think to appeal to her mind. Her intellect."

"He says that she adores them."

"And so she does. But the goal of a present to a Queen is not to impress her, it is to delight her." She looked at me with expectancy, but I failed to respond.

She spoke to me slowly and with great elucidation. "How does one delight a Queen? With a gift that tells her she has no weakness."

In spite of my mood, my curiosity was piqued. "And what weakness can a Queen have?"

"Vanity. She fears growing old because she fears losing love. She is closer now to her death than to her birth. She must fear that men circle her, not because they wish to be near her but because they wish to survive her after she has gone. Men come not to give love, but to get gain. So Lytham must not give a gift that she will adore; he must give a gift that speaks to her of *his* adoration. She must be convinced that she is still worthy of admiration as a woman, not as a Queen. Any man can admire an intellect. Not every man can admire a body in decline."

"Then what must he give?"

I took Lady de Winter's answer straight to Lytham.

———

"A length of damask?" *That* was Marget's marvelous idea? "Her Majesty has more clothes than she can possibly wear. Every town she visits gives her gloves and fans and sleeves in abundance." I hated to dampen her excitement. There had been so little that piqued her interest since the babe had died.

"Aye. They give her a gift they have fashioned themselves. The best that *they* can make or imagine. But how can they know the mind of a Queen? Why would she wish to be dressed in a design of someone else's making?"

At least my wife was talking to me again. That was something. I pushed my chair away from my desk, took her by the arm, and settled her into my lap. "And what do you suggest?"

"Give her a length of fabulous embroidered satin. Tell her you would not dare to dress Her Majesty in a fashion of your own choosing, for how can a Queen be made in the image of any man?" She could not stay settled on my knee and took instead to her feet once more. "You cannot hope that your gift will match her beauty; you hope only that she will be able to use it to fashion something that pleases her."

It was good to see animation at work in her face again. "And you have in mind such a length of cloth?"

"I know how to get one."

She did, although it cost me plenty to wrangle it from another's hands. The idea was sound, though I might never have thought of it, and in the end it was worth the effort. Some several months later, I came to know that Her Majesty had indeed ordered the satin fashioned into a gown. And when she wore it, she made certain that I had noticed.

Surely the Queen would agree to visit Brustleigh now! Once more, Marget had been useful indeed.

———

Under Lady de Winter's prodding and Joan's ministrations, life began to take on a sharper focus. And slowly I began to see color and hear music once again. And then, one day, I heard myself laugh at a jest Lytham had made. After that, everything seemed to settle back into its place.

Except that a babe-sized hole had been left within my heart. And my hands still suffered. If I had expected to shed my malady with the child, I had been mistaken. But life was still mine for the living. And I once more watched with devotion and listened with attention to the goings-on at court, watching for the next opportunity in which I could make myself useful to Lytham.

As soon as it was deemed safe to return to London, Her Majesty called a parliament. Lytham was obliged to sit. And in that I could be of no use at all. But he immediately summoned a tailor, and I watched as he chose a new set of clothes. By opening day, he was resplendent in his new doublet, ruff, and cloak. He did not return until late that night, and when he did, it was to find me playing the lute in order to keep from falling asleep.

"How goes Parliament?"

"Exactly as the Queen would have it. She made haste in reminding us that she would assent or dissent to anything she liked."

"So why call the lords?"

"To prosecute the Catholics. And the dissenters."

"Even more?"

"Aye. It is to become a crime."

"A crime? When any man of good sense would bow before England's altar just as quickly as the Pope's? Why would one not wish to save his head before his soul?" Had I just spoken those words? It used to be that I had believed in God with steadfast faith . . . but that was before I discovered He dressed himself in Her Majesty's gowns.

Lytham turned to discard his cloak before my words could elicit a reply. When he had shed it into the hands of his chamberer, he spoke of different things. "She wants money."

"For what?"

"For everything. For this thing and another."

When it became apparent that Parliament would be sitting for some time, I made plans to return to Holleystone. Why suffer the indignities of life in the city when I could go home to the estate and enjoy the benefits of the country?

I wished for Lytham, but I could not say the same for my paints.

The respite from court was pleasant in more ways than one. Refreshing to both body and soul. Freed from the confines of ceruse and vermillion, my face and indeed my spirits grew more animated. Would that I could have gone without the paints at court, but to do that would have risked Her Majesty's wrath and damaged Lytham's chances. It would have meant the loss of everything I had worked so hard to gain. But at Holleystone, with no one's eyes upon me and without the necessity of regarding everyone else, I was able to be only and exactly myself.

Of course, I missed court, the opportunities to listen, to gather information. I missed being useful. But I found other ways in which to be useful at Holleystone. I made ale and produced apple wine. I had wool delivered to the poor so they could card and spin it. I gathered what plants there were and processed them in the still room for medicines and then took my maids with me to the village to educate them in the nursing of the sick.

But news from London began to find me. And as it found me in greater quantities, I began to gather myself to return to the city. The poor were still lining up, every day, outside the gates. They had deteriorated much, purple chilblains turning into bulbous and oozing wounds upon their toes. Faces had become bonier, hair had turned grayer. And they had become quieter through the winter. There was no more singing on the work sites and little shouting. There was no longer any jostling for food. But I noticed their resolve had become greater. They had survived thus far. With God's help and a good harvest, they would survive still.

31

When finally I reached Lytham House, I received a marvelously warm welcome. Only it did not come from the quarters from which I had expected. It was Lady de Winter, rather than Lytham, who first greeted me.

"I have a gift for you." Her tawny eyes were sparkling.

"I am in need of gifts. Pray, tell me what it is."

"It is something to befit your station."

I felt my brow rise. What could it be?

"Follow me and I will show you."

We passed out of the house and into the day. The April weather was ambivalent, unable to decide whether to settle on winter or spring. The sun had shown herself, but neither in any great splendor nor any great warmth. Lady de Winter led me to the stables. When we entered, she called to her groom.

"You may fetch Lady Lytham's gift."

The groom bowed and went off in search of whatever it was that Lady de Winter would give me. When he returned, I did not recognize at first what it was that he carried. He headed toward his

214

mistress, but the lady gestured him to me. He bowed once more and then deposited his tiny bundle into my arms.

It wriggled. And then it bit my finger. "What is this creature?"

Lady de Winter smiled as though I were not astonished at her choice of giftings. "'Tis a dog."

"Aye. And for what purpose? Lytham has dogs aplenty. And this one looks to be puny in the way of dogs." The beastie had decided to chew on my necklace. I thumped it on the head and removed the pearls from its mouth.

"No purpose."

"For no purpose at all?"

"None but display."

"But why . . . ? You thought it fitting for my station?"

"Is your head so dull? Think on it. In possessing a dog, you proclaim that Lytham has so much influence that you have wealth enough to support a creature that has no purpose."

I held it out in front of me toward the groom. "Take it."

He relieved me of the creature and placed it on the ground.

"Tut, girl. You must make a friend of it."

"Not if it is to devour the best of my jewels."

"But you see, it does not matter, does it? Because you can buy more!"

I looked at the pup as the meaning of her words sunk in. Of all the fabulous displays of wealth at court, a pup could, in fact, be the most extravagant. And, as Lady de Winter had said, the pup declared that we had wealth enough to feed it and keep ourselves in clothes. And jewels. It was better than a new pair of sleeves or a new rope of pearls, for it might consume wealth even as I displayed it. I knew too well how Lytham longed for the Queen's favor. And if it could help Lytham at court . . . "Aye, I can. I can buy more." I began to see how the creature could be of use. "Is it male or female?"

Lady de Winter shrugged as we turned to watch it skitter along the floor. "I did not think to look."

With a yip, the creature rolled onto its back, exposing its pale underbelly.

"'Tis a male." We were both agreed upon it.

Lady de Winter had the groom pick it up and give it back to me. And after we had walked about in the garden, after Lady de Winter had left for her own house, I took the beast inside with me to show him his new home.

———

"What is this . . . thing?" I heard my own voice echoing through the Great Hall.

Marget looked up from her book, her eyes at first ignorant of what I was speaking.

I pointed to the floor, toward my boot the creature was nibbling upon.

She turned her eyes back toward me. "'Tis a dog."

"Aye. And no hunter from the looks of him." I lifted my foot from the floor. The pup dangled a moment and then slipped to the ground.

"'Twas a gift from Lady de Winter."

"She wished to curse us?"

"Nay. The intent was to help people to understand your position and influence."

"Through a runt of a cur? You know some say she is mad?"

"She is brilliant! Only one who has great wealth can support a creature with no purpose."

"No purpose but to destroy me." I cast a glance toward the pup. He had now decided to scratch a hole in the woven rushes. "It will cost me a fortune." A fortune I did not possess at that particular moment, though I would, once the Queen visited Brustleigh.

She smiled. "That is exactly the wanted effect."

"To cost me my fortune?"

"To have others realize your fortune is so vast that it cannot matter what a pup does. It cannot matter how much he eats."

"It matters to me." I nudged the pup with my boot, coaxing him from his task. But then he gained his feet and ran to the refuge of my cloak.

"Come, Lytham, he is a gift. From a powerful and influential woman."

I followed the pup and pulled the cloak from him, tumbling him from his hiding place. "What do you call him?" The creature was trying to gain his feet.

"I had thought to call him Cerberus."

I could not keep myself from laughing. "The hound from hell? He may be hellish, but he is no monster."

"Argos then."

"As in Odysseus' faithful, loyal dog?" I heard myself sigh. "Do what you will. I only wish not to see him."

———

I was able to fulfill Lytham's wishes for the first week of the dog's residency at Lytham House. It was not difficult when Lytham kept himself at court for half the night. But then there came one night when he forsook his cards for my company. And when he did, he discovered the pup guarding my chamber. From the inside. Nestled into his very own pillow of feathers, which had been placed beside mine.

The dog was promptly removed to the floor. But every time Lytham approached me, the creature yipped at him.

"I cannot make love to you without some privacy."

I laughed. "So now you claim to be modest, my lord?"

"Make it go away."

"He will only begin to bark in earnest."

Lytham pushed himself from the bed onto an elbow. "Who is the man and who is the dog that I should be reduced to beggary?"

"If you could only whine, my lord, just a little, you might find you get your way."

"Is that how the beast does it?"

"Aye. He whimpers from the foot of my bed, and creeps up until he gains the pillow."

I heard Lytham stalk around to the foot of the bed. Then he pushed the curtains aside and began to climb up over the bed. "Like this, then?"

"Are you suffering, my lord? Because when the creature whines, it sounds as if his heart is breaking."

"There's other things here breaking, lady, like my knees. Have pity!"

"Much better." I threw back the coverlet to let him in. "See? You have only to ask."

As he slipped in beside me, the pup growled at him.

Lytham sighed. Then he left the place he had gained, took Argos by the neck, carried him from the room, and then closed the door in his face. "I will not fight some wretched beast for my territory."

"I had not known, my lord, that it was in dispute."

Lady de Winter returned later in the week to see if the pup and I were becoming friends. I offered him up to her to carry, but she frowned and pushed him back toward me.

"I cannot stand the creatures, although they do serve a certain purpose. You need to take him to court, girl. He does no good for you here."

"But he is still so young!"

She shook her head over my display of sentiment. "Enough of pups. There is one thing Lytham still lacks, girl."

Of course there was one thing Lytham lacked. He lacked an heir. And was I not trying everything I could think of to provide one? I was already drinking beer that had been boiled with tansy. I took a wretched syrup daily made of arrach, wild and stinking. And I would even eat calendula once it came into bloom.

"He is not a Knight of the Garter. You must do something about it."

I blinked. Lady de Winter's thoughts had not been my own, but she was right. If Argos could elevate me in the ways of fashion, Lytham lacked his own distinctive accoutrement. He lacked the garter knight's purple velvet vestment and gold collar. I wished that I could do something to help him obtain that honor, but I knew not what to do. "I would like to, but how can I gain access to Her Majesty's ear?"

"For you, that may be an impossibility, but you can find someone to speak to her on your behalf."

"Who?"

"Think, girl! If it is she who appoints the Knights of the Garter, then they must have obtained her favor in some way."

"I could speak to one of them?"

"Aye. But *speaking* might not produce the desired effect."

"I could . . . I have some jewels." Though not as many as I once had.

"Those might prove fruitful."

Those? In plural?

"Now, listen well. I have a plan."

32

The next forenoon, Lady de Winter conspired to have me meet with one of the garter knights at her own house, in her own chambers, so there would be no witness to our meeting. I took Argos with me.

"Sir Thomas, Lady Lytham. I will leave you to conduct your . . . business." Lady de Winter took her servants with her as she closed the doors to her chambers.

"Sir Thomas." I extended my hand toward him.

He grasped it with his own clammy fingers and kissed it. "My lady."

I sat in one of the several chairs in the room. My hand reached out, as was now its habit, to stroke Argos's head. How did one go about arranging these things? Did one just . . . ask for what one wanted? Knowing the arts of the courtier, I doubted it would be that easy. Or that straightforward.

"The Lady de Winter suggested that I may be of some aid to you."

She had? "I was hoping . . ."

He looked at me, brows raised.

"That perhaps . . ."

"I had heard I might help you in . . . influencing . . . a certain process, my lady."

"Aye. Aye, I had hoped that you might be able to help my husband, the Earl of Lytham."

He nodded.

"Obtain a . . . that is . . ."

"Had you hoped, perhaps, that I could present his case before Her Majesty, my lady?"

"Aye." Exactly. In my lap, Argos yawned, then placed his head upon his paws and closed his eyes. "If there is a way to go about it."

"There are ways, my lady . . . and there are ways."

"I see." I said the words though I saw nothing at all. There are ways . . . ? What was it that he wanted? Oh! He wanted to be paid. Trying not to jolt the pup, I pulled a hand from beneath his chin to find the purse which dangled from my waist. I removed a jewel from it. "I would consider it a very *great* favor."

"I see." From the way he said it, it was quite clear that he did not, in fact, see any ways forward.

"I thought perhaps . . . perhaps I have been mistaken, Sir Thomas. I would not want you to do something that would not be of profit." I had not brought any more jewels with me, in spite of what Lady de Winter had implied, for I had hoped I would not need them.

"For a lady such as yourself, who keeps a pup, it could be said that there is nothing too costly. Nothing which might not be obtained. For the right price."

"You are right, Sir Thomas. But it is my misfortune not to have brought any other . . . tokens of my wealth with me this forenoon."

"Surely, my lady, I could take your jewel just as well as I could take gold."

"Of course." But I had not offered him any gold.

"But there are certain rewards of a . . . sweeter kind . . . that might do just as well."

I could not pretend to know where his words were leading.

Suddenly, he got to his feet and walked toward me. He knelt before me on one knee, face flush, his golden collar glinting. "I would consider it a very great honor indeed, my lady, to do as you suggest if only . . ."

My cheeks flamed as I finally understood precisely what it was that he wanted.

He wanted me.

I tried to think of some way to extricate myself from the situation. Surely Lady de Winter had not suggested that I actually . . . Nay. She could not have done so. The man must have thought of that reward himself. And I had been closeted, alone, with him for . . . far too long. It was imperative that I escape. Now! But still he knelt before me, looking quite hopeful that I would agree to his proposition.

God, what am I to do? If you would rescue me from this situation, if you would . . . make certain that Lytham will never find out, then I will . . . What?

What could the Almighty God want from me? What could I possibly offer Him? I had no jewels that He had not created. I had no gold that He had not forged himself in the bellows of the earth. But if He would not act on my behalf, to help me honor the vows I had pledged before Him, then my virtue would be tarnished beyond redemption.

Think!

If I refused the man, if I shamed him, then I could not count on him to support Lytham's candidacy. And I very well could count on him to sour the other knights against the earl.

Now the man was reaching for my hand!

I pulled it from him and lowered my head as if I were being demure. There must be something that I could do!

Argos stirred beneath my hand.

Argos! My heart filled with thanks to God for hearing my prayer.

With the hand that remained beneath the dog, I pulled at the hairs on the underside of his belly.

He woke with a snarl. And when he saw a stranger's face before him, the snarl turned into a growl.

I pulled the pup to my chest and took to my feet. "I am so sorry, Sir Thomas! The creature has never liked men. I apologize. And, oh—" I extended a hand toward him.

He extended his.

I dropped the jewel into his palm and withdrew my hand before he could capture and kiss it. "Thank you so very much for your considerate attention. I wish you great success in this endeavor." At last I made it to the door and pushed through it, not even stopping to bid farewell to Lady de Winter before rushing into the courtyard to regain my horse.

My knees were trembling as I handed Argos to the groom and took to the saddle. As I rode for Lytham House, I thanked God once more for the runt of a cur that had proven to be my savior.

Alone in my chamber that night, the darkness allowed me no sleep. My actions filled me with shame. How had I gotten myself into such a predicament? How had I become like the women my father had used to mock my mother? And how had I allowed a marriage, and all that was right, to turn into such wrong?

God had rescued me, of that I was quite certain. He had allowed me to remain faithful to my vows; He had allowed me to retain my virtue. The only question was what He might want in return. If those were the gifts He had given me, then did it not stand to reason that He might want me to preserve them? As I walked the path that had been placed before me, might it not become increasingly more difficult to do? How could I maintain my integrity in a court devoid of anything decent? But how could I be of use to Lytham if I refused to be at court?

It was a riddle to which there appeared to be no answer. If I were to be of any use to my husband, it seemed as if I must stay precisely where my faithfulness would be most tested. There seemed to be no route of escape. And so, just before drifting into sleep, I prayed to God that if, indeed, He was asking of me the impossible, that He would himself open up a way.

My savior, Argos, soon proved his worth in other ways. When my maids took up their embroidery, my stiffened fingers found gainful work in feeding the creature sweetmeats and other choice bits of food. And though, by times, I could not gather my thoughts swiftly enough to provide a prompt retort to Lytham's skillful speeches, stroking the pup's sleek fur provided a reason for my distraction.

I discovered that I could not do without him, and so, as Lady de Winter had suggested, I took him with me to court. In fact, it was Argos and I who witnessed one of Lytham's greatest feats. It took place at Windsor. The court had lingered there due to plague in London. When I heard talk of a leaping contest being staged, I knew the earl must have a part in it. And so I joined in the company of lords and ladies, who were gathering in the space outside square-walled Winchester Tower.

Lytham had divested himself of his cloak and his sword. I did not know what my lord could hope to accomplish, for he was not the tallest among the courtiers. But after several rounds of leaps, he was still among those competing.

One of his competitors called out a protest. "We must check your shoes, Lytham. Do you not have a set of rabbit's feet hid inside?"

The crowd laughed.

"Nay. 'Tis simply parentage."

There was some movement among the onlookers, soon explained by the sight of the Earl of Essex pushing through their numbers.

He watched one round and then asked if he might compete. With his height and athletic prowess, there was no way he could lose, so it did not surprise anyone when he proposed a wager.

The courtiers still competing gambled such paltry sums that they were mere tokens. Except for Lytham. He bet twenty pounds. I turned away during the next pass, not wanting to see him fail, but instead of appearing to collect his cloak from Nicholas, he remained among the competitors. Two more rounds and then three and still he stayed, until, at last, Essex was his only opponent.

Lytham may have been confident, but I feared for him.

I closed my eyes and buried my head in Argos's fur and so did not see his winning leap.

———

I could not keep a smile from limning my face. In truth, might not be able to for the rest of the forenoon!

Marget approached me, Argos nestled in her arms. "You are satisfied then?"

"Tremendously."

"How did you know you would win? He has a certain advantage of height."

"Aye. And I wager he has never worked so hard at leaping in his life."

"But what can you hope to gain by garnering his disfavor?"

I leaned close as if to impart a secret, but I wanted simply to tickle her ear with my words. "Essex's second glance. You can be sure he will no longer underestimate me."

Marget tucked her ear toward her ruff even as a smile curled her lips. "At the potential loss of twenty pounds?"

"A bargain, my sweet, I assure you. He will never again take what is mine." Or if ever he was tempted to think about it, he might think first upon this humiliation. I spied Nicholas coming toward us across the courtyard and made quick work of cupping Marget's elbow.

The crowds of people engaged in various amusements made it safe to take my place at her side, and I did not wish to miss a moment of it. "Perhaps we could take some exercise in walking about the grounds? To the Upper Ward, perhaps?"

"As you wish."

Taking her hand in mine, I directed us toward the keep.

"Could you not walk a bit more slowly? With this jostling step I will wake the pup."

I slowed my step to accommodate my lady and her beast, but in the doing made it possible for Nicholas to catch us.

He hailed me, and then, once he had come close, spoke in a tone that only I could hear. "My lord? 'Tis Her Majesty. She desires a word."

The old witch. She ruined everything. I dropped Marget's hand and bowed to take my leave. "'Tis Her Majesty. Nicholas will accompany you."

———

Did she have her spies watching us? Why else then would she always part us just as we came together for the pleasures of simple amusements? Lytham left Nicholas and me with a swirl of his cloak. I sighed and hugged Argos close as we completed a tour of the grounds. And as I walked, I tried to work out a puzzle. It had to do with Lytham and Essex. For if my lord's words had not belied him, the two had entered into at least one contest before that one.

The list of names to be added to the Garter Knighthood eventually became known early in spring. Lytham's name was not among them. I had failed. Unfortunately, I was not the only one to know it.

"Are you mad, girl?"

"Lady de Winter." I tried to drop a curtsey, but she continued to advance upon me in the Presence Chamber, the ladies around us parting to let her pass as if she were Moses himself.

She came at me hissing and spitting. "I gave you Sir Thomas and you did nothing with that gift!"

I wished she would speak more quietly. "He wanted me to . . . he expected me to . . ."

"Be a courtier? Is that what you mean to say?"

"I could not—"

"Spare me your excuses! I tried to do you a favor. A very *great* favor. I had to pay him so that he would not speak of the disaster." Finally, she stopped her advance. "What was it? Was he not comely enough?"

"Nay. I mean, aye, he was . . ."

Her eyes narrowed. She leaned toward me to peer into my own. "He was not Lytham."

I could only shake my head.

"You suffer from a constant heart, girl! I told you love would ruin you. How can you hope to help Lytham succeed if you insist on being in love with him? He could have had a knighthood. And now he has nothing at all. What am I to do with you!"

My heart both trembled and rejoiced at the thought that she might be done with me. That she might leave me, for better or worse, to my own devices.

32

On May Day, while watching maids dance and observing the selection of the May Queen, I felt a quickening inside me. I made a quick calculation. We could expect a babe in October. My thoughts traveled ahead through the months, thinking of linens to be laundered, cradles to be found, and nurses to be employed. But then, the next week, I had a flux bloody enough to keep me abed.

And after that, I felt no more movements.

I told no one. Only Joan knew my flowers were other than normal. And I instructed her to advise all who inquired that I was ill. And I was. But there was no remedy for sickness of the heart.

Distraction came from an unexpected source. Lady de Winter, no doubt guided by providence, had decided to put away her grievances. She approached me one forenoon with several of her maids-in-training in tow.

"We go to see the lions. Will you come?" Her offer was made dispassionately, as if she did not care what I might say, and she did not clutch my hand in friendship as she once had done, but she had made the offer. And I had nothing better to do.

We took several of Lytham's and de Winter's men with us as

we rode to the Tower. When we got there, we were handed off to an attendant, who directed us toward the Lyon's Tower. Once we got there, Lady de Winter told the man waiting at Lyon Gate what we had come to see.

"Aye. Everyone what comes here comes to see the lions. But look you first to the wolf. 'Tis the only one left in all of England . . . least of the kind what has four legs instead of two . . . if you take my meaning."

We took his advice and observed a pale, mangy dog-of-a-beast lying in a cage in front of us. He lifted his head from his paws at our appearance, then put it back down.

The keeper walked before us into the gloom. Ahead were six cages, each one of them containing a lion. Lady de Winter, the maids, and I walked up to them, squinting to see through the dark.

They were all of them lying upon their sides, steadfast in ignoring their visitors.

The keeper lurched away from us. "I'll have them out for ye . . . just give me . . . where did I put . . . ?"

He came back brandishing a torch. Then he slid behind the cages and pushed the flame through the bars toward a beast.

The lion leapt to its feet, snarling.

In our haste to step back, Lady de Winter and I nearly stumbled over each other.

"They hates the fire. Always gets them moving." The keeper moved toward the other cages and drove their occupants to their feet. And then he plunged the torch into a water bucket and came to stand beside us. "They have a hundred years, the two of them here."

"One hundred years, girl! Imagine."

"Have they names?"

"The one here, the pale one, his name is Edward. For the King, God rest his soul." The keeper let out a spasm of a laugh. "An' this one here . . ." As he pointed, the other lion stretched its claws through the cage and then curled them around the bar and pulled. Its eyes were orbs of golden fire, their color not unlike those of Lady de Winter. As one person, Lady de Winter and I took another step back. "This one here, she's Elizabeth." He leaned toward us and whispered in an ale-soused voice, "She's the grasping female one." Silent laughter made his shoulders shake.

Elizabeth opened her mouth and let out a great roar.

"She don't like it when I say that." He pointed a gnarled finger at her. "But it's the truth. Still, we takes good care of them. If Elizabeth dies, they say our Elizabeth will surely die too."

I looked at him sharply. "Edward still lives even though *our* Edward is surely dead."

He screwed up eyes and scratched his chin. "Aye, that's a fact. I'm just telling ye what I know."

Elizabeth roared at him again.

"But this one here's healthy as Her Majesty's horse. Quit your moaning, beastie. I'll feed ye."

"What do they eat?" I could not pretend to mask my fascination.

"Anything what moves. And sometimes even things that be dead."

Elizabeth roared and the keeper growled back.

Elizabeth lifted a paw and batted at a bar of the cage. She shook her head to produce fantastic roars. And she kept it up for several minutes before I became aware of a strange noise. A scream that lay just under the register of the lion's growls. It rose and fell in a manner that made the hairs at the back of my neck tingle.

Lady de Winter must have felt the same sensation. "Keeper! What beast makes that noise? Can it not be kept silent?"

"Not a beast, my lady. 'Tis a man."

"A man?"

"Aye. In the Tower. It's the rack what turns a man to mewling."

"And what has he done to deserve such?"

"They don't know. Not yet. But they will. I wish they'd get to the end of it. Drives the lions mad. 'Specially Elizabeth—the ladies have the thirst for blood. She knows there's something out there what's close to dead, and she wants him."

I turned away from Lady de Winter and her maids and retched. I needed, of a sudden, bright sun and fresh air. I started back the way we had come in.

"But ye can't go without seeing the tiger. And there's a porcupine what has more pricks than a—"

I fled. I could not bear to hear more.

"What ails you, girl?" Lady de Winter had to lean close to be heard above the noise in the streets.

"Nothing."

"A person then?"

"Nay."

"A babe?"

I looked up sharp to find her staring at me. "How did you know?"

"You have the look of it about you. Your shade of pale has nothing to do with paint."

"I have lost another."

"And so, you will try again. And again until you have one that survives."

"But how can . . . how do I . . ."

"How do you survive? You concentrate on the task at hand. You make yourself useful in other ways."

"And if I cannot . . ."

She shrugged. "If you do not have one for your own self, then you can always take one."

"Take one?"

"Aye. It is quite possible that Lytham already has a child."

"Already has a child?" There was a ringing in my ears. A shallowness of my breath.

"Most courtiers do. And his would not be the first illegitimate child suddenly legitimized."

"He cannot. He would have told me."

"Would he, now? Are you certain?"

There was something in the way she asked the question that sent suspicion creeping through me. I beat it back. "He would have told me."

"Well. *If* he does not have his own, then you could take one from elsewhere."

"From where?"

"From the people. They seem to have enough of them. And 'tis done more often than one might think. There are many ladies in this court who have never had a babe. But their husbands all have heirs."

"But I cannot . . . just . . . *take* one."

"You can if you must. And why should they care? 'Tis just one more mouth to feed and they all seem to have so many."

"I cannot—"

"You *can* do what you must. You can. You will. You cannot let yourself begin to think otherwise."

"But if I cannot be the wife he needs . . . Lady de Winter, surely you know I am not the first of his wives."

"Aye. I know it well. Elinor and I were maids together to the Queen."

"And she loved him?"

"Theirs was looked upon as a love match."

"What happened?"

She searched my eyes before she answered. "What happened was an Act of Parliament that granted him an annulment. If you want to know more than he told to obtain it, then you will have to do your asking of him."

———

"Lytham?"

We were closeted within the curtains of the bed in my chamber. Marget lay beside me. I lifted myself onto my side and planted a kiss on her shoulder. "My sweet?"

"Did you love her?"

Her: Elinor. Had I loved her? I returned my head to the pillow and stared up toward the top of the bed. It was a familiar position. I had lain exactly so many nights during that marriage, though I had been absent a companion on most of them.

"Lytham?"

"You speak of Elinor?"

"Aye."

"Nay."

"They say you did. They say it was a love match."

They said. How would *they* know? "Then it was a love come from hell."

"But if you did not love her, why did you marry her?"

Oh, sweet Marget. "Who better than someone close to the Queen to advise me? Who better to take to the Queen my petitions than an old intimate?"

"Did she?"

"She tried."

"She failed?"

"She did not fail. The Queen was generous. She leased us Brustleigh Hall. But she never gave any other sign of preferment."

"What happened to her? How could . . . I mean to say, if the Queen approved the marriage . . ."

"How can a marriage be annulled that the Queen herself approved? The answer is, how can there be a marriage between two consenting people when one of the couple cannot be said to be in her right mind?"

"But was it . . . it was not . . . from the first?"

"It must have been."

"You did not see it?"

"Perhaps I did not know where to look."

"They say she loved you."

"They can say whatever they want."

"And are you . . . glad . . . you married me?"

"Exceedingly so."

"I love you."

"Hush, you now, my love." I took her into my arms and willed the specter of the past to die.

34

*L*ytham's explanation of his marriage to Elinor ought to have lightened my spirits. It ought to have bolstered the love that grew between us. But my strength began to desert me. I would return to my chambers after a day of doing nothing but standing and talking and be too tired to stand still more while I was being undressed.

I felt truly terrible, as if by God's curse I had caught my death but managed, in spite of it, to live. Joan applied my paint as was her habit, but I told her to apply it in increasing layers. For though I felt awful, I did not want to proclaim such to the court. I hoped that perhaps some extra sleep, some extra paint would carry me through that season of sickness, but what I assumed was temporary soon became permanent. My strategy of employing extra paint continued through the next month and the next and on into summer. It seemed that instead of masking my illness, each layer of ceruse added more weight to the burden of my malaise. Each dreary day turned into the next with no end in sight, and then the plague crept once more into the city.

"Marget? Marget!" Where was my wife? Of late she had not been herself. But I had not known her to have grown deaf.

I ran along the upper passage of the house and thrust open the door to Marget's chambers. I did it with such vigor that it struck the wall and then swung back at me toward its frame.

"My lord?" She had put a hand to the seat of her chair as if to push herself up, but then stopped in the process.

"There is plague."

"Plague? Where?"

"Along the docks. They are deserted as if never a man worked there. In a short time, it will overtake the city."

She blinked at the news. Then finally her eyes sought mine.

I strode to her chair, squatted beside it, a hand on her arm. "You must leave. Now."

"Of course we must go." She did not move.

"Nay, my sweet. I must stay. *You* must go."

"You must stay." She said it aloud, but it sounded as if she spoke the words to herself. She turned her head toward me. "*Why* must you stay?"

"I expect any day to have a report from the Continent. News of the wars and of my interests in the Low Countries."

"But . . . if you stay . . ."

I waited with some impatience for her to finish the sentence. Why could she not command her senses? There was news to be reacted to. There were things to be done. There were dangers to confront, decisions to be made. And yet she only sat and stared. "Marget? Are you well?"

She seemed to consider my question and then she nodded.

I grasped her hands.

She gasped as if in pain.

"You must go before you are trapped. As soon as the plague spreads from the docks, there will be no travel allowed from the city. I want you safe. At Holleystone."

She nodded but made no move to leave her chair.

"Joan!"

The girl rushed to my side. Curtsied. "My lord."

"Is she ill?" Had she already caught . . . ? Nay. I would not even think on it.

Joan shrugged. "There is no fever. No pain . . . least, no more than normal. She is just slow to move. For some time, she has had no . . . vigor."

I peered more closely at her face. "She looks well." And she did.

" 'Tis the paint, my lord. It casts the illusion of health. Without it . . ." She shrugged once more.

I lifted Marget from the chair and carried her to her bed. And then I gestured for Marget's companion. "Joan, you will have to see to the packing. You will leave, all of you, as soon as you are able."

———————

My maids busied themselves in the packing while I lay on my bed and watched them. The plague. In London. We had to get out. I could not get myself to move, and so I burst into tears. No one noticed, and I scarce had the strength to lift my own hand to my cheeks to wipe them away.

I watched as my gowns were flung into trunks. As my books were tossed into coffers. I saw my jewelry casket dropped to the floor and all my jewels spilled out onto the ground. I noticed a pearl roll toward my bed, but I could not cry out loudly enough for anyone to pay attention.

Later, when Lytham pulled me to my feet and dragged me out of my chambers, I had no power to protest. Frustrated with my sluggish gait, he bent down and swept me into his arms, carrying me out of the house, down to the stables, and placing me on top of my horse.

And then, finally, the words I had searched for arrived at my lips. "Do not make me leave you."

"I cannot come."

"Then let me stay."

"I cannot do it." He handed the reins of my horse to one of his men. And then he slapped my horse on her hindquarters, setting her to trotting. I grasped the horse's mane in order to remain mounted. Turning, I caught Lytham's eyes before he returned to the house.

"I will come when I am able."

When he was able. But who could know, with the plague, if ever he would be.

Leaving Lytham House, we took to the road along with half the population of London. Would that we could have left by the Thames, but those watermen who had not died already would soon be quarantined. No one with a wish to live would step closer to the docks than was needed.

Church bells clanged. Chaos spun through the streets. Clothing and possessions were being thrown from many a window into carts waiting below. Pigs and dogs ran through the crowd, around people's ankles and between horses' hooves. And with such a press of persons, there was no way to avoid the gutters. The month's filth was churned up with every step, its slime carried into the very center of the crowd and distributed throughout the street. I had never been more thankful to sit atop a horse, away from the refuse, away from the people who coughed and spat and wiped their noses on their sleeves.

Everyone was suspect. Every person assumed to be a carrier of the plague. And yet, so great was the tide of people flowing toward the gates that none could help being thrown up against his neighbor in the flight. As one, we pressed together toward the safety awaiting us outside the walls.

But among those of us intent on gaining the city gates, there were a few who wandered with red faces, cheeks glazed with sweat, arms lifted away from their sides—a certain sign of buboes growing beneath. The crowd tried to shift first one way and then another, to create a berth for the sick to pass. We succeeded only in stopping our progress forward.

One of Lytham's men tried to make a path. "Clear the way for her ladyship! Make a path for the countess!"

None moved, save to turn their heads and give us ugly looks.

From my vantage in the saddle, I could see the gate. Could see clearly the heads of traitors adorning the wall above it. And I did not know whether my head too would soon be eaten to the skull by the worms of death.

God have mercy.

In my state of stupor and anxiety one phrase fixed itself in my mind. A childhood prayer, half remembered. The only part I could recall was, *Pray for us sinners, now and at the hour of our death.*

Now and at the hour of our death.

The hour of our death.

Death.

Was the prayer Catholic or Protestant? Would it help me or bring down upon my head the fires of hell? I did not know, but it seemed to be the only thing that I could do. I was trapped between the plague and the gate.

Then the crowd surged forward.

My horse was set to dancing by the sudden frenetic movement around her. She rose up on her hind feet, snapping the reins from my fingers, and started toward the gate at a run. My hands were useless. I could only wrap my arms around the beast's neck and try to hold on. I added my voice to the cries of Lytham's men. "Aside! Stand aside! Get you back!"

At first, the crowd closed in around us, probably loath to see us once more try to escape the city ahead of them. Then one man stopped his progress and cast a glance over his shoulder, noting my horse nearly upon him.

At his cries, the man beside him pulled him out of the way and the men before him cleared a path with frantic, waving arms.

I had almost gained the gate when a pig trotted into our path, followed by a child. I could not say whether it was a he or a she, for the slight figure was clothed only in a soiled jersey, tied up with a rope around its waist. It did not see me coming.

And the pig had decided to stop and root around in the filth.

"Get back! Clear the way!" I pulled on the horse's neck and tried to swing her course, but she only saw one way out.

She put her head down and picked up her pace.

I only had time enough to see the waif turn, see its eyes grow wide in surprise, its mouth circle in terror before the horse trampled it beneath her hooves. And then we clattered beneath the gate and were free from the crowds.

Behind me, there was the sound of the thunder of hooves. And then, after, a thin wail of grief.

As I worked to loose myself from the saddle, my maids surrounded me.

And then one of Lytham's men broke through their ranks. He rode toward me with a hand held up, staying me from leaping to the ground. "Nay, my lady. You must not stop."

"But the child."

"You cannot help it now."

"But I—"

"It was not your fault. The child should have moved." He urged his horse forward, and when my own horse tossed her head, he grabbed the reins and pulled us into a trot. My maids took up their places behind me. We did not stop until we had passed Knight's Bridge some several miles farther away. As I held my seat, I repeated his words. Over and over and over until they became a sort of litany.

"It was not your fault. The child should have moved."

We gained Holleystone on the fifth day. Our journey over, the wait began to determine if all had left the plague behind them in London. If we had brought the sickness with us, then there would be no escape. Once it broke out, it would be too late to take precautions. Too late to closet ourselves from one another.

As much as possible, I ordered the servants living at Holley-stone to keep among themselves. As much as possible, those who came with me from London were expected to keep company with themselves. And with me.

But still, a muffled cough sent a vibration of panic through the air. A reddened cheek meant instant isolation for its owner.

Constantly we watched ourselves. And just as closely we watched our companions. We noted every weakness in our bodies with suspicion. Did a hand tremble because of illness or because of overwork? Was a sudden shudder caused by the presence of a draft or by the onslaught of sickness? Was there sweat upon a brow because of exertion or fever? Was a pain felt beneath the arm only the ordinary stiffness upon waking or was it a bubo in formation? Did a black stain upon the skin signal a simple bruise or the spread of the blackness of death?

We waited and watched and grew weary from constant vigilance. We were tempted toward madness with our unending thoughts of illness, our supposition of the plague's approach, and our anticipation of a slow and excruciating death.

Ten days passed, and with several days more, two weeks. And then, finally, we declared ourselves saved. We celebrated by collapsing onto our beds from fatigue and partaking in sweet sleep.

At least that is what my maids did. Whenever I closed my own eyes, I saw before me the face of that child, forever frozen in my memory, just as it had looked before my horse trampled it into the ground.

May God have mercy on my soul.

35

*S*oon as we had begun to breathe again, I found there was one more reason to be thankful I had survived. I felt a quickening within me and knew there would be a babe early in the coming year.

And so began another wait. A different kind of waiting, a restless sort of waiting. I rose each morning in hope of having some word, some message from Lytham. And I went to bed each night in disappointment. But at least I had regained my senses. As ever at Holleystone, slowly, my strength was being renewed.

One morning as I stood at my window looking off into the horizon, hoping to conjure some word from Lytham, the line between land and sky blurred, and the road seemed to shimmer darkly.

"Joan? What do you think of this?"

"Of what?"

"The road. There is something upon the road." I stood aside and gave up my view.

She looked for only a moment, then returned to her task. " 'Tis the people."

"Which people?"

"Them that come from London."

"From London?"

She looked at me as if I had taken leave of my senses. "Aye."

I declined my bread and wine and had Joan dress me plain, in a robe. Then I gathered Argos into my arms, summoned the steward, and asked him to take me to the gatekeeper.

He bowed at my approach. "My lady?"

"Those people out there, walking the road. They come from London."

"Aye, my lady. Any who can escape the city does."

"Hail one. I wish to speak to one of them."

"'Tisn't safe, my lady."

"I need news."

"His lordship would see me hung if any came sick onto the estate."

"I do not want you to open the gate and let one in, I just want you to call one of them over."

"If they come from London, they carry plague, my lady."

"I need news."

The keeper sighed and then bowed. "As you wish. Only hide yourself behind the gate there." He pointed to the tall brick and dressed stone pillars that supported the iron gate.

I was loath to move, not willing to trust him at his word. But he stood firm, unwilling to do my bidding, until I withdrew.

I relented and he called out, "You, fellow! Come you here!"

I could not see the one to whom the keeper called, but I could hear their conversation.

"Aye? Have you any bread?"

The keeper stepped back so I could see him. I nodded a violent assent.

"Bread for news."

"Bread for news, then. What news would you have?"

"How goes London?"

"London is well. It's her people what keep dying."

"'Tis bad?"

"Worse than last year. Worser than '63, maybe. Bodies thrown to the streets. The Searchers of the Dead afeared to go near them, and the Bearers of the Dead afeared to collect them."

"And the great houses?"

"Stopped up tighter than Her Majesty's purse. Won't give no bread nor ale. There's no one goes into those places and no one what comes out."

"No big funerals?"

"No funerals at all. It's them deep pits and quicklime for one and all. Ain't no nobility in death. Not when it's the plague that gets ye."

"My thanks, then."

"And the bread?"

"You'll have it."

The steward crossed into and then out of my vision as he hurried toward the kitchens.

There was the silence of birds and wind, and then the man summoned to the gate cleared his throat. I heard his spittle splat on the ground. "You would news of someone by name, my lady?"

I did not hesitate in responding. "Lord Lytham."

"He's in one of them great houses, then?"

"Aye. On Poultry. Near the Stocks Market."

His reply was stayed by a hacking cough. "If he hasn't come out and no one's got in, then I suppose he's safe enough."

"Thank you."

"Your ladyship. I don't suppose you'd have some ale to wet a poor man's throat."

"I cannot let you in."

"Nay, my lady."

"But I can ask the steward to bring you a drink."

"Thank you, your ladyship."

I stepped out from behind the pillar to take my leave and to thank the fellow for his news, but I was astonished by the sight that lay before me. I had knowledge of but one man. But in between the steward's calling him to the gate and my conversing with him, the one man had been joined by a dozen other persons. They were standing silent like a cordon behind him. Their gazes were hollow, their faces marked by their journey. Their clothes, such as they had, flapped insubstantial around them in the breeze. They had the presence of statues, but I had never seen stone dressed so rude.

"I cannot—I am not—I must not—" I turned on my heel and fled up toward the house.

After the encounter at the gate, I did not spend any more time looking to the road. I busied myself with the people of the village and the affairs of Holleystone. And I kept a close eye on the accounts.

One forenoon, a knock sounded at the door and the steward entered. "My Lady Lytham, I need consultation on the accounts."

The accounts? I had been to the kitchens just that morning. Though our stores had decreased from lack of trade, we had laid up food in abundance. And there was nothing owed to the accounts that existed. "What is your meaning?"

"My lady, there is money owed the workers."

"Which workers?"

"Those who labor on Brustleigh Hall, my lady."

"How much?"

"All of it, my lady." He lowered his eyes.

"All of what? And which workers?"

"All of the wages, my lady, for all of the workers."

"All of the wages since when?"

"Since the year's start, my lady."

My eyes widened. "But that is—"

"Since Lady Day, my lady."

Lady Day? But that was in March. "Surely . . . my lord must

have . . . are the monies stayed in London? Because surely they will understand. Not one can get out."

"Nay, my lady."

"Nay what? Speak plain!"

"Nay, my lady. There are no monies in London and there are no monies here."

"Then how do I pay them?"

"I rest upon your advice, madam."

Why had Lytham not let Nicholas come with me? That gentleman would have known what to do. "He made no provisions?"

"None, my lady."

Then how was I to pay them? "But if . . . on account of the plague . . . I ask them to—"

"They say they will stop, my lady."

"Stop?"

The steward gave a quick nod. "If they are not to be paid, my lady, they say they will not work."

"I cannot imagine . . . my lord must have the monies in London. Tell them they will have to wait."

"Excuse me for saying, my lady, but 'tis what my lord said in June."

He had no monies in June?

The steward, my maids, Joan, even Argos were looking to me for some decision and I could make none, for I could not believe the information I had been given. There had to be monies. Somewhere, there had to be a means of payment.

"Bring the ledgers to my chambers after supper, and I will tell you the solution."

As the steward bowed and left, I cursed both Lytham and Nicholas for leaving me in such an embarrassing situation.

Oh, Lytham, come home.

36

My examination of the accounts cost me a night's sleep and more than a few tapers, but at the end of my work, I could find no answer different than the one I had been given. There were no monies. And there had been none since shortly after my marriage, when most of my dowry had gone to buy Holleystone.

I did not understand how an estate—how three of them, in fact—could operate without funds. There had to be something of which I was unaware. Some account, some source that had not yet run dry.

I had nothing to tell the workers, because I had nothing with which to pay them. I decided the easiest course would be to wait until Lytham's return and leave him to untangle the mess.

Please, Lytham, please come home.

Though no news reached us from London, Lady de Winter had been sent into the country as well. And when she came to visit me, she brought word of the world beyond Holleystone's walls. And beyond England's borders. It did my nerves good to stroll through the gardens with her.

But I could not keep my thoughts long focused on politics. They drifted too often to Lytham's accounts and his inability to pay the workers. My strategy of postponement worked through August and into September, until one day the steward returned to my chambers.

"My lady, the overseer requests to see you."

"The overseer?"

"Of the work on Brustleigh, my lady."

"He is come here?"

"Aye, my lady. Do I show him in?"

"Nay!"

The steward froze mid-bow.

My maids paused in their singing at the sharpness in my tone.

"Nay. Nay, I will go down to the Great Hall to see him."

The steward accompanied me down the stairs and into the hall. The overseer was a large, dark man, who was twisting his cap within his hands. He dropped it when he saw me, bent to pick it up, but then paused mid-reach, realizing perhaps that he should instead have bowed, which, finally, he did. "My lady."

"Overseer." I did not encourage any remarks, for I knew I could not propose any solution. If he wanted anything from me, he would have to ask for it.

"My lady, I have come about the work on Brustleigh Hall."

"Aye."

He wrung his cap so hard he pulled a feather from it. It floated to the ground before his feet. " 'Tis work, my lady, for which we have not been paid."

"Aye."

"I was hoping, your ladyship, I was coming to ask . . . to see if perhaps we might now be given what we're owed."

Oh, how I wished I could say aye. "You must know that my lord the Earl of Lytham is kept in London."

"I had just heard, my lady."

"And his monies are stayed there with him." If it sounded like that was the final pronouncement, it is because I hoped it would be. I did not think I could bring myself to deny a request for payment for work that had already, long before, been completed. Work which should have, according to the accounts, never been contracted. Work for which I could see no hope of ever paying.

"Your ladyship?"

"When my lord returns, then you may approach him with your request." I could not credit the words to my own mouth. That I should speak such a lie! That I should give such hope when I knew it could not be offered! I could not bring myself to look upon his face, and so I turned to leave.

"Begging your pardon, your ladyship, but what if . . . I mean, the plague takes the rich as well as the poor."

I did not try to offer a response. But if the plague looked for Lytham among the rich, it would never find him.

Perhaps he would live after all.

One forenoon at the end of October, Lytham and Nicholas rode right out of my prayers and into the courtyard at Holleystone. I tried to stand, wanted to make my way down the stairs to greet them, but my legs would not support me.

Lytham found me, seated still in my chair, with my face crumpled in relief and my cheeks marked with tears.

He came and knelt before me.

I pushed Argos from my lap, drew Lytham's head toward my bosom, and buried my face in his hairs.

"You cry, my sweet."

"I had no news."

"You did not think the plague would take me?"

"I knew not what to think."

"I think a weary traveler deserves some sweet refreshment for having found his way home."

I thought so too. I grasped his head between my shaking hands and brought it toward mine with a kiss.

———

It was only when my hands touched her belly that I left off my pursuits. My hairs stood on end. My stomach roiled in protest at what my fingers had felt. I rolled away from her. Sat up. "What . . . ?"

She smiled up at me, as if she were proud to share her news. "There is to be a babe."

There is to be a babe. I could hear Elinor's voice in my mind. Could see her lying in my bed in exactly the same manner. Smiling in exactly the same way. I threw the covers from Marget and stared at the mound of her belly. Blinked. Tried to remind myself that she was not Elinor.

It cannot be mine. Did the words only echo within my own head or had I spoken aloud? For I'd said those words before.

God, please tell me I have no need to say them once more. I beg you! Not to my sweet Marget. Had she too succumbed to the depravity of court?

I closed my eyes once more. Opened them.

Marget's face had crumpled . . . crumpled into Elinor's. Was it her voice or Elinor's that cried out through the tears.

"It *is* yours."

Was I going mad? I slid to the floor. Stepped away from the bed. "I have been in London these three months. And at court before that."

Marget pulled the sheet up over herself, seemed to shrink beneath it. When she spoke, her voice was dull. "The babe is to be born in February."

"February? But then that is . . ."

" 'Tis no one's but yours."

How could Marget's voice have become Elinor's? How could the yearning, the desperation be the same?

And please, God, tell me how I could know the truth!

"How do I know there has not been another in my bed?"

Where Elinor had recoiled in shame, Marget's eyes sparked fire. Her voice grew fierce. "Because I have never had another. How could you even think that I would betray my marriage vows? I pledged myself to you in front of God!"

"But . . ."

" 'Tis one thing to cheat you, but another thing entirely to stand faithless before the Almighty. Please! You must trust me."

Would God that I could. What was I to do? What was I to think? I plucked my clothes from a chair and pulled them on before leaving the room.

———

After he left my bed that night, Joan came to comfort me. "Hush now. Do not cry. It can do the babe no good."

"He accuses me—" I could not bring myself to say it. "He accuses me . . ."

"He accuses you of something you cannot have done."

I had not done it, but I had been offered the opportunity. Was this my punishment? And had I not flirted with the men at court? Why should he believe me? What evidence did he truly have that I had not done what he had said? Though God had saved my virtue, He had done it in spite of myself. "I did not . . ."

"Hush you now."

"I cannot . . ."

"Nicholas will talk some sense into his thick head."

"Nicholas was not here." If I could not be trusted, then neither could any who had been at Holleystone with me.

———

Elinor had cuckolded me once. I would not be made a fool of again.

"Nicholas! I have want of Nicholas!" At my demand, one of my chamberers ran from the room in search of the man. If I could not sleep, then I would have company in my misery. It took Nicholas several minutes to reach my rooms, and when he finally did, sleep still clung to his eyes.

"Marget is with child."

"Felicitations, my lord." He lifted a hand to stifle a yawn.

"I sent her away from me in . . . one state . . . and have returned to find her in another entirely."

Nicholas frowned. "Babes take no little time before they begin to show themselves, my lord. Surely you cannot accuse my lady of—"

"The very same thing which Elinor did? Did I not tell you she was a devil in women's weeds?"

"My lord, surely you cannot mean the words you say."

"I do not know what I mean!" My voice cracked with emotion.

"When is the babe to be born, my lord?"

"In February. Least that is what she tells me."

"Then it cannot be any man's, my lord, but yours."

"But how can I truly know it? How can I trust her?"

"How can we know anything? How can we trust anything? One first must know of whom one speaks, my lord, and then one may do the judging. Surely you know the countess is incapable of—"

"I need you to ask the servants, to find out if . . . whether . . ."

"My lord, please do not ask me to do this."

"I must know."

"You will lose more in the asking than you will gain, my lord. And if, as you must already know, there was no assignation, then you will have ruined your marriage forever. For nothing."

"I fear it is already ruined."

When Nicholas found he could not dissuade me from my course, he left, fairly slamming the door shut on his way. I remained within my chambers for two days. I longed for sleep, for the obliteration of reality that only dreams could provide.

I looked for it in my cups. I looked for it in my books and in song, but still it eluded me. Finally, I fell to my knees on the high-backed stool I used for prayers and I wept in my misery to God.

God, how can I know? How can I be certain that Marget is telling the truth?

But how *could* she be telling the truth? No one at court told the truth. Truth was weakness. Truth could be turned into a weapon. Truth could always be wrested from the hand of its possessor and then turned and plunged into his heart.

But had I ever known Marget to tell a lie?

If she had told me the truth, then surely I was a despicable creature. I had questioned her constancy, I had impugned her honor, and I had abandoned her at a moment that should have been heralded with great joy.

Surely, then, I was the greatest of wretches.

But surely, given the court in which we lived, I could be forgiven my transgression, God, could I not?

But why would there come no peace?

Perhaps . . . perhaps because I had not asked for it? Perhaps because I had not . . . prayed for it? There had to be something, some prayer, some invocation that would work.

I grabbed the *Book of Common Prayer* from the shelf of the stool and flipped through its pages until I came to one.

"From all blindness of heart, from pride, vainglory, and hypocrisies, from envy, hatred, and malice, and all uncharitableness. Good Lord, deliver us."

Good Lord, deliver me.

"From fornication, and all other deadly sin, and from all the deceits of the world, the flesh, and the devil. Good Lord, deliver us."

Good Lord, deliver me.

With my head in my hands I thought about the words I had just read. And then I began to laugh. For what had I just done than prayed that I might be delivered from court? For where else in all the kingdom could be found pride, vainglory, and hypocrisies in abundance; envy, hatred, malice, and all uncharitableness; fornication, deadly sin, the deceits of the world, the flesh, and the devil than in court, before the Queen's own throne.

Well, if God could deliver me, then let Him do it!

But as for me, I could see no other path than that which I had chosen. No other way to fortune than that of the courtier. If there was any position for me to maintain, any influence that could be gained, it was at court that I would accomplish it. Two things were certain: I could never give up my title, and I could never leave the court.

But now, at this moment, there were many choices to be made. The next step along my chosen path was deciding how, exactly, I was going to apologize to Marget.

———

I stayed in my chambers for two days. On the third day, as I was reading to my maids, after a sharp rap on the door, Lytham appeared. He looked at me and then pointedly looked at my maids. He wanted me to dismiss them.

I would do no such thing.

He bowed and then came toward me and knelt by my side. "Tonight I have commanded radishes for supper."

If he had hoped to make me smile, he had failed.

"Bowls of them."

I turned a page of my book.

"And I shall eat them all."

I continued my reading in silence. Until he placed a flower upon the page.

It was a pink late-blooming rose nestled in ivy.

Love and fidelity.

"Nicholas verified that . . . you were . . . are . . . constant."

I lifted my eyes from the flower and looked into his. "Because my own word cannot be trusted?"

"Because I am a fool." There were all sorts of misery at work in his eyes. All manner of pain. All kinds of anguish.

I fingered a petal. "Aye. You are." But if he was a fool, then so was I, for I loved him. God had cursed me with love for him! I suffered from a constant heart that nothing could shake, and I could do nothing else but love him.

37

The next week, after supper one night, after all in the household had taken themselves to bed, I threw on my night-robe and knocked upon the door to Lytham's chambers.

He bid me enter and I shut the door behind me.

"My lord, I must speak to you."

"Pray, speak then." His eyes reflected back a taper's light, looking at once both daunting and inviting.

"It is about the accounts."

"Aye."

"The workers at Brustleigh have asked, several times, to be paid."

He dismissed my concerns by returning his attentions to the ledgers in front of him. "The workers are always asking to be paid."

"Have you no . . . sum . . . set aside, perhaps?"

"Set aside?"

"Is there no money anywhere?"

He glanced up from his ledger. "Of course there is money; I have the rents."

"The rents!" That was it. I had forgotten about the rents. But . . . I had looked at all the accounts.

"When they come in, I put a bit into foreign ventures. And another bit into whatever expedition is going to the Americas or the Indies."

"To foreign ventures and the Americas? But . . . it could take months for there to be any return. If there is ever to be any return . . ."

"You are worried about the accounts?" He placed his arm across the ledger and leaned upon it, fixing his glowing eyes upon me.

"Aye! How can we ask people to do work for us for which we cannot pay?"

"When I have the money, then I will pay them."

"But people who work need to be paid when we make use of their labors. We cannot spend at the rate we have been spending. We must begin to set aside some of the . . . something . . . some monies . . . in order to pay off our debts."

———

Debts. She said the word as if they were some foul thing newly discovered. As if they threatened our very existence. As if, in my folly, I had no knowledge of them. No knowledge of them? They haunted me! I lived with them as my closest friends. And everything I did, every action I took at court, every venture I took part in was calculated to relieve them. How could she not know that? Did she think me a fool? But all would be remedied once Her Majesty visited Brustleigh. They would all disappear in an instant.

"Set aside some monies? You mean, save them?" She had to be mocking me. I rose to my feet and crossed the room in quick paces, letting my eyes dart toward all the corners. "Where? Where shall I hide them? Underneath . . . underneath the bed?"

She gave me no answer.

"And then what would you have me tell all those people? All

those poor. And not even those who are poor now, but the almost poor. How do I explain to them that I have pulled my wealth from circulation so that the monies I pay to the merchant tailor cannot be paid to the sempstress which cannot be paid to the baker and the fishmonger and the water carriers and the tanners and the—" I halted in my tracks and stood there, panting from my efforts. "Aye. We should look to our own interests and not to the interests of others."

"I beg your pardon, my lord, I—"

"What would you have me do? What would you have me do other than what I have done?"

"I do not . . . I have no . . . I do not know, my lord."

"*La noblesse nous oblige.*" She had to understand that. Nobility obligated me. Obligated us.

"But if we fail, if we are ruined, how can we fulfill the obligation?"

"They cannot afford for us to fail, and so they will make certain that we do not." That truth was the only thing that kept me standing beneath debt's heavy burden. That, and the hope of Her Majesty's visit.

After a week's stay at Holleystone, Lytham took me to court with him by way of Brustleigh. I was shamed to have to show my face to the overseer, but Lytham appeared to harbor no such qualms. Once there, his attentions were entirely devoted to the renovations. He hoped to entice Her Majesty into Berkshire while on Progress. And then to host her visit at Brustleigh Hall.

But first the estate needed to be grand enough to engage the imagination of a Queen. Brustleigh, little though I liked it, had become even less pleasant. Everywhere I looked, I was confronted with Her Majesty. She seemed to have taken over the estate. If not with her symbols, then with the expectation that her person would soon be present. It was not enough that I be harassed by her at court; she had invaded my private life as well. Her visit was now the only thing of which Lytham spoke.

"I had thought to turn the workers to your chambers," my lord stated.

"My chambers!" If there was anything good about Brustleigh, it was knowing that the renovations had to include my own rooms. And in this case, I was more than willing to have my rooms redone to blot the image of another woman, Lytham's first wife, from them.

"They have the best view of the estate, out over the gardens."

"I thought perhaps a theme of the three graces? Painted panels in pinks and yellows and greens on a surface of gold, separated by wainscoting? And plasters on the ceiling repeating the images between the ribs." He did not respond, so I continued on. "The wardrobe as the domain of Joy with an emphasis on pink, the bed-chamber to be Radiance, perhaps with more gilt than paint, and the outer chamber to be the Flowering, with green and yellow all over. What do you think?"

"Of what, my sweet?"

"Of my chambers. On the theme of the three graces."

"For Her Majesty's Grace?"

"Nay. For my use. Something filled with light. And pretty." To make my stays at the estate more tolerable.

"But when Her Majesty comes, there will she stay." His eyes took a tour of the gardens and then he paused, turned round, and stood staring at the house. "Nay . . . not the three graces. On the theme of Flora, perhaps. We could push out that window, there." He turned to look at the gardens again before looking back at the house. "Come. Let us go up there to look down from that spot."

We returned to the house and went to my chambers. He walked toward the window in question and, opening it up, leaned out to gaze below. He spent some time in looking about. "There is no view."

"None but the garden. And the hills. And the trees and the sky."
The world as the Creator himself intended.

"We can make a view. If we push out this window, we can have
a garden made that stretches away to the hill. Then place a viewing
platform—or better, a banqueting house—on top! And perhaps not
a theme on Flora. Maybe . . . pelicans!"

"And have the birds piercing their breasts all over my walls!"

"To feed her young, to nourish her kingdom."

"Not on my walls. I want no blood dripping forth into buckets."

"Perhaps Hebe! The goddess of youthful beauty."

"So the Queen can spend eternity serving nectar to the gods?
You know she will serve no man."

"Then . . . Minerva."

"Of course. A wise old goddess with a clunky helmet on her
head."

"Then we play upon our loyalty to her person. We will decorate
with the royal coat of arms and Tudor designs of green and white.
She cannot find fault with that."

But I could. "I wanted the room to be done . . . fanciful. And
pretty."

Lytham drew me close and kissed me. "And you will have anything you fancy, pretty girl, when we can gain access to Her Majesty's ear."

But I did not want access to Her Majesty's ear. I wanted Lytham's
attentions. I had grown jealous of the time and effort he devoted to
a woman who was . . . not me.

The men went quickly to work on my chambers. As my maids
and I looked on, they began to dismantle the wall, removing the
window and wreaking havoc on the rooms. And while they worked
on the interior, an army of men worked below them. Slowly, over
the following days, they consumed the ground which spread from
the window up to the hill. And then they began to install a garden.

I looked on the work with interest until I realized they intended a knot garden. And then I sought Lytham.

I found him in his bedchamber, having his beard trimmed and starched by a barber.

"You do realize that they are laying a knot garden below my window?"

He turned his eyes in my direction though he dared not turn his head.

"You cannot have asked them to do it?"

He put up a hand to stay the barber's razor blade. "I *did* ask them to do it."

"But knot gardens are so . . . formal. Why can I not have raised beds with twig fences?"

"Because, my sweet, I cannot have the royal coat of arms worked into a bed. But it can be worked into a knot garden. We spill the theme of your chambers out your window and up the hill. It will be glorious. Think on it."

I did. And I did not like it. I did not want to gaze each morn on the symbols of someone else's glory. Did not want Lytham's interests so fixated on the Queen. But I should not have worried. I should have known that my own glories could never be far from his thoughts.

Once back in London, he leaned close to me one forenoon while we were watching a play, *Love's Labour's Lost*. "Did you see Lady de Winter? Wearing velvet?"

"I did."

"I had wanted you to be the first in velvet this season."

"It cannot matter."

"It does to me. I will send for the tailor and have him alter the design."

"And what would you have him do?"

He drew a finger from my ruff down to the neck of my partlet and tugged upon it. "I would have him make the neck lower."

I cast a glance to the crowds but found them to be watching the play. I smiled. "By how much?"

"Enough that every man may guess what you have in abundance, but not so far that any man might see it."

"You would taunt your enemies?"

"Nay. I wish to make friends."

I unhooked his finger. "You cannot be *my* friend if your new design gives me catarrh. Think on the babe."

"Your health is not worth my admiration?"

"You must hide your admiration to increase its value. You overplay your hand, sir. You are too generous with your praise."

But when the gown and partlet came back from the tailor, like the renovations at Brustleigh, my gown had been shaped and reconstructed to better showcase my assets. They were made from a velvet that turned from the color of a pale sky to indigo with every movement. Lytham swore that in the middle of the colors' change, the hue matched my eyes exactly.

The first day I wore it, I had the chambermaid fasten to it my silver lace sleeves.

Lytham smiled as he approached me that morning. "You look ravishing."

"Do you not think on it! One movement and all will explode."

"I can be careful."

"Nay, you cannot." I chanced a deeper breath and felt the partlet slide.

"You tease me."

"Then you are caught in your own trap and I can feel no sorrow."

Once at court, Lady de Winter saw me and, with a queer smile twisting her lips, glided to my side. "I see you have laid all of your cards upon the table, girl."

My eyes dove toward my chest, but my ruff blocked it from view. "I am playing partners, so I can only do as I am advised."

"Then your advisor has no need to bluff."

"I shall die if I do not breathe, and if I take the breath I need, the force will tumble me from this gown."

"That is what a fan is for." She fluttered her own in front of her chest and made a show of taking a breath, letting her eyes roll into her head. "Breathe deep, girl." She cast me a smile as several women joined us.

Their conversation was also one of fashion. Particularly the pamphlets that had been distributed decrying the use of paint.

"They say it loosens the teeth."

"They say it grays the skin."

"And corrupts the bones."

Lady de Winter used her fan to sweep away their words. "And they also say our Queen is a virgin."

"Then she has come by it late."

"After Dudley perhaps?"

"Or has it been since Essex?"

The women around me laughed, hiding their rotted teeth behind the fabulous colors of their ostrich feather fans. But the laughter could not drive away their words.

The paint loosened the teeth?

It grayed the skin?

Surely if it did so, the Queen would not use it. I looked toward Her Majesty's throne. From my vantage point, she looked as if she had never aged.

The pamphlets could not be true . . . could they? Of course not. Why would one paint one's self to look more youthful if the paint only stole one's youth?

But what if it were true?

Had my skin not taken on a certain pallor of late? Had my thumb not become misshapen? And had I not come by more energy when

I had been confined to Holleystone, when I had not bothered to have myself painted each morning?

What if it *were* true?

Even if it were, I could not stop painting. Everything I had gained, all the friendships I had made, all the good favor I had received . . . all of Lytham's attention . . . had come after I had begun to paint. After I had molded myself into the image of a courtier. I could not stop.

Would not stop.

To stop painting would put everything I had won in peril. I chanced one more glance at the throne. Hurry to your death, good Queen, and save us all.

38

As he had before, Lytham sent me back to Holleystone for the babe's birth. It was the first Christmas I had ever spent on my own. Without relations, without husband. At least, however, I was with child. And I intended to stay that way. Daily, I had tansy applied to my belly. Daily, my maids came up with some new scheme for my amusement. Daily, I prayed God would grant me the desire of my heart . . . and that the babe would resemble its father.

Just before Twelfth Night, I gave my maids leave to go home. Perhaps it was foolish, but I was swept away by the good cheer of the season. They made great haste in leaving me. And then it was just Joan and I, whiling away our hours.

"Joan?"

"Aye?"

"Would you not like to go home as well?" I was hoping that she would not, but I felt churlish not to give her the chance. It would be a long trip, and it would keep her away past Christmas, but I could not keep her with me if her heart mourned for home.

"To King's Lynn?"

"Aye."

"Nay."

"Do not feel as if I will not be taken care of. I would survive your absence. Though perhaps not in any great cheer."

"But I would not survive the visit. King's Lynn is no longer my home. In truth, it never was."

And so we spent the season together. But if there were only two of us, there was an estate filled—yea, even a village filled—with people to help us celebrate. And a full twelve days in which to do it.

I did not take part in the dancing nor in the revelry, but I did make certain the Earl of Lytham's table did not run out but over during those days of Yuletide. There was a small cake of marzipan given to all who called at the house, from the very least to the very greatest.

The constable had been selected the Lord of Misrule by lots, and he chose both the earl's High Steward of the Courts and the bailiff to be on his council. Together, the men planned the village festivities and managed the revelries, planning a masque and a play and a bonfire for the last day of Christmas on Twelfth Night. There would be babes aplenty in the autumn.

Of a night, Joan kept watch at the gates with me as carolers came to sing. With merry applause, we rewarded them with ale and cakes. There were children among them equipped with bowls, begging. We gave them ale and cakes as well, not chancing to invite bad luck into our estate.

The bailiff commanded felled the largest tree he could find, and I sent men to drag it into the courtyard. It took six men to carry it to the hearth. But once rolled into the fireplace, it burned for all twelve days of Christmas. The parks keeper opened the park gate so the servants could collect holly and ivy, and the house was filled with the greens.

On New Year's Day, I offered to Joan the present of a purse filled with coin, and she offered up to me a cushion she had embroidered. It was the perfect size for the small part of my back and excellent for easing the strain I had so lately begun to feel.

We were joined by a band of traveling mummers and then a pair of jugglers. Had Lytham been there, he might have asked them to produce a license, but being Yuletide and a season of good cheer, I could not see the sense in heaping trouble upon anyone. And besides, their diversions were well done, though I did warn Joan to tell the servants to be on guard and to keep our silver plate under lock. I did not mind giving food and drink for amusement, but I did not want to be made to overpay. Nor to explain to Lytham how his estate came to be stripped of all things valuable.

That night, amidst the dancing and feasting, I realized that Joan no longer waited in attendance upon me. Curious, I pushed up from my chair and walked away from the table, skirting the crowd, to see if I could spy her. At length, when I had almost given up my search, I saw her in conversation with Falconer. They stood beyond the reach of the bonfire, where there were only shadows to shelter them.

As I watched, he turned several times toward the recesses of night as if he wanted, very much, to leave. But then he would turn his head once more toward Joan. And at last, she clasped his hand and with several tugs succeeded in moving him forward, toward the feasting.

It was perhaps then fate which led Falconer to find a bean in his piece of cake and be declared King of the Bean. And seeing that happen, it was no surprise to me when my own Joan found the pea in hers and was dubbed Queen of the Pea. A dance was called for and a lute player began to play, after which the people persuaded me to lead the chain dance of a carol.

Joan came into my chamber late that night. I had been unable to sleep for pain in my haunches. She was quiet in slipping into her bed, letting only the rustle of her feet crossing the rushes betray her.

The house was soon emptied of all signs of Christmastide. After the yule log had burned itself out, the charm and warmth of the season waned. And so I put my thoughts to the new year. To the babe. To the monies I hoped would soon be ours.

I received a letter from Lytham that cheered me. Raleigh had set sail once more both on his perpetual search for gold and to restore himself to Her Majesty's favor, which had been distinctly lacking since the discovery of his marriage. Lytham made mention that he had been one of the backers of the venture. He said it could not fail. I fervently prayed that his risk would be rewarded.

I was brought to bed at the end of February. The babe took me by surprise, in my sleep, waking me with a drenching of waters and the feeling of knives stabbing at my back.

It was over quick and the babe born before sunrise. He was small and scarce made a cry. My work successful, I succumbed to sleep with him nestled in my arms. But he only tarried for three days before he closed his eyes one morn in slumber and failed to wake again. My attendants waited until my tears had stopped and I slept from heartache and exhaustion before they removed my boy from my arms.

Upon waking and finding my hands freed from their sweet burden, I slipped into sleep once more and did not emerge for several days. When I did, it was to find Lytham pacing the floor beside my bed. Seeing him, I tried to shut up my eyes before they caught his attention. I had failed once more at my most important duty. I could give him no heir.

———

I could not help thinking that the babe had somehow heard the words I had used to deny his parentage. That somehow he knew he had not been wanted. I had started from court before I had heard of the birth. But even so, I had been too late for his birth. And his death.

I sighed. Ran a hand through my hairs.

I only wanted Marget to wake.

The midwife swore she had no sickness and Joan said she slept only from her heart's pain. I had reached the foot of the bed with my pacing and had naught to do but turn around and walk once more to its head. In doing so, I caught a glimpse of Marget's eyes.

They had opened!

And now she was burrowing beneath the coverlet.

"Marget!"

She curled into herself at the sound of my voice.

I climbed up onto the bed and tried to unbury her. But the harder I tried to wrest the sheet from her grasp, the tighter she clung to it.

"Marget. My sweet . . . I am sorry. For saying . . . what I said."

"It was *you* who did not want him. Leave me!" She thrust an arm behind her to push at me.

I grabbed on to it and used it to drag her closer. "Do not ask me to go. I will not do it."

She kicked out at me. "You would do better without me. Leave me and go find another. Some other that can give you an heir."

"You do not know what you say."

She turned on me then, twisting herself up in the sheets. "I know precisely what I say! I am useless. I am worthless. I am worth less than a Southwark stew. I can give you no children, least none that will live." Her lips parted to dispense terrible laughter. But the laughter soon changed to tears, and the strength that had enabled her to push me away deserted her. She sunk back onto the sheets and turned her back to me.

But I would not let her go so easily. I clasped her around the waist and pulled her toward myself. The misery at work inside me wanted only to have her. To hold her.

She beat at me with her elbows, but still I would not let her go.

That show of fortitude turned her tears into wailing. "I want my babe."

I wanted him too. "Hush you now. I know."

"I want my babe, Lytham. I just want to hold my babe."

I clasped her tighter.

"I never even got to say good-bye."

I cupped her head to my shoulder and sheltered her within the curve of my body.

She wept there for a long while. And then when she quieted and found her voice, she used it to share with me the gift of those few days that she had been given.

"He was so . . . sweet. He had the face of an angel. And your eyes. He had your eyes. I wish you could have seen him. . . ."

And then it was my turn to weep.

39

After I was churched in March, it was judged best for me to return to court. At least I knew what would be expected upon my return. At least I knew no one would wish to share my private grief. And so I practiced as we rode to court; I practiced pretending that I had not lost another babe.

The blue violets along the roads had pushed their heads from the ground and begun to perfume the air. So with them as my example, I also took on the courtier's robe of gaiety. By the time we reached court, my sorrows had been put away and I was ready to take my place once more.

———

Marget had been pretending a certain joviality since we had returned to London. I doubt that anyone had noticed. But I had. I wanted to persuade the bloom back into her cheeks. To hear her laugh in earnest instead of under pretense.

I sent a messenger out for a handbill one day to see what would be played that forenoon. When the boy came back, there were several options. Two I knew to be not worth seeing. The other two were tragedies. I hesitated at choosing either, but then wondered whether coaxing tears from her might do even more good than coaxing laughter. I chose *King Richard the Second*, which played at The Theatre.

I found her in the Great Hall, gave over the handbill to her, and removed Argos from her hands so she could read it.

The beast tried to chew my finger and I dropped him to the floor.

"Lytham!"

"The creatures have nine lives."

"'Tis *cats* who have lives to spare."

"My mistake."

She looked at me beneath her brow as if she doubted the veracity of my implied apology.

I raised an eyebrow. "What do you think?"

As she read the handbill, her nose began to wrinkle. But when her eyes met mine, it stopped.

"What does not please you? The play or the house?"

"Neither. Do you not think Marlowe superior to Shakespeare?"

"I had not thought on it."

"Then think. *Tamburlaine* or *Titus Andronicus*?"

"You do not like The Lord Chamberlain's Men?"

"I prefer The Admiral's Men."

"The Admiral's Men?" I shuffled through the other handbills. "*Tamburlaine* is at The Rose. How fortunate for you."

She smiled. And it seemed to me a smile of some substance.

———

Lytham and I took a wherry across the river to Southwark and arrived at The Rose in time to take a lords room with cushioned seats from which we could see all. Below us, in the pit, there was a great jostling about for seats . . . and for women. But then the play began and I forgot the crowds. I thought I recognized a particular countess's frippery on one of the players. And then a baroness's sleeves on another.

It was nearly an hour into the play when I became aware of a commotion in the theatre. I pulled my gaze from the stage and saw Nicholas in heated conversation with some man. Prodding Lytham with an elbow, I made a broad gesture, attracting Nicholas's attention and motioning in our direction.

He made his way to stand beneath our seats, but not without causing a string of curses to lift into the air to mark his progress.

We could not hear him speak, but he made a show of doffing his hat and dropping to one knee in a courtly bow.

Seeing his pantomime, Lytham pushed to his feet and hurried from the box without a word, leaving me to stare at his rapidly disappearing back.

A minute later he was replaced by Nicholas.

"Her Majesty." The gentleman did not offer the information by way of apology but only by way of explanation.

Again? I was tiring of being constantly jilted for another's company, even if the other happened to be our Queen.

———

A summons from the Queen! I hurried to the palace, prodding my horse into a gallop whenever I could. Once there, I paused only to adjust my hat and drape my cloak more gracefully over a shoulder. That done, I walked in a measured pace through the palace halls. By the time I reached the Privy Chamber, I had gained control of my thoughts. And my breath.

I was bid to enter.

Her Majesty was pacing before the fire, speaking to her maids. She paused, and with loud voice put an ending to a story that made the ladies around her rock with raucous laughter. She laughed herself for a brief moment. And then she turned and saw me. "Lord Lytham!"

I bowed. "Your Grace."

She walked toward me and extended her hand. It was a hand grown bony and disfigured with age; in fact, it looked as if with a brief tug I might pull her thumb right off. But I took it as if it were the loveliest I had seen and kissed it in reverence.

"I grow weary of the city."

She wished to travel! "Perhaps a Progress this summer, Your Grace?" Work on Brustleigh was far from being done, but if I hired more men, if I purchased more supplies . . . ?

"I cannot travel this summer. But speak to me of your estate. Of Brustleigh. Perhaps you can convince these aging bones into a Progress next summer. I have heard it is an estate grand enough for a sovereign."

She had? But who had told her? And to which challenge should I respond first? "The only bones aging here, Majesty, are mine. I fear you sit a horse far better than I."

"You fear it, do you? But do you not have horses at Brustleigh?"

"There are horses aplenty at Brustleigh, Your Grace, and a park in which to hunt. But I fear you would find my estate lacking in refinements."

"There is no garden?"

"There is, Your Grace."

"Then there must be no suite of rooms."

"On the contrary, Your Majesty."

"Perhaps, then, there is no fish pond to supply your table?"

"There is, Your Grace. A small one."

"Tennis court?"

"One, Your Majesty."

"Then there must be no banqueting room."

There was no banqueting room. I felt perspiration dot my upper lip. How dearly I wanted to claim one, and yet I could not lie. She had already been informed. "There is no banqueting house, though I have plans for one, Your Majesty."

"Ah. Well . . . perhaps there might be one by next summer? If there were, I might be persuaded in your direction after all, Lord Lytham. Even in spite of your ties to that gypsy girl."

She wished to visit! She planned to visit! By next summer my debts would be paid, my fortunes assured, my destiny forged. I could not wait to tell Marget.

————

Her Majesty had let it be known that she intended to visit Brustleigh. Lytham was beside himself with joy. He intended to visit Brustleigh as well, to oversee the work, but he could not travel for heavy rains. That did not stop him from sending letters, however, one after the other, to the estate's steward.

The miserable and continual torrents soon drowned the country's wheat. The price of flour, indeed, of bread, became quite dear. And without the harvest, the people could neither pay rents nor place food into their mouths.

Lytham's plan for those at Brustleigh was to put them to work on a banqueting house. Letter followed after letter. He made plans aplenty, and kept speaking to me of them all.

"I envision an intimate setting with seats carved from stone, supported by an English lion and a Welsh dragon as befits the theme of Her Majesty's royal arms." We were standing side-by-side, gazing out of one of the windows at the interminable rains.

A banqueting house. When we had a perfectly respectable hall in which to dine and no money at all with which to build it. If only Raleigh's ships would return; if only he could find his gold and my lord could be returned some of his.

"My sweet?"

"My lord?"

"Does this not interest you?"

"Of course it does." In only the most banal of ways.

"And I had thought, perhaps a shelter with colonnades or grotesques holding up the roof."

I sighed. "Why not lions rampant?"

"Lions rampant! Brilliant. Lions holding up the roof with their paws, just so." He struck the pose, one foot lifted, one hand stretched up in front of him, the other held above his head. And then he brought both hands together in a clap. "You are so very clever! I will command it done this day."

It was not difficult to know how to please one obsessed with a single idea, moved by a sole purpose. I did not know what would happen to Lytham should Her Majesty fail to visit.

40

*B*rustleigh was all he spoke of that summer. And the syllables of that word came to echo the fall of the rain, came to pelt upon my nerves with such insistence that I thought I might go mad. Brustleigh presented itself between us even in bed.

"You do not sleep, my lord?"

"I cannot decide what diversions to offer Her Majesty. At Brustleigh."

"A masque?"

"Perhaps."

"A play?"

"But on what theme?" he pondered.

"Diana?"

"It has already been done."

"Venus?"

"'Tis been done to death."

"I do not think she would protest." Did she ever?

"But I want something . . . new."

"There *is* nothing new. Her Majesty is a Queen of thirty-six years. She has heard every flattery that one can offer. And even those which cannot."

"There must be something."

I heard myself sigh. Turning from him, I wanted only to sleep. My head had pained me that month without reprieve. But once set to the tune of Brustleigh, my thoughts began to march on their own. And they fixed upon my responsibilities. There were curtains to have made and tapestries to be commanded. I would need to order Her Majesty's initials embroidered on her bed linens. *My* bed linens. I would have done it myself, but my fingers would no longer guide a needle. My hands were useless.

September brought no harvests of the normal kind, but it did bring Raleigh's ships to harbor. And with them came such incredible tales! For a while they were the only topic spoken of at court.

"They say there are men living along the Orinoco who . . . eat each other."

"Nay!"

"Aye! And their heads grow beneath their shoulders instead of on top!"

I tried to imagine such a person, but confess I could not do it.

"But he has found El Dorado?"

"He has located the gold mines?"

In fact, he had not.

There was no use in berating Lytham. And no use in mourning lost monies. We went on with our activities and took part at court in the ways we always had. I vowed that if Lytham were able to keep thoughts of insolvency from his conscience, then so would I.

Despite the winter's cold, we went once more to Brustleigh. I could remember the gripping, grasping cold of previous winters there and came to the house with great reluctance. That year, however, the cold did not assault me. Even without a warming box, my toes stayed warm. My nose also kept its heat. When I might have ordered a fire built high, I asked instead for logs to be pulled to the side. While my ladies shivered beneath their cloaks, I cast mine off. And several weeks later, I was made to know why. Within me, I felt a quickening. I resolved not to leap before myself to the birth. And I guarded the precious secret, sharing it only with Joan. But I caught myself smiling at my maids' needlework or humming to myself when I took exercise in the gardens.

Her Majesty's officials came to visit us at the end of February. They were planning Her Majesty's Summer Progress. It seemed Lytham's dream was about to come true. The men looked among the chambers. They toured the kitchens. And the stables. And the storehouses. Lytham showed them all that might be of interest and even those things that probably were not.

I idled about the Great Hall, waiting for their return.

They stepped into the room with the air of men having finished their business. But then Lytham spoke. "Do you wish to see the park?"

"You have a park, my lord?"

"I do. It would be my pleasure to offer it to her Majesty for a diversion."

"It has been stocked recently then, my lord?"

"Four years past."

The officials frowned.

"Of course, I was planning to restock it again this spring."

"We need to know, my lord, if the plague has been here recently."

"In this parish? The last appearance was some dozen years ago."

The men bowed and turned to leave. Lytham and I escorted them into the courtyard.

The officers nodded their thanks. One of them spat into the

straw while the other surveyed the property. "That, on the mound over there, my lord. Is that a banqueting house?"

"Aye."

"You may take us there, my lord."

In turning to walk with them, Lytham made a frantic motion to me.

I interpreted it to mean I should offer them refreshment.

Returning to the kitchen in haste, I commanded food and drink be taken to the mound. And quickly, without being seen.

Cook loaded one servant with plates. Another with cups. A third with figs and dates and a fourth with sweet cakes. And then she sent them off at a run.

I climbed the stairs to my chambers and stood in the window, marking their progress. Lytham was walking slowly and with much gesturing down the right side of the gardens. On the other side, bent at the waist, ran the servants. Lytham and his men had started toward the mound first, but the servants had the advantage of speed.

As I stood there, wringing my hands, my maids joined me.

There was a hiss of indrawn breath as Lytham began to lead the men toward the fountain in the middle of the garden. And then a sigh of relief as their attention was drawn toward a statue behind them and to their right.

That distraction gave the servants time to reach the mound and distribute plate and food.

By the time Lytham and the officials had reached the banqueting house, the servants stood at the side of the table, waiting. I only hoped they would not be doing so with great huffing breaths or hacking coughs.

Two weeks later, once we had returned to London, Lytham laughed in delight when the itinerary for Her Majesty's Progress was published. It had Brustleigh Hall writ upon it for all to see.

Lady de Winter was generous in suggesting those things that

might impress Her Majesty most. Chief among them was the provision of a throne. The very idea of providing the Queen with a new throne became Lytham's newest obsession. He seized upon it like a child presented with a new amusement.

"A throne? But already she must have at least a dozen!" Even to my own ears, my voice sounded shrill.

"But she does not yet have one at Brustleigh." His tones were measured, as if he were speaking to an infant.

"Surely she will bring one of her own."

"Not if we let her household officers know that we have one."

"And will that impress her? Will that cause her to grant you a sign of preferment? Or will it be perhaps one thing more? Can you not see? This leads only to ruin. Our ruin! We have stacks of bills that have already come due. Must we add to their number still one more?"

"What can one more possibly matter?"

"If you cared for my thoughts half as much as you cared for hers, you would know that it does!"

"You know that I care for you."

"Do you? Truly? Because all that I know is that you have spent all of your time, all of your fortune, and all of your future on a woman who demands from you everything and promises nothing in return. You respond to her every wish, her every whim as if you were her lapdog. And it is I who am your wife!"

"Shall I order a throne made for you as well? I could enthrone you as queen of my heart."

He was trying to make me smile, but I would not do it. "I would rather be queen of your monies."

"Ah, but there, I fear you might become a ruthless tyrant."

"No more ruthless than she." We both knew of whom I was speaking.

"It is only because she is the Queen, my sweet—"

"Then why do I feel as if I am your mistress?" I could bear no more. I turned and left the chamber.

"I am a courtier! How can you fault me for what I have done? What else would you have me do?" His words followed me down the length of the passage.

When he did nothing that day or the next to assuage my hurt, I realized that his distraction was complete. He could not see past the great glittering crown on Her Majesty's head. In spite of my protests, he ordered a throne made to his specifications and then, once he had obtained it, we galloped to Brustleigh with it to confer with the parish officials on the visit.

As they met with Lytham in the Great Hall, and I listened to the conversation, I realized their thoughts were the same as my own. There was no excitement, no joy in discussing Her Majesty's summer visit. Only great consternation at the wealth of food, fuel, and fodder that Her Majesty asked to be provided.

―――――

I could not understand it! The men should be rejoicing at the prospect of Her Majesty's visit, but they protested at every opportunity. "But you will be reimbursed at a reasonable price, man!"

"It is not the reimbursement we mistrust, my lord. It is the quantity of stores that must be provided. How are we to come by them? And where shall they be kept?"

"If you need storehouses, I will supply them."

"We need storehouses."

"Then I will supply them. Now, what about the painting to be done and the gowns to be made?"

"What painting? Which gowns?"

"Of the buildings. For the churchwardens."

And so it went. The parish officials bristled at the inconvenience and decried lack of funds while I pulled open my purse strings and bid them take what they needed. If only they knew how very little there was.

There were presents to be thought of and ordered. A large one for Her Majesty and lesser ones for the courtiers and officials accompanying her. Each day brought new crises. Things to which I had not given a moment's thought. Things like horses.

"Nicholas!"

"My lord?"

"Why did you not ask me to think on the horses?"

"Which horses, my lord?"

"Those which will come. With all of the court."

"I—"

"We must have feed. And hay. And grooms aplenty. And we must provide fresh mounts."

"I will see to it, my lord."

Several days later, I stood with Marget in her chambers . . . rather, Her Majesty's chambers, gazing out at the park stretched before us. All had been arranged in a knot garden. The old trees and shrubs had been dug out and carted away. And then, I realized of a sudden, what that portended. "What have I done!"

"To what?"

"There is no shrub. No screen." I had truly lost my senses. And worse, there was no way to fix it.

"But is that not precisely what you commanded be done?"

"Aye. But, I did not mean . . . what will . . ."

"Did you not order the plants and flowers to be put up in their place?"

"Aye. But . . . there is no shrub. No screen."

Marget looked at me as if I were daft.

"No rose alleys for use as a *common privy*."

Her eyes grew wide as she comprehended my words. "They will only be here for one night."

"One hundred people for one night means . . ." I stalked from the rooms, muttering to myself. Maybe . . . perhaps the area behind the stables could be used.

When I returned to court, I left Nicholas to oversee the work in my place. The steward was eminently capable, but I needed a man who knew the court. A man who could think of the visit as I had done. In truth, who could think perhaps a bit better than I had done. A man whose work would not be found wanting. All must be perfect if I were to find favor in Her Majesty's eyes.

And I had to find favor in Her Majesty's eyes. Everything depended upon it.

41

The weather turned and Lytham sent me to Holleystone. By March, the air had warmed considerably. I was certain the babe would stay. It grew stronger within me each day, like a wych elm sending out shoots.

But like a wych elm, it must have developed some inner rot. For one week later, all came crashing down upon me. A bloody flux came, beginning with an all too familiar cramping in my back. By the time the midwife had been summoned, I delivered myself of a dead girl. As if knowing my need for warmth had been met and that she had served some purpose through the winter, the babe had expired.

I was inconsolable. Worse, I did not wish to be comforted.

Only Joan was brave enough to risk my ire.

"Why can I not keep a babe?"

"I do not know."

"What secret sin do I harbor that God will not give me a babe?"

"We cannot know what God, in His mercy, keeps to himself."

"What is worse? For my lord to know I have lost another babe or for him to think me barren?"

"Hush you now."

"In the end, the result is still the same."

I kept to my bed for two weeks. And when I rose, I did it with the knowledge that I would never hope or dream or laugh again. In those bleak days, spring mocked me. Life was flowering, life was singing, life was cavorting through the fields. Everywhere I looked, life was in bud.

Everywhere except my womb.

I did not want company. I did not want companionship. I did not want any but the ones I could never have, nor hope to hold. My only goal was to keep in perpetual motion, for when I stopped, I knew my grief would overtake me. I took to walking—great long walks about the estate. Keeping to the paths and roads in order not to soil my clothes, I walked its boundaries over and over. And then slowly my walks took on a meaning and a purpose. And more often than not, I would set my feet on the path to Falconer's.

Falconer rarely spoke but to his birds. When the servants brought him dinner from the kitchens, he made me to eat and drink of it. But mostly, I just watched him work. For a man so rude, he had such gentle hands. When he took the birds into the park, I would follow.

"They are a little like children, are they not?"

"In what way, my lady?"

"They depend upon you."

"Aye. But only because I have trained them to, my lady."

"What happens if they do not?"

"My lady?" My question had pressed a crease into his brow.

"What happens if they do not depend upon you?"

"If I cannot give them food, provide them meat, then they fly away in order to find it elsewhere."

"But if you do provide it . . . then they stay?"

"Aye, my lady."

When the birds were fed, when they were sustained, they stayed.

I felt my face fold in upon itself and saw Falconer gaze upon me with horror. But I could not stop myself from weeping and I could not stay the words which followed. "Why do my babes not stay? What is wrong with me? What is so misformed within me?" I wept as I had not since the birth.

Falconer, caught between an apparent abhorrence of tears and a lady who would not dismiss him, could only stand and watch. But then, as if by a miracle, Joan appeared to console me. She shepherded me away from poor Falconer toward home.

Following that outburst, Joan made certain I carried always a portion of Melancholy Thistle about me. She pierced a stalk and threaded a string through it, then draped it over my head about my neck. I could not care how I appeared; I had not even painted in weeks. And so I went around, bedecked with it for some days until the stalk went brittle, the string pulled through its hole, and it tumbled from me. After that, she soaked some of the thistles in wine and in the forenoons, when I was most apt to be overcome by dark moods, she set it before me and urged me to drink of it.

With Joan's ministrations, I was ready to face Lytham by the time I met up with him at Brustleigh. Ready to pretend that the child had never been. And indeed, as far as the earl knew, she had never existed.

Lytham had returned to survey the roads within the parish and found them in shameful disrepair. At one point, from cause of rains, the whole width of the road had sunk into a huge hole. He ordered the track remade around it. The lesser holes he ordered filled with stones. There was some dispute over the hedgerows lining the way. Lytham considered that they crowded the road too much. The parish insisted that two horses abreast could pass without problem. When he tried to inform them of the many carts and the traffic expected with Her Majesty's arrival, they could not conceive of it. He ended by pledging the men and monies to complete the work himself. And then, finally, all was ready. We awaited only Her Majesty's visit.

But for cause of rains, the Progress was delayed. And then pushed back and rescheduled. There were rumors that it might be cancelled entirely, but as Brustleigh was one of the first estates on the itinerary, Lytham insisted that she might arrive at any time. And that we must be ready.

Due to the long delay, the meat of the animals we had slaughtered in June was no longer fit for serving. Spices did not hide the rancid taste, and stewing did nothing to disguise the texture of rotting flesh. We sent it all out into the village. Other provisions had expired as well. And with the constant rains, the roads soon needed further work. Lytham commanded men out into the drenching downpours to fill in what holes they could and make a way around the parts of roads which were impassable.

But all his work was worth the effort, for with a break in the weather, we were sent a message that Her Majesty had finally started out upon her way.

Six days before the Queen's visit, carts began to roll into the courtyard. Two hundred of them, pulled with six horses apiece. They were led by a Gentleman Usher, and he had with him an army of men to disgorge the bounty.

And so began the invasion.

In my chambers, they threw up ladders to pull down the tapestries.

"But those are the finest of work. Ordered especially for—"

Lytham's hand squeezed my own, causing enough pain to stop my words.

Swiftly, they were rolled up and taken from the room. And

another hanging was put up in its place. And then they started to dismantle the bed.

"Surely you do not—"

"Perhaps, Lord Lytham, you and the lady would seek entertainment elsewhere."

And as easy as that, we were dismissed.

Under their exacting eyes, most of our furniture was carried out and the Queen's carried in. The Great Chamber at the head of the stairs was transformed into a Presence Chamber, complete with the throne Lytham had ordered constructed. Lytham's rooms were turned into a Council Chamber and space for Her Majesty's clerks to work. And once all was arranged, there were guards posted at each door.

I had become an intruder in my own home.

42

Three days before the visit, we were joined by an officer of the Wardrobe of Robes and three of his men. Two days before the visit, a man from the Controller of Works appeared to change the locks on all of our doors. Once the locks were secured, staff from the Tower's Jewel House brought the Queen's baubles. There were silver perfuming pots for her bedchamber and gilt water pots for her Privy Chamber. Beautiful jeweled salt cellars and vessels of gold to grace her dining table.

One day before the visit, an officer of the Keeper of the Council Chamber advised that it might enhance the rooms were they garlanded with branches and flowers.

Lytham ordered the grounds to be sacked for greenery. Only the knot work garden, which could be seen from my window, was spared.

The day we were to expect her, people began to trickle in as soon as the sun had woken. Before I had taken my breakfast, clerks were already at work within their chambers, and Her Majesty's personal cooks were at work in the kitchens. Those from the village taking part in Lytham's play had appeared and they worked on practicing the entertainments. But in the forenoon, when we should have received word of her approach, we received a lone man on horseback instead.

Lytham went to intercept him. "Her Majesty comes?"

He dismounted, bowed stiffly, and then rose. "Her Majesty does not come, my lord."

"There is some delay?"

"My lord, there is some change."

"So she will come tomorrow?"

"Nay, my lord."

"Then . . . the day after?"

"Her Majesty's Grace, my lord, comes not at all."

Without further explanation, the man strode past us into the house and began urging people to gather the royal possessions.

Lytham followed the man inside and I followed Lytham. We had to force our way through the halls. The officers of Her Majesty's household who had installed themselves in our quarters were leaving the house at a run, heading toward the stables, eager to rejoin their Queen.

"You say she is not coming? But why?"

"She has shortened her visit to My Lord de Winter's. On the morrow she is on to Windsor Castle, my lord."

"To Windsor?"

"She has deemed the roads impassable. She has cancelled the Progress."

Lytham spun on a heel. He ran to the stables so quickly that I had to trot to keep at his heels. And even then I had to jump from his path as he mounted his horse and galloped away out the gate.

I was left to oversee the packing up and leaving by myself.

The Gentleman Usher bowed when he became aware of my presence. "It is good you had so many useful objects, for the leaving is much more swift, my lady."

Behind him, a man carried the crimson and gilt-covered throne from the house.

"But, the throne . . ."

"Her Majesty takes great joy in such splendid, lovely things, my lady. And surely you have no use for a throne."

"Nay, of course not."

"You will be reimbursed for normal expense, my lady."

"Of course." But we had soared well past ordinary expense on our climb to greatness.

I stood in front of the house, along with those from the village, and watched the carts sway out of sight. Her Majesty's Grace was not coming. And still the kitchens were filled with food, the stables bulged with hay, and the villagers stood unused with no thanks or recompense for their great efforts. And so I told Nicholas to ask them all to come within the gates and stay and be fed and show their fellows the entertainments they had planned.

When Lytham finally returned, it was to the sight of bonfires and feasting.

His eyes glinted rage, though he slumped in the saddle.

I met him at the stable.

"Why the crowds?"

"I invited the townspeople."

"So they can be party to my disgrace?"

"So they can profit from their efforts. What else are we to do with all of these provisions?"

That night Brustleigh was the site of great revelry not seen by the Earls of Lytham since Empress Mathilda was defeated and returned to France some three hundred years before. The sitting Earl of Lytham passed the long night in his chambers alone.

The next morning I haunted the passage between his chambers and my own, hoping for sounds of stirring. For the melody of a lute or a horn.

I heard nothing.

I dined alone and supped alone.

It was only the next day that he made an appearance, and that at supper. We ate in silence. But when my lord made to leave, I left with him. When he took himself outside into the gardens, I followed. We took a turn about the fountain. Its water splashed silver in the moonlight. Rather ironic, considering the amount of silver it had cost to build.

"What are we to do, Lytham?"

"I do not know. I have no means left of holding Her Majesty's attention. No hope left for advancement. I shall never obtain a Garter Knighthood now. I am worse than my brother. He only gambled with money. I have gambled all I own . . . more still than I own . . . and I have lost everything."

Rage pushed at my chest, suffocating words, overriding reason. An unholy rage directed at a sovereign so indifferent, so needy. She consumed without discretion. She stole without knowledge. She had dictated every aspect of my life. She had stolen my husband's attentions, stolen my chambers, and she had stolen my money. "She has no right to treat you in this manner!"

"She has every right. She does not even know she treats me thus."

"Even now you defend her?"

"Have a care. That woman is your Majesty's Grace."

"Grace!" A gurgle of wild laughter escaped my lips. "Grace? She has none. She is a beggar. And what she cannot beg, she borrows or steals! She is no better than a common thief. Nay, worse! For she has no need. Need she men? She hath in abundance. Need she money? She has but to mint some. Need she castles, carriages, and gardens? She has only to order them built. She has all and I have *nothing.* Because everything I had, I gave her."

43

We quit Brustleigh as soon as we were able, as soon as the rains lessened, and returned to London. The trip did nothing to buoy Lytham's dark mood. The constant rains had ruined another year's crops. People had taken to the streets in riots. Bread cost a small fortune. There was death from starvation and disease stalked the land.

Upon our return to Lytham House, Lady de Winter was my first visitor. She came as I was walking to the stables in preparation for going to court. She reached out a gloved hand from her cloak to clutch my arm. "I have come to offer my condolences. On Her Majesty's Progress."

"We ruined ourselves in preparation for the visit . . ." I made a great effort to blink back my tears. "We have nothing left." I could hardly bring myself to whisper the words loud enough to be heard above the rain. The wind had already whirled our cloaks about us and left our ruffs exposed to the rain. They lay flaccid on our shoulders.

She removed her hand from my arm and offered it to me.

I took it. We could not meet above them due to our farthingales, but I clung to it for my very life. And so we stood there allowing the rain to bleed our gowns of their dyes. The colors ran and then dripped down into a puddle of mud that was soon painted with all the hues of a flower garden.

"Do not give up hope."

I tried to smile. "You assume that I still have some left."

"If Lytham could obtain a Garter Knighthood . . ."

"You think I have not tried?"

She squeezed my hands. "You may have tried, but have you tried *every*one? Every*thing*?"

"Of what do you speak?"

"Who has Her Majesty's ear?"

It did not take me long to realize her intent. "Essex?"

"Aye."

With Lady de Winter's help, I soon obtained a meeting with the Earl of Essex. Knowing Lytham's strong feelings about the man, I confess that I felt a bit guilty about my actions, but what else was there to do? Lytham's plans had been ruined. It was up to me to help him. And so I set my thoughts on my meeting with Her Majesty's favorite. On how I would appeal to him.

Could he really be in love with such a one as the Queen?

I supposed power was a strong aphrodisiac; even if he did not truly love her, he had bet his fortunes on the illusion. And if he had, then so had I. I told Joan to paint my face white and then to black my teeth in imitation of Her Majesty.

When I took myself to Wanstead, I was accompanied by four of Lady de Winter's men. Upon my arrival, I was taken straight to Essex's chambers. He was attired according to his usual negligence. I failed to see how anyone so inclined to dishevelment could figure so prominently in Her Majesty's affections.

"Lady Lytham. I welcome you to my humble estate. You grace me with your presence."

"Thank you, my lord."

"What shall I have brought for you? Can you stay?"

"I am at your leisure."

"You are too kind."

Having never been adept at courtly games and the manipulation of truth—and knowing that Lytham's future depended upon this meeting—my nerves were frayed as at the point of a knife. The pricks in my hands and feet were turning to tremors. "My lord, may I be plain?"

"Is that a possibility for the most beautiful woman at court? Pray tell how you would do this. What sort of magic would you use?"

I tried again. "My lord, I have a confession."

"Tut. There is no one in the realm who would mistake me for a priest."

I began once more. "I discover myself to be anxious of late."

"Then what balm shall I apply to your nerves?"

"Tell me, please, how can I obtain a Garter Knighthood for the earl?"

"Of Lytham? Her Majesty alone makes those appointments. I do not know why everyone seems to think that I can read her mind."

"May I be blunt?"

"As the axe of Mary Stuart's executioner, may God rest her traitorous soul." He paused and smiled, baring wolfish teeth. "Although, now that I think on it, He cannot, can He? For she was a papist. It does one no good in life, neither does it do one any good in death." His smile disappeared and his eyes lost their gaiety. "As you were saying . . . ?"

"It is said you possess Her Majesty's ear."

"Among other things, I would imagine."

I inclined my head toward him, unwilling to confirm the gossip whispered throughout the court.

"Please, forgive my lack of couth. Continue."

"He who controls Her Grace's ear might, perhaps, control many other things as well."

"He might."

"Then can you tell me, sir, how I might obtain the appointment?"

"One might suppose that pleasing me would be the same as pleasing Her Majesty's Grace."

So there it was, just as Lady de Winter had said. I had not yet tried everything. She had given me the chance with Sir Thomas, but I had not done it. But maybe this time . . . for Lytham. I curtsied and held it longer than I had need so that I could gain control of my emotions. Upon righting myself, I was able to speak. "I only wish to serve." But I knew even as I said it, that I could not do *that*.

Essex crossed the floor and came to stand in front of me. "What a noble sentiment of English virtue. And what great things might be accomplished by such service. Would that all of the Queen's subjects had hearts so fully devoted as your own."

"You must only tell me what I am to do, my lord."

He turned my chin with a fingertip so that I had to look into his eyes. He examined them for only a moment and then he began to laugh. "So, Lytham has sent me the most powerful weapon in his arsenal. But tell me, lady, does he know your heart is already engaged?"

"He does not know . . . that I am here. He has no knowledge of our meeting." My words came out in a whisper. O God, save me. I have made a terrible mistake.

"You are far worse than a spiked cannon, for those cannot be expected to work. You are a cannon forged with an invisible flaw. Only upon engagement is it discovered to be defect. And do you know what happens then?"

"Nay, my lord." I could only whisper the words.

"It backfires into the face of the man who intended to use it."

A cold sweat broke out behind my ears. How would he use me?

To my surprise, he bowed before me in the manner of a courtier. "Have no fear, Lady Lytham. I am in the habit of playing only with faithless hearts. The faithful will find themselves in no danger from me. I accept as gifts only those things given freely. I am quite willing to make a different arrangement."

Blood buzzed in my ears as I tried to understand the meaning of his words. Was I . . . had I been saved then?

Thank you, God.

He took himself from me and settled into a chair. "Do you have any idea what it takes to please Her Majesty the Queen?"

Had I? "Nay."

"If I must keep your secret, then you must keep mine. It takes baubles and sonnets and trinkets and diversions. And the next must be more amusing, more perfect than the last. It is enough to drive a man to an early grave."

"That must be quite taxing, My Lord Essex."

"Ha." He barked a laugh that seemed to take the both of us by surprise. "Taxing, aye, and in several ways. I find that I am bereft of ideas and . . . well . . . monies. And this, perhaps, is where you can help me. I have heard Lytham is having made a pair of fabulous bracelets for Her Majesty's New Year's gift."

"Aye." And only because he had sold some plate in order to do it.

"Then I would like them."

"I . . . I am sorry, my lord, I do not quite understand—"

"You will give Her Majesty something quite different and I will give her the bracelets. Is it quite understood?"

Was that, then, all he wanted in order to speak on Lytham's behalf? "It is. I will have the goldsmith render the service, then, in your name."

"Ah. Well, this is how we conduct our business. I take what is yours and you take what is mine. I am not unjust. In fact, I take nothing; we only exchange the one for the other."

"I see. And where is your gift . . . rather, *my* gift to be found?"

He tapped his head. "At the moment, it resides just here, but I am certain you will be able to find precisely what it is that I envision."

"And what is it, precisely, that you envision?"

"It is the most wonderful and amazing of amusements. I hardly have the words to describe it. But I am certain that when you see it, you will know it."

Clearly, our meeting was at an end. I curtsied before him and then straightened. "Thank you, My Lord Essex."

44

As I was riding through Cheapside, I decided to stop at the goldsmith's and see to the bracelets I was having made for Her Majesty's present.

The goldsmith looked up from his work as I entered. "My lord."

"Goldsmith! I have come to discover how the bracelets are coming."

"They have come, my lord. And they have gone."

"Gone? Gone where?"

"To My Lord Essex."

"Essex?"

"Aye. He said that you had sold them to him."

"To Essex!"

"Aye, my lord."

"You gave my bracelets to Essex!"

"Aye."

"And . . . then what am I to give the Queen?"

"I . . . can you not . . . use, perhaps, the monies that he gave you, my lord . . . I have very many pretty things."

"I did not want just any bauble. I wanted the bracelets! He asked for them in particular?"

"Aye, my lord."

"For my bracelets."

"Aye, my lord."

"And you gave them to him?"

"He said . . . If he had not spoken to you, my lord, how could he have known . . . ?"

I felt like strangling the man, but in truth it was not his fault. I had been cheated, but I had no recourse. Especially not at this late date. I laid a hand on the counter, and tried to do it gently. "May I see what else you have?"

———

When Lady de Winter asked for a report on my visit to Essex, I told her it had gone well.

"Better than the visit with Sir Thomas, I trust? I know that Lytham does not like the man, but if you can get him a knighthood, why should he care what you had to do to obtain it?"

"We were able to reach an agreement."

When she pressed me for details, I took my time in answering. And before she could ask me once more, providence answered my pleas in the form of an official delegation that paraded through the Presence Chamber.

I was able to distract Lady de Winter with a question. "Who is that man?"

"An ambassador. From Polonia."

We watched together as he bowed before Her Majesty, offering up a letter. We all must have assumed it was some letter of thanks to Her Grace for having contracted a peace between Polonia and the Moldavians several years before.

One of her ladies took the letter from the ambassador and handed it to the Queen. As she read it, the ambassador was seen to step backward, one foot behind the other, looking still, with each step, at Her Majesty. A strange way for an official to conduct himself.

"What are his designs?"

Lady de Winter frowned. "I do not know."

We saw him continue to step away.

"Does he mean to flee the palace?" Lady de Winter turned to see if Her Majesty had noticed.

"Perhaps this is the practice of Polonians?"

"He must know he cannot long go in that direction. He will run himself into a wall."

But just as the words were spoken, he stopped. He cleared his throat and threw back his head. And then he began to speak.

Her Majesty looked up from the letter she was reading. For a moment, she looked annoyed. And so she should have been at a person daring to address her without first being addressed by her. But as he continued, the corners of her mouth plummeted toward her chin and the rings on her fingers glinted as her hand convulsed around the letter.

At first we could not believe what he was saying, as no one, not even Essex, had ever dared address Her Majesty with such words.

First, he complained that Her Majesty had unjustly entrained the rights of the Russians and Polonians in trade. Next, that Polonian goods on their way to Spain had been impounded. And then, as a friend of Spain, he declared he could not remain silent.

"So we hear." The words came from a baron standing beside us.

"Hush!" Lady de Winter had no shame in using her rank as a weapon.

He demanded reimbursement for the goods that had been seized and wanted the liberty to trade with the Spaniards as Polonia wished. If not . . .

I felt my brow rise. "Did he just make a threat?"

"He just . . . . Did he say they would attack us?" a man at my elbow questioned.

The court was abuzz with persons trying to decipher the riddle of his words.

And then Her Majesty condescended to speak. "Your king is young and has come to his crown by *election*, not by royal birth. He cannot hope to understand those things which passed between me and his predecessor."

"Your Majesty, I—"

"Although princes are governed by the Law of Nations and are presumed to have sovereign rights, those same laws allow a prince to stop supplies from reaching an enemy."

"But—"

"Especially in time of war."

"If you would just—"

"You will not speak to me!" At that, Her Majesty withdrew to her Privy Chamber.

The Privy Council rapidly conveyed the ambassador into conference, leaving the court to gossip in their absence.

"But did not the King of Polonia confiscate the goods of our *own* merchants on the way to Muscovy?"

"Did he . . . He was not demanding an answer, was he?"

"What would be of more interest is his answer to Her Majesty."

Unfortunately, the ambassador had not been given of an answer, but only charged to carry back to the King of Polonia Her Majesty's reply. But it remained a topic of conversation and provided many a night's discussion upon which characteristics, exactly, the ambassador had failed in his attempt at courtiership. And how our own ambassador to Polonia had failed to warn Her Majesty of such a missive. Surely he could not hope to keep his post for long.

I was trying not to fail at my own attempts in courtiership that season, but there was a pain in my mouth that would not be stayed. It was probably good that my fingers had lost their feeling, for I began to chew upon the littlest one. It took an edge off the ache in my teeth. I soon noticed that I was not the only lady in court driven to the same action. In fact, I had noticed Her Majesty doing that very thing quite often.

Spring bounded forth as we rode to Windsor for St. George's Day. But it was a mean year, for though there were five inductions, Lytham was not one of them. In spite of my hopes, my prayers, and my alliance with Essex, for Lytham, nothing had changed.

———

One more St. George's Day come and gone and still no Garter Knighthood. I sighed. Tried to tell myself it did not matter. As I rounded the Lieutenant's Tower, Essex came around the corner from the opposite direction. I stepped aside so that I would not have to speak to him. But instead of continuing on, he stopped in front of me.

"Good day, Lytham."

"Essex."

"Is Lady Lytham with you?"

"Nay."

"Would you be so kind then as to pass on a message for me?"

"To her?"

"Aye." A smile played at the edges of his lips. Would that I could have wiped it off with a sword. To the heart.

"Tell her, if you please, that I am but one man."

"You are but one man?"

"Aye. If she wishes to obtain you a place in the Order of the Garter, she must attempt to influence more persons than just me." He bowed and then continued on his way.

If I had not been a person of honor, I might have . . . murdered him. Right there. Instead, I made haste in finding Marget.

———

I had just finished dressing when Lytham burst into my chambers. I stood, expecting a kiss or at the very least an embrace, but then I looked into his eyes.

I sat back down in my chair.

"Essex asked me to deliver a message to you. From him."

Sweet heaven.

"You have been trying to buy me a Garter Knighthood?"

"I have only been trying to help you to succeed."

"By treating with my enemy?"

"You know influence must be . . . purchased . . . in order to obtain such a position."

"With Essex? What did you have to give him for his help?"

"I—"

He pulled me from the chair. "What did he ask for? Tell me the truth."

"He asked for"—I could not look him in the eyes—"something I would not give him. And then he took the bracelets instead."

"*You* gave him the bracelets?"

"I was only trying to help you."

"Help me? You only succeeded in turning me into a . . . joke. Stop trying to help me! You are only harming my cause. Just leave me be." He turned on a heel and left, slamming the door behind him.

45

The weight of Lytham's anger and the burden of our insolvency bore down upon me. Daily I searched for some way to bring the subject of monies to Lytham's attention. Finally, one day I knew I must speak of it or let my mind be ruined by worry.

It was not, perhaps, an ideal time. We had scarce finished dinner and he was already in his cups. Melancholy. Morose. Unshaven. He had become disheveled in dress, going about with his doublet unfastened. His years had begun to find him.

"My lord, we must talk."

"Of what?"

"Money."

"You mean to say its lack?"

"I mean we must be clever. We must begin to see how we can live. We must survive."

"You think I do not know that?"

"I think knowledge is prudent, but action is better."

"And what do you suggest?"

"I suggest we forgo the lease on Brustleigh Hall."

"Nay."

"Surely we do not need it. It has devoured everything we once owned."

"I will not give it up."

"Then we must look to Holleystone."

"Holleystone?"

"If you cannot give up Brustleigh, then you must let go of Holleystone."

"Let go?"

"You must sell it."

"Sell it? After I finally retrieved it? It will never leave my family again!"

"My lord, can you not see? We cannot keep both. We have no monies. There have been no crops, so we are receiving no rents. There are no monies left and there are none coming in."

"I will not sell Holleystone."

"Then what else do you propose to do?"

"I will not sell Holleystone."

———

The woman plagued me. Could she not see that I had nothing? Could do nothing? Could she not see that there was nothing more *to* do? "It is *you* who do not see. It is *you* who does not know. How can you know how it feels to watch your family's inheritance handed to a son of no reputation, simply because he is the eldest? How can you know how it feels to watch your heritage traded away, piece by piece, for gambling debts? How it feels to watch your legacy carted away to embellish some mistress's house? It feels wretched . . . abominable . . . to see everything your family stands for exchanged for ridicule, mockery, and derision. To have your own name spoken with scorn because of the actions of another. A person who was to have vouchsafed it—vouchsafed everything—for those to come. The only smart thing he ever did was to die without an heir."

Her hand reached out to touch my arm. "I know you feel . . ."

I shrugged it off. "How do you know how I feel? How do you

begin to know how I feel? Let me tell you. This will be a good lesson: I will tell you how I felt when I heard Holleystone was up for sale and I had nothing with which to buy it. I had put Elinor behind me. I had sworn never again to marry. And my monies were pledged to Sir Francis Drake's disastrous campaign against Spain. Or was it Portugal? The estate, my family's own home, was there for the saving and I had nothing with which to rescue it."

"I cannot imagine—"

"Imagine this. Imagine hearing that in Norfolk there was a newly knighted merchant, who was dangling his daughter in front of nobility like bait set before a pack of dogs." I heard the words I was saying. I winced to hear them, but I could not stop speaking them.

"I do not want to hear more." She was pleading with me.

I should have stopped, wanted to stop, but I had no control over my tongue. "But what one wants is so rarely what one obtains. Do you know how your father baited the trap? Did you imagine that it was with your beauty?"

"Please stop." She took a step away from me.

"You did?" I laughed because that was funny. Truly funny. "You did! Then that is the amusing part. Because your beauty was the last thing I learnt of you. Nay, the first thing, the very first and most important thing was your dowry."

"I already know he spent more than he had intended." My brave, sweet Marget.

"Oh, it was far, *far* more. And I intended for his great expense to fund my greatest triumph."

"So . . . you never wanted me." She was going to cry.

I had brought her to the brink of tears. Once that might have moved me to tears as well. But now? I could not bring myself to care. "Wanted you? I abhorred you. You were so very beautiful that I almost cancelled the marriage contract. You were a beautiful angel, but I knew you to be wrapped in the devil's own cloak. And now I am so bewitched by you that even your words have the illusion of soundness." I took another drink.

"You did not want me?" The words came out in a whisper.

Aye, I had. I did. In truth, I wanted her still. But I did not deserve her. She deserved someone successful. Someone who had made something of himself. She deserved someone like Essex. I could hardly speak for the lump in my throat. I clamped my jaw together and tried to swallow it down. "I tried so hard to hate you. I tried so hard to despise you. But, God save me, I could not do it." To my eternal shame I broke down. I could not stay the sobs that ushered from my throat. I covered my eyes with my hands, trying to stop up the tears. Trying not to see the pity in her eyes. "Sweet heaven, what is to become of me? If I cannot hate you, then I love you. Do you not understand? I must love you!"

She waited to speak until I had composed myself. "But . . . I thought . . . I was given to understand . . ."

"That I was some beast? Some monster?" I lashed out with my arm, trying to make her go away.

"That you wanted me. The sonnet."

"What sonnet?"

"The sonnet you gave me as a betrothal gift."

"I wrote no sonnet."

"But you did. I committed it to memory. And still I carry it with me." She reached down to unfasten her Book of Hours and pulled a document from some hiding place.

> "Every man who claims a destiny
> Is giv'n a ship of fate on which to sail
> Some guide their course by basest treachery
> While faint hearts anchor far from life's travail
> But take to hand the Astrolabe of Love
> And soon you find that your course does run true
> Through day and night, gales thundering above
> All the sailing leads to naught but you
> To you alone I give Love's astrolabe
> That in your sailing you might find the same
> Gale winds that blew my soul to you to save
> Might in return give you to me to claim

Coupled, may we kneel before love's altar
Clasping hands that bear faith's ancient color."

I found that I could smile after all. "Love's astrolabe . . . a clever device. And a very good sonnet." I had recognized Nicholas's work at the first quatrain.

"You seemed as if . . . you wanted me."

"The man who wrote that made it seem as if I wanted you. But I did not write it." I wished that I had. Nicholas had always been the better poet.

"What do you mean?"

"I did not write it. Who gave it to you?"

"You did."

"So you say. But when?"

"As a betrothal gift. Along with the astrolabe. And—"

"Let me guess: my mother's ring." I had become of a sudden so weary. I only wished for sleep.

She nodded.

"But who was the man who *gave* those things to you?"

" 'Twas Nicholas."

I held her gaze, willing her to understand. Willing her to comprehend so that I would not have to say it. So that I would not have to disillusion her in still one more thing.

" 'Twas Nicholas?"

"Aye. It was Nicholas who kept hounding me, begging me, nagging at me to send something. I finally told him to choose something. And since he was so bleeding concerned about your welfare, to take them himself. He did rather well, do you not think?"

She came to me then and knelt beside my chair. Took my hand in hers, threatening once more to undo me. "But even if you did not write it, you became that man. You are the man I love and you have become the man of the sonnet. I need you."

I could not look at her. "I was never that man."

"You have always been thus, Lytham. You have always been that man to me."

46

And so Lytham and I began an intricate dance. It was set to the tune of austerity, though the words *reduced, impoverished,* and *insolvent* were never sung. With a household staff of nearly one hundred, I could not reduce the expense of food by much, though I began to water our soups, ales, and wines. And, though we had paid for our annual flesh-eating license, we began to eat fish on Wednesday, Friday, and Saturday.

We forwent sweet oranges, melons, and other culinary luxuries. And when our French cook was enticed to the household of the Earl de Winter, we let him go. The former assistant provided admirable, though less cunning, meals.

The work at Brustleigh was halted and the workmen dispersed. Without that army of men to feed, the burden on our purse was lightened. I broached the idea of selling some of our horses but was quickly taught that it was an imprudent idea. In all of our dancing around words, we made not one mention about clothes. There was no need. When we had to force savings from our clothing, then all at court would be lost.

We could not hide our secret long. Not from those who ran

our estates. And not from the beggars who came seeking food. Joan told me the word had spread that there was no charity at the Earl of Lytham's house, that beggars had warned each other away from us toward more generous hearts. They were right, those indigents. But only God could save them from the knowledge I had: there was no charity anywhere.

Lytham returned to court that spring only to ask permission to leave. Expenses were significantly reduced while we lived in the country. But when he returned to me at Holleystone, he was accompanied. By an alchemist.

There was nothing overtly sinister or malevolent about the man. He both comported himself and dressed himself as a gentleman, although once or twice I noticed the lining of his cloak to be shredded and the cuffs of his sleeves to be worn. But I confess I did not like the way he looked about with his eyes. He gazed upon all as if he might own it, and he made no distinction in his interest between person and thing. I put up with the man for a fortnight, with his impudent glances, his lurking in the estate's halls, and the malodorous fumes from the room Lytham had assigned him. And then I could delay no longer.

I went to my lord when I knew he would be at work. But the alchemist had preceded me and he sat, ensconced, across the table from Lytham.

"My lord, I must speak with you." As he glanced up from his paper, his companion turned around in his chair to face me.

"Proceed."

"My lord, I desire a word alone."

At my statement, the alchemist leered.

Lytham dismissed the man, then addressed himself to me, his mouth lined with displeasure. "And what would this word alone entail?"

"My lord, an *alchemist*?"

His lips went straight with impatience.

"Where did he find you?"

"In St. Paul's."

"St. Paul's! And you believe him to be honest? You might as well search for a virgin in Southwark! He cannot be licensed."

"The Queen herself employs an alchemist in order to build the treasuries."

"And has he?"

"Has who what?"

"Has her alchemist contributed to them?"

Lytham blinked.

"Has he actually added any gold to the treasury?"

"Why else would she employ him?"

I threw up my hands. "Why does Her Majesty do anything?"

"You told me once that I must sell one of the estates."

"And so you must."

"Not if I can obtain some monies."

"And how will this alchemist help you?"

He sighed and folded his hands in front of him. And then he proceeded to address me as if I were Tom Fool. "An alchemist makes gold."

"He *makes* it?"

"Aye. Everything changes state. An acorn turns into an oak tree. A cloud turns into rain. An alchemist turns things into gold."

"And what are we to give him to do this miraculous work? Eggshells? Ham hocks?"

"He does not work in transmutation. He works in multiplication."

"Multiplication."

"He multiplies what we have and turns it into more."

"My lord, one cannot take what we have, which is nothing, and multiply it. There can be no multiplication when there is nothing to begin with!"

He shook his head and turned back to his work. "I have given him some silver plate."

"Sweet heaven, why did you not just give it to a band of gypsies?! At least then it might have been honest charity!"

"I have no other options."

"You have *three* other options. Brustleigh Hall, Lytham House, and Holleystone."

"This is what I have decided must be done."

"Lytham, hear me. The only way to make money is to exchange something for it. Listen to me. I am a knight's daughter. A knight who began as a merchant and amassed a fortune."

"There, you see: he began with nothing."

"Aye. And he *worked* for what he gained. And what he gained enabled you to buy back Holleystone."

"You cannot understand."

"I do understand. I understand that trusting this stranger, this . . . alchemist . . . is as big a gamble as your brother ever undertook. And just as certain to fail."

He did not bother even to look at me before returning to his accounts.

A week had not passed before I saw the stranger carrying a silver goblet down the hall.

"And where did you get that, sir?"

He did not even honor me with a bow. "My Lord Lytham has given it to me."

"For what purpose?"

He leaned to the side and peered past my shoulder, then he crept close enough that I could feel his breath touch my cheeks. "For the alchemy, my lady. I must not be delayed. The dragon and the eagles have begun to fight."

"The dragon and the eagles?"

"Aye, lady. And the dead of the battle will birth a crow." He turned and continued on down the hall, clutching the goblet to his breast.

I went on a search for the steward and found him in the store-house.

"My Lady Lytham." He bowed and offered his hand so that he might better escort me.

"Good Steward."

"I may assist you in some way, my lady?"

"In regards to the alchemist." I had hoped to read his face and discern there some sign of approval or disproval, but I was disappointed, for I could find nothing.

"My lady."

"I would wish him . . . watched."

He bowed. "From now until you bid me cease, my lady."

"I also desire an accounting and cleaning of the silver plate."

"Aye, my lady."

"Then I would like it closeted. And I wish to retain the key."

"Of course, my lady."

"And I wish it done as soon as is possible."

It was done within the week. There were two platters and two goblets missing. But after the accounting, there remained nothing in the house that gleamed. It was all locked away into a cupboard.

The next week Lytham went on a search for me. Joan warned me of him and so I had enough time to enable him to find me out of the house on a stroll through the gardens.

"What have you done?"

I glanced at the rose in my hand. "I have plucked a rose, my lord. Might I be forgiven for such a temporal pleasure?"

"The silver plate! Where is it?"

"I have had it collected for an accounting and a cleaning."

"And where is it?"

"I do not know."

"Stop playing with me, Marget! Steward says you keep the key."

I opened my hands and let fall the rose. And then I held my palms out toward him. "Then he is mistaken, for I hold nothing."

"The alchemist needs more plate."

"And what would keep him from needing more and more and more until all the plate is gone?"

"Would you see me in debtors' prison?"

"Nay. I would see you guard what fortune you have."

"He must have more for the multiplication."

"My lord, why can he not first make a multiplication and then employ the new supply of silver that he has just made for his future use?"

"How can I know how it works? I only know what he tells me."

"Here is how it works: he will demand your supply of silver and then, once he has obtained it, he will leave. And he will take with him what is ours."

"Nonsense."

"My lord. You have already given him two platters and two goblets. How much would those fetch from a pawn?"

"Two pounds? Five pounds?"

"Aye. And so the only one whose wealth will be multiplied is the alchemist's. He is the only one here who will have started with nothing and obtained something. Seven pounds' worth of something! Why can you not see that?"

"Because I have faith! And you cannot see because you do not."

"It is not a question of possessing faith; it is a question of lacking sense."

"Give me the key."

"Nay."

"Give it me!"

"Nay, my lord. I will not be made partner to your folly."

He raised his finger in warning. "If he fails in the multiplication, then the blame will rest entirely upon you."

I wrapped my hand around his own, kissing his fingertips. And then I looked into his eyes. "And I will take it. I will take all of the blame. Better his failure than your fortune . . . what is left of your fortune. After you give him all the plate, then what? Will he demand the jewels from your doublet? From my sleeves? Will he then ask for the tapestries? And the Turkey carpets? At least your brother had an honest whore for a mistress. At least he obtained some small pleasure for his possessions."

At that, my lord went white. And then he flushed red. He gazed beyond my shoulder at the house which sat in the distance. "He will not do it."

"Will he not?"

His eyes found mine once more.

"He will not do it." He sounded as if he was trying to convince himself more than he was trying to convince me. And then, leaning against me, he clutched my arms as if some massive blow had rendered him senseless.

I staggered under the sudden burden of his weight.

"What have I done?"

"Nothing which cannot be undone. Simply ask the man to leave."

"How can I . . . how did I . . . how could I have let this happen?"

"You are a good man, Lytham. Do not ignoble yourself in trying to maintain your family's honor. You have enough of it in you if only you would know it."

47

*L*ytham asked the alchemist to leave that very forenoon.

"But . . . the multiplication is not yet achieved."

"And will it ever be?"

"I . . . beg your pardon, my lord?"

"Is there more needed for the multiplication to be accomplished?"

"How gracious of you to inquire, my lord. I need only silver plate."

"A platter? Another goblet?"

"Perhaps . . . a salt cellar."

"A salt cellar?"

I coughed to cover my surprise at his boldness.

Lytham looked at me in reproof. "I cannot give you a salt cellar, for we have none."

"But—" The alchemist's words vanished with one glimpse at the look on my lord's face.

Lytham glanced in my direction before continuing. "Perhaps . . . might I suggest, perhaps, a jewel?"

"A jewel! Of course."

"Nay. I forget myself. For you are undertaking multiplication, not transmutation. Only silver will do, will it not?"

"At most stages, my lord, although at this step, the dragon must be fed. And rubies are the only thing upon which it will feed."

"I see. Well, I am sorry to say that I have no rubies to give you. Perhaps . . . would a tapestry work just as well?"

"A tapestry, I assure you, will be quite necessary after the dragon has eaten and he takes to slumber again."

"A tapestry, I assure you, will never be granted. And I suggest, once more, that you take your leave of this estate."

The fellow must have known he had been discovered, for he offered little excuse. Nicholas walked him from the hall to the stables and had him placed on his horse.

We watched him ride away up the hill and vanish from our sight. It was the only miraculous feat he accomplished, for when we entered his rooms, we opened his chest to discover a walnut resting upon a moldy apple. And fixing them together, the putrid remains of an egg.

We never did find the platters and the goblets, but assumed them to have already been given to a pawn. No amount of visiting London's shops uncovered the plate. But I considered it a small sum to pay to be rid of him.

As Christmastide approached, we journeyed back to London. One could not possess a noble rank and not be present at court for Christmas. One evening, once we had returned, we were needed for supper at the palace. There was to be a banquet for Christmastide festivities with entertainments following. We were to dance in a masque. My part was easy to accomplish, though I was in no mood to make merry. Not before the woman, the Queen, who I held responsible for my husband's ruin.

I spoke no words but stood at the back of the group pretending to be a tree. Later word went round that Her Majesty desired a dance in the Presence Chamber. When we arrived, she was already reclining upon her cushions. And someone had placed a tassel in suspension, so we knew it was to be a galliard. A dance at which Lytham excelled.

The music started.

We stepped right and then left. Right and left. I derived no pleasure from the dance, and knew my countenance to be sober, but at least in dancing a galliard, all attention was focused on the men. On Lytham. While I stood for the next step, he leapt into a cadence, landing one foot stretched out before the other in a posture. Together, we moved to the music, performing the steps that made the dance our own. And at the end, bounding into the air, Lytham reached out a leg and kicked at the tassel.

Our reward was Her Grace's applause.

Again we danced. It was another galliard. First stepping left, stepping right, and then joining hands together. But then Lytham let go my hands. He took hold of my busk with one hand and pressed the other to my back, turning me to the side. It was then I knew my galliard had turned into a volt.

I placed my hand to his shoulder and fixed my lips into a smile. We stepped into a turn, leaping first onto our outside feet and then lifting our inside feet forward. Together. One long graceful step and then I sprang into the air.

Lifted high by Lytham's arms, supported by his thigh, I yearned to take flight and fly beyond the confines of the palace, but then my feet touched the floor once more.

Again and again, caught in the turns, I was lifted into the air, then brought back down. Though my heart longed to weep, I could only smile. But by the last lift, my emotions were no longer under my command and I stumbled as my feet touched the floor.

"Here, here!" The musicians halted their music at Her Majesty's word.

She pushed away from her cushions, gained her feet and came to stand in front of us.

We made swift reverence.

"What ails your wife, Lytham? Rise then, girl. You must not land so heavy on your feet!" She dismissed me with a wave of her hand and gestured for music with the other. And when the music began, Lytham danced with her around the chamber.

———

I awoke on the morning after the dance, filled with good cheer. The Queen had chosen me as her partner the previous night. Perhaps *this* was the way preference would find me. Perhaps it was the sign of a changing of fortunes.

A summons to court that day for an audience with Her Majesty did nothing to diminish my optimism. I chose my best cloak and my best doublet. I had Nicholas place a gold chain around my neck, and then I galloped off to meet my destiny.

"Good Earl of Lytham!"

I bowed and approached the chair where Her Majesty was engaged in correspondence in her Privy Chamber. "Your Grace."

She did not ask me to sit, but she did wave away her clerks and set aside the letter she had been reading. "It has been too long since we have spoken of monopolies."

"Your Majesty."

"I have become enamored of your ideas. Though why you should be so interested in a monopoly for starch . . . ?"

"My greatest interest is only ever of your greatest interest, Your Grace. Ruffs continue to grow in size. You can obtain nothing but profit from granting such a monopoly."

"But do you not find the ruff tiring, Lytham?"

I hid a smile by bowing my head. My ruff was only a trifle compared to the size worn by Her Majesty. Though she was wearing only a simple robe, she wore a ruff no one could ignore. "Not when wearing one reminds me of your vaunted . . . person . . . Your Majesty." It was said her ruffs were meant to disguise her time-ravaged neck.

If that were so, it worked. Admirably. Beneath its folds stretched only pale, unblemished skin.

"Well. We shall see. I will take it into consideration." She motioned her clerks forward.

I bowed. "Your Grace."

As I stepped back, she spoke once more. "Your gypsy wife must be such a disappointment to you."

I could not think what I should say.

"It is not seemly for those to dance who have no grace."

It is not seemly for those to dance who have no grace. That was the real reason for the audience. She did not wish for Marget to be noticed. Of all the unjust . . . ! My wife had the lightest foot of anyone I knew. She might not be able to leap as high as the Queen, but what she lacked in strength, she made up for in grace.

Those who have no grace.

So what was I to do? Praise God that she had not told me to retire Marget to the country! I did not wish to live without my wife.

But still, we would have to be very careful. I had gained Her Majesty's favor. Now I only had to keep it.

———

First, an upgrade of apartments at court and then a waiver from taxes was given to Lytham. And then he heard Her Majesty was considering the possibility of granting a monopoly for starch.

He was exultant. Jubilant. And completely enamored with his Queen.

He could not seem to decide, in my disgrace, whether I was an asset or a liability. And so he vacillated on my attendance at court. One day commanding me to go, the next leaving me at home.

And so I made friends with my thoughts. But thoughts such as those were vagrant friends. The worst kind of friends. They were enough to drive me mad. There was only one thing I knew with certainty: that I was not made with a faithless heart. I could only pray that in his success, he would remember me. And so I did. For long hours. Days at a time.

———

The days that followed were filled to overflowing with activity. There were politics to be discussed in the mornings, advancement to be discussed in the afternoons, and dances to be danced in the evenings. And all of it done within the circle of those closest to the throne. If I did not dance with Her Majesty, then I danced with one of her maids-in-waiting.

Finally, I had access to everyone with the ability to influence the Queen. I had only to decide who it was I wished to speak to her on my behalf. I had already laid my case before her for the starch monopoly. Now it needed only a push from the proper direction. Essex, of course, was not an option. Neither was Cecil, her secretary; he was too bent on strengthening his own sphere of influence. In short, I did not trust him to have any interest in strengthening mine. The choice fell, finally, to one of Her Majesty's maids. For a price, I knew I could get one to speak for me. So I sold some of my plate and chose not the most beautiful, nor the most merry, but rather the most grave, though, in truth, one could not long remain solemn in Her Majesty's court.

I drew the girl from the Presence Chamber one forenoon on the pretense of viewing the monthly roses in the pleasure garden. "I hear their beauty rivals only your own."

"Then I shall have to see them. And if their loveliness is everything you say, then I shall have the gardener cut them . . . and give them to you."

"I would press them between the pages of *Astrophel and Stella*. I have ever been a lover of stars. Particularly those which glitter closest to the moon." The moon had long been used as a symbol for Her Majesty's Grace. I was certain the girl understood exactly of what I spoke.

She smiled. "Sometimes I can be persuaded closer to the earth."

"Nay, my dear, do not bend too close to this dusty sphere; your beauty is greater appreciated from afar."

We paused in front of a bench. I took my cloak from my shoulders and draped it over the bench so that she could sit upon it.

She sighed. "It costs dear to remain so long suspended." She extended a hand to me.

I grasped it and knelt before her on one knee.

"Sometimes, I long for my feet to touch the ground." She drew her hand from mine and pressed it to my cheek.

I removed her hand and kissed it. "But if you leave your orbit for the earth, then how are you to sing my praises to the moon?"

"It would only have to be a fleeting stay."

She was offering me everything, for nothing. She was a courtier's fantasy: a girl who wanted but a brief moment of time abed for which she professed herself quite willing to do anything. And I ought to have agreed right then to her terms, but oh, for the love of Marget, I could not. The love between us, our constancy, may have been sweet, but it had just become quite costly.

I might be able to explain away a dance or two, but a prolonged flirtation? That, Marget would never understand. And the fact that I had been propositioned? Regardless of my response, it would be the death of everything between us. I could not be about my business and worry over Marget's perceptions as well. There was only one thing to do.

48

*S*oon Lytham's vacillation about my role at court turned to resolve and he dismissed me. It was one thing to excuse me from attendance day-by-day, but another thing altogether to bar me from going. I ordered the household back to Holleystone. What else could I do? But I retired there with much relief, even in my disgrace. I meant to stay until I was recalled. And it was not I who would do the asking.

I had been spurned for the Queen. But had that not been my goal? Had I not been trying, for years, to push Lytham closer to the throne? Well, I had succeeded!

Oh, bitter victory. My success had robbed me of a husband.

For what sin was I being punished? For stumbling during a dance? It was my error that had catapulted Lytham into the Queen's lap. And *I* was being banished? Were I to rend my heart from my chest, it could not have ached any more than it did.

Life without Lytham was dull. There was no laughter, no diversion to separate the morn from afternoon and the night from day. But then, there was no need to take great pains in appearances. My ladies and I went about in our night-robes until dinner. I had no need for paints. After several weeks of restless activity, I began to settle into a country routine. The window seats wanted new cushions, so I set to work selecting designs. Then I ordered up the colors of wool and put my maids to work. As they stretched out the canvas, I read to them from a new play.

One of them had clumsy fingers, and one day, with impatience, I took the canvas from her hands, picked out the stitches and then reworked them myself. It was only later that evening as Joan helped me into bed that I realized what I had done.

"My hands!" I held them out in front of me, wiggling my fingers. Clenching them into fists and then loosing them.

"Aye. And these right here, these are toes."

"Joan, look at them."

"Aye. You've ten of them even."

"They work! They are not swollen."

She grabbed at them. Turned them over. "Hold them out in front of you."

I did as she asked.

"They do not even tremble!"

I lay back into the pillows, pulled the coverlet up to my chin. "'Tis Holleystone. The country. I like it here." Even though I did not like my reason for being there.

"Nay: 'tis the paints. You are not painting."

Whatever it was, my health improved. The constant knots in my belly were loosed. I was less irritable. Less tired. But the new energy within left me with a desire to do more. To be more.

I consulted first with the Clerk of the Kitchen and then the Chief Cook on ale, ordering the bushels of malt to be ground, having it brewed thrice over a furnace, and then seeing to the barreling. We tried a new receipt for metheglin, a drink made of fermented honey, water, and herbs. With some of the orchard fruits in the storehouse, we also tried our success with brandy.

In a visit to the stillroom, I noted a dwindling of supplies. I also noted a complete absence of simple tonics for healing wounds.

And so I commanded a supply of mineral water and oversaw the restocking of the herbs.

There were babes born among the people. And several deaths. There was the distribution of flax and wool to the poor for carding and spinning.

As long as I kept myself at some worthy task, my thoughts were not able to wander. But abed, at night, they either spun into the knot of Lytham's desertion or they unraveled, leaving me staring into a void of space.

And as the weeks passed, the staring happened all too often.

"Marget?"

I started and took up the book on my lap. But I could not hide myself from Joan.

"You are too pale. You have kept yourself inside too long. You should go hawking. Falconer would take you."

"Nay." I hawked with Lytham. The attraction of the sport lay in the partner, not the activity.

"Why so melancholy?"

"I am not." And I was not. I was just . . . changed.

Lady de Winter and her husband came to visit on the way to one of their estates that winter. If they had been excused from court, had taken the chance to leave, then surely might not Lytham do the same? And if he might, then why had he not?

Lady de Winter spoke to me of nothing while her husband flirted with my maids. A hand circling one of their slender wrists drew my attention for its indiscretion. And when Lady de Winter perceived me not to be listening, it drew hers as well.

"He finds something to engage his affections wherever he goes." She took my arm and pulled me around so that our backs were turned toward them.

"And this does not bother you?"

"Bother me? It delights me! If he is talking to some maid, then he cannot be talking to me. God rot them both. God rot them all. The man and *all* his paramours."

I could not understand the alliance of the de Winters. In my observation, he was far more solicitous of other women's health than his own wife's. But if Lady de Winter did not please him, he could well send her away. As Lytham had me.

In thinking of him, I could not stop myself from speaking of him. "How goes Lytham?"

"You have had no word?"

"Of what?"

"He probably lacks the time to write. He is day and night at the Queen's side."

Day *and* night?

She must have seen my frown. "Well, 'tis what is *said*. I have not seen him of late, for I have not been well. But, come! 'Tis a triumph."

"Of course, 'tis a triumph."

"Then why do you look so grieved?"

"I just . . . it is just . . ."

"You love Lytham too much, girl. Can you not see how I despise de Winter?" She had turned us back around to view the merriments, and her eyes were throwing daggers at him.

Aye. I saw too well how much her own heart was hurting.

"Love will do you no good. And much more harm."

I hoped for Lytham into spring. Surely, I thought, we would see him for St. Matthias's Day. And then I was certain he would pass through for Shrovetide and then for Easter. But he did not.

It was nearing summer when he finally returned. And when he came, it was with Nicholas and all of his men. And he embraced me right in the middle of the courtyard.

"Have you missed me as I have missed you?"

I could not allow him to guess that my heart was beating furiously within my chest. "Miss you? I have not had time to think about you."

He led the way into the Great Hall, triumph evident in every step.

"I gained some more rents and a waiving of some more taxes."

"Excellent. See the new cushions on the seats?"

He blabbered on about Her Majesty. About this thing which she had said. And that thing that he had answered. By the time supper was over, I was sick unto death of them both. And so I took myself to bed.

But I woke that night with a start. Someone's cold toes were begging warmth from mine and clever lips nibbled at my ear.

I pulled the covers up over my head.

I felt a hand caress my hip and quickly nudged it away with my elbow.

"Marget, my sweet."

He tried again, running his hand up and down my back. Usually I responded by curling into him like a kitten, but that night I rolled onto my back.

"What is it, lady?"

What is it? What else could it be! "I have no taste for another's bone."

"Of what do you speak?"

I sat up, clutching the warmth of the covers to my chest. "Think you that I will be content with another woman's leavings? You cannot spend half the year with the Queen at court and expect me to be grateful that she allows me the scraps of one week's end."

He stared at me with something close to amazement, and then he began to laugh.

"And I will not have you laugh at me in my own chambers. Get out!"

"I cannot—"

"Away!" I gave him a shove that sent him sprawling onto the floor. And still he laughed.

"But 'tis just that—"

"I am sure the royal bed has finer pleasures than I can offer."

"Marget, my sweet, your rage does nothing but endear you to my heart."

"You come here with nothing but words and cold toes expecting that all will be forgiven? I remind you, as others so often have, that I am but a knight's daughter. And among such classes there is still a thing called honor!"

"And upon my honor, I will tell you, lady wife, that I have never even glimpsed the inside of Her Majesty's bedchamber."

"And further you—have not?"

"I have not."

"But . . . Lady de Winter said . . . she said you were at the Queen's side day and night."

"And so I was. For Her Grace plays like a fiend at cards and she loves to dance. And if she cannot dance, then she takes pleasure from seeing others do the same."

"So you . . . played cards and . . . danced? This six months?"

"Aye."

"And 'tis all that you did?"

"For the better part. There were some masques. There was some intrigue. There were quarrels betwixt Essex and Raleigh. And then quarrels betwixt Essex and Cecil. I never wanted for entertainment. And I have never worked harder in my life. How many ways are there to flatter a sovereign? One can compare her to the moon and to the sun. To Gloriana and Diana. To Astraea and Flora. And then one begins to worry. And so I galloped toward home the first chance I found only to have my own wife round on me and push me from her bed! Must I think of some pretty compliment for you too?" He pushed to his knees and extended an arm toward me. "Dear lady, your affections are as enduring as a boulder . . . and just as able to crush the life of those standing too close." His eyes ranged my face. "It does not please? Then I offer you this: 'My lady is like the white rose, offering excellent hips and sweet perfume to those that gaze upon her beauty and naught but pain in the plucking.' "

I blanched. It was true. I had done that very thing. I let go the covers and extended a hand toward him. And he came forward to clasp it with a kiss. It was one of the sweetest I had ever known.

"Why did you send me away?"

"Because I thought you better entertained here at Holleystone. And in truth, I was afraid that if you stayed, I could not court the Queen the way I had to."

"It was not because you did not want me?"

"I ever want you. You cannot doubt the truth in that."

I blushed to hear it.

49

When Lytham went back to court in London, I went with him. I hoped and prayed during the next few weeks that the seed of love that had been planted and renewed would produce a babe. But it did not happen.

What if like so many of the women at court, I was destined to be childless? What then would happen to Lytham's estate? And what would happen to me if I failed in this duty? Even as I grieved my dead babes, I also grieved for myself. For my position. For my failure. Though I tried to keep it hidden, Lytham tried to search it out.

I sighed one forenoon as I listened to him play the English horn.

He stopped his song. "Why so sad, my sweet?"

"I am not."

He put the horn back to his mouth and played a progression of notes in a sad, mournful key. "Says she of wounded eyes."

"My lord . . ."

He set the horn down and came to my side. "Must you address me as my lord? Could you not call me Lytham? When you call me Lytham, you speak to me of amusements and trivialities." He looked at me with a hope I could not return.

"My lord."

"So it is to be of business, then?"

"It is to be of posterity."

"Then say what you will."

"What if . . . what if I cannot . . . ever . . . have a babe. One who lives?"

"Your flowers have not stopped?"

I tried to smile. I tried to shake my head, but I discovered that I could do nothing at all. Little surprise for one who had failed at the very first responsibility of marriage. "Nay. They have not. It is only that, considering what has happened in the past, it is very difficult to consider the future."

There was no change in his visage. No lowering of his eyes. But I noticed that the light had gone from them.

"I must ask you, my lord, is there no one, no close relation of blood, that you might recognize as your heir?" Some person, as Lady de Winter had hinted, heretofore gone unrecognized to preserve my dignity?

———

She was asking me if I had an illegitimate child! And what was I to say? I needed words, divinely inspired. Oh, sweet Marget, why are you asking me to betray your trust? I could answer in the negative, but that would do nothing to quiet the concern in her eyes. And it would not have been the truth.

I looked away from her. Sighed. "I have one son."

Her gaze dove from mine. She folded her hands and placed them into her lap. "How . . . old is this . . . son?"

"He has seven years."

I could see her do the calculations. Not ten and seven? Not twenty and seven? Seven years before we had been joined in marriage? But it was not as she was thinking. She closed her eyes. Bowed her head. "Then he must be brought into our household."

"Truly—"

"Do not say it."

"I must tell you—"

"I do not need to know." The words sounded as a hiss escaping between her teeth.

"But he is—"

"I will not hear it. Whatever words you speak, I cannot care. The boy may be brought into this house, and he may be raised as your own. He must be. I know this. But I cannot hear how it was for you those years ago when I remember still how it was for me."

"How it was for you? For you? Let me tell you how it was for me! I had vowed never to look upon a woman again. Never to touch one. Never to trust one. And then I arranged to have myself married to a veritable raven-haired Helen with which half the court fell in love."

"Truly, my lord." She said it as if she scoffed at my sentiments.

"Truly! And so, even as I doubted her constancy, I was ever confronted by examples of her fidelity. And even when I thought her a Clytemnestra, eating at my very soul, she changed into a Circe and had me lying, like a dog at her feet! It was enough to drive me mad!"

"You love me." Why did she have to sound so resigned?

"Sweet heaven, how could I not? There is not strength enough given to man!"

"But then, this boy . . . ?"

"He is *Elinor's* son. He is called William."

"But why did you annul the marriage if—"

"She did not tell me until after the annulment."

"But why?"

I felt my hands claw my hairs. "I do not know." I never had, and always it had puzzled me.

"Forgive me for asking, my lord, but how do you know that he is yours?"

I lifted my eyes to hers. "One has only to look upon him to know."

We gazed at each other for several long moments. And then she broke the silence. "What is being done with him?"

"I do not know."

"He is your son and you do not—"

"It is not my place to know. He does not bear my name. I *have* been informed that he has been placed into service in a nobleman's house. The home of Elinor's brother."

"And what is to become of him?"

I shrugged. "He will become part of the man's household."

"But not the *son* of such a household."

"Marget. *Our* son will be the son of such a household."

"But what if there is no son?"

I knelt before her and took her hands into my own. "There are many years left, my sweet, before that will be determined, but *if* that happens, then I can officially adopt William as my own and make him the heir to my estate. There can be nothing about which to worry."

"As long as your future is secured."

"My future *is* secured. And I prefer to spend it with you." There. Those words, at last, had made her smile.

————

In some ways, knowing about William eased my mind. In others, it only underlined my complete failure as a wife. I wished, more than anything, to do something, to be somebody of use to my husband.

Thankfully, I had a friend who understood my wishes.

"I know, girl, that Lytham has gained some rents, but still, there must be a certain barrenness to his coffers." Lady de Winter had come to see me at Lytham House.

I did not know how to answer, for she was right. But I did not want to make our humiliation complete.

"There is one way that you could help him."

"How?"

"He needs, perhaps, influence more than gold. Money might save his estates now, but power will help him line his purse for some time to come."

"What must I do?"

"Have you never noticed that those closest Her Majesty seem those most able to dispense fortunes in pursuit of their pleasures?"

"I had not—"

"No one approaches the throne except her maids or ladies-in-waiting know of it. And they are always able to turn such audiences into transactions. Do you understand what I am saying?"

"I do not know if—"

"Do not be stupid, girl! Could you obtain a position as a lady-in-waiting to Her Majesty, then not only would Lytham gain influence, but *you* would gain money. People will pay, gladly, for a conference with the Queen. And pay even more if they do not have to meet with her, if you pledge yourself willing to speak on their behalf."

That might solve all of Lytham's problems! Only . . . I would have to spend all of my hours near the Queen. I trembled at the thought. "She does not like me."

"She does not know you. As one of Her Majesty's previous maids, I am willing to recommend you to her, but first . . . well . . ."

"Please, speak freely."

"You must first be seen to be worthy of such a position."

"How would I do it? I would not want to presume . . . and I would not want to surpass Her Majesty in—"

"I do not speak of beauty. You have learned that lesson well. I speak of status. You must appear already to have gained the position. You must order the finest gown that your money will buy."

"But—"

She held out a hand. "I know you have no money, girl, but you must still possess some of your jewels. I will pay you for them."

"I could not presume upon your kindness."

" 'Tis no kindness, I assure you. I have had my eye on one of your rings. I will give you forty pounds for it."

Forty pounds! I rose, walked to the table, and picked up my coffer. "Which one?" I set it on her lap.

She opened the lid and plunged her hand inside. "This one." It came out with Lytham's betrothal gift upon her thumb.

I could not long mourn the departure of Lytham's ring. There was too much at stake. Quietly, before doubts could overcome my courage, I ordered the draper and the tailor to Lytham House. Together in my chambers, we planned a gown that would delight Her Majesty with its finery. Only the best of satins, the finest of sables, and the most opulent tinsels. It was to be embroidered with silk, dotted with spangles, and bedecked with lace. It took two months to be made, but finally it was delivered.

The day of Lytham's redemption had arrived.

It took all of the maids to help me into the gown, two maids to dress my hair, and a full hour for Joan to paint my face. My belly had tied itself in knots; I could not eat. Joan tried to converse with me, but I had no words to give her.

"Come, Marget. You will be a great success. How could Her Majesty not deem you worthy?"

She could and indeed she often had declared me very unworthy.

"At least take some bread."

I shook my head.

"Then drink some wine. 'Twill calm your nerves."

I pushed the cup back toward her.

She pushed it back to me with more vehemence than I had expected and I fell into the slopswoman.

At least she had not yet completed her chore. She only bobbed her head and continued toward the stool, as was her habit, humming that tuneless melody.

But that day I could not have it. "You! *What* is that irksome tune you sing, you beslubbering shrew? If you insist on singing it, then let us all hear it!"

The woman looked up from her pail with surprise. Shifted first to one foot and then the other.

"Now!"

> "Death's finger paints my lady's face all white
> *While underneath the mask, her skin turns gray*
> *'Tis just a matter of time, once all goes tight*
> *She'll leave this earth's delights for Grave's decay."*

Her warbling voice died at the end of the last word. She stood there silent, still shifting first to one foot and then the other.

"Out!" Her words had shaken me to my innards. The image of Death's finger painting. Skin turning gray, getting tight. It was all happening to me. But Grave's decay was a matter I refused to contemplate.

After the woman shuffled away, Joan took my hand. "She is a hideous creature, but you cannot fault her for speaking truth."

"Her truth is terrible."

"But 'tis truth none the less. Please, Marget, stop painting."

"How can you ask me to stop on the day I go to see the Queen!" How could anyone ask me to? I wished I could! I wished I could stop plucking my brows and dying my hairs as well. But what would I gain? Only the court's derision and Her Majesty's wrath. Only everything I had once suffered. Were the paints robbing me of my health? There were worse pains to suffer in this world than grayed and tightened skin. And besides, I did not paint for myself. Would never have started if it had anything at all to do with me. I painted because I had to; there was no other choice. I painted for Lytham. I painted for his benefit, for his future. I painted for his Queen.

"I just—"

I left her. I walked from the room and went to the stables for my horse.

———

I had been idling in the gallery waiting for Marget. I had heard that the Queen had once more been speaking of selling monopolies. Excited, I began to speak to one of the other lords of the idea and together we walked into the Presence Chamber. It was not long before we were joined by some others and then the talk had turned from trade to politics.

But once the conversation had turned from Spain to France to Scotland, I confess that my thoughts began to wander, my eyes began to scan the crowd. Across the room, Lady de Winter caught my eye for the simple fact that she was doing nothing at all. Her eyes alone moved as they watched something mid-room. Knowing Lady de Winter, that thing was bound to be a person, and so I turned my own eyes in the direction of that lady's stare.

It was Marget.

She was dressed in a shimmering, glittering display of jewels, tinsel, and gold spangles. She looked the very picture of the Queen herself . . . some thirty years before. It was a splendor that rivaled the Queen's own. And it was then that dread clenched its fist tight around my innards.

Although she was not approaching the throne directly, her wandering path put her in danger of attracting Her Majesty's attention. And if she did, if I knew the Queen as well as I thought, then all was ruined.

I glanced back toward Lady de Winter. She was marking Marget's progress, a smile lurking upon her lips.

Pushing through the men around me, I was desperate to reach my wife before she caught the Queen's attention. But even as I broke through the group surrounding me, I saw Her Majesty lean forward upon her throne. And then I saw her stand.

It was too late.

50

I had tried hard to shake the slopswoman's words from my head, but they had taken root, had grown, become more voluble on my way to the palace. I looked at the faces of the ladies around me. How many had turned their faces gray from paints? How many had, like me, skin that stretched too tight? How many were speeding themselves upon the way to death?

I felt like one of the Tower's lions.

All the courtiers were staring at me. They were backing away from me, making a space for me, as if they considered me dangerous. Had I not just then gained the center of the chamber, I might have turned around and left. But now, Her Majesty was standing. She was speaking. To me.

I curtsied as low as I dared.

"Lady Lytham."

"Your Grace."

"Come here!"

Her voice did not sound as if she were pleased with my appearance. In fact, it sounded much cooler than Lady de Winter's promised warm response. I held my curtsey one instant longer and then, eyes lowered, did as I was bid.

"I suppose it is the fashion for monkeys to go about dressed as children?"

"Your Majesty?"

"If I had a face as brown as yours, I suppose the only thing to do would be to dress as a doxy and join some traveling gypsy band."

"Your Grace?"

"If you wish to play at being Queen, then find your own court in which to do it. And since you appear dressed to travel, I suggest you leave at once and do your maundering elsewhere. Perhaps . . . in Berkshire."

My gasp joined those of the courtiers behind me. If I was not mistaken, she had just dismissed me from court. Banished me to Holleystone.

Unable to control the trembling in my knees, I curtsied once more and backed away on wobbling legs. I had offended Her Majesty the Queen. Again. And this time, there was no mercy. This time, no grace. My career as a courtier was over. I only hoped Lytham's still remained.

There would be no hiding of Marget's error. Her Majesty's voice had rung so loud, her sarcasm had been so pointed, her command so plain, that no one in the palace could deny having heard it.

But Marget could not have started upon such a course by herself. She would have had to have been set upon it quite deliberately. And only one person could have done it.

As I watched Marget exit the Presence Chamber, I was torn between following her and confronting the engineer of her downfall. I decided, finally, that I could not leave without receiving an explanation.

I found Lady de Winter, grabbed her by the elbow and spun her toward me.

"Lord Lytham! How pleasant to see you."

"Did you put her up to that?"

She said nothing, but her eyes shouted defiance.

"How could you do it? Did you not know the Queen would have her head? Why did you not stop her?"

"Because you would have!" She spit the words from her mouth.

"Of course I would have!"

"And why?"

"Because I—"

"Because you love her." Coming from her mouth, the words sounded vile. "You love her and so you allow her to ruin you. You forget yourself. You forget your position. You forget your Queen!"

"You pinch-spotted trug!"

"You should thank me."

"For ruining my wife?"

"For doing you a favor. She will be banished from court—and then you can think with your brain instead of your heart."

"I despise you!"

"Despise me as you wish, but this is twice I have saved you. I saved you from Elinor before I saved you from this girl."

"This girl is my wife. And so was . . . Elinor . . . What did you do to her?"

"I only helped her to see that the best way she could help you was to detach your heart from her."

"I will have you—"

"It worked, did it not? When was it you gained the lease on Brustleigh? How was it you were able to remarry and regain Holleystone?"

"You are despicable."

"There is no place in this court for love. Unless that love is directed toward the Queen."

She only told me what was true. Chastened, I sighed and allowed my gaze to drop. It fell upon the lady's hand from which my mother's ring of rubies and sapphires sparkled. I grabbed at her fingers. "You wear my mother's ring!"

Her brow rose. She glanced down at her fingers. Withdrew them from my grasp. "I do."

"How did you get it?"

"It seems Marget needed some money to purchase a new gown . . ."

I dropped her hand and turned on my heel.

————

He caught up with me on the road to London. "Marget!"

I drew my horse up to wait for him. There was no purpose served in running away.

"Why did you not wait for me?"

"Wait for you! I do not know why you would even wish to speak to me. Nor why you would wish to know me."

"My sweet."

I pulled the cloak tight around me, trying to cover up the evidence of my folly. "Do not say such things to me. I have ruined you. I have turned your name into a mockery."

"But how could you not have known?"

I looked into his eyes then. I should not have done it. There was such kindness there, such gentleness, but also a clouded confusion. As if he had discovered something about me that he could not reconcile with what he already knew.

I had discovered that same thing as well. It was a stupidity, a blindness, an unfounded trust. "Do not look on me. I do not know how I could have been so foolish. But Lady de Winter was so . . . persuasive. She said that it would help you. That you would gain influence, and monies, if only I could become a lady-in-waiting to the Queen."

"A lady-in-waiting? Is that what you hoped to accomplish?"

I could not bear to look at him. "Aye."

"Then you would have had to have known Her Majesty from birth . . . or be a blood relation."

Oh, the betrayal. "I did not know."

The day dawned gray the morning I left London. A thick fog had wrapped away everything from view as if I was not to be permitted even one last look at the city. Lytham was not there. It was necessary for him to be at court. Now more than ever. He promised to come to me in the new year, but I would not hold him to it. He would have to prove his loyalty to the Queen for some time before he could risk a visit to me.

But he did leave me a message. Of one word: *Fortitier.*

Bravely.

In reply, I left him a message. *Fideliter.*

Faithfully.

United under the St. Aubin family motto, I could go on to Holleystone bravely knowing that he would stay in London faithfully. Nothing more needed to be said.

One thing I did not take was my paints. Where I was going I would have no need for them. And further, I had decided that I could only be who I was. I had never had any hope of being the person the Queen had wanted me to be. And now it no longer mattered. I had tried to be a good wife, tried to help my husband succeed. But in the end, at that too, I had failed. And so I left the city being only myself.

51

I took great comfort in being at Holleystone. In knowing that, though Lytham was at court and I had been banished, I waited at the one place he longed to be. It was quiet in the country. My maids had been called back to their own families, for no one wanted their daughter to be tainted by my scandal. Finally, I was as I had always longed to be: without paints, without artifice. I had even decided to let my hairs revert to their usual color. And I helped them along with one last bath of dye. Only this time it was with the intention of turning them black. The paints had ravaged my skin, as Joan had always warned they would, but I was hopeful that in time all might be righted. I was very nearly the image of the girl who had left King's Lynn one autumn day so long ago.

But as I installed myself in Holleystone, my thoughts worked at something to busy them. And they fastened upon a puzzle from the past. Like Lytham's first wife, I had in effect been banished from my marriage. But what exactly had happened to Elinor? And why had she gone mad?

I decided I had to find her.

The decision was easier made than done. Most of the servants of the house were unquestionably loyal to Lytham. There was only one person I could ask without risking another person's presence, another person's ears. Only one person on the estate worked alone: Falconer. And so I took myself out to the mews one day.

"Lord Lytham said you were to train up another bird for me."

"Aye, my lady, I wait for one to be born. Should be in a week's time. Then I'll wait another month to start the training."

"Can you not just trap one?"

"A grown one, my lady?"

"Aye."

"Nay. They are hard to teach to return because they are used to hunting for themselves. They fly away."

"Can you not buy one?"

"Aye, I could. But then he'd have to learn his loyalties all over again. Best thing is to wait and raise one for your own, my lady. A falcon you cannot trust isn't worth the time to train."

"And how do you teach them to kill? How do they learn it?"

"It's their speed that kills. Once they spot their prey, they grasp their talons like this"—he clenched his fists—"and dive straight toward the target. Fastest bird there is. It's not the claws or the beak that kills; it's the impact. And the falcon's always careful to hit a bird on the wing so there's no danger to himself."

"So cruel."

"Nay, lady. The birds aren't cruel. Less cruel than most of us." He turned his head and looked straight into my eyes. "They mate once. For life."

I walked around the mews, looking at the birds. And they looked right back at me. Peregrine falcons with their shadings of cream and blue. Their heads sleek with black feathers, angling toward their beaks like helmets. Their black eyes, encircled by yellow, stared at me, unblinking.

"Falconer, you knew Lady Elinor."

"Aye, my lady."

"Was she truly mad?"

" 'Tis what they say. She came here once. Tried to set her bird free."

"Did she hawk?"

"Loved to hawk. Thought like a bird. And her bird missed her. Flew away rather than stay with me."

"What makes a bird fly away?"

"When you lose their trust. If they think they can do better on their own, then why should they stay?"

"Do you know, Falconer, where Lady Elinor went?"

He drew a deep breath as he picked up the strap of a jess. Then he let it out as he went to work on the polishing of it. "Went to where she'd be taken care of. She flew home." He kept his attention so focused on his task that I almost did not hear what he said next. "Home to North Moreton."

North Moreton? But that was only a few short miles away.

Elinor may have only been two miles away, but she might as well have lived in Ireland for all the good it did me. How would I go about seeing her? How would I introduce myself? As Lady Lytham? If I did, why should anyone allow me entry? But the thought of Elinor being so tantalizingly close worked upon my thoughts until I knew I would have to find some way to meet her.

Knowing she had been one of Her Majesty's maids, I fastened at last on a plan. I may not have been a maid and I might never have served Her Majesty, but I knew what they did and how they did it. I had a periwig as orange as any court lady's. I no longer had my paints, but I could make a paste of flour and turn my face nearly as white as any courtier. And I could make myself appear a bit older, as if I were Lady de Winter or another of Elinor's contemporaries. In fact, I could *be* Lady de Winter. I could declare my intention to remember myself to Lady Elinor. And if I did, how could anyone forbid me access?

And so, with the help of artifice, I did it. Since it was so close, I rode only with Joan and one of the younger grooms from the stables. A groom young enough, I hoped, that he would never have encountered Lady Elinor as Lady Lytham.

I need not have worried overmuch. As soon as I announced myself and my mission to Lady Elinor's household, the steward was notified and he himself led me up the Great Stairs.

"You may find her . . . much changed . . . if I might be pardoned for saying so, my lady."

I nodded as if I might have expected such.

"We try to keep the Lady Elinor quiet in her thoughts, my lady."

"She is troubled?"

"Aye, my lady." He signaled a page, who pulled a key from his waist and opened a door. "Light disturbs the mind, you understand, my lady." The steward entered the chamber, clearing his throat as he went. "My Lady Elinor, you have a visitor." He bowed and signaled me to enter.

I did so and then made of him one request. "You may leave."

He bowed once more and retreated down the passage, without closing the door behind him, leaving light to mark a trail into the room.

In the gloom of that chamber I could make out only a shape seated on a bench. But then the shape turned and found its feet, threw a hand up to block light from the eyes. "You have come finally? To see me?"

"Aye, Lady Elinor."

"And do you see?"

"Forgive me, but I can see . . . nothing."

She stepped forward into the shaft of light leaking in from

the hall, cringing and pressing her hands more tightly to her eyes. She waited some moments before lifting them. Then she stepped forward once more. The light touched her features, throwing them into relief.

Flesh had fallen from her bones and puddled into wrinkles. The absence of teeth had left great hollows in her cheeks. Her hands shook even as they clasped each other. I could hear the slopswoman's voice in my head: *"Death's finger paints my lady's face all white, while underneath the mask, her skin turns gray. 'Tis just a matter of time, once all goes tight, she'll leave this earth's delights for Grave's decay."*

A ripple of dread crawled up my spine.

Our eyes met.

"You have come, Lady de Winter! I have waited all this time and you have finally come. How does it go for him?"

"I have not . . . I mean to say . . ."

She suddenly dropped to the floor and crept toward me on her knees. "I failed him. My heart never learned to listen to my head . . ."

As she advanced, I retreated. But I became tangled in my far-thingale, and she caught me by casting herself before my feet. "I tried to do as you asked. I tried to do as you commanded. But my heart was not yours to own. I loved him."

"Lady Elinor—"

"I could not do it! You asked too much."

"Lady Elinor, listen to me—"

"I did everything you told me to, but it did not disengage my heart."

"Lady Elinor—"

"But still, when you told me my love would ruin him . . . I did the only thing I knew to do."

"What did you do?"

She tried to speak, but her words left off as tears stole her voice. She grasped my feet and pressed her forehead to my boots.

"Lady Elinor!"

"Please . . . please . . . tell me . . . tell me he has succeeded." She rocked on her knees and pressed her head once more to my feet.

I tried to shake her from a boot but she would not be moved. And if I could not move, I could not call for aid.

She thought me Lady de Winter? Then I would play that role to the hilt. "Lady Elinor! To your feet this instant!"

She stopped her rocking.

"Is this any manner in which to speak to me?"

She pushed herself from me and, with much scrambling, stood.

"Now then, I wish you to tell me the whole of the tale."

" 'Tis not a tale. 'Tis truth."

"Then make it plain, girl!"

"I betrayed you. I lied to you. I never have stopped loving him."

"And I am willing to overlook it if you will tell me what you have done."

"My lady?"

"Make haste!" The steward might be lurking in the hall.

"What do you wish to know?"

"I would know what you did to Lytham."

"I cannot say it."

"I command you to say it!"

She pressed her lips together and shook her head.

"Out with it!"

The shaking became more violent and I worried she would throw her head from her shoulders. "Then tell me what you did to save him."

"To save him from my love? I made him divorce me."

"I thought your marriage annulled."

"It was. But I began by giving him grounds for divorce."

"Which were?"

She raised her head then and looked me full in the face, eyes streaming with tears. "Infidelity."

"And what happened?"

"I broke his heart. And I broke my own along with it." She collapsed into a heap upon the floor, shuddering with sobs.

"And why did you do this?"

"You told me to. *You* told me to. You said to declaim everything that is good about him. No one could believe that you love a person you do not respect. But it did not work."

I had heard those words before. The hairs at the back of my neck stood on end. "So you . . ."

"I made him divorce me."

"So that . . ."

"He could do what he needed to. Obtain what he wanted. What else could I have done?"

I had plenty of time on the ride home, and in the weeks which followed, to ponder Elinor's words. But more so, Lady de Winter's involvement in her sad fate. She had told Elinor what she had told me; she had goaded Elinor into action the same way that she had goaded me. And if the result for Elinor was a betrayal of marriage, then that must be what she had intended for me . . . and had intended all this while. But what was it that she hoped to gain? For there was no doubt now that she was acting on anyone's behalf but her own.

52

With Marget gone, I had nothing to distract my thoughts, no one to coax me to laugh, nowhere to go. Not only had Her Majesty's attentions cooled toward me, so had the attentions of those who wished to please her. My rents had mysteriously dried up and my waivers from taxes had been revoked. There was no hope of my being given a monopoly now.

I lived within a courtier's nightmare.

I had fallen from favor.

I picked up my treble viol, played a few chords. Set it down. I threw on my cloak and walked a few turns in the garden, but quickly tired of the effort. I showed myself at court each day, made certain that I was seen, but with no one to talk to, the pretense soon grew old. It was while I was contemplating Her Majesty's response to Marget that a thought began to implant itself in my head.

The Queen has only ever come out against my wife because she was jealous.

At first, I nearly laughed at the thought, but soon I knew it to be true. The Queen *was* jealous. It was vanity that had made her react as she had. If vanity were the way to her wrath, might it also be the way to her heart?

I had little money, I had no wife, I had no friends. But I still had my pen. And, given enough time and hard work, I could write sonnets that would make heaven weep with their beauty.

I would write a sonnet. A cycle of sonnets.

I would dedicate it to Her Majesty.

She would forgive all, and further I would entreat her to give me a pension just like she had done with Spenser.

A sonnet!

How could I go wrong? And why had I not thought of it before?

All I had to do was portray Her Majesty as the most beautiful woman in the world. As the ideal beauty. As the Aphrodite of the Atlantic. If I could praise her beauty and get others to do the same, then my fortunes might be restored.

I went to work on it that very night.

It needed to have something to do with wisdom and temperance. With peace and grace. And beauty, of course.

I spent several difficult weeks in the writing of it and another in the correcting and the organizing of it. And then, at last, it was complete. And I had only to convince the Queen that she wanted to hear it.

That took a full two months.

I dressed in my best hose and doublet and threw my finest cloak over top. As I approached the center of the Presence Chamber, a hush fell over the crowd. I bowed. Straightened. Pushed my cloak over one shoulder, held the sonnet out in front of me and began to read.

At first, Her Majesty's visage remained cool. She continued to summon her councilors, to issue orders to her clerks.

But soon she stilled.

And then she listened.

"Those angel's feet, so lithe, so filled with grace
Which whirl and bound and leap about the air

> *So nimbly dance among this fallen race*
> *And touch all hearts with gladness everywhere . . ."*

I dared a glance at the throne. Aye, she had smiled. I continued on for some verses before coming to one of which I was especially proud.

> *"Look! Wisdom's silken mesh of gilded hairs*
> *Have birthed within the sun a jealous rage*
> *Fueled by envy, Apollo, war declares*
> *But he is dazzled ere he can engage . . ."*

Another smile.

It was working! I could almost see her softening with each word. I read on, each line provoking a reaction which exceeded my expectations until, at last, I had come to the end.

> *"That such an eye of blue could spark Sun's rays*
> *Within a heart, and raise it from its sleep!*
> *That with one look, one azure-colored gaze,*
> *One sole regard shall maketh all life sweet.*
> *Lay down your weapons you who need not fight*
> *And heed our Sovereign Queen—she makes all right."*

I had expected a smile, perhaps applause from the throne. But I was disappointed. All the goodwill the previous verses had created seemed to vanish in an instant. I received only a steely-eyed stare from those legendary gray eyes.

Gray.

Oh . . . sweet heaven, Her Majesty's eyes were gray.

'Tis Marget's that were blue.

It did not take long to ride back to Lytham House. I waited there in growing terror for several days, knowing that at any moment I might be clapped into the Tower. Men had been sent there, had their heads removed from their shoulders, for less than I had done. But after a week's time, I began to realize that my fate was to be much worse. I was simply to be forgotten.

I had tried everything I knew to succeed at court. I had spent all of my monies, exhausted all of my influence, and used up all of my favors. And what had I gained from all of it? Nothing. Not one thing.

If my situation did not change, and soon, I would have to let go of the lease on Brustleigh. Even Holleystone might be in jeopardy. In what universe could that be considered just? All I wanted was to be with Marget. At Holleystone.

I smiled at that thought. When had my life become so very simple? I had been a poor excuse for a courtier ever since I had married Marget. It used to be that I wanted money and estates and honors . . . but now I only wanted what it seemed I could not have. One thing was certain: I could not leave court. There was no way out for me, not even if no one spoke to me, even if the Queen herself did not deign to recognize me. I was a noble, I had responsibilities. Responsibilities of which I could never be shed. And I could not just renounce my title. Could not flee court. I was well and truly stuck unless the Queen excused me. Or unless she could find a use for me elsewhere.

The wars?

Nay. I was too old for wars.

Perhaps I could find myself a position somewhere. Become an authority of some port city.

Nay. Once, perhaps, I might have, but I had no money left to purchase such rewards.

Once more my thoughts returned to Her Majesty. Unless she excused me, unless she found a use for me elsewhere . . . perhaps Polonia. She needed an ambassador, a better one, in Polonia.

Perhaps I could offer myself to her for that position. It was certain she would have no volunteers. Not for a post beyond the borders of civilization. Not for a post in the savage wilds of the eastern part of the Continent.

She might just let me go there.

But in going I would have to leave everything. There could be no hope for retrieving any preference or preferment; I would no longer be in court to present my case before the Queen. I would not be present to buy or trade influence, to exchange favors, to deal in secrets. Of course, I would be given some small pension for my services, some pitiable allowance for my expenses, but I would have to forgo any dreams of amassing a fortune. Fortunes were made at court, and I would be far from the throne.

I could, perhaps, leave the courtier's life without too much regret, but in going I would also be leaving Holleystone. I would be leaving my home. Mine and Marget's. I had toiled for years to be able to regain it. But then how could I stay at court, in possession of Holleystone, and be separated from Marget forever? Her Majesty's banishment of my wife was a test. A test that would reveal in which woman lay my loyalties. Aye, I could stay at court and try to regain my place, but rare would be the chance to regain my bride.

So, after weighing my options, it came down to one choice. A simple choice. Marget or the Queen; Polonia or the court; all or nothing. And then it occurred to me that perhaps this was the way. *The* way. Had I not left my destiny in God's hands, certain that He could find no solution if I could not? Perhaps, then, this was His answer, His way of setting my feet on another path. An honorable path. Some path other than that of the courtier.

I wrote to every friend and ally I once had. I wrote to Cecil, Her Majesty's secretary, and even to Essex, who was about his duties in Ireland. I pleaded my case to anyone who would hear it. But still the months passed by, autumn turned to winter, and I heard not one word from the throne. Not until just before Christmastide. It was then that I received the summons.

The Queen made me wait for hours before finally granting me admission to her Privy Chamber. And when she did, she did not even look at me, but continued with her reading as if I were not there.

I bowed and stayed bent for many minutes waiting for some sign.

At last, she spoke. "I will not have a man reciting poetry to me in front of my own court which is clearly meant for another woman's ears."

I straightened.

She continued reading for some minutes and then, finally, sighed and put the book aside. "What am I to do with you?"

"I do not deserve to remain in Your Grace's presence."

"So I should throw you into the Tower? Like I did Raleigh?"

"My life is yours to command."

"But not your heart."

God, help me! Please help me. I bowed again, and stooped even further. "I am not worthy of your esteem, Your Highness. My . . . inconstancy of heart—"

"You never were like the others."

"Your Grace?"

"You seemed to be quite sincere. For a courtier. But I have never asked for sincerity or for constancy. I have *hoped* for those things, but I have only asked that one be discreet. Behold Essex and the debaucheries that take place at Essex House." Her words seemed mild compared to the fire, the wrath in her eyes.

I did not know where to look or what to say.

"Come, you think I did not know of them?"

"I cannot account for what Your Grace might—"

"Tsk. One may only react to what one acknowledges. And I *will not* acknowledge his . . ." She seemed in imminent danger of exploding from rage.

"Essex, being the sort of man that he is, Your Majesty, perhaps if you gave him something—"

"Something to do? Some mission? Is that not why he is in Ireland, trying to fix the troubles? I have given him a rope. He can either use it to save himself or use it to hang himself. I care not which."

Clearly, she did care. But still, I felt that I should warn her. And so I set aside my own worries to address hers. "Forgive me, Your Grace, but one such as he is too proud to be used so slightly . . . and he covets the people's hearts."

"One always longs for what one cannot have. And I love the people more than he. He may ask of me many things, but the people, I will not give him!"

"His roots betray him, Your Grace."

"His roots? You mean to say his mother, Lettice? That grasping whore?" Then she threw back her head and laughed. "Do you know she has paraded herself through the streets pretending to be me?" She cast me a keen glance. "And so must my roots betray me?"

"You are your father's daughter, Your Majesty. Your parentage ensures that one man, though he be the Earl of Essex, might never be sufficient." Could I get her to drop the man for spite, then many would thank me.

"And you, Hugh St. Aubin's son? That Earl of Lytham was married some . . ."

"Twenty years, Your Highness."

"To the same woman?"

"My mother, Your Majesty."

"Happily?"

"Quite."

"And so your roots betray you. You are fixed upon this gypsy girl?"

"I cannot pretend otherwise."

"Have you not heard me? I only ask for what I can see. I only react to what I choose to acknowledge. If you could just keep her out of sight . . . out of *sonnets*! You have made this quite complicated, Lytham."

"A thousand apologies, Your Grace, but might I propose a solution?"

"Outside of the Tower? Is there one?"

"Perhaps there is an ambassador, one of your emissaries to a foreign court in the eastern part of the Continent. An ambassador who, if I may be frank, is an embarrassment to Your Majesty's Grace. Perhaps, if he could be recalled and another sent in his place, several of Her Majesty's problems might be solved at one and the same time."

"You speak of Polonia. And I suppose you would like to be that man?"

"It could only be an honor to serve Your Highness at home or abroad."

"And I suppose you would want to take your gypsy girl with you?"

"Your Majesty would never have need to see her again."

"Happy marriages are hard to come by. Or so I have been told. And so, if you find yours to be . . . happy, I do not wish to hear of it. Ever. And you had better leave soon! Before winter makes the Channel impassable. I am feeling unaccountably merry this season, but if you stay in the realm until spring, I *will* see you in the Tower."

53

The golden days of autumn in Berkshire had given way to the mean, cold days of winter. They were made chiller still by the knowledge that Lytham had fallen from favor at court. Due to a sonnet! He had told me all how he had written it while thinking of me. How the vision of my face had transformed the poem from one of love for the Queen to one of love for me. It seemed, even in my absence, that I could do nothing right.

Every morning I woke with the knowledge that he could be sent to the Tower that very day. I spent most of my time in silence. In prayer. But one forenoon, a great commotion disturbed my solitude.

"Girl? Girl!"

It was Lady de Winter's voice. I had just pushed myself from my chair when she burst into my room. Her hat was askew and her clothes in disarray. She had not even bothered to remove the traveling shield from her skirts.

"Lady de Winter." I gestured toward Joan to move one of the chairs closer to the fire.

"I come with news."

I found within me the will to be civil. "Sit then, and speak."

She crooked a gnarled hand and motioned me close. "It is not for everyone's ears."

I had to recover from the foul scent of her breath before I could order the maids gone.

"And that one as well." She pointed to Joan.

I looked at Joan.

She looked at me.

"What news, Lady de Winter? Have no fear. You may speak in Joan's presence. She is my dearest friend."

She opened her mouth to speak, but I stopped her.

"Before you tell it, you should know that I recently made a new friend. I visited Lady Elinor. In North Moreton. She had a strange tale to tell." I tried to smile. "And most of it involved you."

"How is Lady Elinor?"

"She was most anxious for a visit from you."

"Was she?"

"Aye. She wished to know of Lytham's success. Somehow she seemed quite assured of it . . . since she had removed herself from his life. Just as *you* had suggested."

"I . . ."

I took a chance with my next words. "When did Lytham catch Lady Elinor?"

"You mean with the Earl of Essex?"

The Earl of Essex? I had learned more than I had hoped for. "Aye."

"Just before Lytham petitioned for annulment. He caught the two of them together in his very own bed. Tell me what you wish to know."

I did not want to know more than I already did. In fact, I wished I knew much less. For now I knew Elinor sane enough to do the one thing that would have made Lytham cast her far from him. She had slept with Essex, in Lytham's bed, where she could be certain she would be caught. The very same Essex with which Lady de Winter had me make an alliance. "Nothing you have ever done has been calculated for my success, has it?"

"I—"

"All that you have counseled me was only meant for my destruction."

She looked truly offended. "That is not true!"

"Then explain yourself."

"Everything I have counseled you was meant for your success."

"Sir Thomas?"

"I brought you Sir Thomas because I thought he would help you. 'Tis your own fault that you bobbled that chance!"

"Essex?"

"Again—'tis you who fumbled that opportunity."

"And your lies about love? Your education about how to navigate through court?"

"The only lie I ever told you was the one about becoming one of the Queen's ladies. But for that you *must* see that I am to be forgiven! Everything I have ever done was meant for Lytham's success. Even when he chose Elinor over me, still I worked for his success."

And then I comprehended everything. "*You* are in love with him."

"There is no place for love in court. If I have loved him, then at least I have always only acted for his good. To remove from his path everything that would divert him from his goal. You cannot tell me that you have done the same, you selfish witch! At least *I* have the sense to know that love means nothing. That love can do nothing."

"But there, you are wrong. You have always been wrong. Love is not some tool for manipulation. Love is a gift—love is from God. Love means *everything*. And unlike everyone else's marriage at court, when I pledged my vows, they meant something." I had once promised myself that I would not have a marriage like my parents'. And now I knew for sure that I did not. If I had failed at everything else, at least I had achieved that.

"Are you still so young? Do your vows still mean more than Lytham's success? Because if you truly loved him, then you would do as I have done. You would remove yourself from him; you would retreat, so that he could advance."

"You have done nothing but destroy everything that means something to him. First Elinor, and now me."

"He might have found success through you. At first, I was only trying to teach you how to be useful. But then you fell in love with him. Even that might not have been so terrible, except that he fell in love with you. And that could help no one."

"And so, you removed me."

"Aye, I removed you. And you might have thanked me, except for the fact that with the sonnet he removed himself. But all is not lost. I do have news. News that might be of interest to you *if* you love him as much as you profess to."

Now the haste of her journey made sense. Something must have happened in London. I could not speak. Neither could I stand. I groped for a chair and sat in it. Hard. "Her Majesty . . . ?"

"Aye."

"What has she commanded to be done to him?"

"What she wanted and what she commanded are two different things."

It was the first time I had known hope in days.

"She has been counseled against acting too hastily."

"Thank you, Lady de Winter." For who else would have persuaded Her Majesty to listen to reason? In spite of my newly proved distrust of the woman, I would be indebted to her forever.

"I had very little to do with it. One cannot insult Her Majesty's Grace, and simply go on living."

My heart seemed to stop itself up within my chest. "Go on living?"

"Aye. Have no fear. He is to live. But it is to be in a place far from here."

"It is not the Tower?"

"Nay. 'Tis worse. He is to be the new ambassador to Polonia."

"Polonia!"

"Aye. 'Tis the best that could be done, everything considered."

"Praise God! Then he is to come home? To pack? We must pack! We must make arrangements, we must—"

"Nay. First, we must think."

"Think? Think of what?"

"Of *why* the earl fell into these troubles, of course."

But I could not think of why—of what the cause might be.

Lady de Winter left her chair and crept toward the fire. "After all of this, can you not see some common theme to all of the earl's difficulties?"

"Nay. I fail to see any—"

"'Tis always difficult to see beyond one's self!"

Beyond one's self? Was she saying . . . ? "You are saying that the cause is me? But now I know you. Now I know what you are about. What you have always been about."

She whirled from the fire toward me. "Aye. You have won. You have him. You hold his heart. I admit it. Well done." Her words sounded strangely humble. "But can you not see *this*? The cause *is* you. 'Tis always been you! His position was secure before he married you."

"But—"

"From the first time she saw you, the Queen despised you. She called you a gypsy! In front of the entire court!"

"I—"

"The decline of his star began and ended with you."

"That cannot be true. I only ever wanted his success. I only ever wished for his influence to increase. All I ever did was—"

"What? Cause the Queen to hate him? Cause his friends to revile him? And all because you loved him?"

"I did not mean . . . I never meant, never thought—"

"Aye. The one thing you did not do: you did not think! But now there is time. *Now* we must think. Lytham has secured a position for himself from the Queen. She has given him a second chance to prove his loyalty. When did all of his luck desert him? When you came. When you decided to *love* him."

I had no comment. Love had never before sounded so base. So selfish.

"And now he has an opportunity. Now he can set right everything that has gone wrong. Now, my dear, finally, you may begin to help him."

"How can I? What can I do that—"

"Since you profess to love him, one must assume you are committed to his success. If that is the case, then you must do what you have failed to do thus far: you must stop hindering his ascent."

"I have tried everything I can to—"

"Just so! *You* have tried. I have already told you, 'tis yourself at the root of all of this evil. Let him go, girl. If you truly love him as you say you do, then let him go!"

"To Polonia?"

"Aye. To Polonia. By himself. Unyoke yourself from him, and the Queen will see his worth once more."

"By himself . . ."

"Come, you must act quickly! You are the strong one. Men are weak. If he finds you here when he arrives, he will not have the strength to do what he knows he must."

"But how can I leave without seeing him? How can I let him go without saying good-bye? I love him."

"Your course is plain, girl! There can be no love at court. You must do yourself what he is incapable of doing. If he will not give you up, you must do this thing for him. Can you not see?"

Aye, I could. Like Elinor, I could see too clearly what must be done.

I told Joan to see to Lady de Winter's departure and I started up the stairs. Anguish found me before I reached the top. Was this what love was? Grief and sacrifice? Was this, then, what love felt like? Submission, surrender. A giving up, a yielding of hope. I loved. Clearly this was what I must do.

Had I not once thought, after the encounter with Sir Thomas, that God had wanted me to preserve my integrity? Had I not told Him that if He wanted the impossible, that He would have to open up the way?

This, then, was how He meant to do it.

Maybe virtue from afar was preferable to the sharing of love in proximity. But how could I do it? How could I live without Lytham? How would I survive?

It was there, on the stairs, that I collapsed into tears, and there that Joan found me.

"We must go."

"Go? Go where?"

"Back to King's Lynn."

"You cannot tell me you believe her?"

"She only told me what is true."

"Her truth has always had a strange way of sounding like lies."

"We cannot go with him."

"And why not?"

"Can you not see? She is right."

"How can you know what you do about her, hear the confession of all of her deceits, and then tell me that she is right?"

"She has always been right. Can you not see it? No matter what she has done, no matter what she has said, she has always been right when she says there can be no love at court."

Joan sputtered, working herself into an explosion.

"The earl has been able to redeem himself from Her Majesty's wrath. But it could only have come at great cost. In order to aid him any further, I *must* let him go. Alone. The only way left me to aid him is to let him unshackle himself from me."

"But he loves you!"

"I know it. And I love him. But there can be no love at court." As I repeated the words, I knew finally the accuracy of them. Lady de Winter had never spoken a truer thing.

54

In the end, there was not much to be packed. What need would I have in King's Lynn for gowns of tinseled silk, velvet, or cloth of gold? If I was going home, then it was in disgrace, for I had failed at the courtier's tasks. I had failed to provide my husband with an heir and I had failed to advance his position at Her Majesty's court. Indeed, I had figured largely in hastening his destruction. I would take only Joan with me. And several of Lytham's men to see us safely there.

I desperately wanted to leave a letter for Lytham. To explain to him why I could no longer be with him. But Lady de Winter was right. It would only have caused his resolve, and mine, to weaken.

We started out the next day and rode fifteen hard miles.

When the men wished to travel through London, I commanded them to ride a different way. Toward the north and the east. I had no wish to be reminded of all that I had lost.

———

Three days later I was ready to leave Lytham House for Holley-stone. All had been readied for the voyage to the Continent. Those items I had packed would be sent to the port at Dover, where they would wait for Marget and me. A week of hard riding and we could gain the port before winter closed the seas. I could not wait to tell Marget of my good fortune. Could not wait to sail with her from England's shores and leave the past behind us.

———

Every day, every mile, every minute, Joan pleaded with me to turn back.

"Please, Marget. You cannot go without telling him why."

"I left a letter."

"You did not!"

I kicked my horse to pick up the pace. Lytham's men spurred theirs to keep with me.

"Marget!" She had to shout now in order to be heard above the fury of the north wind. "How can you call yourself a wife and then separate yourself from your husband?"

"I do not! I call myself a countess and so seek to do my husband whatever good I still may."

"Marget—"

"I will not change my mind!"

"Then think on this: how can you give him a babe if you separate yourself from him?"

Her words nearly made me weep. I did not want to be reminded of just how much I was losing by returning to my parents' home. "He does not need me to have a babe."

"Marget—"

"He does not need me! He already has a son. His name is William. And with me gone, he can finally give the boy his own name."

Joan's face registered shock. William was the only secret I had ever kept from her. I spurred my horse into a canter as I crested a hill. I only meant to increase the distance between myself and Joan.

But what I had meant for good, fate turned to evil. My horse stepped into a hole and broke her leg.

Her tragedy succeeded where Joan had failed. My friend caught up with me. As one of Lytham's men freed the horse from her earthly woes, I wept. And then I had to ride with Joan. There was no help for it. I had forgotten to command that a spare horse be brought along. By the time we reached the next village, it was too late to acquire another and take up our journey anew.

"Marget?" Joan's voice echoed plaintive through the bedchamber, like the honking of a goose.

"Do not speak to me."

"Marget, I have only ever wanted your good."

"If you cannot stop speaking to me, then I will stop speaking to you."

"I know you think that you are doing this for Lytham's sake. But 'tis not only you going back to King's Lynn. 'Tis me as well. You think you go back to disgrace? Well, I go back to hell."

I had closed my eyes to wish for sleep, but upon Joan's pronouncement, they had flung themselves open. "If you go back, 'tis not as Joan Hybby. It is as the Countess of Lytham's lady."

She laughed, but the sound was tinged with derision. "I am no lady."

"Perhaps not by birth—"

"Marget! Did you never wonder how my father kept hold of the Green Griffin Tavern when he could not keep hold of a penny?"

"Joan, do not—"

"Did you never wonder how he could operate selling watered beer and bowls of rotten stew for a half-penny?"

"I do not—"

"Nay. You have never wished to know, but I will tell you. 'Tis because he also sold poor Joan at a penny a feel."

Nothing she said could have stunned me more. "I never knew it."

"Nay. You never did. 'Tweren't such a bad life. The boys we grew up with could never do me wrong. 'Twas the *gentle*men that came to town that used me bad. Like dirt under their feet. And still I might have stayed but for John Stump."

"Of Fisherfleet."

"Aye. That one. Being *paid* for what I did . . . well, that was one thing. But being expected to do it? That was another. I prayed to God that He would find me a way out of it, and He did: He rescued me through you."

"If I had—"

"Do not pity me. I only say it for one reason: the man you have is a good one. There is not one like him among a hundred. I have only ever found one other."

She had? Whom? And then I remembered the New Year's Day at Holleystone. Had she and Falconer come to a sort of understanding? In fleeing to King's Lynn had I taken her away from her only hope of happiness?

She clutched my arm with a vengeance, ridding my mind of all thoughts but the pain. "Marget, listen! Lytham loves you. If you let yourself be drawn from him on Lady de Winter's advice, then you do not deserve him. And I will tell him that myself. I will not go any farther with you."

"You have to come."

"I do not. I break my contract with you, here and now."

"You cannot break your contract! Not until Lady Day."

"You break yours. Was it not you who stood in that church and took vows? Was it not you who pledged to the earl to be his wedded wife, to have and to hold, from that day forward, for better, for worse, for richer, for poorer, in sickness and in health, to love, to cherish, and to obey, till death you depart? If you can break your contract before death, then I can break mine before Lady Day. And I do. Now."

"I did not know him then. I did not know myself."

"Neither did you know me. Not truly. So for ignorance, I leave you."

"Why did you never tell me, Joan? I could have . . . I might have . . ."

"I did not tell you because you could have done nothing. And if I did not tell you, I could pretend to be the person you thought me. I did not wish to lose your love." She turned her back to me, pulling the coverlet with her. "Seems as if I was right to worry."

I did not sleep that night. I thought of Joan. Of what she must have endured throughout our childhood. I thought of myself. Of Lytham. Of what choice love would make.

I had chosen sacrifice. But had I not chosen it for myself? Had I not made a choice so that I would not have to hear that same decision come from Lytham's mouth? In making my choice, I had made myself out to be brave, stout-hearted, ever-faithful, a good wife. But had I not also chosen to protect my heart above all else?

Lytham himself might have asked me to return to King's Lynn, but in hearing those words from his lips, I would gain only humiliation. In fact, I had chosen my pride over the possibility of humiliation. I had not chosen sacrifice at all. If I had taken an easy path, it was only to make the road easier for myself. Not for him.

I had been traveling like St. Paul on the road to Damascus. I had been bent on doing those I ought to love great harm. But now that the scales had fallen from my eyes, I could see. I could see that those who had commanded me, whom I had let command me, intended only great evil. But knowing it now, there was only one thing left for me to do.

55

My great joy on gaining Holleystone was soon turned into frustration. Marget had gone.

"Where?"

"I do not know, my lord." The steward looked as if he would rather have been caught sleeping than be called to address me in my chamber.

"How could you not know?"

"She did not tell me, my lord."

Odd. "Perhaps . . . did she go to visit a neighbor's estate?"

"She spent three days in packing, my lord, and then when she left, she took Joan and two of your men."

Three days? "Did she mean to join me in London?" But if that had been the case, then why had we not crossed in our journeys?

"I do not know."

"Had she word from . . . East Anglia?"

"Nay, my lord."

"Any visitors?"

"Only the Lady de Winter, my lord."

The Lady de Winter? Then my plans had just been turned into one merry mess! "The Lady de Winter came and . . . ?"

"And then my lady began to pack, my lord."

That witch had tried ever to part us. It seemed as if she may have succeeded. I would not leave for the Continent without Marget. And if I could not leave before the week's end, then I was Tower-bound. For all eternity.

"She left no word? None? No message? No missive?"

"Nay, my lord."

I ransacked my room in spite of the steward's words. And then I ransacked hers. I learned nothing but that she had left her best gowns, best ruffs, best gloves . . . best *everything* here at Holleystone. But she had taken that which mattered most: she had taken the coffer she had been given upon our betrothal, the astrolabe, and Nicholas's sonnet. The one she swore I could have written.

If she took what she loved best, she did not mean to return in haste. And if she did not take clothes for court, it only meant one thing. She was headed for King's Lynn. She was returning to her home.

But if I had not met her on the road, that meant she had not traveled through London. So which way had she gone? At this date, riding constant, switching horses, I might be able to overtake her. And if I did, there still might be time to make the ship. But how was I to know which way she had gone?

———

"Next time you decide to run away from home, could you not do it in the summer?"

"I do not intend for there to be a next time, Joan. The earl will take me to Polonia or he will leave me at Holleystone. *Together* you and I will do as he decides."

"Now is not the time to become docile!" She pulled the hood of her cloak further over her head, but not before I saw her smile.

I followed her example. I had grown tired of the snowflakes' game: first following the gusts of the wind down my neck and then melting to join the stream of drips cascading down my chest.

"Could we not find a place to stop?"

I dared to lift my head and gazed at the snow-covered fields around us. Tried to peer through the gray blanket the flakes had made of the sky. I thought I saw the blink of a light, but it was far off and bobbing like a ship through the driving snow. "I cannot even see! How can I find a place to stop?"

One of Lytham's men suddenly appeared beside me, his cheeks flushed with cold. "My lady? The road will soon be covered. And then we will lose the way. There is a light ahead. We must find some place to stop or risk becoming lost."

"Can we not go one more mile?" In fact, I was hoping for two. Now that we had turned our horses south toward home, toward Holleystone, I could not get there fast enough.

"We could, my lady, but then we might not live to see another. And we are far from any grand estate." I heard the rebuke in his words. If I had allowed us to use proper roads, then we might not have found ourselves in such dire straits.

I consented to stop and soon the horses crunched up to the door of an inn. We must have been the only people foolish enough to have traveled that day, for we were their only customers. We were served some beer hardly worth drinking and some stew hardly worth swallowing, but a fire roared from the hearth and soon the meal had warmed our bellies.

Lytham's men played at cards for a while and Joan and I played chess. But soon the snow-dampened dark and a day spent riding through the cold made my eyes grow heavy. The next morn we set out once more upon the road. It took some time and an enormous amount of energy for our horses to wade through the snow. The storm began again in earnest, and so we were only able to reach Ware that night. We took refuge at The Anchor Inn.

———

I had to travel light and fast. I chose Nicholas and two of my men to accompany me. We were joined at the stables by Falconer. But he was an unwanted guest. He barred the door, blocking us from leaving.

"I have no need of a bird, man!"

"If you search for the lady and find her, then what I search for will be found at her side."

"I must travel fast."

"And so must I." He did not look as if he were planning to move.

"Who will take care of the birds?"

"You cannot think that I would not leave them without provision."

He had better not. I ground my teeth and then nodded at Nicholas.

Nicholas ordered up a horse for the man. And then together the five of us rode back the way I had just come.

Knowing that Marget must have passed London already, I decided the quickest route was to head straight for the city and then turn north on the postal road toward Huntingdon. We made quick time in gaining London, but our pace slowed once we turned north when we rode into snow. By the time we reached Ware, our horses had grown weary.

"We will leave these horses in the city and exchange them for others."

"We had better stop altogether, my lord." I could hardly hear Nicholas's voice for the wind.

"We cannot stop."

"We cannot proceed, my lord."

"If we stop, then I might as well just offer myself up to the Keeper of the Tower this instant."

"Better him than the Keeper of Hell, my lord."

I paused. "Then where would you like to stop?"

He pushed back the hood of his cloak and looked round at the street we were on. "'Tis either The Anchor Inn or The Albion, my lord."

I wanted a drink more than I wanted sleep. "The Albion."

"As you wish."

While the men saw to our horses, Nicholas and I warmed our boots and bellies beside the fire.

"Are you certain of this course, my lord?"

"Aye."

"You are leaving the Queen, you are leaving the court, you are leaving . . . Holleystone."

Holleystone. Though I had made my decision with much deliberation, it had not truly hit me until now. I was leaving behind everything. Everything I had ever wanted . . . everything I thought I had wanted.

"The Queen cannot live forever, my lord."

"But then neither might I. And what sort of life would I have without Marget?"

The question was not asked of him, but he answered it with one of his own. "The marriage did not turn out as you feared, then, my lord?"

"Nay. It turned out much worse: I fell in love with her. As you might have predicted had you not wished to keep your position." He hid a laugh with a cough. "But for that, I will ever praise God."

"Amen and amen, my lord."

I shifted positions to better warm myself. "There is one thing that lies heavy on my mind."

"My lord?"

"The young William."

"What of him, my lord?"

"I pray God might bless me with an heir, but Elinor's lad might be my only hope. Have you found out anything of him? Does it go well with him?"

"As well as it can, my lord, for a young servant at a grand estate."

I mulled over that thought as I gazed into the fire. Young servants were never treated very well. And Elinor's brother had never been known for his patience. If God did not grant my prayer, then I would have need of this son. And would it not be better that he be raised where I could get to know the look of him? "Perhaps . . ."

"My lord?"

"Perhaps in the spring, once the weather opens the Channel once more, I might find myself in need of a squire."

"Aye, my lord. It would be a great honor to fetch him for you myself."

I lifted my eyes from the fire and looked at him. "Thank you."

The door opened, and the wind pushed snowflakes into the room. Behind the snow stomped my men, with Falconer bringing up the rear.

"Why did Falconer insist on coming with us?"

"I would guess, my lord, that it has something to do with my lady's Joan."

"With Joan?"

"Aye, my lord. I seem to recall that you also once wanted, very much, to marry that woman yourself."

I turned a bit more in my chair toward the men to see just what kind of man Falconer might be. He was brilliant with birds, of course, but was he good enough for Marget's closest friend?

As the man turned toward the fire, he saw me looking at him and he looked right back at me.

He might just do. And in the wilds of Polonia, one thing was certain: there would be land, and plenty of it, for hawking.

"Nicholas?"

"Aye, my lord."

"I may have need of one thing more this spring . . ."

As soon as my men had joined us, the publican brought our food. "A fearsome day for traveling, my lord."

"Aye."

"And you head north?"

"Aye."

"Then you will be more miserable still."

———

Joan and I rose with the sun, could not in fact help it since its rays gleamed off every snowflake. At least the storm had gone. She helped me to dress. We ate with the men and then we saddled up and took once more to the road, traveling south.

We were hardly a mile into our journey when, in looking round, I realized I had left my coffer at the inn. I drew my horse to a stop.

Joan pushed back her hood. "Have you changed your mind?"

"Nay. I left my coffer."

"I have it here."

"Not that one. The other. The one the earl gave me . . ."

She glanced back at the road we had just traveled. "He can give you a dozen others just like it."

But I wanted that one, for it had the sonnet in it. The one that . . . he had not written. And yet I could not leave it behind.

Beside us, the horses of the men stomped and snorted.

I pulled on my reins, causing my horse to turn, hardly daring to glance at the men as I did so. "We must return. I have forgotten a thing at the inn."

"Good heavens, Marget!"

"I cannot leave it."

"But you can leave us dead or dying on some road in the dead of winter in order to reach Holleystone!" Joan muttered all the way back to Ware.

———

The next morn, we awoke to a world bleached by snow.

"'Twill be hard to follow any kind of road in this stuff, my lord."

"I have no choice."

"You could turn south, my lord. To Dover."

"Without Marget?"

"I could accompany her to Polonia in the spring, my lord."

"Nay."

"The further north we go, my lord, the worse the roads may become."

"I have no choice."

"You have *two* choices."

"One of which I am unwilling to choose. And so there is only one. And my Gentleman of the Horse had better see to the horses!"

While Nicholas stomped out of the place, I ate more bread. Drank more wine. Stood closer to the fire to try to persuade the remaining damp from my boots.

At last, Nicholas opened the door, noted that he and the men were ready, and met with the publican to settle our bill. As I hoisted myself into the saddle and began to start out, Nicholas gestured to a path beaten down into the snow that led from the side of The Anchor Inn across the road from us. "Those people have the right idea, my lord. They ride *south*."

I turned to follow that lonely track in the snow. Squinted against the sun's glare and saw a group heading toward us. "And those people?"

Nicholas looked farther down the path at a group toward which I was pointing. "Must be as mad as you. My lord."

I tried to hide my smile from him as I nudged the horse out onto the road with my knee. But I looked back once more and was startled to perceive two colors, crimson and azure, in a familiar combination. And even more surprised to see the very person for whom I had been looking.

"Marget!"

Was it . . . ? It was Lytham! He was sitting upon a horse right in front of us in the middle of the road as if he had nothing to do but watch us ride toward him. He was so very . . . dear . . . to me. And he could either take me to Polonia with him or send me back to Holleystone.

Please do not ask me to leave you or not to follow you.

I advanced until our horses were nose to nose.

And then he urged his horse forward two steps more and we were side-by-side. "Why did you go?"

It was cold. So very cold. But the snow's chill could not compare to the sudden freeze spreading through my own heart. "Congratulations on your appointment. I am sure you will be very happy in Polonia."

"*We* will be very happy there. I came home to take you with me and found you were not there!"

"I cannot go."

"But why?"

"Because."

" 'Because' is a child's answer."

"I cannot go because . . . I love you."

"And I consider that love to be the most valued of all of my possessions." He reached a gloved hand down to caress my cheek.

"I am the cause of all of your troubles."

"Who told you that?"

"Lady de Winter, and she said—"

"She is a serpent."

"But she is right!"

"About what is she right?"

"About my being the cause of all of your troubles. Since the first day the Queen laid eyes on me, I have done nothing but degrade you in her eyes."

"You have done nothing but love me with a constant heart."

"But what has that love done for you? Nothing."

"It has done everything! It has comforted me and sustained me; it has made me whole."

"But I embarrassed you at court. I was banished. And you were disgraced."

"And it has all been made right. We will go to Polonia and we will start our lives anew. Together."

"But then you will have to leave Holleystone behind. If you would just let me leave, go back to King's Lynn, then you could return to court, you could resume your position, and you would not have to leave Holleystone."

"And how could I remain at Holleystone without you? You

are its heart. You are its soul. 'Tis only with you in it that it means anything at all."

"But if you go, you leave court . . . you leave the country. You leave the Queen. You give up everything."

"Not everything. Do you not remember? 'To you alone I give Love's astrolabe / That in your sailing you might find the same—' "

" 'Gale winds that blew my soul to you to save / Might in return give you to me to claim.' But you never wrote that."

"I would have if I had known of this end from the beginning. And I would sail to the ends of the earth to find you. But do not make me do it. Claim me now. Love me."

"I do. I love you. I will ever love you."

"And I, you." He pulled me close and kissed me. "Now, please, may we go to Polonia? There is a cell in the Tower waiting for me if we miss the last ship to the Continent."

And so we rode to Dover together, our past behind us, our future before us, and not without a little fear. For in the wilds of the East, who knew what we might find? But greater than our fears were our hopes. And our dreams. God was for us, how could we doubt that? With constant hearts we had chosen love, and He had perhaps not rewarded us, but He had rescued us. He had set our feet on a new path. An honorable path. And with our love now fixed between us, we would let nothing separate us again.

A NOTE TO THE READER

Marget, Lytham, and Lady de Winter never lived, but their experiences were all too real and occurred all too often during the reign of Queen Elizabeth I. Lead poisoning was not uncommon when court women began to follow their Queen in fashion. Queen Elizabeth I used lead paint foundation and mercury sulphide rouge to hide the ravages of smallpox and disguise the advance of age. Noblewomen happily followed her example. Ceruse, or lead paint, was the Renaissance's answer to wrinkles and aging. We now know that it only caused premature aging of the skin and sped women along the route toward death. Queen Elizabeth I died on March 24, 1603, from blood poisoning. Some suspect the poisoning was due to lead.

The first symptoms of lead poisoning were only cosmetic. The paint dissolved hair follicles and then loosened the teeth. Continued use of the paint led to the rapid aging of skin, to which the answer was simply to coat the ceruse on in thicker layers. It was inside the body, however, where lead poisoning left its most insidious marks. Early on, the user would begin to have trouble with speech and recall and would manifest the symptoms of carpal tunnel syndrome.

Later, the women would experience tingling in their hands and feet, lethargy, and irritability, along with miscarriages, premature births, or stillbirths. With long-term use came difficulty in concentration, general fatigue, tremors, abdominal pain, headaches, vomiting, and weight loss. Eventually the women might experience paralysis, severe abdominal cramps, seizure, coma, and death.

ACKNOWLEDGMENTS

I owe many thanks and much gratitude to the people who encouraged me as I wrote this book: to Beth Jusino, who gently nudged me forward; to Dave and Sarah Long, who graciously offered me both time and space; to Lanna Dickinson, Narelle Mollet, Trudy Mitchell, and Maureen Lang, whose enthusiasm for these pages sparked my own; to Linda Derrick, who prayed; to Ginger Garrett for sharing the dream; and especially, and always, to Tony.